HE CAPTU

“Was it truly a you in Cairo City, Aisha?” he asked.

“I have lived a wonderful life! I harbor no regrets! I was birthed in a palace that offered me all there was for luxury, security and high status . . . while all around the world people live lives of abject want and despair.”

“But this,” he whispered, leaning down to put his mouth lightly against hers. “This cannot be said to be a small thing.”

He moved his mouth to her eyes and brushed her lashes with his lips. “I would like to see you emerge, fly from your cocoon . . . to nest in my arms. On this altar of snow, life is making an offering to you. You cannot have everything, that is true, but you can have this.” He kissed her hard then, his arms tightening round her, until her lips parted and their breaths mingled. When he released her, Aisha whirled away from him, her head spinning, her stomach, too.

“As Allah is my witness,” she swore, “I will not love you.”

“But you will. Any day now.”

ENTHRALLED

Georgia Taylor

AN ONYX BOOK

ONYX
Published by the Penguin Group
Penguin Books USA Inc., 375 Hudson Street,
New York, New York 10014, U.S.A.
Penguin Books Ltd, 27 Wrights Lane,
London W8 5TZ, England
Penguin Books Australia Ltd, Ringwood,
Victoria, Australia
Penguin Books Canada Ltd, 10 Alcorn Avenue,
Toronto, Ontario, Canada M4V 3B2
Penguin Books (N.Z.) Ltd, 182–190 Wairau Road,
Auckland 10, New Zealand

Penguin Books Ltd, Registered Offices:
Harmondsworth, Middlesex, England

First published by Onyx, an imprint of Dutton Signet,
a division of Penguin Books USA Inc.

First Printing, April, 1996
10 9 8 7 6 5 4 3 2 1

Printed in the United States of America

TO MY NEPHEW AND MY FRIEND

WARREN MICHAEL KAUFFMAN

"—there hath passed away a glory from the earth."

—Wordsworth

I am the God Thor,
I am the War God
I am the Thunderer!
Here in my Northland,
My fastness and fortress,
Reign I forever!

Thou art a God too,
O Galilean!
And thus single-handed
Unto the combat,
Gauntlet or Gospel,
Here I defy thee!

—Longfellow
The Saga of King Olaf

In the year of the Prophet Muhammad, 465, Egypt-Land had for three centuries been the most civilized region in the world. From the windows of rich houses that banked the Nile an hundred vessels could be seen unloading the wares of half the earth upon the wharves of Cairo City.

Christian monasteries loomed, ancient and immutable along the banks of the Nile, surviving by the grace of Muslim tolerance. For the monks of Egypt the monasteries were sanctuaries of Christianity within an infidelic and degenerate world. Five times a day the monks heard and ignored the echoing, lyrical chants of muezzins calling faithful Muslims to prayer from minaret towers. In silence they continued with their daily tasks, unaware of and uninterested in the civilization outside the high stone walls that closed out a world they had turned from in search of peace and salvation.

The descendants of Odin, who called themselves the Asar, inhabited northlands that did not exist on the maps of Islamic navigators. Often the Asar sailed the Sea

King's Road to the Nile, entering Cairo City harbor in ships that were as strange and as brazen as they; barbaric oddities in a civilized world that distrusted but tolerated them and their ships as automatically as it tolerated the unobtrusive monks in the monasteries. The Asar did not believe there would ever come a day when they no longer ruled the seas, as they had for twelve centuries, or a day when Odin and Thor would be vanquished in battle.

It was the year of Christ, 1034.

CHAPTER ONE

Aisha, born of Abdullah bin Abi Kilabah and Dunyazad, lived contentedly in the house of her husband, Kamar al Zamen, the physician. She was fully aware of her good fortune in having become, through marriage, a citizen of Egypt and of Cairo City. In this year of the Prophet, 465, everything was as it should be and, Allah willing, tomorrow would be a duplication of all that had gone before.

Aisha stood at a window enjoying a jasmine-scented morning breeze and the privacy and comforts of the *harim*. She did not consider herself in any way imprisoned in these luxurious quarters, would have vehemently resented as an insult any negligence on the part of her husband in maintaining this seclusion.

Her black hair, perfumed and adorned with tiny stones, fell to her thighs. Countless lengths of black silk thread had been intricately hidden in her hair to fill it out around her face. She wore a loose gown over satin trousers that were caught tight at her ankles, and a snug, embroidered vest. The gown was diapered with cloth of gold and brocaded with figures of beasts; the eyes were of gems, the claws of red rubies and green beryl. Her almond-shaped eyes were shadowed with powdered antimony, and scarlet lip paint brightened her mouth.

Kamar al Zamen, on the anniversary of the fifth year of his marriage to Aisha, described her in poetic lines. *My evening star measures five feet and two. The snows of her bosom are like two globes of ivory from whose brightness the moon borrows light, a seduction to all who see it, and joined thereto two upper arms smooth and rounded, and a stomach like little waves as it were a figured cloth of finest Egyptian linen made by the Copts, with creases like folded scrolls, ending in a waist slender past all power of imagination, based upon back parts like a hillock of blown sand, and those back parts upborne by thighs smooth and round and by a calf like a column of pearl and all this reposed upon two feet, narrow, slender and pointed like spear blades. My cherished one is as some limber, graceful branchlet, or the slender stalk of a sweet basil, to amaze and bewilder my fancy.*

Aisha sighed, thinking that Nur al Huda would return this day. Kamar al Zamen's fourth wife was a thorn in the backside, worst of all, not removable. The child's half-month visit to her parents was over. The peace of this day, of the past fourteen days, was near an end.

Suddenly Aisha gasped excitedly—and her hands flew up to catch hold of the intricately carved wrought iron grillwork of the window. Squinting, she stared hard at the horizon line of the Nile, far to the north under a cloudless azure sky. A flashing redness had caught her eye. It streaked now across the slate-like surface of the river like a giant, winged bird. Then another showed itself, fast behind. Swiftly they took form. The first ship's sails were blood red, the other's white as snow. Their oars sparked silver and gold in reflection of the glaring sun.

"Alhomdolillah!" Aisha cried, a hand flying up to her mouth. "Dragon ships."

She swung around and ran across the expansive hall, silk veils fluttering a trail behind her. She caught hold of the stair banister and took the steps two and three at a time. At the third-floor landing she whipped left and sped toward Kamar al Zamen's bedchamber, dashing through the red silk draperies that framed the entrance and across the room, without so much as a nod in her husband's direction.

Before the old man sprawled upon his mattress had quite focused on his wife, she was gone, beyond his sight upon the balcony of his chamber that overlooked the river.

"Bismillah," Kamar al Zamen shouted to her in a palsied voice. "Wife, I fear you have lost your senses. Come here to me and let me feel your brow."

"I am perfectly well," Aisha called out to him from the balcony. She leaned over the railing, straining her eyes to see over the rooftops of Cairo City to the ship-pocked face of the Nile. "Dragon ships have entered the harbor. I feel the strangest sense of excitement whenever I see such a sight. Come, my husband. Behold how beautiful they are."

Kamar al Zamen threw back the satin coverlet and, with some gasping and creaking of joints, lifted his frail body from the mattress. Catching up a white, silk robe, he wrapped it round himself. Moving with satisfactory agility for a man of sixty and seven years, he stepped up beside his wife. His ancient eyes could find no more than a reddish blur where her finger enthusiastically pointed, but he would not admit the fact and cheerfully agreed that the ships made quite a striking picture.

"They will be carrying furs," she commented excitedly.

"Most certainly furs, my lovely."

"Look! See how the prow lifts, arches from the water like a great neck. The stern also lifts, to form a tail."

"A dragon, yes."

"No. The head of a beast not of this world, lace-horned and lovely." Abruptly she whipped her face round to Kamar al Zamen and pleaded, "Your permission, husband, to venture to the city this day. I would bid for their cargo."

Kamar al Zamen could now clearly see her face. He raised an arm to lightly brush her cheek with a quivering forefinger. He smiled and murmured, "Thou art as guileful and radiant as the day you first entered this chamber, my evening star."

Aisha laughed, much pleased by the compliment. Momentarily diverted from the ships, she purred, "Ah, husband, you flatter me, seek to deceive me. Am I not the mother of two married children, the grandmother of three? I am old, now, hmm?" knowing full well the unlined, youthful perfection of the face which he gazed upon so adoringly. "I was still ten years of age when I came to your bed. You do not see that I have greatly aged since then? It has been twenty and two years and I am thirty—"

"Now you seek compliments, so you will hear no more from me." He smiled indulgently upon her. "You wish to purchase furs? First wife, soon you will be wealthier than I, and out of injured pride I will be forced to divorce you, hmm?" playfully patting her cheek with the flat of his hand.

"You will never divorce me," Aisha said soberly, turning her eyes back to the far scene. "But you are right. One day I *will* be wealthier than you, Blessed Allah willing."

"What was your last accounting, eh?"

"Ten million dinars," she replied matter-of-factly.

"Truly!" he exclaimed. He let his lower lip form an amused pout. "Tell me, my sweetmeat, what will you do when I am gone? Will you retire to our son Ajib's manor? Stitch and dream away your remaining years?"

She turned apprehensive eyes to her husband. A coldness had formed round her heart. She did not wish him dead, Allah knew, but she longed for the day—an emotional paradox and a painful one. Ah, the plans she had laid for the filling of those years ahead, years of independence. She tried to be light, laughing, "Will you leave to me a fourth of your estate, my husband? My mother, Allah bless her in Paradise, left me two million dirhems, my father, thrice that sum. I am terribly clever in my investments, but, truly, inheritance is the sweetest kind of money. After you, dear Kamar al Zamen, and our progeny, I love gold best in all the world."

Kamar Al Zamen laughed appreciatively. "You did not answer my question. Will you go to Ajib when I have gone to Paradise?"

Forced to reply, she said emphatically, "No, I will not go to Ajib." She turned away from him. "I will not be put to pasture as if I were a mare without strength enough to run another race. I am only thirty years and two. The *law* is specific. When you are gone from me, I will have become lord and master of my person and of my estate."

"You are that this moment, my evening star," he said huskily.

"Master of my estate, yes. But not of my person. As I owed Ajib and our daughter, Budur, mothering, so do I owe you love and lifelong duty. When . . . when that dreadful day comes, I shall owe only to Aisha."

"You have only to ask, and I will free you."

She could not look at him. She knew his feelings, understood him completely. When he could no longer treat her as a man, he had offered her a divorce, but she had refused. Allah had decreed that she should be wife to Kamar al Zamen. Only Allah, or her husband, could release her from that responsibility. Freedom would be a feeble treasure if gained by cruelty, if overshadowed by guilt. To leave him would surely kill him. "Let us not speak more of this," she whispered, reaching back to take hold of his cold hands.

Kamar al Zamen swallowed a rising emotion that moistened his faded eyes.

Aisha whipped round to him and quickly added, "But you could offer Nur al Huda her freedom, instead." It was a happy thought. "You should never have wed her. She was far too young, and you were far too—"

"No," he interrupted firmly. "There will be time enough for Nur al Huda after I am gone to Allah's Paradise. I do not care enough for her to free her."

Aisha shrugged. Having harbored no real hope of escape from Nur al Huda's bad temper, she found his refusal quite easy to accept. She returned her full attention to the ships.

The dragon ships were at rest, oars hovering motionless over the river. As the vessels moved with the current, the beast heads slowly turned and seemed to be surveying the land with arrogant eyes. The lead vessel was a monarch of ships, at least an hundred feet in length, with sails of red-dyed skin, its planking painted sun yellow above the waterline. The rising head and tail was gold-plated and appeared to be jewel-studded. A banner flew from the masthead, but Aisha could not make out the design. Slowly the ships eased between two hulking, graceless Andalusian merchant vessels. It would be nearing sunset before the captains could obtain berths and be prepared to accept bids for their cargo.

"Husband? Do I have your permission to—"

"Of course!" Kamar al Zamen exclaimed, flourishing an arm. "Why do you persist in this? You are free to go anywhere, anytime. Do not pester me with such requests. That is for mere wives. You are far more than wife to me. Twenty-two years past, two golden eyes looked into mine, over veils, entered into me and captured my soul completely. Go. Invest in furs if you must. But take care. Savages man those ships. Armanus must accompany you."

"Savages?" Aisha protested. "I have heard it said that slaves do not man the oars of these strange ships, but *princes*." At his skeptical expression, she insisted, "Actually. Men of means and property man the oars for a person of just higher station."

"Nonsense. Romantic nonsense. Pagans. They eat their own children. That is what I have heard."

"Husband!"

"Ach; forgive me, my sweetmeat." He brought her into his arms, kissed her cheek and sent her off to the zenana. He watched her depart from him with much regret in his tired eyes.

As Aisha efficiently arranged for a litter and escort to take her to the wharves in search of a bargain in furs, David of Saint Monica took the first steps toward the crossing of their destinies. He, too, would seek out Northmen on the wharves, but for a very different reason.

David stumbled blindly down halls that were like long, tenebrous tombs, his hands trembling against chill stone walls that guided him toward the outside world. At the monastery of Saint Monica candles were reserved for ceremonials. The use of artificial light of any kind was considered intemperate.

At last under a glaring morning sun he straightened his frail shoulders and moved purposefully across the courtyard toward the enclosing masonry and stone wall, toward the gate that slowly swung ajar in the wind. There had never been a need to lock the gate, for those who wished to enter were welcome and no man inside had ever wished to leave. The closer he came to the gate, the more slowly David stepped. He had always thought of this portal as an entrance only. Now it seemed to bear a mocking sign, *Exit*.

David came to a halt and stood frozen on the threshold of his future, his blue eyes fastened to the hard-crusted earth at his feet. The gate swung back and forth, its hinges screeching a mournful dirge and denunciation. The shrill, repetitious song of the Muslim call to prayer echoed on the wind, a beckoning . . . a warning that dangerous unknowns existed beyond the sanctuary looming behind him under a sky painted red by the rising sun.

A sudden explosion of emotion propelled David through the exit and whipped him about to pull the gate closed. He dropped his forehead against the rough metal, breathing hard, hanging on to the iron bars while strength returned to his quaking knees.

At last he turned, lifted his chin a little and let his eyes stray to the palm-fringed Nile. The trees formed a swaying, verdant canopy that followed the river through a countryside so arid as to seem lifeless.

Steeling himself against an impulse to look back at Saint Monica, David stepped in the direction of the river. Brother Sebastian had said he had only to follow the river's direction. Over his shoulder he carried all his possessions, a small leather bag that contained a bit of bread and cheese, and a copy of the Bible that he had lovingly printed by candlelight during long, silent nights in his cell. His drab, soiled brown robe, buttoned down the front from collar to hem, brushed the parched earth as he moved more swiftly now. His skirt kicked up a thin trail of dust that hovered in the still air behind him like an illusory rope connecting his escaping feet to the fast-vanishing monastery, representative of bonds that could never be broken, no matter how swiftly he stepped, or to what far place.

As he hesitantly stepped toward a new life and duty, the past moved in vivid detail before his mind's eye. There had been so little variation that recollection was in no way difficult. He could not recall any other place, any other family than seventy and two monks. When he had asked the much younger, less rotund Brother Sebastian how he had come to Saint Monica, he had been told, "You were consigned to us, David." But what did *consigned* mean? "Given," was the stingy reply.

Given. When he was six weeks of age an unknown woman with yellow hair and blue eyes had knocked upon the gate, to deliver him unto the Lord and His service. Whoever, whatever, she might have been was Brother Sebastian's and the abbot's secret. After that day he had not asked questions about his background, but naively accepted his coming into the fold as little short of a divine miracle. He thereafter enjoyed childish illusions of kinship to Holy Jesus, imagining himself immaculately conceived. God in Heaven was his singular father, the Blessed Mother herself the one who had delivered him through the gate now being left behind at last, after thirty-four years.

In silence, forbidden to laugh aloud, to talk unnecessarily, to run, shout or weep, he had grown to manhood. At fifteen, he took the tonsure unquestioningly, though it was not required that he become a priest to remain at Saint Monica as a monk. He had thought it was expected of him by God and Christ.

He had rarely pondered the outside world, not until recently . . . it had been a place as far divided from reality as the worrisome dreams that on frequent occasions disturbed his sleep.

For nineteen years he had followed an identical routine to that of his brothers in Christ. He rose at 2:00 A.M. and repaired to the chapel to recite the nocturns. At dawn, the matins, again at 6:00, at 9:00, at midday and at 3:00. At sunset, vespers. At bedtime, when darkness prohibited work, the Completion. Between canonical hours, a lonely cell wherein his eyes burned and watered in the bad light, as he copied and illuminated countless numbers of Bibles.

He could not recall when the change in him had begun, only that he had, with apparent suddenness, come to the conclusion that living in devotional refuge was cowardly, that he had a duty to mankind. He had waited two full years for the abbot's permission and another three years for the sanction of His Holiness the Pope.

David halted his step, to gaze upon a dark-skinned, ragged young man occupied in lifting water from the river with a *shaduf*, a long pole from one end of which hung a wooden bucket, the opposite end weighted by a heavy ball of dried mud. The farmer looked up and his mouth split into a wide grin that showed broken, badly rotted teeth. He spoke to David in greeting.

David nodded in response, suddenly aware of a deficiency he had not before considered. He knew only one language, the Latin of Holy Church. Conversation had, all his life, been an indulgence that was strictly forbidden. He had entered the world of infidels, determined to bring men to Christ, and he possessed no means of communicating the word of God to them. The thought stunned him, but within a few moments he had convinced himself that language barriers were the least formidable obstacles in his path. He would listen and learn. If he saved but a single soul from damnation in the future ahead, he would be fully rewarded and vindicated. As a recluse his individual soul was being saved, but at the cost of all those souls he might have rescued as a missionary.

David tried to raise his chin before the curious young

man, but it pained him to do so. So long accustomed to submissive rest upon his breast, his chin was a down-pulling weight. All his past weighed heavily upon him. He had never been strong. Now he would have to be. Now he must speak, and in tóngues. Now he must eat to improve his physical strength that he might prevail upon the people he approached. His only working task was to be that of conversion, the bringing of the unholy to grace.

In a later age, men such as David of Saint Monica would consider themselves highly educated. David, traveling to the northernmost corner of the earth, knew that his ignorance was the most formidable barrier in his path, that it was, perhaps, insurmountable. He had been taught to copy the Latin in a fine hand and to read the Holy Bible. He had memorized the nocturns and matins. The stricture against conversation had precluded questioning.

The Bible spoke of sin, blasphemy, a multitude of worldly transgressions, but without life experiences, no real comprehension could be achieved. He had never met a man that was not Christlike. There were no extenuating circumstances, no possible compromises; the Word of the Lord was inviolable and unerring. That the conclusive doctrinal of Holy Church could lose or alter meaning in translation, vary according to geographical location and according to the inclinations of diverse peoples, was simply too incredible to have occurred to him. Quite soon, however, it would be made brutally clear to David, by a person of indisputable authority, that Christianity was, indeed, variable. To be a Christian, or a priest, was not synonymous with saintliness; nor was the Word beyond analytical inquisition.

En route to his mission in Nordland, David was confident in his noble convictions and optimistic about the future. He made no *effort* to be a saint; he *was* one.

Aisha's four heavily oiled Ethiopian bearers carefully placed the curtained litter down upon its stout ebony legs, full center of the frenzied wharf street. Armanus, her personal attendant, had ridden ahead and was standing near the wharf edge. He was almost lost to Aisha's searching, curtain-hampered gaze in a hustling, caterwauling crowd of merchants, stewards, seamen and not a few half-naked children scampering everywhere underfoot in search of carelessly guarded purses or merchandise.

A mountain of sacked mint teetered near a wagon loaded with fat oranges. Long rows of squat wine barrels formed a barrier around which the crowd absentmindedly flowed like the Nile round a sandbar. The stench of fish, combined with the aromatic fragrance of mint and oranges, the stagnant putridity of the muddy river, utterly confused the senses. Behind the litter's draperies, Aisha was uncertain whether to cover her delicate nose with a kerchief, or to breathe deeply of the familiar aggregation of scents, which was in a way pleasant but discomfortingly vigorous.

Armanus turned, searching the crowd. He saw the litter and elbowed his way toward it. His hulking frame, draped in white linen, rose head and shoulders above those he jostled so arrogantly. Upon reaching the litter, he leaned his turbaned head so that his wide brow brushed the curtain and said in a resonant, low voice,

"The dragon ship long boat approaches now, my lady, but seems to be veering toward the Street of the Flowers."

The draperies split apart and impatient golden eyes met his. Armanus lifted his brows to express his regretful sympathy.

Aisha's glance turned to seek out the ships, but walls of goods prevented sight of them. "To the Street of the Flowers, then—" she called out sharply to the bearers, and the litter lurched upward, throwing her back against the richly upholstered wall of the box.

"Allah protect thee, thou art mad, thou soul of whimsy!" Armanus shouted at the retreating litter in outrage. But even as he argued, he rushed to mount his waiting black mare, knowing his mistress to be willful to a fault, the most obstinate, insuppressible female a man could have the misfortune to serve. Allah bless him with increased patience and fortitude.

Continuously muttering dramatic predictions of doom, Armanus rode close ahead, clearing a path for the litter along the filthy, narrow streets of Cairo's river section. The balconies of houses met overhead to completely block out the sunlight. The air in the murky caverns thus created was a thick weight upon flesh and lungs.

Inside the litter, Aisha removed her face veil, unable to breathe behind it. She snapped her long, henna-painted fingernails in furious impatience, complaining loudly when the clumsy bearers tilted or too suddenly halted the box as they literally rammed through the loitering, seemingly aimless crowds.

The Street of the Flowers was a conspicuous example of fanciful misnaming. Better if it had been named

Street of Foulness, Aisha thought, as she raised her kerchief to place it tightly over her mouth and nose for a moment's relief from the stench. Here the human sewage of Cairo City kept company with rats and insect vermin to produce an atmosphere of fetid, depressive corruption. Death, disease, and all the evils of which men and women were capable festered this entire district like a spreading, devouring cancer. Blind, crippled and hunger-driven human beings stumbled against the litter, their dark arms, like hideous tentacles, slithering between the litter's curtains, their foul mouths hissing cries for alms, alms for the love of Allah.

Suddenly the litter came to an extremely abrupt halt. Aisha clutched the sides of the box to keep her balance. She heard Armanus shouting obscenities at the clamoring beggars in such terrible, booming tones as would have caused Allah himself to tremble. Clawing hands vanished as by magic. The litter dropped but with amazing gentleness settled upon its legs.

When Aisha had regained her composure, her veil fastened in place over the bridge of her nose, she leaned to her left and split apart the curtain. She instantly sucked in her breath. She had squarely met the curious, ice-blue gaze of a giant straight out of *The Tales of a Thousand Nights and a Night.*

The man stood about five paces from the litter. His arms were crossed over his expansive breast. He had hair the color of summer wheat, parted in the center and falling straight to his massive shoulders. Across his forehead he wore a gold diadem, narrow and intricately carved. His head was long, with heavy features in comparison to the men of Islam, but artfully designed in pleasing proportions to the size of him. His beard was neatly trimmed and he wore a short tunic of embroidered linen with snug-fitting trousers banded with gold braid from ankle to knee. A gigantic sword hung from a jeweled leather belt round his narrow waist, the blade sheathed in a tooled leather casing.

Aisha held the giant's confident, amused gaze for long moments. He nodded to her, his eyes filled with dancing lights of mockery. She lurched backward, the curtain falling closed to shield her. Her ample bosom rose and fell with her fury. The savage. Uncivilized barbarian from Allah knew where, how dare he mock her that way.

"Armanus!" she called out in an unnatural voice.

"My lady?" his deep voice queried from outside the curtain.

"Approach the Northman in my name," she whispered urgently. "Determine whether his ship carries furs of a quality as might delight the most discerning. Twenty dinars per skin; I will pay no more. Begin at five dinars."

"But," Armanus argued in a hoarse whisper, "the Northmen can sell a single fine skin for one *hundred* dinars in any marketplace. Look again into the man's eyes and note that he is neither ignorant nor a fool."

"I have met many men who were reasonably intelligent," Aisha snapped, "but never *one* who was not to some degree a fool!"

Aisha heard, with satisfaction, Armanus' outraged intake of breath, then she watched intently as, with fluid grace and confidence, he moved to speak to the Northman. She was unable to read either of their expressions through the silk draperies. Again she began agitatedly snapping her long fingernails.

Two more giants joined the first, standing close to him and a hand-waving Armanus. The eunuch could not utter two words without drawing pictures upon air with hands that were truly more articulate than his eloquent tongue. Tall as Armanus was, the Northmen towered over him as minarets rising above the highest rooftops of the city.

Aisha's eye was caught by a figure wavering behind the Northmen. A Christian monk, she guessed, though all images were so diffused by the curtains it was difficult to be certain. Something about his hovering, meek outline wrought a curiosity so strong in her that she leaned to split the draperies, just wide enough apart to see him clearly.

For a moment the man was lost to her inspection, as Armanus shifted his stance. Then the monk stepped around the group, wearing an expression on his face that reminded her of Hasan, her seven-year-old grandson, when he was being punished for some infraction of etiquette. He also reminded her of the Christian Jesus, Allah bless him, as depicted by the artists of Rome, though one would hardly expect to see the gentle rabbi so unkempt and soiled. The similarity was in his guiltless eyes, in the vulnerability and tenderness of his expression. His features were at once feminine and masculine, his mannerisms also. He seemed desperate to speak to the Northmen and at the same time in dread of them, as if his tongue were tied by fear and self-consciousness. Not one man in the group so much as noticed him. He did seem so . . . superfluous was the only word she could think of. Poor soul, she thought, he thinks that the meek shall inherit the earth, when, in reality, it is the strong and the brutal who rule, who will always prevail. Allah bless the man and protect him. Her pity for the strange monk was relieved somewhat by the truth that all good men who led good lives would see Allah in Paradise, despite any delusions they might harbor in life as to prophets, saints, rewards and punishments.

Startled by a raucous laugh, Aisha's attention was drawn back to the Northmen, who wore leering grins upon their pale faces. Armanus threw up his hands and swung round to stride furiously in her direction, the Northman close on his heels. The unnoticed monk was left behind, looking utterly defeated.

"My lady," Armanus growled against the curtains of the litter, "the ship's captain will not discuss with me the purchase of his goods. He bargains only with the holder of the gold and not with a mere"—he swallowed fury, lifting his arms to clutch hold of the litter roof with stiff hands—"with a mere *messenger*."

"Ridiculous!" she exclaimed. "Tell him it is the custom in—"

"My lady?"

It was a husky, surprisingly civilized voice speaking passable Arabic that had interrupted her. Aisha strained to see his face through the curtains. She did not reply.

"My lady," he said again. He stepped closer to the litter, forcing Armanus to sourly step aside. Then he leaned to stare curiously through the curtains. "If you would purchase my cargo, I would, first, see the color of your eye, to determine if it be honest, then the color of your gold, if it be true. I have no time for intermediaries . . . back and forth." His long head nodded vigorously in jovial emphasis.

"Alhomdolillah," Aisha raged on an outrush of breath. She was not used to being thwarted. Never in her entire life had she suffered such abuse. She did not know quite how to cope with the situation. In desperation, she finally called out, "Armanus! In the name of the Prophet, let us take leave of this place. I find I am not interested, after all, in the purchase of furs."

"But, my lady," the giant said again in heavily accented Arabic and with exquisite patience, "you would never forgive yourself if you failed to deal with me today, for I carry upon the *Sea King's Deer* not only furs, the most rare and beautiful, but *live* fur as well. Live, hmmm? The animals. Cubs."

Aisha's eyes widened and turned shades of gold, in reflection of a vision, the fortune to be gained from the acquisition of live, strange beasts from the north. The zoo owners of all Islam, and there were tens of thousands, every rich merchant, physician, tradesman, every man of means possessing a zoo, would jealously bid for any and all such rare animals as she could obtain from these northern men. Delay, and every merchant in Cairo City would be bargaining with this northland captain.

Aisha dramatically threw the draperies apart and met the Northman's gaze with a hard and calculating eye. "Live beasts, you say? What species? Quite unusual? Speak, man. My time is also valuable!"

The man stared at her for long moments, then thoroughly examined the interior of the litter, as well as her silken, bejeweled form, still more curious and amused than businesslike. "Harp seals," he said pleasantly, his glance sliding from the pointed toes of her satin slippers to the dangling rubies fastened to her veil over each ear.

"Seal! There is nothing extraordinary in *seals*."

The Northman laughed, and the sound was as a rumble of dancer's drums, vibrant and lusty. "No, not a rare beast, unless it wears markings like a harp and is white as Nordland snow when a cub." When her expression remained blank of interest, he added patiently, "I also carry the white bear of Snowland, and the *hrandeer* of Scatanavia," nodding questioningly, encouragingly.

Aisha frowned and bit her lower lip, hoping to convince him that she was little interested. "I could not sell such ordinary beasts."

"Your eyes are extraordinary," the Northman abruptly commented. "Could the rest of your features possibly compliment such beauty?"

Aisha stiffened and backed away from him into the box. Admittedly, his tone had not been mocking, more boyishly sincere, as if he had not intended speaking thus, the words slipping from his tongue as an involuntary expression of his thoughts, but she was angered, nonetheless.

"We were discussing *beasts,*" Armanus cut in icily. "If you have beasts, show them."

"If you have gold, *show* it!" the Northman snapped with equal severity, not offering Armanus the satisfaction of so much as a glance.

"Khattaf!" Armanus swore between tight lips. He moved threateningly toward his adversary, who continued to ignore his presence.

The Northman remarked blandly to Aisha, "It seems

a foolhardy custom, indeed, my lady, to send slaves to bargain in your name."

Armanus' dark eyes blazed at this. "One could not expect *barbarians* to comprehend the amenities and time-honored customs of civilized, intelligent people. A lady of quality and honorable house, carrying sacks of gold about, would constitute irresponsible boasting and pure folly, an invitation to thieves. Her signature upon a *chek* . . ."

"Oh, no!" the Northman protested vehemently, snapping erect at last to face Armanus again. "No *chek*. That custom I do not comprehend. Gold and exchange, these I understand."

"Inshallah," Aisha said exasperatedly, "gold you shall have, Saíd." When the Northman turned quickly back to her with a triumphant smile, she returned his smile and added, "When I have examined the beasts, the quality of your dressed furs."

The Northman bowed to her in agreement. It was as if he had been meticulously instructed in the politeness of bowing, on the premise that it would benefit him greatly amidst heathen peoples, not at all natural to him. As his fair head bent low to her, Aisha thought that he was decidedly not a man of ingratiating disposition, that he would not bow his head to Allah with any sincerity. The gesture strangely degraded him.

"My lady," he said with a flourish of his arm toward the river, "the *Sea King's Deer*, the beasts, await your noble inspection."

"No!" Armanus shouted. "Father of deceivers, you will not entice us aboard your foul vessel!"

"*Us*, slave? I do not recall inviting *you* to board my ship."

"Lady, Aisha . . . you cannot," Armanus insisted, his face reddening.

"Hush, man," Aisha scolded. She would have liked very much to inspect the gleaming ship, but said flatly, "I cannot possibly board your ship, Saíd. But if you will bring to me, at the Inn of the Nightingale, before the sun has set, a sample—one live beast, several dressed skins—I will discuss with you a price for your cargo, based upon the excellence of your samples." She hesitated, suffering a sense of misgiving. His eyes showed compliance. She said carefully, "But I will not pay gold for what I cannot examine altogether. As I must trust in your honesty, so must you trust in mine. I will show you samples of silks and jewels, which I will be prepared to offer in fair trade."

"The Inn of . . . ?" he questioned, grinning down at her.

"—of the Nightingale. Any man, woman or child can direct you."

The Northman thought a moment. He lifted his head and spoke in a harsh, guttural tongue to his companions. His comely face writhed in altering expressions, from perplexity to stern concentration upon their quick replies, to a wide grin suggesting an erotic jest had passed between them.

He turned to Aisha and said, "Before the sun has set. Let your goods be rich, for I am not so coarse and lack-witted as you might suspect. I will not be easily deceived, nor with impunity cheated."

Aisha flinched. It was as if he had read her thoughts. Choice silk wrapped, a thin shell, round a bolt of inferior cloth. How could he know lest he unroll the entire bolt? His warning succeeded in building caution in her.

She would instruct the better material to be thicker round than usual. The extra cost to herself would be nominal. She found it impossible to believe that such a man could examine a jewel and judge its value, discern between a flaw and a mark of excellence. She nodded in agreement.

Drawing the curtains closed, Aisha ordered the bearers to proceed to the inn. She would rest there and take refreshments while Armanus gathered samples from her storehouses.

CHAPTER TWO

The Inn of the Nightingale presented a bare, noncomittal face to the narrow street, indistinguishable from its equally unobtrusive neighbors. Its grounds were secure behind a high screen of vine-covered walls and rising, intertwined shrubbery, stretching several lush acres in either direction of its rusted, iron gate. The two richly appointed, well armed blackamoors that stood guard at the gate constituted the only broad hint as to the luxury within. Outward embellishments were considered an announcement of inner opulence to all passing by, consequently an open invitation to thieves. Thus the streets of Cairo City were cliffed by windowless, gloomy constructions, a pretense in such general practice throughout Islam that no thief worthy of the title was for an instant misled or daunted by the architectural deterrent.

Inside, beyond the marble walls and illuminated tile floors of the foyer, a lobby as large as that of the Caliph of Cairo's palace, wide halls avenued in spokes from a central, open court. In the garden court fountains spun spidery, perfumed webs of moisture. Orange trees blossomed along winding, delightfully landscaped, marbled and graveled footpaths. Wrought-iron benches encircled the trunks of umbrella-pruned willow and fig trees. Most of the halls were partitioned into private salons by extravagant lengths of brilliantly dyed silks, or carved and braided strips of bamboo that clacked incessantly as waiting women with bare abdomens and oiled flesh gracefully rushed in and out of the occupied salons.

The ordinary citizen of Cairo City gloried in the majesty of the caliph and shared gratefully the dinars taxed into the city, carrying themselves with the pride and dignity of capitalists and numbering themselves among the rulers of the world. They wore silks and fine linens and ate with keener relish than those feasting from golden plates at the Inn of the Nightingale. If their lot was slightly less than paradisiacal, they were solaced with the promise of a Paradise to come.

The wealthy sought Paradise on earth. No man or woman privileged to enter into the Olympian splendor and profusive gratifications of the Inn of the Nightingale expected to find more in Allah's Paradise. The most exotic, masterfully prepared foods were served, the fairest slaves shown and bargained for. Palaces were lost with the turn of a card. Scented steam eased the tense and weary, cleansed flesh and soul in the Romanesque baths. Naught in haste, but all at one's leisure. It was a house of pleasure, comfort and beauty, of commerce and trade, dickering and bombastic, grandiose thievery, but not a place where one sought the satisfaction of fleshly desires. No man entering the Inn of the Nightingale sought sexual gratifications outside his home, where more women dwelt than he could, with equity, appease. The inn's lovely serving and dancing girls were much admired, often with a jeweled hand to their firm backsides, or voluminous bosoms, but never molested, a crudity that was beyond the dignities of those refined, silk-shrouded gentlemen who frequented the inn.

Aisha, wife of Kamar al Zamen the physician, a man of prominence and immeasurable wealth, was well known at the inn. Upon her entrance, a flurry of waiting maids rushed to satisfy her every wish. She lounged on blue satin pillows, and nibbled at the fruit, cheeses and delicate curries set before her on a richly woven Arabian carpet. A black boy, somber and diligent, slowly arced an enormous fan of multicolored ostrich plumes over her, causing a pleasant stirring of the air that was heavily scented by delicate clouds of burning incense.

Her hunger satisfied, Aisha dipped her fingers into a bowl of scented water and dried her hands upon the provided linen. She sighed contentedly and leaned back into the pillows for her daily afternoon nap. Beyond the draperies that secluded her, the steady hum of low voices, discordant, silver music, the rustle of skirts and the soft tinkling of glass was all a familiar lullaby, sweetly opiate.

An uproarious confusion startled Aisha awake. Armanus stood glaring down at her from the salon entrance, holding the silk curtains aside with a hand.

Aisha stared past Armanus into the open hall. Four Northmen stumbled toward her with a monstrous, drooling box upon their shoulders. Their captain was encouraging them with much verbal noise. They howled like drunken men with a laughter that shook the rafters and caused crystal goblets to vibrate in sheer agony.

"Praise Allah," Armanus growled, "I have unleashed a nightmare upon this house. The beasts, mistress—as you requested."

Aisha calmly reached for her face veil, tying it fast at the back of her head. As double protection, she lifted her silk shawl and held it across the bridge of her nose. She could not help smiling. The Northmen gamboled across the slick tile floor that, as it became wet from slopping water, rendered them flailing, hilarious clowns. They were quite as carefree as little children.

"If you . . . *please*!" Aisha cried as the captain stumbled through the curtains and nearly trampled her where she lay upon the pillows.

He whirled about, startled, then stared down at her, his mouth dropping open in amazement. At last he said, "If you had a proper seat, you would not be stepped on."

"This *is* a proper seat," she argued. "Now, if you will be so kind as to explain . . . that," distastefully pointing at the wooden box high above on four herculean shoulders.

"It is a sea-dog pup," the captain said pridefully. He motioned his men to lower the box.

Aisha sat up and cautiously stretched her neck to see over the metal rim of the ponderous barrel. "Ahh," she purred, delighted, as two black, button-like eyes met hers. Its adorable white head rose, then vanished in a wave that splashed over the side. The pup came up again, exactly as if it were playing a peep-game with her. "Never before have I seen a white seal. I am enchanted, Saíd."

"Ah," the captain said, nodding, obviously pleased at her reaction to the pup. He said soberly, "Unfortunately, Good Fellow will not remain white. But his unusual markings, when he is grown, will please you greatly, I guarantee." He reached into the water and lifted the silken creature into his arms as if it were a child he adored, then gently put it down on the carpet.

Aisha clapped her hands together happily, for she loved all infant creatures, touched deeply by their sublime innocence and amiability. The captain spoke to the beast and from its throat erupted a coarse bark, and another, which drew the clients and servants of the inn like the muezzin's call drew them to prayer. The sea-dog slid about, rolling over on command with a great deal of help from the coaxing captain.

"Delightful," a gray-bearded gentleman onlooker commented.

"A magnificent white coat," another said.

"How many of these?" Aisha asked eagerly, unable to further conceal her enthusiasm.

"Six. But several have already begun to lose their infant coats, not as perfectly white as Good Fellow, here."

"Ah, only six?"

"Two snow-bear cubs." He gave a signal to a black-haired giant, and the man immediately strode out of the salon. "Two hrandeer. A pair of wolf-dogs from the heaths of Eire. Three rare black foxes. That is my live cargo in all."

An enthusiastic groan of delight emerged from the group of curious onlookers, who broke apart to allow through the Northman who had moments ago departed. In his hulking arms he carried a large, cuddlesome ball of white fur that proceeded to show Aisha two frightened black eyes and a button nose.

The captain smiled at Aisha's evident pleasure. He swung his cloak from his shoulder and spread it, lining side out, for her inspection. "This cloak is lined with the pelt of but one beast. Of just such unmatchable quality are the hundred adult-size snow-bear pelts I carry on the *Sea King's Deer,*" stretching out his long arms to indicate approximate size.

"You exaggerate," Aisha said, laughing.

"I speak the truth," he replied testily, obviously unused to having his word doubted.

"Send your men and beasts away, Saíd, and we will begin the bargaining."

As the curious backed away and the Northmen stumbled off with their sea-dog ashoulder, Aisha moved so that her back leaned against the salon partition. She crossed her legs Buddha-fashion and took note of the bolts of silk and caskets of jewels stacked neatly in the far corner of the salon. Armanus had somehow managed to have the merchandise delivered soundlessly while she slept. The captain paced before her, keeping his eyes upon his finely worked boots, or the draped ceiling, waiting for her to begin.

When calm had been restored, Aisha said sweetly, "Might we know to whom we speak? Do sit down, Saíd. There is no need to pace thus. I am as amiable as your sea-dog. I have yet to bite a tradesman."

The captain's discomfort increased as he searched futilely for a chair or bench. Armanus sat on his heels beside Aisha's couch. Sourly the eunuch picked up a large, fringed cushion, waved it at the captain, then tossed it to the carpet. The captain walked to the cushion, let his knees bend and fell back to land his backside on it.

Aisha said with a smile, "You are not used to our ways, Saíd. I would guess that this is your first visit to our land."

"Yes," he replied, preoccupied with getting comfortable. "This is my first trade voyage to Egypt."

"Yet you adequately speak our language. Not the easiest tongue to learn. How is that?"

"I was schooled in the languages of all the world."

"But by whom? Who in your distant land speaks our tongue?" She leaned forward, fascinated, the beasts and furs forgotten. The man was as interesting as his beasts. "Your name, Saíd?"

"I have several names," he began, clearing his throat. "Gudrid, my mother, did not like the name my father fastened on me when I was water-sprinkled. Snorri, it was. When she divorced my father and took me to Ransay, she changed my name to Dan. I am Dan Thorfinnsson. Then my foster father name-fastened me Sea Kingsson. I am renowned as Dan Sea-Kingsson, which name is to my liking."

"Well, who taught you our language, Dan Sea-Kingsson?"

Dan's glance moved to Armanus' inscrutable face. He was reluctant to answer her question. At last he said somewhat apologetically, "Thralls speak . . . I mean to say, *slaves,* Egyptian slaves, speak your language and teach it to us. Yes, *slave* is your word."

Aisha's eyes rounded in surprise. "I see," she said coldly. She was stunned by the realization that members of her own race were somewhere slaves to savage tribes. She envisioned one of her personal women upon a Northland slave block and could not bear the thought. To serve herself, or men such as Kamar al Zamen, was in many ways a privilege. But to be subjected to the depravities of *barbarians.* Ghastly. Simply appalling. "Please inspect the cloth and jewels," she said sharply, nodding her head in the direction of the goods. She had lost interest in the man. Kamar al Zamen had been right. Savages.

Dan awkwardly rose from the pillow. He strode past the still somber black boy who rhythmically wielded his fan, to finger the bolts of silk and to lift the lids of the tiny caskets.

"Do you know jewels?" Aisha asked softly.

"Well enough," was his preoccupied response. He reached into a casket and removed a pale blue stone. Lifting it to the light of a flickering overhead oil lamp, he studied it carefully. "For instance, this is a star sapphire of poor quality, too light in hue and carelessly cut, causing the star to be misshapen." He added, after a more scrupulous inspection, "This star is like the pupil of an eye in its roundness, the points diffused."

Aisha's head snapped round and she met Armanus' eyes, silently speaking of her amazement and rude awakening. She turned a guarded eye back to Dan and said carefully, "Truly you have been well schooled in the art of trade, Saíd. I would not have supposed that your people shared the same values as ourselves . . . regarding jewels."

"Perhaps you were right," he said with a grin, returning the stone to its casket. "I was taught *Saracen* values, that I would not be cheated. Personally, I place little value upon colored rocks."

"Indeed. Then, what *do* you consider to be of great value, hmm?"

He eyed her soberly, then looked away. He lifted a bolt of green, printed silk. While inspecting the cloth, he said, "My *ship*, my sword—many things which you would consider of small worth. My son."

"Ah, you underestimate me, Saíd. I, too, have a son. A young man worth far more to me than all the gold of this earth." She added curiously, "Of what faith are you, Dan Sea-Kingsson?"

"I believe in my own strength," he replied confidently.

Dan threw the heavy bolt of green silk away from him, holding to the cloth edge, unfolding a long length for his inspection. "This is indeed fine silk. But I would accept such cloth only in dress lengths, folded, that each piece might be examined upon exchange of goods."

Aisha could not suppress a hearty laugh. "Name your price, Dan Sea-Kingsson, and you shall have it. Fair is fair. I will make a fortune from the sale of your beasts."

Dan dropped the silk and moved to stand at her feet. He grinned down at her, greatly satisfied with himself. "Five hundred dress lengths of silk. All three caskets of jewels." His smile widened. "All my people are not as astute as I. I will make a fortune from the sale of these inferior stones on the Dublin wharves."

"A bargain. When can you deliver the beasts and pelts?"

"On the morrow."

"Excellent. Deliver the beasts to the house called the

Golden Gate, the manor house of my husband. We have a zoo that can temporarily house the animals. Deliver the furs to my storehouse. Armanus will direct you to it."

Aisha brought her silk shawl up over her hair, rose to her feet and offered her right hand to the Northman. He took her offered hand and for a moment both her flesh and her eyes were fastened to him. Aisha felt a strange warmth pass from his hand to hers, a warmth that caused her to quickly remove her hand from his. "It has been a pleasure bargaining with you, Saíd," she said softly. "If you come again to Cairo, with beasts, knock upon the door of the Golden Gate and ask for me. A good day to you. Peace be with thee."

With a rustle of satin and silk, Aisha turned and left Dan Sea-Kingsson there. If she had thought upon it, she would have supposed never to see the man again.

A condition of lonely restlessness had settled upon the crew of the *Sea King's Deer.* Dan and his four companions gulped three flagons of ale in a murky cellar inn with much effort at joviality. At last they wandered back to the Street of the Flowers wharf, for want of a better direction to turn.

The Northmen had departed from Dansfiord three weeks past, looking forward, with vigorous talk of delectable Egyptian wenches and orgies of pagan lechery, to this first day in Cairo City. But women were only veiled apparitions with downcast eyes that swiftly passed them on the streets. Now that dark had settled, not one could be seen anywhere about. At night, in Christian lands, harlots flocked like scavenger gulls upon the streets, energetically hawking their wares.

"Muslims take so many," Dan's standard bearer grumbled aside to his captain, "so many into their homes, that none are left to please destitute seamen."

"Some possess as many as fifty, or one hundred," Dan exaggerated absentmindedly. His eyes cast across the now almost deserted wharf, to his ship. The *Sea King's Deer* lolled there, magnificent, and stirred a warmth of pride in his breast. He sat himself down on an empty wooden crate, turning his glance to the starlit sky. "It was good," he muttered, "to make so quick a bargain. We will easily return before Hayjannir."

"One of the lechers must have more women than he can handle. If we could discover such a husband, perhaps . . ."

Dan laughed and slapped his friend on the back with the flat of a hand. "The pain is bad, hmm?"

"Unbearable!"

"Truth; polygamy is an abomination. For Muslims, at any rate." He made a smirking face and said, "We would not want to deprive our good King Magnus of his three wives, Christian though he swears to be, now would we? Let us praise Christians, one and all, for not only preserving harlotry, but for progressing it."

"Speaking of Christians," Thorvald said aside, "look what approaches. Holy Jesus himself."

Dan's mouth turned down into a fierce, rigid line. A Christian monk hesitantly moved toward him out of the darkness. He brought his arms up, folding them across his chest, as if controlling an impulse to plant an axe in the monk's skull. He lifted a foot and nudged Thorvald's boot, a signal to give the Christian a trying time of it.

David halted before Dan, rocking uneasily from foot

to foot, his fingers nervously fluttering over the skirt of his robe, his chin refusing to rise. He was exhausted. The walk from Saint Monica had drained him of what little strength he possessed. He managed to say, falteringly, "Latin? Do you . . . speak Latin?"

Dan shouted every obscenity he knew at the monk, in the language of the Asa people. When David only smiled helplessly, bewildered in the face of such grossness, the five Northmen howled with mocking laughter.

David flushed. "Nordland," he said apologetically, in a whispering tone of voice.

"Nordland, Nordland," Dan echoed, thrashing his head like a brainless man.

Hurt and frustrated, David lifted an arm and pointed at the *Sea King's Deer*. "Orkney," he said in an attempt to discover a word that would communicate his need.

Dan instantly sobered. In excellent Latin he shouted at David, "What in the name of Hel do *you* know about Orkney?"

David flinched and backed away. His lips quivered as he tried to form words in his throat, but intelligible sound did not emerge. At last he managed, "Passage." His entire body was trembling. He had taken too little food with him and was weakened by exertion almost to the point of fainting. "To Nordland," he said hoarsely. "I seek the office of Bishop John Hoskuldson. I am commissioned to—to the Orkney islands."

"Not on *my* ship!" Dan said explosively.

"But," David stammered, stunned by the loathing for him that he saw in the man's eyes. "I have only a little gold. But I—"

"If you offered me a thousand raven stallions and ten thousand *dreki*, each sixty oar, I would not allow one of your paws to *touch* the *Sea King's Deer*. Off with you! Enough Christians infest our lands these days. Like flies upon sweetest Saracen sugar. Scat! You offend me."

David's mouth dropped open in shock. Numbly, he turned to depart, tears of helplessness and incomprehension in his eyes.

"Well, if you *must*. If you insist." Dan had been suddenly struck by the frailty of the man, both of the flesh and of the spirit. "See the captain of the *Raven of the Wind*. That white-sailed vessel. Mord, he is called. He is a Christian, thus could probably stomach your presence."

David whipped around, his face alight with gratitude. But Dan's unfaltering scowl discouraged any comment.

"Did I hear my name mentioned?" a bass voice drummed from behind the group.

David's eyes rounded. Emerging out of the darkness, elbowing a path between Dan and Thorvald, rose a man of unbelievable proportions. A whale amidst a school of sardines. He was at least seven feet tall and as wide through the chest as a wine barrel. His hands and feet were three times normal size.

"Mord Baptized-One." Dan grinned up at the giant. "This person seeks passage to Nordland, or to Orkney."

"He has it," Mord boomed, investigating David with cold eyes. In clumsy Latin, he said to David, "Get you aboard, monk. We cast away at a moment's notice."

"So soon?" David murmured, clearing his throat against a shaking fist.

"Possibly tonight," Mord replied, offering Dan a knowing smirk.

"Have you made bargain for your cargo already,

Mord Baptized-One?" Dan asked, a definite note of triumph in his voice.

"In less than one full day?" Mord roared, glaring down at his seated rival. "Hardly!"

"*My* cargo will be exchanged on the morrow, for silks and precious stones."

"Liar!"

Dan erupted to his feet, one hand flashing to the hilt of his sword.

"Sit down," Mord commanded. "We are peace-sheathed. Will you undress the Flinging One? Begin a war on this far shore? So, you have bargained for your goods. Jesus love you, you are the soul of cleverness, Dan Sea-Kingsson."

Dan's mouth twisted into a reluctant smile. "It was extreme good fortune," he sourly admitted. "No cleverness on my part was involved. She came to me, seeking—"

"She?"

"She. In veils. Jewels dripping from her as icicles from a gable."

Mord's massive, rubbery face writhed at the mention of jewels. He leaned down and asked confidentially, "You will fleece her, eh? and fast away?"

"This is not a coastal village," Dan objected heatedly. "It is a policed city half a day inland from the sea. I hear tell Muslims send birds from stronghold to stronghold that carry messages about the movements of their enemies. In Cairo City we are traders, peace-sheathed, our shields inheld as we sailed into port. Enough that I receive goods for goods."

"Where do you exchange goods?" Mord asked, grinning and sucking on his teeth.

"At a manor called the Golden Gate. Just beyond the city walls."

"Outside the walls, you say! To the north?"

"North," Dan admitted, frowning against a strong suspicion.

Mord said thoughtfully, "On the path toward the sea . . . I saw the grand houses as we entered harbor."

"Do as you see fit, Mord Baptized-One," Dan said warningly, "but not until my goods are exchanged. Understand? The woman has made bargain with *me*. If you in any way interfere, I will have you outlawed at the Thing as a thief!"

"Dan Sea-Kingsson! Would I commit such an act against a fellow?"

"You would. Do not play the fool. Loot along the route home. Here, the risk is too great."

"Pardon me," a fragile voice interrupted.

Both captains turned to stare at David. They had completely forgotten about him.

"Well, speak up," Dan said sharply.

David stared at Dan Sea-Kingsson and was suddenly overwhelmed by the realization of just how difficult his task of conversion was going to be. *I of the faint heart and trembling knees, I whose single strength is good intentions, cannot hope to completely alter the lifelong convictions of a man like this, a man of such remarkable physical beauty, limitless pride, and almost god-like self-assurance.* The captain's companions were his equals in every sense, looking at this intrusive monk before them with equal distrust and hatred. They were not poor, or meek, or downtrodden, but carried themselves like kings. David could not imagine such men as these on their knees praying for the salvation of their souls.

Stunned by the direction his thoughts had taken, David said unsteadily to Mord, "I beseech you, do not sail without me. I must go to the church of Father Jonas . . . who will instruct me in my mission and . . . I will return quickly." With that, he hurried away from the group along the wharf.

Mord roared after the monk, "Here! Hold on." When David had turned and was attentive, Mord called out, "I will send a man along with you to protect you."

"Thank you," David said gratefully, "but God is my protector." In a rush of coherence, he exclaimed, "The Lord sent you to this shore, a miracle, that I might be transported to my mission!"

Dan groaned and doubled over in pretended agony. "I am going to puke! A miracle . . . a miracle. What hangs between his legs, do you think, Thorvald? Keys, eh? A woman's keys. Swing-sway, tinkle tinkle." His four companions were exploding with laughter, which did nothing to discourage Dan. "Oh, do be sweet and gentle, fellows. It is not nice to kill people you hate. It is naughty to hate. Cut off your pricks and replace them with keys. We dream of a world of one sex, all *women.* Jesus . . . Thor dissolve him in thunderstorm . . . was not a *man,* he was—"

A shattering bellow emerged from Mord's throat, cutting Dan's dramatics short. The goliath's head was red as the sun when seen through smoke.

"Take your hand from your sword, Mord Baptized-One," Dan said pleasantly. "Did you not remind me, but a moment past, that we are peace-sheathed?"

"Heathen wearer of Hel shoes," Mord gasped. His flaccid jowls quivered with his increasing indignation.

"Do I see *hatred* in your eyes?" Dan asked, mocking

stunned amazement. "Tch-tch. Where is your *other cheek*? Show it to me, and I will strike it gladly. You must love me, Mord Baptized-One. I am your brother and you are my keeper."

Dan's companions were doubled over, completely overcome by Dan's wit. Mord shook on his legs like a tree about to fall.

"When next we meet on Orkney soil," Mord said at last, swallowing in great gulps the erupting rage within him, "take care to have the Flinging One in hand, Dan Sea-Kingsson."

"Mord!" Dan wailed. "You are doomed. The Church hates blood!"

CHAPTER THREE

The four wives of Kamar al Zamen sat cross-legged on their cushions. The thick, red carpet on the floor before them was crowded with serving dishes that had been artfully heaped with morning cakes, whole and sliced fresh fruits, sweetmeats, dates and creams, and carafes of steaming, thick coffee. Partitioned apart by transparent lengths of silk, the ten concubines shared a setting of their own, their overlapping chatter and laughter an incessant clamor. Several servant girls moved about the two areas swinging ornate brass incense pots that filled the room with billowing clouds of jasmine scent.

"What was that you said, Nur al Huda?" Aisha asked frigidly, dropping her demitasse into its saucer.

"I said," the child boldly cried, shaking a braceleted arm over the table, "that this is a wretched house and that I cannot *wait* until the foul son of a she-goat is dead!"

"Allah forgive you!" Aisha exclaimed, genuinely horrified. "Beg Allah's forgiveness this instant. You are hell-bent for certain, Nur al Huda."

"I am hell *driven,*" Nur al Huda argued. "Why is it I must pine away within these walls, allowed only one half month's visit a year to the house of my father, while you—you spend days, whenever you please, in the city? I ask you, is this *equitable*?" She nodded her dark head to each of the others, seeking support, but received not so much as a sympathetic glance.

Aisha fought to control her temper. Reaching for her cup, she sipped the heavily sweetened and creamed coffee. Coldly she inspected the child. Nur al Huda was quite beautiful and preposterously young, not yet sixteen years. Her raven hair fell to the pillows she sat upon in a gleaming horse's tail, and crisp ringlets framed her oval, virginal face. In truth Nur al Huda was a virgin, or should be. Kamar al Zamen had been impotent when he took her, a child of twelve, as wife. A foolish indulgence, but Aisha had understood why he was marrying so late in life. A man could not admit to impotence at any age. It was his way of telling his friends that he had not lost his virility. However, she did *not* comprehend Nur al Huda's churlish resentment of that impotence. It had been somewhat of a relief to herself when he had ceased calling for her. She had never taken any particular delight in copulation, despite the thoroughness of her early training that began at the age of five, and Kamar al Zamen's practiced expertness.

"I say . . . why must I die of boredom?" Nur al Huda insisted. "While you—"

"Because," Aisha interrupted tightly, "you are an irresponsible child and have no purpose in the city save wickedness. It has been *my* decision that you remain confined, not our husband's."

"Wickedness," Nur al Huda wailed, her voice breaking. Tears glistened behind her eyes.

"Adultery. Is that specific enough? Is that not what you have in mind? If I recall correctly, it was yourself I apprehended, planted under an orange tree, intent upon committing the grossest insult against our husband and our Blessed Allah in Paradise. And with a *kitchen* boy!"

"Allah render me deaf! I cannot abide your saintly lectures another instant!"

"I will not quarrel with you," Aisha said disdainfully. She selected a frosted cake from the platter, took a dainty bite of it and chewed with deliberate detachment. After long, tense moments, she sweetly offered, "Fascinating new animals will be brought to the zoo today. Perhaps that to look forward to will render the remainder of this day less unendurable for you, dear."

Nur al Huda exploded to her feet. Choking on strangled sobs, she wailed, "I despise you! Loathe you!" She ran from the room, then through the open pavilion doors into the garden courtyard.

The red-haired wife sitting to Aisha's left quickly got to her feet, moving to follow Nur al Huda.

"Sit down, Zarífah," Aisha commanded.

"But I . . . I only wish to—"

"I *know* what you wish to accomplish, second wife. But I think Nur al Huda can do without the kind of comfort you hope to dispense." She faltered. It pained her lips to speak of it. "Those obscene compensations that you incessantly attempt to inflict upon the women of this house. If you lay a hand on that child, I will instruct our husband as to your monstrous perversion and you will be punished."

The woman paled and shivered, falling back upon her cushions. The punishment, according to law and custom, was death, though seldom was worse than divorce and public shame meted out in these enlightened times.

"Inshallah!" Aisha cursed as the gong sounded, a warning that men sought entrance to the house. The next minutes were spent clearing the expansive manor of all females. "Whoever could it be at such an early hour?" she cried, furious at the interruption.

Aisha quickly counted those present. All were accounted for except two servant girls, who could be depended upon to take refuge in the cookroom. Nur al Huda rushed in from the garden, to throw herself upon her sleeping mattress. Silence descended upon the harim, the concubines having been drawn from petty conversations by the prospect of sneaking to various secret places where they could enjoy happy hours of eavesdropping.

Kamar al Zamen entered the harim and moved purposefully toward Aisha, who leaped to her feet at the sight of him. She bowed slightly to her husband as he approached her and said sweetly, "Allah's mercy and peace be upon thee this day, my husband."

"Good wife," Kamar al Zamen said, smiling upon her, his eyebrows raised questioningly. "A veritable Apollo stands within my anteroom. He delivers beasts?"

Aisha slapped her forehead in dismay. "Praise Allah! I am not prepared. So early! The men have not begun making room in our cages. The monkeys must be . . . And Armanus will not return from Cairo City with the trade goods for hours! Whatever am I to do?"

Her husband shook his head, his still handsome face

wearing an expression of paternal, affectionate tolerance. He said, "Perhaps I can entertain the trader. For an hour. Then I must keep an appointment with Asaf ibn Barkhiya."

"That old fraud," she complained, thoroughly unnerved by the confusion. "Why do you waste your time with him, my husband? He will outlive us all."

"Indeed he will," Kamar al Zamen replied agreeably, "but he pays so well. Who am I to destroy the delusion which is his greatest comfort in life, that I can somehow give him immortality? I do not nurse his flesh so much as his supreme fear of death. If Asaf had a proper faith in the hereafter, the here and now would not enslave him so in chains of terror. Enslaved. Ah, are we not all enslaved, to one thing or another? Myself, I cannot imagine how I existed forty years and five without you by my side, my evening star. . . . I will take pleasure in entertaining the tradesman. A curious breed. Quite interesting. He strongly suggests Apollo to me, or Hercules." With that, he touched her cheek with a palm and moved toward the draped exit, quickly moving out of sight.

Dan Sea-Kingsson stood, uncomfortable, before the old man, searching for a place to sit. He took note how the old one sat upon his heels, in what would appear to be a knee-breaking, muscle-agonizing position. At last he fell down upon a cushion, slid the calves of his legs under him and sat on them. He leaned backward in stiff repose, half on the pillow and half off.

"Saíd?" Kamar al Zamen purred, sipping the wine in his crystal goblet. "Would you do me the honor of enlightening me as to your land and people? I would truly be fascinated. All my days I have heard of Saxons and of their unusual vessels."

Dan sourly eyed the old one, who wore jewels worth ten years' trading upon turban, robes and fingers. The ruby of the man's thumb ring caused Dan to writhe in speechless temptation. His pirate's blood ran hot. He was, in fact, surrounded by priceless artifacts—statues of silver, jasper and jade, precious woods, ivory. The carpet under him was hand-woven and of intricate design; it was at least two inches thick. The wine decanter was of gold. The crystal he held in his hand was ringed with gold filigree.

"You admire my thumb ring?" Kamar al Zamen asked graciously. "I can only hope Allah has not sent a pirate to my house. Such princely men as you . . . lawless raiders? Difficult to believe, Saíd."

Dan smiled, his wide mouth rising impishly at the corners. "My *ship* entered Cairo harbor with shields inheld, Saíd, which is to say that this moment I am not a pirate but a trader."

"Which often is the same thing . . . trader, pirate, eh?"

Dan laughed at the old man's easy wit. He began to relax. "Truth you speak, Saíd."

"You call yourselves Saxons."

"No. That is what we are called by those ignorant of us. My sword is single-edged and called a Sax," shrugging as if to say, thus the unimaginative workings of heathen minds. "We are the Asar. Northmen."

"But from what land? How far? Across what seas?"

"Do you have knowledge of a land called England, Saíd? Eire?"

"By name only. I own several merchant ships, but

they do not venture west beyond the Pillars of Hercules."

"West of the Pillars. Then north, past the great firth. There lie islands called Orkneys. One of these islands, named Ransay, is mine. From Greenland, Snowland and Nordland, the Asar people sail to your ports. For many centuries we have considered England a colony of the Asar, though the English like to think of themselves as independent. Long ago Nordland became overpopulated and the Asar migrated to England, peopled the coastlines. They are subject to the Asar whether they will admit it or not."

Kamar al Zamen frowned and shook his head, perplexed. "You are Christian peoples?"

Dan's broad face twisted into a scowl. He said stiffly, "Some have forsaken Odin and Thor in the past hundred years, submitting to a knee-bending degradation. Not I, Saíd. I meet Thor's eye squarely, with my sword upraised. I bow and whine before no man or god."

"I bow several times a day to Allah," Kamar al Zamen said, smiling tolerantly. "I am a knee-bender of long standing. This is not manly, eh?"

Dan did not reply, but met the old one's eyes with his unspoken answer clear to read in his own.

"You treat your God—Thor, you named him?—with such aggressive defiance?"

"He would turn from me if I so dreaded his might as to tremble before him. Tremble before the gods, tremble before the battle . . . tremble before death. The battle is lost for want of courage. Valhalla is lost for want of a valiant death. All purpose in living is lost if a man is allowed no pride, honor or valor."

"Christianity, I admit, allows for small degrees of

pride and valor, but Jesus Christ, Allah bless him, was of noble mind and heart. Loving one another is not an altogether distasteful philosophy."

"Distasteful? A weak word. I define Christianity as the ridiculous ravings of emasculated life-lovers, who squawk and flurry like terrified chickens before the specter of death. I am not a chicken but a *man,* and I fear nothing but the loss of my pride, honor and valor. I would not so *honor* Christianity—by fearing it. I am stunned at how it has spread across Europe. What ails people, I wonder, to pay such general homage to a man as ineffectual as Jesus Christ, a man with so little pride that he accepted a *thief's* death."

Kamar al Zamen studied the flush of the Northman's face, then thoughtfully refilled Dan's goblet and his own. His mind reflected upon the specter of Christianity, which, he believed, would one day be a serious threat to his own people. If the pope was, as it would appear, entrenching himself in the northlands, commanding the minds and souls of such men as this one before him, less persevering, perhaps, but nonetheless racially vigorous, no other conclusion save defeat could be imagined. Nothing so ensured defeat as luxury and the physical and spiritual fragility resultant therefrom. He sighed, thinking that he would not have to face those black future days when Christians, rather than Muslims, ruled the earth.

"You were born on your island in what year, Dan Sea-Kingsson?" Kamar al Zamen asked, curious as to the man's age, which could have been anywhere from twenty and five to forty years. His face was a sun-baked, unlined mask of general good health and robust youth.

"I was not born on Ransay," Dan replied. "I entered this world upon the shore of Vinland, twenty-eight winters past."

"Vinland?"

"West-over-seas. A land first sighted by Bjarni, later explored by Leif Ericsson."

"West, you say," Kamar al Zamen commented doubtfully.

"*West*, Saíd. From Snowland to Greenland, and from there across the northern sea, five days with fair wind, to Vinland."

"Praise Allah!" Kamar al Zamen exclaimed. "How vast that sea must be. One is sometimes appalled by a suspicion that the waters are infinite, without any final shore or cataract. But then, that the waters could pour over a world's-end cliff is equally inconceivable. One cannot help wondering if that overflowing tide would not form another sea below, which in turn . . . Ach, the mind stumbles and halts before such ponderations. A land called Vinland. Quite remarkable."

"Thus did I come by the name Sea-Kingsson. The men of Orkney found it difficult to conceive, though they did not for a moment doubt the validity of my mother's experience, of land so far west. They were awed. My foster father affectionately imagined me to be a son of the Sea King, the Sea King impregnating Gudrid, my mother, at the brink of the world in a furious, fiery storm. We enjoy fanciful tales. I take pride in the title, uniquely mine."

"Your mother took such a hazardous journey?" Kamar al Zamen asked, amazed.

"And dwelt on that hostile shore three years. My mother is a very remarkable woman, in many ways."

"You astound me, young man. Your manner is refined, your mind educated, and your tongue is fluent. Hardly what I had expected from the tales that are told about your people. Fathers of sea monsters, they say."

Dan turned a slow smile upon his host. "Perhaps you would not think me so civilized were I where you sit, host to yourself at my homestead at Dansfiord. When in Rome do as the Romans do, was my first instruction. I am what is called 'prime-signed,' which is to say I am allowed to condone and pay homage to false gods for the sake of fruitful trade. Thor is not as insufferably jealous as Allah, or Jehovah."

Kamar al Zamen laughed so abruptly that he choked on the swallow of wine in his throat. He hastily wiped away the little that had splashed upon his white robe, then asked enthusiastically, "And how, exactly, would the occasion differ, eh?"

"I would be rousing drunk by now. Then I would shout a great deal, wrestle with a friend, throw a few meat bones about, which is to say that I would be having much more fun than I presently am, no insult to your noble self intended, of course."

"And none taken . . . none taken," Kamar al Zamen said with a broad smile. "Politeness is a virtue notoriously inimical to revelry." With slight difficulty and a creaking of joints, he rose to his feet. Dan quickly followed his lead and stood before him. "Now I must *politely* and reluctantly end our very interesting conversation, Dan Sea-Kingsson. I have an appointment to keep."

Following a fleeting handshake, Kamar al Zamen asked, "Do you understand our custom of female seclusion, Saíd?"

Dan's expression tightened slightly, indicating a disapproval which he had no intention of voicing. He nodded affirmatively.

"I shall assume that, since you so firmly adhere to the adage—when in Rome, eh?—I can trust you to keep faith with this custom. I leave you to the servants. The zanana is sufficiently set apart. You will not find it difficult to avoid. A good day to you, Dan Sea-Kingsson." He bowed deeply from the waist. "Peace be with thee."

Dan returned the bow, replying with the proper "And on you be peace and the mercy and blessing of Allah, Saíd."

"Excellent," Dan heard the old one mumble as he walked stiffly out of the room, vanishing behind the richly embroidered drapery that served as a door. "Indeed, Hercules."

When his host was gone, Dan stood motionless for long moments. He regretfully eyed the rich furnishings surrounding him. Sighing, he stepped to the window, hoping to catch a glimpse of his waiting men and wagons of beasts. But he saw only vast stretches of lawn and shrubbery. A slice of the sullen Nile was visible between two spreading shade trees.

A black manservant entered the room with a bowl of fresh fruit. He placed it upon a low table, then turned a dark, suspicious eye upon Dan.

"I am free to . . . to wander about?" Dan asked, striding across the room to snatch up a red apple.

Obviously opposed to his master's leniency, the servant only stared rudely and refused to answer.

Impulsively, Dan darted toward the servant and roared like a lion, baring his teeth. The black man lurched back in round-eyed terror and made a hasty retreat.

Satisfied with himself, Dan took half the apple into his mouth with one bite, then strolled out into the anteroom.

Nearing the end of his inspection of the ground floor of Kamar al Zamen's house, Dan came upon a sternly guarded curtained archway. Two black slaves stood at either side of the entrance. They were garishly attired in balloon, yellow satin trousers and purple vests, their muscular arms ringed with bracelets.

The harim, Dan surmised, halting to draw his mouth into a thin line of contempt. He could not imagine men so addlebrained as to imprison their women so cruelly. It was an act of stupidity, to take more women than they were capable of gratifying, then living in such dread of being cuckolded, they were compelled to set guards upon the pitiful wretches.

Dan thought about Freydis, his wife. He saw her striding competently through his house, across the fields and at the marketplaces, her keys proudly fastened to her girdle, her golden head back-held in haughty self-confidence. And Gudrid, his mother, a veritable tigress, physically and mentally the match for any man and the better of some. He could imagine the wounds Gudrid would have inflicted upon a husband who was so distrustful as to insult her with imprisonment. What manner of women must these of Islam be to abide such treatment?

Dan had been raised to admire and respect all womankind, unwearying, warm, unfathomable creatures, delivered to man by the All-Father as helpmates and solace, mothers, lovers and partners. In the northlands a wife was the equal of her husband, not a plaything or a servant. This moment, Freydis, with unquestionable ability, was keeping his house, his fields and his financial affairs in order during his absence. She would take arms, if need be, to protect the homestead. That she might take a man to her bed concerned him not in the least. Adultery, to be sure, was a convenient and lawful tool in the obtaining of a divorce, but until such time as he felt inclined to take a new wife, Freydis could take solace with whomever she chose, as would he. Asa men could be as rabid before adultery as any Muslim or Christian, but Dan considered himself intellectually above such perverse vanity. Freydis commanded too much respect from him to ever suffer shame or hurt by his hand.

Dan moved away from the harim entrance, out into a garden courtyard. He wandered impatiently along the graveled paths, then tried to relax by lounging under the shade of a flowering orange tree. All the while, he suffered a strong sense of being watched. But not a face or eye showed itself to him from any of the dozen high windows and balconies overlooking the courtyard. It finally occurred to him that as long as he remained on the premises, the women of the house were forced to remain secluded. His tongue flashed out over his lower lip, as his eye raised to a ground-floor window that must belong to the harim, thinking of the ten, twenty, perhaps thirty lovelies there who were so in need of comfort.

"Saíd?"

Dan leaped to his feet in surprise. He had been so

engrossed in a vision of himself gratifying twenty eager harim wenches, he had not heard Armanus' approach.

"I beg your benevolent understanding," Armanus began, bowing stiffly from the waist, "and your continued patience, oh worthy captain. An unfortunate delay. I fear you will have to return empty-handed."

"Empty-handed!" Dan shouted, rising to full and suspicious height.

"Most unfortunate. But you insisted upon dress lengths. You must realize the hours required to cut so many bolts of cloth. Much care is necessary, that the lengths do not reach you in less than perfect condition."

"Curse you, slave! Why did you allow me to pace half the morning, like a beast in one of your master's cages?"

"Oh most worthy captain, my most humble apologies. I made every effort, I assure you, and came as quickly as possible when I knew it could not be done this day."

Dan kicked at a small white flower that was growing up through the lawn close to his boot. The man was being insufferably polite about it. He snapped, "What about the beasts? I paid silver for the rental of those wagons stalled all the forenoon outside the gate."

"Leave the beasts, Saíd," Armanus purred, smiling excessively.

"Leave them! I would never see a length of cloth!"

"My mistress is not a thief!" Armanus protested, his glossy veneer giving way.

"My standard bearer was to deliver the pelts to you. Did you receive them?"

"I did. Excellent quality, worthy captain."

Dan hesitated, torn between distrust and an intuitive confidence in the woman's integrity. Then he gave thought to Mord Baptized-One's hint that he might loot this house. He quickly discarded the idea. Mord was a fool only in his choice of gods, never at the helm of his ship, or in the battle. He had been adventure-dreaming, no more. The tameness of this trade mission, though it was vital to the economic survival of their *odels,* was beginning to gnaw at the spirit, his own, as well as Mord's. No, Mord would not attack this suburb. "I will leave the beasts," Dan abruptly agreed. "Give me the caskets of jewels as part payment, and I will be gone."

Armanus fairly exploded with triumph. He led Dan into the house, where, from a locked cabinet in his own lavish quarters, he produced the caskets.

Dan opened each box, giving cursory examination to the contents of each. He nodded approval and made straight for the hall, and out of the house to his companions, where they sprawled under the wagons for shade from the hot sun. The crated animals were unloaded and left on the road for Aisha's men to do with as they pleased.

The very moment that Dan lifted himself to a wagon seat, sourly snapping the reins to begin the short journey back to the Street of the Flowers wharf, Mord Baptized-One ordered the anchor to be raised and the *Raven of the Wind* eased out of its berth, moving northward toward the suburbs. Dan Sea-Kingsson would have had the entire day to make good his bargain. Mord's cargo had been hastily dispensed with for less than half its value. He had made a decision—to add zest to this trade venture by effortlessly effecting the transition from tradesman to pirate.

CHAPTER FOUR

There was no moon. The *Raven of the Wind,* with her white sails furled, was as invisible on the river as a coiled snake in tall grass. In the close-away suburb unaware families entertained friends, put children to bed, sat intently over chess or backgammon boards, or strolled through their beloved gardens to the strains of whispering fountains and the exultant songs of night birds. Monkeys chattered in their zoo cages. A woman's vibrant laughter rose on the cool breeze. From the manor called the Golden Gate, infant seals barked a chorus familiar only to those fifty and two pirates tensely waiting on the dragon ship for the order to attack.

David of Saint Monica stood near the bow of the *Raven of the Wind,* utterly bewildered by the behavior of the crew, who had gone from boisterous activity to complete silence. Every man was frozen like a statue with breath held—seemed to be waiting for something. A sweetly scented breeze caressed his face and hands, and gently flapped the skirts of his brown robe against his trembling legs. His hands were trembling as well.

He had never before experienced such excitement, such exhilarating joy; it rushed about under his ribs, upset his stomach and caused him to gasp for breath. God had blessed him by providing this ship to his mission so soon after his departure from Saint Monica—truly miraculous.

David flinched as he recalled the mocking laughter of the yellow-haired captain and his men when he had spoken to them of the miracle of their presence at the Cairo City wharf at this precise moment in time. Anxiously, he strained his eyes to see through the darkness to the men closest to him. Their faces were drawn into grim masks, their breathing strangely heavy, as if they had been running. When he had boarded this ship near sunset, not one member of the crew had shown the slightest inclination to honor him as a priest, though they all wore Christian crosses round their necks. He had learned that though he was among Christians, he was as isolated from them as if he were a pagan, that to be Christian did not necessarily mean kinship.

In the city, Dan Sea-Kingsson stood high upon the forecastle of the *Sea King's Deer,* tensely listening for the sound of the horn that would tell him whether Mord Baptized-One had attacked somewhere in the suburbs, or intended to. He had sent Thorvald up river in a smallboat, with two men, to investigate the whereabouts of the *Raven of the Wind.*

When Dan had returned to the wharf from the Golden Gate, the *Raven of the Wind* had been gone from her berth, a forewarning not to be taken lightly. He would have broken loose from his moorings immediately, except for the five hundred dress lengths of silk to be collected on the morrow. His sails were furled, the mast lowered, the men in place at their oars. On a moment's notice he could be away.

Dan's mouth was dry. His fingers ached, where they had tightened round the rope that held the *Sea King's Deer* fast to the wharf. The Flinging One was no longer peace-sheathed, but in his hand and glinting reflected light from the oil lamps that lit the Street of the Flowers wharf.

In the house of the Golden Gate, servants bustled about the kitchen preparing the next day's foods. A kettle of wine simmered on the fire. Chickens were being killed and plucked, and morning cakes were baking in the brick ovens.

Kamar al Zamen had not returned from the city. A slave boy from the house of Asaf ibn Barkhiya had arrived at sundown with a message, saying that the master would take meal with his patient and spend the night.

In the harim servant girls were laying out the sleeping mattresses, arranging pillows and coverlets, while Aisha and the three other wives occupied themselves at cards. Five of the ten concubines sat round a lute-strumming sixth, singing a lilting, discordant love song.

Aisha had been deliberately losing so that Nur al Huda could win, which had brightened the fourth wife's outlook considerably. Nur al Huda was fairly exploding with a gloating triumph, her gleeful taunts ringing through the harim.

At a signal from Aisha, the women scattered to their respective beds. Servant women removed scented oil lamps, and darkness fell upon the physician's household.

Three men stood guard. One at each street gate, front and back, and one at the entrance to the harim. Armanus made his nightly inspection of the house and grounds, then went to his bed.

At midnight the captain of the *Raven of the Wind* launched the smallboats. Forty men silently scrambled out of the boats onto the riverbank, then in groups of five, swept into the hushed streets. A man was left with each of the four small boats. Each of the pillagers carried a large skin bag tied round his neck and falling down his back. The captain's order had been to be silent, and they were not to set fires that might awaken the entire suburb and adjacent city.

No monumental, gilded portal showed them the way to the most splendid of all the manor houses. A beggar had been paid to guide them to the house called the Golden Gate, which was hidden behind trees and shrubbery.

Aisha's eyes sprang open. She lay motionless, listening. No unusual sounds. She heard only Nur al Huda's shallow, whispering breathing close by, and the song of a nightingale from the garden. Still, her heart skipped and she remained tense. Taking in a deep breath, she told herself a dream had disturbed her, forgotten immediately upon awakening She gazed at the draped ceiling, noting the dark waves marked upon the silk by a breeze blowing in through the open pavilion doors. Turning her head, she looked across the room, through the open pavilion entrance to the garden beyond. The darkness was brightened in ethereal patches by oil lamps set along the paths.

Aisha forced her eyes closed, but a sound, carried on the breeze, jolted her to a sitting position.

"Allah be merciful!" Aisha cried, leaping to her feet. But her knees would not hold her and she collapsed to the mattress.

A looming black shadow had appeared in the garden entrance. A nightmarish *jinn* of monstrous proportions. Then four other figures emerged out of the shadows. A low growl rumbled through the harim, and the women mewed in disturbed sleep.

Aisha knelt on her mattress, frozen, staring in disbelief at the shadows. They were not real. In truth, she was dreaming. But within moments the apparitions came alive, rushing in. The enormous one fell to his knees with laughs and unintelligible throat utterances at the foot of Nur al Huda's mattress. Taking hold of Nur al Huda, he shook her as a child might shake a new toy, and the terror-stricken child screamed.

Women dashed hysterically about the harim, like birds flushed from a thicket, their shrieks and sobs, their terrible gasps, like a music from hell.

Blindly, Aisha lunged backward and with shaking hands found the jeweled knife she always kept under her mattress at night. She whipped about, holding it tight in a fist. A black figure loomed over her. As his arms reached for her, his body bending close, she lunged upward with the knife, plunging the blade into his groin. He fell on her with a grunt, a crushing weight. She managed to wrench herself out from under him, then, without hesitation, she leaped upon the back of the giant covering Nur al Huda with his loathsome body.

The brute threw Aisha off, but the blade of her knife caught him a glancing, wounding blow on the left arm. He reared to his feet, bellowing like a great bull, to express his rage. Then he laughed uproariously. No larger than a hummingbird, this harim whore thought to attack and kill an elephant.

Aisha stumbled to a standing position, defying him, cursing him, her head rising no higher than his ribs. He continued to laugh at her and she leaped at him, thrusting the knife toward his groin, but he easily caught her up under one arm and wrenched the knife from her grip with his free hand. He said something to her in a brutal voice, then slung her over his shoulder.

"Armanus!" Aisha cried, kicking and scratching at the fiend who was so roughly carrying her out of the harim.

In the rush out of the house, Aisha's blurred vision briefly focused, and she saw Armanus dead. He was on the floor outside the entrance to his chamber, his head in one place, his crumpled body in another. She watched his body fading behind, then vanishing from her sight. She thought, *Merciful Allah, Armanus has been with me all my life. Never have I breathed a breath without him near at hand. How shall I ever survive without him?* She cried his name again, sucked in a painful breath, shuddered, then fell into a black abyss of unconsciousness.

Northmen rushed from black, tree-lined streets and alleys, meeting at the smallboats. Behind them, the suburb was alive with confusion. Horses whinnied as frenzied men mounted them to dash to the rescue. Gongs sounded a mournful call for the city's police. The screeches of women and children over the bodies of their loved ones was a familiar dirge to the raiders.

The four prisoners taken from the house of the Golden Gate were roughly dumped into the boats with the now bulging sacks. Oars sliced into the placid river, hurling the heavy-laden boats toward the *Raven of the Wind.*

Before the first warning reached the city police, the dragon ship of Mord Baptized-One, with three men at each oar, was streaking northward at a speed of ten knots.

The *Sea King's Deer* soon sounded horns behind the *Raven of the Wind,* then quickly came alongside and held that position. Dan Sea-Kingsson stood on the forecastle, doing his best to subdue his rage. To survive, to prevail against whatever forces would be pitted against him during this flight to the sea, he must accept as allies the might of Mord and his crew.

Dan, imagining message-bearing birds already in flight, saw before his mind's eye the ramparts of the distant fortress that guarded the mouth of the Nile from each side, the chain that could be lifted to prevent ships from escaping to the open sea. Fleet as his *ship* was, he could not hope to outdistance winging birds, who would not twist and meander along the water highway that he must follow. If the sea could be reached before dawn, darkness blinding the fortress guards to their presence, the chance for escape was reasonably good. If not . . .

Dan gave little thought to imponderables. At his

birth, the fates had decided all issues, of circumstance, death, and tide of battle. What was written could not be unwritten. Rather than weakening him, this blind faith in a magnificent destiny rendered Dan akin to unconquerable, utterly fearless and incautious. He attacked life and every happenstance or enemy with the ferocity and daring of a jungle panther, knowing himself to be immortal, untouchable until the day set for his triumphal entrance into Valhalla—and that golden day was not to be feared but yearned for as a weary man longs for sleep. This might well be the battle in which his destiny would be fulfilled. Odin smiled upon him from above. Dan urged his rowers on with cheering cries. His blood ran swiftly. He was grateful that an end had come to long months of merchantman inertia.

The stars had faded in the sky, and pale arms of orange and red reached across the black heavens, as the Saracen fort's chain sluggishly groaned up from the depths of the Nile at the insistence of the turning, screeching cranks. Almost immediately the *Raven of the Wind* appeared as if out of nowhere, with the *Sea King's Deer* at her stern.

The Egyptian captain leaned over a high battlement, calmly studying the two ships that approached. The message he had received, via air, had been necessarily terse, commanding him to raise the chain against two dragon ships. Without having to be told, he knew that warships sped downriver in close pursuit. His task was to stop the ships and to prevent the crews from escaping overland. Fifty mounted guards had taken a single-file position, an hundred yards the length of each bank.

The Saracen captain laughed, noting the canopy that

had been constructed over the ships. The crew were holding their shields up so that one overlapped the other, creating a four-inch-thick roof which could withstand the heaviest fire of arrows. But he had no intention of wasting his missiles. The fools. They were trapped. Within moments the warships would appear behind and destroy them.

Below, the captains of the dragon ships, hidden beneath the shield canopies, ordered the oars raised. The ships slowly came to a halt, bows coming to rest against the iron, hobnailed obstruction. They waited, expecting a barrage of arrows from above. Peering from under a shield, Dan could see horsemen sitting their mounts in full battle array, mocking grins on their heathen faces. It was apparent, to Mord as well as to Dan, that warships would be close on their wake.

Dan slipped overboard. He easily swam the few feet to the chain, which hung rusted and formidable two feet above the waterline. Mord swam up beside him. They did not speak to each other, each giving the chain a thorough, calculating inspection.

Dan turned his head to study the bow of the *Sea King's Deer.* It was heavily reinforced with iron plating for breaking through the ice flows of northern seas, and for the destructive ramming of ships of war.

Mord lunged upward to test the thickness and tensile strength of the chain with a massive hand. "I will risk it," he said emphatically.

Dan sourly ignored the man. His eyes cast up to the granite walls of the fort to his right, in search of the chain's port of entry, then to the other side. No ordinary ship would dare attack this barrier, the hobnails set so as to batter, pierce and sink any vessel usual to these waters. Since no ship could ram the chain with success, no one had bothered to have the chain regularly inspected or repaired. Its mere presence, swinging across the river, was sufficient to hold back any adversary.

Dan muttered under his breath, "Praise Odin, let there be a weak link." With two hard breast strokes, he returned to his ship and heaved himself up over the side, aided by strong hands that slid from under the shield roof.

Within moments the simultaneous commands, "Reverse oars!" resounded through the quiet dawn. To the astonishment of the watching Saracen captain, the two dragon ships leaped backward, skimming downriver in the direction from which they had come.

Dragon ships were designed the same fore and aft. When trapped on a narrow stream, unable to turn, the rowers simply reversed positions on their benches and the ship's stern became its bow. Often these peculiar ships bewildered their opponents with impossible escapes up the most superficial of streams, aided not only by their ability to reverse, but by their shallow draughts. Thus they appeared to be racing backward, tail first—a ludicrous dragon with preposterous aplomb effecting a fanciful water dance.

Five hundred yards downstream, the shield roofs suddenly vanished, the men who had been upholding them dropping down beside their companions at the oars.

Again the cry of "Reverse oars!" and the two dragons sprang forward, charging the chain with a demented fury and purpose.

The Saracen captain stared, open-mouthed and unbelieving. Exactly what was happening at last penetrated. He shrieked an order to fire upon the daredevils below. Arrows snapped from bows, falling short of their targets, whirring over the heads of the intent rowers. The horsemen along the banks were shouting in protest and surprise, but from far above them it sounded like cheering, and their captain's face blanched. The muscles of his neck constricted. His eyes were fastened to the scene below, which could only be a mirage. They would not dare.

With an explosive crash of iron against iron, the *Raven of the Wind* struck the chain an instant before the *Sea King's Deer.* The two ships carried the chain ten feet before it sprang taut. For an instant chain and ships seemed suspended over the river in a ballet leap, an unrelenting force having met an immovable, indestructible object. Then the chain exploded from the cranks that held it within the fortress, carrying great chunks of the granite walls down with it in clouds of powdered stone. Water rose in geysers right and left.

When it was still, the air cleared of dust—all that could be seen of the dragon ships was their gilded tails vanishing into a bank of early morning mist that clung to the surface of the nearby sea.

Dan Sea-Kingsson leaped to stand high at the prow, flinging an arm round the neck of the deer adoringly, as if it were a living creature to whom he was expressing deep-felt love. What man, he thought, what man-made device, could prevail against an Asa man, or an Asa *ship*, each godlike and invincible. Not since Odin had led the Asar northward from the Baltic Sea to settle in Scatanavia, not once since that historic day, had the Asar lost a sea battle.

Dan snatched his sword from its sheath and raised the blade to the sky, shaking the weapon in Odin's prideful face—the son calling the father to task, demanding a duel, a matching of strengths. He was Dan Sea-Kingsson, Odin's son—a god. What men could hope to conquer *gods*? The sky above him was vast, but he felt bigger. The earth was green, beautiful, rich and grand, and his own deeds were one hundred fold. His reward in Valhalla was assured. He had never committed an act against the law, nor broken a sacred vow, nor failed a friend, or to give comfort to his wife; he was guiltless. He feared no man, beast, or god; he was fearless.

"Odin!" Dan shouted into the wind. "Odin!" brandishing his sword and laughing like a small boy at play.

There, between two chariot-shaped clouds, Dan was certain he saw Odin's face, laughing with him.

Greeks, Romans and Saracens, the might of all the ages, had not succeeded in so much as dampening the northern fire that lightning-flashed eastward in omnipotent tongues of flame, to retreat as quickly, again and again, century after century. The Asar hid behind man's ignorance of the earth and its vast seas. The Romans had not known whence they came. The Saracen knew little more. The Franks, the Irish, and the English knew them well and feared them greatly.

That such men as that fainthearted, emasculated monk riding as a passenger upon the *Raven of the Wind* could be wielding the fateful sword of annihilation was a possibility Dan had stubbornly refused to consider. Power rested in the battle axe, and in the fates, who were forever on the side of the Asar—in Thor and Odin, in his own muscular arm, the invincibility of his *ship*. The only weapon the monk bore with him was an idea. But it was an ideology that had already brought most of Europe to its knees, to hold together in a communion of minds a heretofore, and racially still, diverse peoples. An ideology had no power that Dan could see, no blade that could wound or kill. The priests of Nordrey were few. They were impotent, bothersome and persistent, but by no means a threat. A man's thoughts were inviolable. You could drag an Asa man to a cross, but you could not force him to kiss it or to believe in its portent. Jesus Christ would never depose Odin or Thor. Of this Dan Sea-Kingsson could not be more certain. One day Thor the Thunderer would show himself to Jesus the Prophet, and the Christian god would vanish in a cloud of vapor before such magnificence and power.

All men who were wise knew that the Asar were undisputed masters of the seas, and of themselves.

CHAPTER FIVE

The bleached hide of the square sail snapped in the strong northerly, and the *Raven of the Wind* fairly leaped the shallow waves. Her captain lay under a canopy at the stern, snoring vulgarly with his cavernous mouth wide agape.

The sky was overcast, but a glare radiated from the sea to bruise Aisha's eyes. Her stomach felt queasy. Every muscle in her body screamed for rest, but she would not sleep. Nur al Huda clung to her, burying her face against her shoulder, which was wet with the child's tears. Maymunah and Jesimine, the two concubines taken with them, had, upon reaching the open sea, fallen asleep as quickly as had most of the crew.

At least half the crew lay between rowers' benches, asleep inside fur-lined hide sacks. Aisha thought that the crewmen who were on their feet seemed exhausted and not sufficiently alert to safely guide this preposterous boat to a port. A barge, she thought, now that she had closely observed it—an undersized canalboat and not a ship at all. The depth of the ship, from gunwales to the bottom boards resting over the frame that served as decking, was about ten feet, no more. An aisle stretched before her, perhaps fifty feet in length. Benches were lined along port and starboard, between which was a space of no more than twenty feet. At the center of the aisle a monstrous block of wood served as support for the mast. Thirty-foot oars were tied with leather straps along the bulkheads, twelve at either side. Yellow and black shields hung along the outer side of the ship, one overlapping the other.

Far astern, near where the captain slept, stood the pale monk she had studied so curiously on the Street of the Flowers wharf. Strange, indeed, were the peculiar designs of fate written by Allah. She would never have thought to see him again. He stood upon the keel of an overturned smallboat, leaning on the gunwale and gazing out to sea. Since first noticing him, she had tried many times to catch his eye, but he seemed intent upon ignoring her presence.

Aisha eased aside, letting Nur al Huda's head slide from her shoulder and down, gently, to the deck. The child slept there like an infant, exactly where she had been put beside Maymunah. Unsteadily, Aisha rose to her feet. The movement of the ship was impossible to gauge. Clumsily she covered her nakedness by tearing the skirt of her sleeping gown to form an improvised veil. To show her naked face, her hair or the back of her head to strangers was an indecency she had never committed. It would take more than this disaster to bring her to so gross an impropriety.

Holding the frayed linen over her head and across her nose, she stumbled down the aisle, sidling round the mast block toward the figure in the brown robe. "Saíd?" she whispered up to the monk, who kept his back to her. She sensed that he knew she had approached him. With her free hand she touched the hem of his skirt, then tugged it vigorously.

It was as if the man had been dreading just such a touch. He stiffened, then slowly turned to look down at her. He did not speak to her, only raised an unsteady hand to his shaven crown, where beads of perspiration glistened. His dark blond beard was matted and infested, his flesh ashen, as from living for many years beyond reach of sun and air. He seemed as much a prisoner on this dragon ship as she, and the thought wearied Aisha.

"Good monk," Aisha said up to him, "in the name of mercy and Christian charity, we beg your protection."

David cleared his throat against a fist. Carefully he stepped down to face the woman. He supported his weight against the pitch and roll of the ship by leaning back against the smallboat. "Forgive me," he said huskily in Latin, his lips forming the words with great difficulty. "I—I do not speak your tongue."

"Ach," Aisha complained impatiently, understanding him only when he shook his head and lifted a finger to his mouth to pantomime his helplessness. Sternly eyeing the fellow, she said tightly, "Can you not *see* our need?"

David stared at her for long moments, overwhelmed by the contempt for him that was in her tone of voice and in her eyes. Of all the things of the secular world about which he was in ignorance, he had been most curious about women. He had been born of a woman, but, until today, he had never seen one, had no memory of the female who had delivered him into the world and subsequently into the hands of God. Statues and paintings of the Holy Mother had shown him much beauty, virtue and sanctity, but never the true face of woman. Once he had asked Brother Sebastian to tell him about women, and the man had replied, "Perfidious," much bitterness in his tone. The Bible had described the characters of Eve and Jezebel, Esther and many others, but *woman* had remained only an indefinable word to him.

With good intentions, hoping that this woman before him would understand his concern for her, though, admittedly, he did not entirely comprehend her predicament, David dropped to his knees and folded his hands. He began a prayer to the Holy Mother to intercede on behalf of the captive women.

"Alhomdolillah!" Aisha exclaimed. "You *pray*? Prayer I can manage for *myself*, monk!" With that, she turned and clumsily made her way back to fall down in an angry huff beside the other women.

For a long time Aisha sat slumped there, glaring across the rolling ship at the monk, despising him with unreasonable intensity. He was someone to vent her frustration upon. How could she have expected aid from such as he? Only the weak and fearful chose to hide from life behind a monk's hood and monastery walls. The man was more emotionally impotent than she and equally as weak physically.

Aisha had never had to contend with such dire circumstances. Truly, her life had been one of undisturbed peace, lacking spectacular events. From her father's splendid manor, which clung to a cliff top in the Holy Land city of Acre, she had traveled overland as the promised bride of Kamar al Zamen. That caravan journey had been uneventful, the single adventure of her life, the only event in her thirty and two years on this earth that had in any way been nerve-biting and uncertain.

Aisha had been instructed to appreciate the good fortune of going to a husband of advanced years, who was wise in the ways of the flesh. A youth would use her clumsily, without consideration for her tender years. Not once had she doubted that instruction and, beyond question, Kamar al Zamen had proved it true.

She smiled, recalling how handsome Kamar al Zamen had been to her eyes when she first looked upon him. He had been ten years older than her father, but he was still straight of back and dark of hair—the streaks of white in his beard were enormously attractive to her, as decorative as if he wore flowers or jewels there. His smile was devastating, seeming to light his entire countenance; he might as well have had a halo, for what she saw, at first sight of him, was a godlike man that she instantly adored.

She was immediately placed under the tender supervision of Kamar al Zamen's first wife, a Greek woman four years older than her husband, who kindly familiarized her with the house and its routines. Wonderful days and months followed. The Golden Gate was filled with small children then.

It was more than a year before her husband called her to his bedchamber and then only for long talks and hours of reading aloud to him; she was a very accomplished reader and took great satisfaction in the obvious pleasure she gave him during those afternoons.

It was at her own insistence that her marriage was finally consummated. She had been married almost two years, and her pride had been sorely damaged by

Kamar al Zamen's seeming uninterest in her as anything more than an ingenuous child, or a talented reader of fanciful tales. When she put the book down that afternoon and tremulously moved to put her arms about him, and to kiss him affectionately . . . oh, how joyous his instantaneous response had been. His arms had wrapped round her, hugging her close to him. He had kissed her softly on the neck, the lobe of her ear, her chin—so gently, so softly it was as the brush of feathers against her flesh.

Only kisses that first day, but within a month she was completely his wife and could discuss the pleasures of her husband's bed with the other wives and concubines on an equal footing. Her pride had been entirely restored.

Within another year, Kamar al Zamen had divorced his first wife and given to Aisha the place of honor in his house and in his heart, a serene position that she had filled ever since.

Only yesterday she had looked to such a bright future. When Kamar al Zamen was with Allah in Paradise, she would establish residence in the city and spend the remainder of her existence joyfully increasing her fortune. Indeed, Allah had been surpassing generous with her all her days. She did not intend to question Him now. She was strong of heart and mind. In the end, she would be victorious over this calamity. *As it was decreed, so must it come to pass.* To prevail she need only bravely endure what could not be altered, and never give up the struggle to retrieve what had been taken from her.

"La ilaha il-Allah, Mohammad-un Rasulu-llah," Aisha prayed whisperingly. "Let not the worst that is

to come be insupportable. Let my strength be tenfold that I might abide with dignity thy omnipotent will."

Nur al Huda needed her, the others, too—she must, as always, be the rock upon which they leaned for daily guidance. Despite petty resentments and arguments, the three women sleeping beside her looked upon her as children upon a mother. She could not fail them in this desperate hour.

Aisha moved a hand to brush a strand of hair away from Nur al Huda's face—a truly sweet and lovely face. How could she have treated the child so badly?

Nur al Huda's eyelids fluttered, then her terror-filled eyes opened and flung wildly about. She choked on a rising sob and threw herself into Aisha's arms for comfort.

Mord Baptized-One had risen when the sun reached its zenith and now stood overshadowing his captives. The women cringed from him, terror in every eye except those yellow globes that had defied him in the night. He thoughtfully ran a hand over the superficial wound on his arm, grinning down at the brazen wench. Men came up behind him, uttering comments in their vulgar tongue, laughing with sinister anticipation.

"You!" Mord called out sharply in Arabic, brandishing a forefinger at Aisha. He tossed his head in a gesture toward his canopy, which flapped noisily in the wind. "Now, pagan!"

Aisha remained frozen where she sat, unable to speak, holding Nur al Huda's face tight against her bosom. For an instant all faith in Allah's justice, all sense of confidence in her own strength, was gone from her, and she trembled as violently as the child in her arms. Desperately, she looked from face to face above her, in search of pity, but met only lust. Then *his* face was there, the *holy* one's. His blue eyes were bewildered, ill at ease, and it struck Aisha that the stupid fellow had no conception of what was about to happen.

"Monk!" Aisha shouted at him, enraged. "Worm of a man! Will you stand back and allow this?"

Nur al Huda was roughly dragged from Aisha's arms by a giant with red hair and a splotchy face. The child's hysterical screams acted as a battle horn sounding attack.

Mord reached down and hauled Aisha to her feet by an arm, dragging her behind him toward the stern. As she stumbled past the monk, she saw horror in his eyes, a glimmer of comprehension. But he was immobilized, utterly ineffectual in the face of life's most foul act, that of rape. The word froze in her mind and her heart hesitated in her breast. Rape. She cried out to the monk, but he did not move to help her.

Only Nur al Huda screamed. The others were experienced, trained women of Islam and knew well the passions and brutal inclinations of men. Jesimine had suffered the slave block more than once. Maymunah had spent her entire adulthood patiently enduring what to her was distasteful and heart-wearying.

Unused as Aisha was to suffering, she bore the advances of her captor with magnificent disdain, her eyes tight-closed, her mouth drawn into a thin white line of contempt and revulsion. Grunting and groaning, he pawed at her, tore her gown and bruised her flesh. It was over at almost the same instant of tearing penetration when he dropped heavily upon her, wheezing and squealing like a wounded bear. She gasped for air against the weight of him and somehow managed to push him aside enough to catch a breath. The pain had been less because she had not fought him. When he wearied of her, she blindly clasped up the skirt of her gown and held it to her face, stumbling away from him. Numbly she thought of the humiliation, not nearly as disturbed by the exposure of her naked body as by her inability to completely hide her face and the back of her head. All that she could think about was that her face—her head—was *exposed.* She reached midship before blackness began to envelop her. The deck seemed to be rising up to strike her. Clutching out for something solid to grasp and steady herself, she caught hold of the mast block. Then she felt an arm clasp round her waist and she fell back against it. Her feet seemed disconnected, swollen, but she managed to lift one foot, then the other, until the arm about her eased her to a sitting position.

Somewhere, Nur al Huda was weeping—harsh, gasping utterances. Aisha struck her eyes with balled fists in an attempt to clear her blurred vision. Nur al Huda needed her. She must not succumb to exhaustion. But as her thoughts ran thus, she slid to a prone position, the cloth of her gown slipping away from her bruised, blood- and grime-stained face. Her faculties had been overdrawn. Sleep was beyond further resistance.

A black sky met Aisha's gaze as her eyes opened and consciousness returned to her. She thought, there are no stars. Then she bolted upright, suddenly reminded of what had happened.

"Ssh," the monk whispered, a finger pressed against his lips.

Aisha glared at him. He was kneeling before her, a damp cloth in his hand, a bloodstained cloth. She gasped and turned her head to see Nur al Huda lying in a splash of light from a nearby oil lamp. The child was naked. Livid bruises and welts spotted her entire body. Blood was caked on her thighs and it still oozed from where she had been many times stabbed by lust. Tears welled into Aisha's eyes as she thought how the child had longed and plotted for the day of her deflowering. She had been prevented from enjoying a perfect first union under a spreading, sweet-flowering orange tree by a domineering, petulant first wife—to be saved for this rape.

"Give it to me!" Aisha cried, swallowing emotion and snatching the cloth from the monk's hand.

Aisha sponged the unconscious child's flesh by dipping the cloth into a wooden bucket of sea water that was near at hand, squeezing the cool water upon Nur al Huda's feverish brow.

"Cover for her," Aisha demanded of the monk, furiously pantomiming her wish by waving her hands over Nur al Huda.

David flinched and could not meet her eyes. He loathed himself for his inability to express the pity, the rage and revulsion that broiled in him. Tears filled his eyes and his lips trembled in a frustrated effort to find words she would understand.

"Damn you to hell!" Aisha screeched. "Are you pitiless, monk?"

David slowly pushed himself to his feet and put his back to the tortured women. Casting his eyes up to a black Heaven, he silently and desperately pleaded for a sign from the Lord that would direct him. The men who had committed the brutal acts against the heathen women were Christians. The right or wrong of their bestiality was not in question, but how could he ever hope to gain their respect and guide them toward righteousness if he turned against them now, in this first moment of conflict? Then, in his beleaguered mind, he heard words from the Bible— "Charity shall cover the multitude of sins"—and he knew what must be done.

David turned on his heel and with stern purpose strode to where a group of sailors lay in their sacks. With a sharp kick at the nearest bag, he awoke the sailor therein and with uncompromising authority ordered the lout out. The Northman yowled in protest. For long moments general confusion reigned as others awoke and joined him in complaint.

"Captain!" David shouted up at the enormous man who stood on the forecastle. In a voice that was unsteady but clearly heard, he commanded, "Captain, you will order your man to give his sack to me."

Mord Baptized-One stood towering upon the rise, squinting bemusedly down at the shadowed monk. "Give it to him, Bjarni," he boomed.

David glared up at Mord, truly seeing the man for the first time. He raised his voice in condemnation. "The way of the transgressor is hard. The wages of sin is death. How *dare* you name yourself a Christian!"

"I am called *Baptized-One*," Mord retorted defensively.

"The words of his mouth were smoother than butter, but war was in his heart; his words softer than oil, yet were they drawn swords."

"Take the cursed sleep sack, Monk!" Mord shouted impatiently, "take it for the love of God!"

"I also take the women."

"The women! All *four*?"

"All four."

A rumble of protest rose from the crew, and a tight frown creased Mord's broad forehead. "Each is worth three marks of silver on the Dublin wharves," he said in lieu of refusal to comply.

"The women are under my protection, under the protection of Holy Church!"

Mord's shoulders stiffened and he swallowed hard to control his rage. He saw below him the countenance of avenging Jesus and dared not refuse. The Christian prophet had been presented to him as an immortal being capable of ghastly fury when thwarted, of terrible vengeance and reprisal, not as the gentle son of God who loved all men, who had said, "Go and sin no more," to the worst of offenders. This monk wore the mark of sanctity, of communion with the Holy Spirit. To refuse his command would crack the sky asunder and release the lightning of His terrible sword. Mord believed sufficiently in the power of Jehovah, even if he could not altogether comply with all the Christian tenets, to avoid outright heresy. It was the eyes of the priests that watched; God's eyes could not be everywhere at once.

Mord could not control the impulse to spitefully jab the monk. He shouted down at the man, "What is sin for me and my crew is *virtue* for yourself. Eh, David of Saint Monica?"

David did not acknowledge the remark with a look or a reply. He leaned over and took hold of the now vacated sack and dragged it to where Nur al Huda lay, shouting over his shoulder a demand for three more bags. He helped Aisha enclose the shivering child in the warm sack.

When the sick girl was comfortably wrapped, David touched the shoulder of the woman with yellow eyes and smiled at her in an effort to speak of his promise to see her safely home, but she only stared at him, frigidly distant. He did not understand her calmness. It was as if she had not suffered the same brutal act that had been committed against the girl. She had not shed a single tear. But he was grateful that she, and the other two, did not grieve, because his shame . . . his pity for the suffering girl was almost more than he could bear.

He should have known of such inflictions, man against woman. He should have stood hard and fast before the captain then rather than now, in aftermath. Still, he was uncertain whether he truly owed these women charity. They were pagans. All those who were not with Christ were against Christ. But they were friendless and suffering. Had not Christ laid his benevolent hands upon the leper and the harlot alike?

David had, in spite of his doubts, made his choice, and throughout the voyage to Dublin upon the *Raven of the Wind* he would remain optimistic about the future and firm in his resolve to protect the pagan women from further abuse.

To Mord and his crew David had become insufferable. Only *dead* saints were tolerable. While saints lived, lesser men could only stand appalled before a salutary indefectibility which in living, breathing men smacked of unbearably theatrical priggishness.

CHAPTER SIX

The *Raven of the Wind* veered north toward a land mass that rose out of a dawn mist, then sailed upriver to sack towns and a castle high upon a Frankish cliff. Swiftly she escaped to the sea. Two days later, eastern Andalusian seacoast villages were burned after all their moveable goods and staple foodstuffs had found room on the deck of the dragon ship. On the twentieth day at sea the Pillars of Hercules were passed, and the winds became colder and inclined to frenzied whips and lashes. The following night rain fell from churning clouds, soaking all on board to the skin.

Nur al Huda was gravely ill. She had refused all food since the rape, taking only a little water each day that was forced upon her by her persistent guardian. Her fever was high, her limbs quaking as from some inner, violent disturbance. The monk had improvised a shelter of skins and a Spanish cloak lifted from the mountain of loot astern, but the drenching rain could not be kept out, running in tides along the planking as the ship vigorously pitched upon the rageful sea.

Aisha could do nothing for the girl, forced to hold

on with all her strength to avoid being thrown like a pebble from bulkhead to bulkhead. Waves crashed over the beast head as it nosed deep, adding to the depths being systematically bucketed overboard by weary sailors.

As dawn began to lighten the sky, the rain ceased and the swells were reduced to gentle mountains easily scaled and descended. Land was in sight to starboard, a lushly wooded expanse, apparently uninhabited. At the instigation of the helmsman, the beast head turned. The sails were furled, the mast lowered, and the oars were manned. Slowly the ship snaked up a narrow stream, to come to rest under a cover of trees, so closely in that rain-wet branches overlapped the deck.

Gangways were lowered and the crew poured riotously ashore. They built fires in an open heath under the cloudy, threatening sky. Tents were raised for a night on land.

Maymunah and Jesimine stood upon a rower's bench, earnestly searching the heath and surrounding woodland for evidence of a Muslim settlement.

"First wife," Maymunah said excitedly over her shoulder to Aisha, who was behind her tending Nur al Huda, "we must escape this night, make a dash into the woods."

"Ridiculous," Aisha snapped, remaining seated beside the child. "Where can we hope to find shelter or aid upon this hostile shore? And this poor girl cannot *move,* let alone—"

"There is no aid or shelter aboard this vessel," the red-haired one argued emotionally, "or upon that final shore to which we are being carried."

"The monk protects us here."

"Ach! For how long? How *long*? I can see the sparks of lust burning in their eyes, brighter each hour of each day."

Jesimine agreed. "We must escape while we have the opportunity."

"No!" Aisha insisted heatedly. Her temper was ragged. She was cold to the bone, wretchedly dirty and soaked, desperately worried that Nur al Huda might die of the fever that wracked her. "Damn your eyes, Maymunah! Burn the pig that brought you up! You fill Jesimine's head with fancies. What little protection the monk affords us is better than none at all. Lost in those woods we would die, either of starvation or of exposure. Heed what I say, for I do not intend to repeat myself. We remain on board this ship!"

"The *monk*!" Maymunah cried, spitting upon the deck for emphasis.

"Jesus the prophet, Allah bless him," Aisha raged, getting to her feet and moving threateningly toward the woman, "is beloved throughout Islam. To slander one who is his servant on this earth is a kind of blasphemy which I personally abhor."

"Over the face of the earth they make war upon us, your noble Christians!"

"To be pitied for their gross intolerance, but respected as our future companions in Allah's Paradise. The monk is a good man. His level of tolerance is uniquely high, for a *Christian*. We are not of his creed, infidels to his mind, yet he has constructed a wall between the four of us and ravishment. How dare you spit upon his name!"

David moaned and lifted his head, rubbing sleep from his eyes with grimy fists. The high-pitched argument between his charges had awakened him. In three weeks he had learned little of their language, but the word *monk* was the same in either tongue, so he knew it was himself they were discussing so heatedly. He got to his feet and his head struck a branch. He gasped, startled by the unexpected obstacle. The deck was pitching and rolling under him, but at the same time he was aware that the ship was not moving. As he walked toward the women, his legs insisted upon adjusting to a nonexistent roll.

"Peace," David said, raising both arms to Aisha.

She tried to explain Maymunah's foolhardy intention to him, mostly with arm movements toward the wood. He shook his head in objection. He had had a cooperative Northman interpret for Aisha his hope to see her safely returned to Cairo, and now, in clumsy gestures, he attempted to assure her again.

"He tries to make you believe he will see us returned," Maymunah cried. "Ask him how much gold he carries. Ask him!"

"I cannot ask," Aisha raged at the woman. "I do not speak Latin."

"I know he cannot pay our passage. How, then, can he hope to—"

"But I *can*, concubine! Upon reaching Cairo City I could pay any price."

"*Look* at you! Who would believe you if you spoke of vast wealth? Who on this shore could even *understand* you?"

Stunned, Aisha inspected herself and was completely mortified by her appearance. In the debris on deck she had found a soiled gown several sizes too large, a shawl of coarse wool, and miserably uncomfortable leather shoes made for the feet of a man. The colors were brown, green, drab blue, all hideously clashing with one another. She raised a cautious hand that was badly in need of a manicure to her damp, matted hair. It was not difficult to imagine the expression on a man's face if she spoke to him of possessing wealth equal to an hundred million grams of gold. Only two men knew of the splendor from which she had been abducted, Dan Sea-Kingsson and the captain of this ship. Her only hope lay in the greed of the two Northmen, for they were her only means of transportation home.

"My homely appearance is all the more reason to remain on this ship," Aisha said tightly, all inclination to argue having flown with her pride.

"Do as you see fit," Maymunah said, a definite gleam of secret purpose in her eye.

The remainder of the day passed without further antagonism developing between the women. From the forest a bowman brought into the clearing a large beast that was cooked over an open fire. Maymunah and Jesimine kept to themselves, restlessly pacing the center aisle of the ship, or perched on the keel of a smallboat, leaning over the gunwale to soberly watch the men swimming in the river and energetically wrestling, then gathering round the fire to sing cheerful songs.

At dusk bitter ale, meat and flatbread was brought aboard ship for the women and watch crew. David and Aisha sat on the deck across from each other, eating with relish, softly repeating the Arabic words for *eat, meat, mouth* and so on through phrases suggested by the occasion. Nur al Huda awoke, apparently improved, for she asked for food. Aisha dipped bits of the hard, unleavened bread into ale and placed the tidbits on the child's tongue.

The men ashore finally crawled into their small hide tents for sleep. A sliver of a moon slid into view from behind a dark cloud. Aisha and David took themselves to their sleep sacks.

Silently moving to the stern, unable to traverse the gangway because of the burly guard posted there, the two concubines hoisted themselves, with many failures and much scrambling urgency, over the side of the ship into the icy water. They swam the few feet to shore and quickly ran into the cover of tall trees and undergrowth.

Silence prevailed. Then, from a long distance, a choked scream, unheard aboard ship, but the alert men on shore were almost immediately massed in the center of the campsite, bows and swords in hand. Torches were lighted and a search of the surrounding area began.

Aisha and David were awakened by the shouts of the men as they spread out and moved into the wood. David lifted himself and leaned on one elbow, only mildly curious, but Aisha gasped and whispered, "Allah be merciful," covering her mouth with a hand. She knew, without looking at their barren sleep sacks, that it was Maymunah and Jesimine the Northmen hunted.

Within the hour the sound of returning men brought Aisha dashing to the gunwale, her heart racing. In the torchlight she saw they were carrying a body, a horribly mangled woman's body, torn almost limb from limb by a beast with knife-like claws.

The man posted on the forecastle shouted down that

two women had taken to the woods, but not a man was willing to search for Maymunah. They were not concerned. Since it was only a foolish woman and no threat to them, they returned to their beds.

Jesimine was dead. Aisha did not protest, or weep. She turned away and walked numbly back to her own bed. For a long moment she stood over Nur al Huda, watching the child's ashen face for signs of improvement. If the child died, Blessed Allah, she would be alone, for Maymunah was surely dead. For the first time since her capture, tears filled her eyes. But she quickly shook off the sadness, crawled into her sack and forced her eyes closed.

At dawn the *Raven of the Wind* was poled, stern first, to the sea, and from there set a course north by northwest. Five days later, a bleak, mist-enshrouded coastline became visible between widely separated billows of thick, low fog. The air had turned bitterly cold. The little sky that could be seen seemed to be shivering—a slate gray canopy of rippled ice. The dragon's head now veered due north, following the curve of the land mass. The sea broiled as if being vigorously stirred from beneath, waves spraying over the gunwales in a fine, soaking rain.

Looking across the sea to the land, Aisha thought that she had never seen such all-pervading bleakness. Surely men would not tolerate an existence under such skies. She had not seen the sun in days. How much farther could the sea stretch? As the days passed she had become increasingly uneasy, expecting the ship to, any moment, plunge over earth's brink into an infinity of fire and space.

Just after daybreak the next morning, a cry exploded from the throat of a sailor perched high upon the mast. "Dublin!" he shouted again and again to those below, with an emotional quality of voice that suggested the place was home to him.

Poor brute, Aisha thought, with such a dreary place for a home. No wonder the crudities of these giant men, if they came from such graceless soil as this. She glanced down to where Nur al Huda lay in sleep, almost entirely enveloped by the large sack, her gaunt face barely visible. The child's breathing had become more natural, her sleep no longer disturbed by nightmares. Aisha sighed and thanked Allah for His mercy.

David stepped up behind Aisha, lightly touching her shoulder. "Come," he said to her in Arabic.

She looked round at him and smiled. She had grown quite fond of him. He was like a small boy, quick to flush, slow to comprehend worldly manners, guileless and inordinately sensitive. She followed his lead toward the starboard gunwale. The hue and cry, ship to shore, was deafening, crewmen dashing furiously about, chains creaking as the anchor was prepared for lowering. Upon the forecastle, Mord Baptized-One howled an hundred separate commands.

When they reached the gunwale, David stepped up upon a rower's bench and motioned for Aisha to do the same. There before her eyes, like a swarm of dragonflies upon a misty lake, lay a horde of dragon ships, berthed in a curved harbor the vastness of which left Aisha speechless. A ground-clinging, transparent fog diffused the scene, creating a mirage effect. But as the *Raven of the Wind* slowly eased into the bay, the wharves became visible, crawling with people, strangely attired men and women who did, indeed, call this place home. A goodly variety of wares were piled high along the entire curve of the timber wharf, even as in Cairo City, almost as if this were a *civilized* land, this land called Eire.

"One of this multitude of ships will see you home," David said warmly to her, but in Latin.

She did not understand his words, but sensed he was well meaning. Moving a hand from the gunwale, she laid it over his, thanking him with a grateful smile. But she knew that he could not perform such a miracle.

"David of Saint Monica!"

Startled, David whipped his head round to the forecastle, where Mord stood glaring down at him. "Captain?"

"This is as far as the *Raven of the Wind* can carry you. Nordland is north by northeast, many sea days. You must find another ship to take you."

David frowned. "Will you seek out a vessel en route to Egypt," he hesitantly asked, "that this good woman and the child might be returned to their home?"

"Hah!" Mord bellowed. Laughing vulgarly, he turned his back on David.

"Captain!" David managed to shout in a priest's warning tone of voice.

"It is not the long-voyage season," Mord obliged over his shoulder. "Not until winter has passed and the fields have been sown will the long serpents set sail again for the east."

Aisha worriedly watched David's face. Now he knew what she had known all along. But it cut deep, none-theless, the finality there starkly outlined upon his crestfallen face. She would not find a ship in this harbor. Two men existed who could possibly aid her, but she was utterly incapable of approaching that foul man now laughing at her plight on the forecastle. She prayed to Allah that this Mord was not her only means of escape, because she would prefer death to begging a favor from him.

Fear suddenly iced Aisha's heart and she reached for David's hand. Their eyes met and she wordlessly pleaded with him not to desert her now. Out there, upon the cluttered wharves, she had seen women tied ankle and wrist, being sold as slaves. A member of the crew had commented to her contemptuously during the journey that no *thrall* woman was worth more than three marks of silver, that when she reached Nordland soil, when she was a Northman's thrall, she would milk cows, wash clothes, cut hay and brew ale.

"Take us with you," Aisha cried urgently. "We cannot survive without your protection."

David looked away from her, unable to bear the pain and anxiety in her eyes. He, too, had seen the women corraled on the wharf, beside small herds of cattle and horses, as if they also were beasts of burden. The Church did not reject slavery, contending that God had willed some men to be slaves, some to be kings, but this woman was born to a high station; God had not intended that she be treated as a servant. He thought that she was expressing her terror of slavery, and he tightly squeezed her hand, shaking his head firmly, to tell her she would not be a slave if he could prevent it. But what was he to do with the two women? The bishop, John Hoskuldson, would be wrongly impressed, perhaps disastrously so, to find his new cleric, bearing consignment from His Holiness, in association with women. Though purely charitable, it might appear undevout.

Ten days later, despite David's reservations about taking the women with him, he gained free passage to Nordland and boarded the Christian ship with Aisha and the girl at his heels. Nur al Huda was by then physically recovered from her ordeal, though thin and emotionally fragile.

After several weeks of meandering the north seas, making port briefly at several settlements, Nordland appeared, first as a dark line against a murky light on the horizon, then a desolate land mass thrusting enormous, cliffed and snow-capped mountains into the sky.

Aisha's heart froze as the land they approached came into clearer focus: a panorama of barren islands, desolate coastline and formidable mountains. Strange mounds had been constructed upon bare, rocky cliffs of primary formation several hundred feet above the level of the sea. Waves crashed against the cliff bases and the winds seemed to howl a mournful dirge.

All day the winds blew fiercely and the sea lashed against the ship in enormous, foamy waves. After only a brief period of murky daylight, dusk settled over the ship and the land, quickly thickening to a starless night. Winter was at their wake. The three would not leave Nordland until the fiord ice melted under an omnipresent sun.

Ajib restlessly paced the garden paths of his father's house, the skirt of his white linen robe snapping with the rigid urgency of his steps and turns. He was a handsome young man, strongly resembling his beloved mother. A silence, a mournful gloom, surrounding, almost suffocating, was so pronounced it seemed almost palpable on the air.

He came to a halt beside the pool. Water lilies idly swayed there, to and fro with the rippling surface. The wind was chill, as cold as the heart within him that grieved for one too soon wrenched from the world. He saw her there, across the pool, where she had sat upon her pillows each late day when he was a child, laughing as he sailed his toy ships, or swam the length of the pool with confident strokes. He would run to her, throw his dripping body into her arms, while she screamed gaily for mercy.

"Allah," Ajib urgently cried to the sky, "why didst thou bring this iniquity upon the queen of all women? Why?"

Ajib was twenty years of age. He had his mother's yellow eyes and fair countenance, but his father's manly height and lean, supple frame. He had left his house and his family to sit beside his father through the first difficult days and weeks of mourning. The old man lay unmoving upon his bed, unwilling to live in a world not graced by the brightness of his *evening star*, his best beloved. Each day he grew weaker. Each day he protested more loudly against having physicians hovering over his bed, vowing he was not ill of the flesh but of the soul; he was dying because he *wished* to die and for no other reason.

"Ajib, son of my master," a black servant said low, bowing from the waist behind the youth.

"What is it, Abdullah?"

"A courier, most honorable son of my master."

"I will not see him, not anyone. Send Ja'afar to receive the message."

"Son of my master, the one who stands in wait is of honorable station, with letter in hand sealed with the mark of Andalusian nobility, addressed to your most honored and grieving father."

Frowning, Ajib struggled with a heat that was building in his breast, a fire of hope from a spark that could not be quenched . . . somewhere she lived, somewhere within reach of his love and rescue. He swiftly turned on his heel and rushed into the anteroom, striding purposefully toward the resplendent sea captain awaiting him.

The captain bowed deeply from the waist. "I am Sa'ad al Din Saood, your humble servant, bearing a letter from Abd al Malik bin Nusayr, governor of Setubal." Smiling effusively, the man bowed again. "You cannot be the physician, for thou art splendidly attired in youthfulness. I was told that the one I seek is an ancient one."

Returning the man's bows, Ajib said, "My father, the physician, is greatly ill, Saíd."

"Ah. A pity. May Allah bless him with fast-renewed good health."

"My gratitude, most illustrious captain."

The captain considered the matter a moment, then abruptly held out a tiny folded note, which Ajib gently removed from his hand with many politenesses.

"I will return at sunset," the captain said, flourishing an arm. "Peace be with thee, Saíd."

When the man had departed, Ajib broke open the red wax seal, unfolding the multi-creased paper. He read slowly at first, then swiftly. His heart began to race. "Father!" he cried out, running through the house, then up the curving staircase.

Ajib plunged into Kamar al Zamen's chamber, completely forgetful of his father's condition. "Awake, Father! I have wondrous news."

Kamar al Zamen reluctantly opened his eyes, furious with Allah for not taking him while he slept. He was still bound to earth, to his despair. "What news, eh? What news could warm a dead man's icy flesh?"

"Listen," Ajib said breathlessly. "This message arrived but moments ago —'I, Abu al Malik bin Nusayr, write to you, most illustrious physician, in the hope that truth has fallen upon my ear. Your fame is known even as far as this western shore; thus I could not live in good conscience lest I notify you of what has occurred in my town of Setubal. Three days past, my woodsman, set upon his duties with a true heart, fell upon a weeping maiden with hair the color of charcoal fire. This maiden, threadbare and uncommonly distraught, cried out to me that she was wife to you, by the name of Maymunah—"

"Ach!" Kamar al Zamen cried, falling back against his pillows. He had risen with wide-eyed happiness, thinking Aisha had been found. "Maynunah," he moaned. "Only Maymunah. She is not *wife* to me . . . never wife to me."

"Father, do not weep. We have been given hope. She lives. My mother and your beloved wife *lives*! The governor goes on to say that Maynunah escaped overboard on that Andalusian shore, that my mother and Nur al Huda were alive and under the protection of a Christian monk, aboard a ship called *Raven Wind*."

"She *lives*?" Kamar al Zamen asked, unbelieving, raising himself to lean upon an elbow.

"It is true!"

"Then we must rescue her, my son."

"If it is possible. If Allah most compassionate wills it, it will be done. But you are too ill. It is I who must rescue her."

Kamar al Zamen threw off the coverlet enshrouding his scrawny form and rose unsteadily to his feet. "Who is ill? Not I. Have I not said it again and again . . . I am not ill. Eh?" He stumbled forward and Ajib caught him just in time. "A bit weak, I admit. I admit that much."

Ajib insisted that his father should seat himself upon his bed and not strain himself. They talked far into the night, animatedly making plans to rescue Aisha.

The letter from the governor had asked that a reply, verifying Maymunah's claim or denying it, be placed in the hands of him who had delivered his communication. But Ajib suggested it would be better to carry affirmation in person, to save time. Within a week they could be ready to sail. A letter of credit must be obtained, that unlimited resources in gold might be deposited with Andalusian moneymen for the ransom. A ship and trade goods of the finest quality must be purchased, and seamen of sturdy heart and minds must be found, who would not shrink from the wrath of unknown seas and barbarian tribes. They had several clues, the name of the ship she rode upon, the name of an island dropped in conversation by one Dan Sea-Kingsson—Ransay—and Maymunah would provide them with many more details. They would purchase

Aisha from the Northmen, pay thrice a king's ransom if necessary.

Six days later Ajib bid farewell to his two young wives and his children. With his father he set sail for Setubal, which was situated on the Atlantic shoreline of the Iberian peninsula. The same day, Aisha stepped ashore at Hoskuldsfiord, Nordland.

CHAPTER SEVEN

David sat stiffly on the hard oak chair. The man before him, sitting upon a luxuriously carved and appointed high seat, stared rudely down upon him. The bishop did not wear a robe of office, nor was there anywhere within this enormous, high-ceilinged hall any evidence of his holy eminence. He wore a shirt of blue linen, banded at the sleeve edges with a kind of lace, tight-fitting trousers banded from ankle to knee with gold rings set four inches apart, a scarlet girdle, and fringed shoes of fine leather. The man was black-haired, mustached and bearded, and bore himself with the pride of a king.

"This papal communiqué introduces you as David of Saint Monica, Egypt," the bishop said at last in clumsy Latin.

David could only nod affirmatively, utterly incapable of speech before such an incongruous figure.

"Why do you stare at me so rudely, David?"

"I—" he began, but words continued to elude him.

"I am not what you expected?"

"No—. No, your Holiness."

"Dear God! Do not call me 'holiness'! The presumption is too much for me. Ingolf Jarl would please me well." In reply to David's obvious bewilderment, he added, "Jarl . . . means Great Chief. Ingolf . . . that was the name fastened upon me at my birth. On the ecclesiastical records I am known as John; Ingolf was considered pagan and unfit, I suppose. The pope can call me whatever he chooses; my name remains the same . . . Ingolf."

"You are *Bishop*?"

"According to the directive of our good King Magnus, I have the honor of filling that holy office, yes. Though I was not properly investitured in Rome, you will find my authority quite unimpeachable. Frankly, it was not the purity of my soul that gendered my appointment, rather the strength of my arm and of my retinue, the power I already wielded as Jarl—which is to say, I was already, in a sense, bishop over the people. You do not comprehend. Forgive me. But you will have the entire winter to fathom the complications here in the northlands; they are multitudinous, I assure you."

"I am to aid in the conversion of the Orkney Islands," David said uncertainly.

"Perhaps," the bishop replied evasively. "Will you excuse me if I ask a rude question of you?"

"Uh, of course, your—"

"Ingolf Jarl."

"Ingolf Jarl."

"When did you bathe last, hm?"

David's mouth dropped open in surprise and confusion. "Bathe?" he asked weakly.

"We cannot abide filth, within our houses or upon our flesh or clothing."

Defensively, David argued, "To immerse myself in water an hundred times a day would not wash away a speck of corruption, if I were corrupt. Inward cleanliness is of foremost—"

"That kind of exaggerated asceticism," Ingolf Jarl sharply interrupted, "will not be tolerated here, David of Saint Monica. My first command is that you bathe each *Washday*. That is, every fifth day."

"If that is your will," David agreed uncomfortably.

"Now, tell me . . . what did you hope to gain by forsaking your vow of seclusion, by entering the world?"

"Gain? I thought of the world as awaiting what I had to offer it, not as something which had anything to offer me. I have no personal needs that require satisfaction. I came to serve man."

Ingolf Jarl was not impressed. He impassively inspected David for long, suspenseful moments, then said abruptly, "Frankly, I am disappointed in you. I think that you have too strong a sense of your own nobility and have too weak a construction, both physical and mental, for the very difficult task of converting my people. You cannot be aware of what you will have to contend with. Look upon me, as an example."

The bishop rose to his feet, an iron pillar of a man. Matter-of-factly, he said, "I can throw two spears at once and each will hit target full center. I can swim five miles in full armor and not breathe heavily. Jump fifteen feet, backward or forward. I can run the oarblades whilst I juggle three dirks. And much more, David of Saint Monica. A man who cannot perform similar feats at least half as well as I is not a man at all, disrespected by all who know him. In other words, good monk, you are not the kind of man to win the trust of the Asar. The chiefs of Orkney would simply laugh at you and ignore you, and I would ultimately be forced to replace you for your lack of success."

David sucked in his breath and held it, then closed his eyes against a swirling, threatening blackness. He had come so far. It had not been an easy decision to leave all that had been sacred to him. The journey had drained him of strength, his store unduly meager to begin with. Already he had failed, without having been given opportunity to try. He said, without looking at the bishop, "No such physical requirements were mentioned by His Holiness."

"No. Because His Holiness is ignorant of our peculiar situation here. I doubt if the pope knows for certain where I live . . . Let me put it this way, to clarify it for you. A small colony of ants have set upon the conversion of whales to their ways. The whales are too large and footless for a life underground or for the busy march over land."

"Ants?" David said, totally bewildered.

"I have heard that a swarm of ants can devour a human body in a few minutes."

Under the definite impression that the man was being deliberately obscure, David said irritably, "Forgive me, but it is difficult to believe that you are a Christian, sir. By *ants,* I can only assume you see me, and all other Christians, in that light, which is nothing short of heresy."

Ingolf Jarl sighed and his craggy face writhed with unreadable, altering expressions. He sat down upon his high seat, his pale green eyes wandering away from

David. For long moments he remained deeply thoughtful.

"In the year of Christ 1010," Ingolf Jarl began in a firm but somewhat sad voice, "the king came here to my *odel* with his mighty retinue and swore that he would have my head and that of my wife and children if I did not accept baptism. My foster brother was already dead by this king's evangelical fury. I looked into the eyes of my infant twin sons, and I obediently knelt before a new god. Later on, I came to see a certain goodness . . . rightness in the Christian tenets. I am as Christian as I can be while remaining who I am."

The bishop's voice continued to rumble and echo through the hall. He said that he would give the winter to David's training, then make a final decision. Beginning immediately, David was to listen closely and make an effort to understand.

In hesitant, abrupt sentences Ingolf Jarl attempted to define the people David would have to contend with, their manners, superstitions and mores. Until recent years a Christian chief would keep the fact of his conversion a secret, holding Catholic festivals and holy days on Fridays, unable to entirely turn his back on the ancient practices of his followers. The runic writings of the Asar were used for conjuration of spirits and regarded with superstitious fear and awe, so the sole means of conversion was by word of mouth. Animal sacrifice to the gods was still common practice. Human sacrifice was still turned to in time of great calamity.

The Asar believed that future life was shaped by Nornir, the gods spinning the threads of fate at the birth of every child, measuring the boundaries of his doings and the days of his life. The ancient religion was polytheistic and animistic, finding expression in various forms of nature worship, a cult of ancestors and of the spirits of the dead. Thor the Thunderer was the god dearest to the Asar; he was the friend and protector of mankind, the patron of farmers, the peace-maker at Things, the mighty comforter in battle. Odin was the All-Father from whose loins all Asa men had generated. It was a comfortable religion, enjoining no stringent moral code upon its adherents. Sweet to Odin and Thor was the clash and clamor of battle, the smoke of burned dwellings and the vainglory of each victor.

Christianity sought to disentitle them from the freedom to do battle and to ravage without incurring the wrath of Heaven. An Asa man might, without serious misgivings, allow himself to be persuaded to acknowledge Christ as his heavenly master, instead of Odin or Thor, but it was vastly more difficult to complete the conversion and have him pay proper respect to Christ's *teachings.* The partially converted chiefs were always willing enough to fight for Christ, but to *hold back* from doing battle, to deny themselves bloodshed that had pleased Thor, to offer the other cheek to him that smiteth was asking almost impossible restraint.

By the ninth century the Asar had become aware that Christianity was not the special religion of one particular nation. Everywhere they went, south or east, they found themselves among Christians. Brother Germans had forsaken their old gods, and the Franks and Frisians, the Saxons and the English. To become a Christian was to gain a permit to pass unhampered along the golden roads that led to the markets of Byzantium and the courts of the European emperors.

Northland kings were not slow to perceive the advantages of adopting the new faith.

Today, each chief was impelled to the perplexing task of turning his people into Christians, as much by the hope of immediate political gain as by a pure and disinterested evangelical zeal.

"The men you have come into the world to *save,*" Ingolf Jarl said huskily, sternly eyeing David, "are nothing short of magnificent as they are . . . healthy, clean and powerful men, who, to maintain their physical prowess, will swim several miles a day, sometimes carrying a man on their shoulders. They are tall, intelligent, meticulously educated . . . supple, swift of foot, dextrous in motion, with near superhuman powers of endurance. The whale. . . . And we would turn them into *ants,* hm?"

"We would bring them to *grace,*" David replied without rancor.

"Ah, save his soul, that he might see God . . . by destroying his manliness."

"Would you prefer a continuance of *bloodshed*?"

Ingolf Jarl stared at David, his eyes squinting half closed. "*Ecclesia abhorret a sanguine*?"

"Yes! The Church shrinks from blood," David echoed, nodding earnestly in agreement.

"Do you actually believe that Holy Church is *sincere* in this?"

"Of course!"

"God bless you for your sublime naivete. . . . To other concerns. A loft will be provided for you. You may house your thralls with you, or in separate quarters, as you please. When—"

"Forgive me. My *thralls*?"

"Your two slave women."

"Oh, but they are not slaves. They—"

"You have a wife and child?" Ingolf Jarl exclaimed enthusiastically, slapping his hands upon his knees. "I am pleased, extremely pleased. It is said that some priests of Europe and the east are practicing celibacy. I had thought all monks were celibate. Quite a peculiar notion, since the good book has said, 'Who so findeth a wife findeth a good thing.' If I were called upon to forsake my good wife, Ingeborg, I would first forsake Christ. I would not have you in parish upon Orkney without a woman to give you warmth and comfort. A man alone is no man at all. There is no evil in womankind. I abhor the figure of Eve. To me, she was not meant to be representative of woman, but of humanity in general. I am very pleased at this, David of Saint Monica."

David flushed and chose not to explain. Already his status with this peculiar man of God was precarious enough. Let him think an untruth if it would benefit his own faltering purpose. He suffered extreme guilt, but tried to console himself with the fact that he had not spoken an untruth, had merely failed to put a misconception straight. He could not bear to be sent away. The lands of Orkney had been consigned to him by God Almighty; to convert the people there was his calling.

A small concession had been made. The fragile beginning of a far more conclusive and major alteration in the structure of David's faith and its practice was in gestation.

Aisha lay upon a mattress of straw, gazing up to the sky, which was indistinctly visible through an opening in the beamed ceiling that she hesitated to call a window. It was a hole in the roof that was enclosed with something flexible and slightly transparent; whatever the material was, it seemed to resist the onslaught of hail that was now turning to snow on a warmer wind.

The entire land was white now, the waterway, called a *fiord,* quite lost to the eye. The scattered buildings of the homestead and the surrounding wooden barricade were mostly buried under drifts. But here upon her bed, only a magnificent blackness could be seen, belching forth its frozen breath that spilled a billion snowflakes, each like a delicate hexagon of lace, to soften the harsh features of the land. The snow was beautiful; it caught upon barren branches and froze there to reflect the light of torches, or it was swept high with the wind to form mountains and valleys; it could be walked upon with snowshoes, or thin blades of wood attached to one's boots; it could be melted for drinking water and for baths. Snow was truly one of Allah's wonders. Until now she had only enjoyed snow as an ingredient in the delicate sherbets served often at Golden Gate.

"First wife . . . ?"

Aisha turned her head and smiled at Nur al Huda, who lay on the mattress beside her own; she was once again bright with health. "Call me by my name, child. Here we are not wives."

Nur al Huda sat up, moving a hand to sweep her long, dark hair back from her face. "Aisha, my heart is heavy. I swear I cannot abide this torment another day. They will attack us again. I—"

"Ah, no," Aisha interrupted soothingly, reaching for the child's cold hands. "David will protect us. We will not be raped again. Forget that it ever happened, if you can."

"There is a wrongness in me. I feel it, hard inside."

"Only painful remembrance."

"No. It is more. Truly it is."

Aisha looked long upon Nur al Huda, then abruptly sat up. She shivered against the chill of the loft air. Several iron braziers glowed red, but were too little against too much. "Nur al Huda," she began cautiously, "have you recently shown blood?" praying the answer would be yes and knowing it would not be.

"Not since our capture," came the quick reply, no tremor of concern in her voice.

Aisha hastily got to her feet, reaching down to lift a woolen blanket and wrap it round herself. She paced the loft, gathering courage for what must be said to the child. Nur al Huda knew the truth; she simply did not want to face it. She glanced to where David slept in the far corner of the room, but he could not help her in this. At last she moved back to where Nur al Huda shivered under several blankets.

"Will the sun *never* shine again?" Nur al Huda groaned, shivering exaggeratedly. "No daylight—only night. This place is a dark, frozen *hell*!"

Aisha knelt before Nur al Huda, capturing the child's eyes with her own. "Many days of darkness lie before us, Nur al Huda. You must be very brave. Know that sunshine inevitably follows the dark . . . Nur al Huda, you must know that you are with child."

Nur al Huda stared at Aisha in disbelief, then abruptly laughed. "Ridiculous! You have lost your mind. I *cannot* be with child!" Her tone of voice had become brittle at the last, hysteria barely submerged.

"Pray Allah it is not true, but you must admit that it is *possible*."

"No! Stupid woman," she screeched, choking on a rising revulsion. "I will not be with child, cannot be. You must take it from me, the filthy thing . . . you must!"

"I cannot do that! I am not a physician, have no knowledge of such—"

"You *do*!" Nur al Huda wailed, dissolving into frustrated tears. "You loathe me and . . . and bask in my torment! Why *me*? You were raped, but you are not with child! Are you?"

"No, child, I am not."

Across the room David groaned on his bed. He lifted his head, to blindly stare toward them in the darkness. "What is it?" he called out huskily, clearing his sleep-clogged throat.

Aisha had spent the past two months learning his Latin, since he was now entirely engrossed in studying the language of Nordland. She carefully attempted a Latin sentence, "A child is to be born."

David exploded to his feet and stumbled across the room, clumsily coming to a halt beside Aisha. "You are with *child*?" he exclaimed, his face reddening.

Aisha shook her head no, and solemnly pointed at Nur al Huda. "Can you comfort? I have no words."

"It is God's will," David said uneasily, avoiding looking at the girl who was weeping on her bed.

"Kuzia Faken," Aisha agreed sadly.

Nur al Huda screamed in rage, burying her face in the mattress, crying out against Allah for singling her out for this additional punishment.

David stepped away from the women. A heavy weight

pressed against his forehead, like a metal band tightening round his head; it was as if his brain were about to explode. The pressures of the past weeks had begun to seem unbearable. Three other men dwelt in lofts under the bishop's tutelage, but each was an Asa man with little to learn save the Word, which was taught them in a sketchy and errant manner.

His eye cast round the dark loft. It had been constructed of timber and turf, and it was tightly sealed with pitch and tar, but it was a cold and dreary place. He felt cold to his very soul. The men of this land looked upon him and judged him *inferior*—inept, naive and weak.

David suffered a discomfort heretofore unknown to him, that of singularity. He felt blown up out of all proportion, isolated and self-conscious. At Saint Monica he had been only vaguely aware of self. Now he imagined a multitude of eyes upon him, judging him according to a bewildering set of standards impossible to fathom. For the first time in his life he wondered what others saw when looking upon him. His hand raised to slide searchingly over his wide-set eyes, long nose and a mouth slightly moving with the urgency of his thoughts. His beard was trimmed short, Asa-fashion, washed and combed. His floor-length brown robe had been discarded for trousers and a shirt of coarse wool. He did not know himself—but had he ever?

When Aisha moved to stand close to him, David turned away, disturbed by her beauty, which was like torchlight in this darkness and caused him to feel strangely uneasy. Under the gaping blanket she had wrapped round herself, she wore a gown cut so low that her breasts were entirely exposed, a style of dress apparently universal among the women of Nordland. Aisha professed an abhorrence of such vulgar exposure, but she covered only her face and the back of her head when in the company of Bishop Hoskuldson, his family and guests. Weeks ago she had ceased hiding her face from David, commenting that they were quite as a family now; it no longer seemed improper. To amuse herself, she often, teasingly, referred to herself as his *wife* and toyed with him in that vein.

"David?" Aisha said, raising a hesitant hand toward him.

"Leave me be!" he snapped, turning farther away from her probing yellow eyes.

"What? I have offended you?"

"No! . . . Yes. Why do you wear such unseemly attire?" continuing to avoid her eyes.

"Because I have no choice!" she exclaimed. "The bishop will only go so far toward satisfying the peculiar tastes of *thrall* women!"

David whipped round with fire in his eyes. "You are *not* thrall women!"

"Are we not! Unless you are blind, you have observed how Nur al Huda and I are treated, have seen the contemptuous light in the eyes of the women of this house. Our hair is not gold. Our skins are not pale enough. Our frames are too modest in proportion. We are *thralls,* for all the games you and I play to convince them we are man and wife. If you did not wear the mark of sanctity, you also would be treated as an inferior, a thrall man. The line between is fragile indeed." Her intemperate speech had consisted of a jumble of commingled Latin and Arabic, so that David had understood little.

"Peace," he said irritably, swallowing a compulsion to shout, to rant against her—against something—anyone.

Infuriated by David's passive bid for 'peace,' Aisha lost control of her emotions and shouted curses at him, including the vulgar *Ya ibn al-aur,* which, loosely translated into Latin, meant 'Son of a prick!' Then, in precise Latin, "No husband could you ever be to woman. You are *without!* A veritable eunuch!"

David flushed and his hands knotted into fists. "Jezebel!" he cried in a hoarse whisper, his throat closing on the brutal accusation.

"Oh!" Aisha gasped, a hand flying up to cover her mouth. She had read Arabic translations of the Christian testaments as a part of her early education and knew exactly what he meant by 'Jezebel.' She whirled away from him, ran across the loft and fell upon her bed. It was beside the point that she had far more grossly insulted *him*.

David followed her and stood over her where she lay, begging her to forgive him. But she would not turn to look at him. He knelt beside her and touched her shoulder hesitantly. "Aisha, I am distraught, weary and soul-sick. I did not mean what I said. I am certain you did not mean to speak so harshly to me, either."

Nur al Huda leaped to her feet and stomped across the loft to David's bed, mumbling between sobs something about hating both of them to her dying day, blaming those nearest to her for her unalterable condition.

"Aisha?" David persisted. "I will be unable to sleep

unless you forgive me. Once I was a gentle man. This coarse land is hardening me, and I am sometimes appalled by the meanness of my tongue."

She rolled over on her back, blinking back tears, pushing hair away from her eyes with the back of a hand. "Words can be swords driven into the heart. I am a virtuous woman. I cannot help it if this is the only dress I can find here."

"Of course. You must forgive me. I—"

"The insult is a wound within me that your apologies cannot heal. I am no Jezebel."

"Nor am I a eunuch."

The pale light from the brazier filtered down upon her bosom, illuminating the rounds so that they glowed under David's eye. Quite obviously, she could have made some effort to hide them, but chose not to. He could not look away from such purity of creative design.

"Ah. Indeed it is true. You are entirely a man." She whispered the words, smiling pridefully up at him.

David's eyes met hers, but he could find no words.

"Chastity was not included in your vows, was it?"

"Yes, I took a vow of chastity," he said uncomfortably, quickly getting to his feet.

"But you are no longer a monk."

"I am a priest."

"But you told me you became a postulant again when you forsook seclusion, and must make new vows." When he merely nodded in agreement, she said provocatively, "In the monastery there were no women to tempt you. How then could you take pride in your temperance?"

David retreated to the Bible and said, "Pride goeth before destruction, a haughty spirit before a fall."

"I will reword the question. How can a man be considered temperate who has never been tempted? The subject was not *pride*."

"I cannot recall referring to myself as temperate."

"What of love, David? And all the tenderness therein?"

He did not reply. Brother Sebastian's voice said to him again, 'Perfidious,' and he was reminded that the way of lust was the road to damnation.

"Never once kissed? How desolate a life, without a single tender touch." With that, Aisha moved quickly to her feet, stepped to him and took his face in her two hands. She brushed her lips against his. "There. You are no longer untouched by tenderness, good man."

David propelled himself away from her touch. He suffered no sense of shame or temptation, only shock and embarrassment.

"Worry not, David. I am no more the adulteress than you are the ravager." She smiled coyly up at him, pleased by his discomfort, by the power of her beauty over him. "You are not bound to those earlier vows?"

He stood frozen before her, a hurricane of new and peculiar emotions blowing within his mind and breast.

"When the bishop accepts you, and you become an avowed priest—will you speak a vow of chastity, good husband?"

"I am not your husband!"

"An answer to my question, please."

"No!"

She deliberately fanned her long eyelashes, turning

upon him her most winsome smile. "Allah protect me," she groaned impishly, "from the temptation to seduce you, David. A virgin man of your exceeding fairness is a treacherous dish to set before a virtuous and loyal wife, one heretofore boastful of incorruptible moral fiber."

"First wife!" Nur al Huda called gaily from across the loft, "cease teasing him. Can you not see how the blood rushes to his face, visible even in the dark?"

Aisha laughed. It was good to hear cheerful words from Nur al Huda. "Come back to your own bed, unpredictable one. No love will be made in our loft this night."

Nur al Huda rushed to her bed and scrambled under the covers, giggling childishly up at David. She turned to Aisha and said, "Pray Allah the infant favors myself. If it has red hair I shall drown it for certain."

"Praise Allah!" Aisha exclaimed, "you have accepted."

"I could find no alternative. Wanting it to go away will not send it away."

"Dear child, you are almost mature! I thought I would not live long enough to see that day."

Nur al Huda leaned and whispered confidentially up to Aisha, 'If you do not seduce him, I think I shall, when I am done with childbearing."

"Ah, but we will be home before then," Aisha said confidently.

"Good night," David said to the two of them, who seemed to have forgotten his presence. He went to his bed and lay there the remainder of the night, until sounds of activity in the freeman's house below told him it was the time of darkness for wakefulness— impossible to call it *daytime*.

David sighed and rose from his bed to face another full day of strenuous mental exercise. The bishop became more surly, more antagonistic to him, more impossible to fathom, no matter how much progress he made or how hard he tried to understand. At first sight of him a prejudice had been born in Ingolf Jarl that was unimpeachable. It had all been a waste. He had lost all hope.

Leaving the loft, David made his way down the precarious outdoor stairway, the wind biting at his face. He silently prayed to God for the strength to fight the temptation to give it up and return to Saint Monica. Within those comforting walls there had been not only a lack of temptations, but no success or failure. No disappointment. Serenity. Dear God, how he missed the absolute tranquillity of the past. He had come to save men, only to discover that men did not want to be saved.

Aisha and Nur al Huda spent the entire morning melting buckets full of snow over the freeman's fire, then lugging each bucket out of his cook-room, up the long flight of steps to the loft. Wrapped in cloaks of rhandeer skin lined with fur, clomping about and slipping constantly in knee-length leather boots, they fought against gravity and the elements for the sake of a bath. Before leaving for his hours of instruction, David had scraped the snow off the steps, using a hot poker to melt stubborn ice, but the water had frozen again before it could run off and rendered the steep staircase treacherous.

At last the clay-lined wooden tub in the loft was full. Shrieking as the cold air struck her naked body, Aisha plunged into the warm water. She and Nur al Huda bathed every day, stubbornly refusing to forsake cleanliness. David went through the motions every fifth day, dipping himself into the tub for several seconds in an effort to meet his obligation to Bishop Hoskuldson.

Nur al Huda scrubbed Aisha's back and aided in the washing of her knee-length hair, then used the same water when Aisha was finished.

When their toilet was completed, they wrapped themselves in the cloaks again and made their way down the steps. A determined wind almost swept them to the drifts of snow below. Heads down, they stumbled through knee-deep snow to the heavy iron-faced door and fell into the freeman's house.

The wife was standing over an iron cooking pot that hung in the fireplace. Smoke filled the large room with a haze and burned the eyes, having no place of exit save a small opening in the high ceiling. The Northwoman was tall, angular and hard-muscled. Around the waist of her trailing linen gown she wore a metal belt, from which hung an array of jangling keys. She smiled stiffly upon Aisha and Nur al Huda, offering them a begrudging hospitality.

The man of the house exploded inside on a blast of wind, stomping snow from his boots and throwing off his cloak. "Good day," he said to Aisha with a grin.

Aisha mumbled a greeting, avoiding his eyes.

"Eat," he said roughly, throwing a muscular arm in the direction of a heavy oak table set with wooden bowls and metal cups. Long wooden benches served as seats.

The meal consisted of dried fish boiled in water, hard bread and ale. The man's wife was not a cook, Aisha thought sourly, she was a torturer, expecting a person to eat such foul concoctions, without spice or sauce. Some days there was fresh meat, but of a peculiar consistency and flavor, simply roasted over the fire on a spit. No fresh vegetables or fruits, or sweet, perfumed wines, no sugared cakes or chewy sweetmeats. As Aisha ate, she dreamed of thick creams, of savory lamb and rice and heavily sweetened, dark, rich coffee.

Nur al Huda was not eating. Aisha jabbed an elbow into the child's ribs and insisted, "Eat, or you will starve to death."

"No," Nur al Huda belligerently replied. "I will throw it back up if I do." Her pale lower lip was drooping in the familiar pout. A temper tantrum was brewing.

Aisha glanced at the freeman, who sat across from her. He was shoveling food into his mouth with both hands. The three children of the house were very noisy; all were under the age of ten. "Embroidery," she said to the man. He understood a little Arabic, which he had probably learned from slaves, a thought that turned Aisha's stomach sour. "My child is weary of idleness. Might we have cloth . . . needle and thread?"

"I am *not* bored," Nur al Huda snapped aside. "I am with child! Tell him to give you a medicine to cure pregnancy."

"Lower your voice," Aisha commanded. "Just before you went to sleep, you swore to be resigned to your condition. Now you are bewailing it again."

"How dare you sit there and accuse me of bewailing! *I* carry the burden. Easy for *you*. My breasts are painful. It is agony to move my arms. But you—"

"Now, hush," Aisha exclaimed. Returning her attention to the curious, bemused freeman, with "Can you afford us a little needlework, Saíd?"

The man nodded and spoke softly to his wife, who fastened chilling blue eyes upon Aisha and spat out a remark in a contemptuous voice. The husband and wife argued calmly. Finally the woman shook her head in disgust and moved to a wooden chest. Two pieces of bleached linen were dropped unceremoniously on the bench beside Aisha, and a woven basket filled with inelegant threads and blunt needles.

"Allah bless you forever," Aisha said sarcastically to the woman. Then, to the husband, "I am grateful, Saíd."

The man grinned, showing perfect, brilliantly white teeth. His stubby fingers juggled a wooden spoon, and his green eyes were fastened upon her rising and falling exposed bosom. Irritatedly Aisha raised a hand to her face, covered appropriately with a length of fine silk given to her by the bishop in a moment of generosity. "Anything else I can do for you?" he asked pointedly.

Aisha squirmed on the bench. Nur al Huda hissed aside to her that rape was in his eyes. She ignored both the lecherous husband and her churlish companion, finishing her meal quickly. Then she rose to her feet, moving to put on the warm cloak and boots.

"The wind is strong," the freeman said, rising from his seat. "I will help you up the steps."

"No," Aisha said firmly. As she struggled with the impossibly bulky cloak, she grumbled under her breath, "Allah, I ask you . . . why did you not design me ugly, that I might not attract every foul male eye?"

* * *

"Hel is one of the nine worlds of the Asa faith and stands under the ash Yggdrasil. Hel is where men go who have not died on the battlefield. When a man speaks of hel-shoes, he speaks of shoes placed upon the feet of the unillustrious dead, for their journey to the lower region. Fire and brimstone are not included in this bargain. Our Hel is not at all an unpleasant place."

David sighed, stretching his neck and shoulders as Ingolf Jarl's baritone lecture continued endlessly. An enormous log burned in the nearby fireplace, warming that half of him facing it, while his other side shivered and goose-fleshed. While the other three postulates learned the Christian tenets, he was forced to study the Asa faith, which, the bishop insisted, was absolutely necessary in order to comprehend the thinking of the Orkney islanders.

In addition to religious facts, David had studied the calendar, memorizing the months. A month was divided into six weeks. There were five days in each week—Tysdag, Laugardag, Odinsdag, Frjadag, and Thvattdag, or bath day.

"Our humble people are buried in mounds," Ingolf Jarl continued, "the body placed upon woolen pillows filled with down. Six oak logs support the frame planking. The chamber is covered and mounded with clay. —The chiefs and all men who have gone a-*viking*, or sailing, with them are put to sea on their burning ship, so that they may join the gods where fire and sea meet. —Aegir is the god of the sea; Ran is his wife. The sea is often referred to as Ran's Husband, or the Sea King's Road."

"Enough," David said impulsively, a hand pressing against his forehead.

"But we have not begun. Already you collapse under the strain? How then can I expect you to stand firm before violent resistance, insults and physical exhaustion?"

David threw his head back angrily. "Go on," he said, clenching his teeth tightly together to control his temper. "I will not forget a word."

"See that you do not. —Most important are the Valkyries. It is said there stands a fine hall under the ash near the well, and from that hall come three maidens who are named Urd, Verdandi and Skuld. They are the maids of Odin, sent by him to determine the issue of battle and to choose those who are to fall and dwell in Valhalla."

"Valhalla is heaven," David said flatly.

"Yes, but only for warriors—for *vikings*. The Asar face death smiling, with contentment. Their faces light as they spy the three maids on charging steeds driving toward them across the sky, fire in their wake, knowing they will soon be with Odin. Your task is to instill a fear of death in hearts that are now light with a true faith in everlasting life. You cannot approach an Asa man and say to him, 'God hath said, whosoever believeth in me shall have everlasting life,' and expect him to eagerly accept baptism on that promise. Odin promised him everlasting life the day he was born. The freemen and the slaves also enjoy a certainty of immortality, if only Hel."

"It appears to me," David argued uncomfortably, "that there is no path to successful conversion. What means can we use, if not the Word?"

The bishop's face creased into a fierce scowl, and he offered quotes from the Bible in reply. " 'What mean ye that ye beat my people to pieces and grind the faces of the poor? . . . Thou shalt not kill. . . . I the Lord thy God am a jealous God, visiting the iniquity of the fathers upon the children.' . . . You use the threat of fire and brimstone, eternal agony in Hell."

"Jesus brought the people to his way with *love,* with forgiveness and understanding, not with *threats*!"

"Indeed. But you are not Jesus. Nor am I. You must instill doubt in the people as to the power of Odin, and insinuate in a strong voice the terror of Christ's vengeance, imagining for them, in graphic detail, the horrors of eternal damnation. Fear is the prerequisite of faith in Jehovah. To exchange a comfortable religion for a hard one, an adoring All-Father for a jealous, vindictive creator, would be an insanity, if it were not a choice based on very powerful persuasions. Fear is a relentless force once the seed has been planted."

"You would have me breed fear in the hearts of your little children?"

"Oh, indeed. They are the most susceptible to fear."

"How can you speak thus, as if devising the destruction of your people?"

"Destruction! Why did you come here, David of Saint Monica, if not to destroy my people? We are speaking of saving souls. When it is all weighed in the balance in the ages to come, the end will have justified the means."

"You do not believe what you say!"

"No, I do not. But I say *this* to you, and most sincerely . . . if you do not save them, by any means, fair or foul, blood will redden the north seas, the very life's blood of my race. I prefer to see them alive and Christian rather than slaughtered sheep on the altar of Holy Church, victims of inevitability. Christianity is fated. It spreads like a windblown seed over the face of the earth, and that wind blows hot, heavy with the stench of *genocide*!"

"You cannot honestly call yourself a Christian," David said heatedly, appalled by the man's heretical cynicism.

"Nor was the king who sliced my brother's head from his shoulders, but first smothered his wife and children to death before his eyes!"

"You lie!" David cried, outraged and sickened.

Ingolf Jarl's face tightened. Glaring at David, he said in a rough voice, his hands tightly gripping the arms of his highseat, "Face this fact, David of Saint Monica . . . the Word is spread by the *sword*! There are no pillars beside my highseat. I took them and plunged them into the sea, thereby forsaking my ancestors and their gods. If I am not Christian, then I am nothing, to dust descending."

"I believe with all my heart that I can teach the Word by example," David responded emotionally, "by living the tenets, as Christ did, by demonstrating the way of virtue and of salvation."

Ingolf Jarl sucked in a deep breath and let it out on a despairing sigh. He looked long upon David and saw a slight man with a gaunt and troubled face, with hauntingly sincere eyes, but he saw no strength, not as he understood it. It was equally difficult for him to see strength in the church's depiction of Christ, so humble and meek in a world keyed to the survival of the strongest. He asked himself, could there be a man who truly loved his fellows, who was genuinely humble and gentle? If so, was this not a disfigurement of the soul, rather than saintliness? The bishop was as immune to absolute conversion as his contemporaries.

Ingolf Jarl's ecclesiastical court was manned by his faithful vassals and champions, few of whom were Christian. As a religious leader his power was negligible, but as *jarl* of his vast domain it was unlimited. His diocese included all of Nordland and her territories: Snowland, Greenland, the Orkneys and Hebrides.

In 1028 the king had proclaimed by law that every man and woman in the diocese must be baptized to Christianity, a law utterly impossible to enforce. Immediately the chiefs had banded together to fight Christianity as they had once fought each other, but it was a plague, a creeping menace that could not be halted, only fought in pointless, bloody battles.

Ingolf Jarl sadly reflected upon his people. They were ruggedly just men, fair and honest, unimpeachably moral; they would rather die with hel-shoes on than to speak a lie, or fail a brother, or steal . . . or murder. It was true that an Asa man had a license to kill, for numerous, precisely defined reasons, but outside those definitions there was murder and it was as abhorrent to the Asar as it was to Christ himself. They loved strongly and grieved for lost loved ones with a wild and inconsolable agony, unashamed of tears. They stood tall, clean and highly civilized, with a literature tracing to antiquity, with arts splendidly developed, but they were considered pagans and barbarians by a world with jaundiced eyes, a world that could see only the rare incidents of human sacrifice, an honest love of war and a boundless audacity. That world would have the

Asar teach their sons to abhor war, to turn the other cheek, but he must also teach those sons that to remain in God's favor they must fight and kill for Him. Holy Church qualified the Word of the Lord that commanded: "Thou shalt not kill," by asking its followers to prostitute their new faith for love of Christ. An interdiction against war in a war-oriented world was proving Christianity false.

"If you are entirely Christian," Ingolf Jarl said tightly to David, "you are a miracle, a second coming, and I have no use for you. I need a man with a sword."

David sucked in a breath and pulled his shoulders back. In as firm a voice as he could manage, he said, "It is God's will that I give my service to the Orkneys, and I will go there, with or without your sanction, as a layman, if not as a priest."

"Very well," Ingolf Jarl growled, his face reddening. Twisting in his seat, hc picked up a rolled canvas which he threw into David's lap. "Scan that map. The northernmost island group is under the spiritual and temporal rule of Dan Sea-Kingsson, Asa Godi and chief. The southern group is under the rule of Mord Baptized-One, chief and Christian. The two chiefs are ruled by Thorfinn Jarl, Jarl of the Nordreys, of Man and of Caithness. He is called Thorfinn the Mighty and he is not Christian, nor is he called the Mighty without justification. Thorfinn Jarl is the grandson of King Malcom of Scotland and the foster father of Dan Sea-Kingsson. . . . On Main Island I have a man, a priest without specific title, whom you will be answerable and obedient to. You will have as parish the entire northern group of eight islands. God help you when Dan Sea-Kingsson sees you coming!" With that, he lunged to his feet. Without another word he strode past David, barking for a servant to bring his cloak and boots.

David sat unmoving, staring down at the rolled map. Slowly opening it, he gazed down at the pattern of lines without actually seeing them. He would never take up the sword against these people; he would rather burn in Hell for an eternity. He wondered how many souls dwelt within his parish. It occurred to him that if he were to be diligent and give equal time to all eight islands he would need a boat. And a house. A church. What was he to do about Aisha, and Nur al Huda?

David thought about Dan Sea-Kingsson and Ingolf Jarl's declaration "God help you when Dan Sea-Kingsson sees you coming!" Recalling the image of that magnificent figure seated on a wooden crate at the wharf in Cairo City, he was moved again by the hatred and contempt for Christianity, and for anyone who represented the faith, that the man had expressed. And he recalled his own disturbing inability to imagine the man on his knees praying for his salvation. Dan Sea-Kingsson's voice had been sharp-edged with a bewildering pain when he cried, "Enough Christians infest our lands!" Suddenly David was overwhelmed by the beginning of understanding.

Whales being turned into ants. The way of conversion was by fear and by the sword. A wife and mother and her children smothered to death before the eyes of the husband and father, in the name of Christ and as a means of forcing baptism. David shuddered and tears filled his eyes. This was not Christianity, but a new paganism . . . a godless corruption of the teachings of Christ the Lord. Fervently he sought verse from the Bible to vindicate his indignation, but the only words that came to mind were threats and warnings, words that could easily be twisted to confirm almost any evil purpose that might occur to men. Jesus had said, "There shall not be left here one stone upon another that shall not be thrown down," words that could have emerged from the tongue of Ingolf Jarl. "Why did you come here, David of Saint Monica, if not to destroy my people?"

David dropped his face into his two hands and prayed to God to show him the way. He had come in peace . . . not as a conqueror.

CHAPTER EIGHT

The snows were melting and Dansfiord was active. The longboats, still under shed, were being polished and repainted, generally made ready for their return to the Land of the Fishes.

A foreign ship bearing the banner of safe conduct of King Magnus of Nordland appeared out of a low-flung, swirling fog. Horns sounded and people ran from all directions, pouring into the compound, where the barricades would protect them against possible attack.

A woman astride a gleaming black stallion nearly trampled to death a dozen or more scampering thralls as she charged out of the compound gate toward the shore. At the water's edge she hauled back on the reins and the stallion reared, whinnying and biting at the silver bit in its mouth. She was of middle age, dressed in a blue cloak with straps set with precious stones down the length of the skirt. The cloak was hooded in black lambskin lined with white catskin. A knobbed staff lay across the saddle before her, tied fast to the horn. Hairy calfskin shoes with long thongs with large tin buttons on the ends covered her sturdy feet. White catskin gloves with the fur inside kept her hands warm. Gudrid, mother of Dan Sea-Kingsson, Chief, wore her silver-gold hair long and twisted into her belt in the fashion of widows and unmarried girls.

Gudrid examined the approaching ship that was moving into the bay, quickly noting that it was of Andalusian design, an eighteen-seater; there were no more than thirty men aboard, eighteen of whom would be slaves. Perhaps ten warriors, no more. Laughing coarsely, Gudrid hauled on the reins, kicking the stallion in the sides with her heels, plummeting up the rise to race back to the compound barricade wall. "Dan Sea-Kingsson!" she shouted into the wind.

Dan stood high upon the barricade, a hand over his eyes, looking out to sea. He looked down at his mother. She stood in the stirrups, shrieking a battle cry. He laughed good-naturedly and shook his head at her.

"Hah! What manner of son are you, *Snorri Thorfinsson*?" she screamed up at him, thrashing an arm at him and using the name she loathed, as she always did when she disapproved of him. "Odin's shame and Thor's humiliation, that you are!"

Dan leaped the twenty feet to the slushy ground, landing easily before Gudrid's mount. "Unseat yourself, witch," he said up to her affectionately. "Fleet Raven is my horse and I wish to ride him."

"To what place?" she spat out, firmly established in the saddle.

"That is none of your business. . . . Must I haul you down?"

"You would not *dare*!"

Dan reached up and took her into his hands as if she were weightless, swinging her to the ground.

"A curse! I shall call upon the spirits of the dead and lay a curse upon you."

Laughing at her, Dan jumped into the saddle. "Call upon my great uncle in Hel, Thorbjorn of the weak knees . . . and give him my best, Gudrid Mother."

"Weak knees!" she screeched after him as he rode away toward the shore. "Weak knees! Thorbjorn the Swift he was called!" But Dan had left her far behind in a spray of mud and slush.

Dan rode to the shore and waited for the ship to lay anchor. A smallboat was lowered and the men who got into it were obviously Saracens; the boat was fifty feet away before he recognized the old man. He sucked in his breath in amazement. It was the ancient one of the house called Golden Gate, in Cairo. Beside him on the smallboat bench sat a finely attired, handsome youth. Dan could not imagine why the physician had come so far. Surely not out of vengeance for the little that Mord Baptized-One had stolen from him. Dan had yet to learn that Mord had also taken women, in particular the one with the magnificent golden eyes.

In the great hall, Freydis Housewife scurried about, seeing to it that Dan's soft-spoken commands for food and wine were fulfilled by the thrall women.

Dan offered to Kamar al Zamen the raised seat of the center bench directly opposite his own highseat, the most honored seat in the room after his own. Gigantic totem figures carved in wood stood on each side of Dan's elaborate chair, representing the spirit and tradition of his ancestors. Fire blazed in two stone fireplaces. The walls were hung with tapestries depicting the historical sagas.

"We meet again, Dan Sea-Kingsson," Kamar al Zamen said in a quavering voice, his palsied hands folded in his lap. His face was far more wizened than when last they had met, his wide shoulders stooped with fatigue and despair. "Now you are host to myself, as months past you attempted to picture for me."

"It is a great honor to have you in my house," Dan said, bowing his head. "Naturally, I am curious as to why you are so far from Cairo."

"Tell him, Ajib," Kamar al Zamen said wearily, motioning to his son.

"Saíd," Ajib began stiffly, frozenly immune to Dan's charm and hospitality. "My father and I search for a woman stolen by you on—"

"Here now! Not by *me*. I stole no women at Cairo."

Ajib ignored the denial. "My beloved mother, Aisha, was taken by pirates aboard a vessel called *Raven Wind* . . . or Wind Raven; we are uncertain. We have reason to believe she is alive, and we intend to rescue her."

Dan was amazed, surprised more by their interest in retrieving the woman than by the fact that Mord had abducted her. He did not reply, merely nodded thoughtfully, inviting the lad to go on.

Kamar al Zamen said, "You made a bargain with her, therefore I assume you remember her."

"Oh, yes," Dan said, "I remember her very well. But how can I help you? The man who took her from you was Mord Baptized-One, and he stole from me as well that day. At the Orkney All-Thing I received only one third of the value of the silks I would have obtained had I been allowed to fulfill the bargain. The contention of the Lawmen was that Mord had kept faith by waiting until the day had passed. I am unable to obtain restitution. I can see no way that I can aid you in your search. I had no idea she was aboard. When we escaped to the sea, we left the *Raven of the Wind* and sailed, without altering course, to Orkney."

"Ah," Kamar al Zamen groaned, sinking deeper into his seat.

Ajib said, "In Dublin we were given to understand that you sold five women on the wharves."

"That was earlier in the year, before I sailed for Cairo. Why did you not seek out Mord Baptized-One, since he was the abductor?"

Kamar al Zamen replied, "We did not seek him out because I felt I knew you. And we hoped one of the women you—" He could not say the word *sold* in relationship to his beloved one.

"I am sorry," Dan said, moved by the old man's visage of grief and despair. He bit his lower lip thoughtfully and said, "I would suppose, since you are sufficiently intent upon rescuing her as to search this far for her, that you plan to pay a ransom?"

Ajib's fine black brows arched, his eyes lighting. "Indeed," he said bitingly, "we most certainly plan to pay a ransom."

"How much for her person?" Dan asked eagerly, sitting forward in his highseat.

"If you could find her, how much would you demand?"

"Ajib!" Kamar al Zamen exclaimed. "We will not haggle for my evening star. She is worth thrice a king's ransom. Do not insult your mother with *bargaining*."

"Thrice a king's ransom," Dan echoed, grinning.

"And what do you consider thrice the ransom of a king, most illustrious physician?"

"One *million* grams of gold," Kamar al Zamen firmly replied.

"One *million*!" Dan said explosively, lifting out of his seat, stunned. "Thor the Thunderer and Odin the All-Father *together* are not worth so much!"

"Dan Sea-Kingsson," Kamar al Zamen said urgently, "my wife is worth far more than that to me. Her personal fortune, separated from mine, is substantially more than that sum. But that is neither here nor there. One million is the ransom price."

"For a *woman*?" Dan cried, choking on his spit. "A single woman, when there are thousands to choose from?"

"There is only one Aisha," the old man said emphatically.

"Truth you speak! No other woman under the heavens is worth so much; she is a veritable living goldmine!"

Ajib said tightly, "I assume we can hope for your alliance, then. We do not know these waters. Without the aid of someone like yourself we cannot hope to succeed, cannot expect to for very long avoid attack. If we were to be slain, my mother would be forever destitute. We must put our trust in someone, then make safe harbor and wait. You, Saíd, can recognize her—a goodly advantage."

"I know only her eyes over veils," Dan said, dropping back upon his seat, still incredulous.

"That is something," Ajib said, shrugging.

"How can I be certain the gold will be forthcoming?"

"If you agree, we will give you one third now."

"You carry gold on your ship? Are you *mad*?"

"If we had feared risks, we would not *be* here! It was a risk merely entering these waters and we knew it. If we lose the one third in gold to you, we will pay another third to someone else, until she is found, or until our fortunes are depleted."

"What manner of woman is this, to so invade the hearts of her men? . . . Why do I *ask*? You have a bargain. I will seek her out. Where will you lay anchor, that I might send word of her?"

"At Setubal, on the Atlantic shore of Andalusia . . . the Iberian peninsula."

Dan laughed abruptly. He had sacked that town a dozen times. Cheerfully he gave Ajib a banner bearing a black horse. Any message sent would ride upon a ship carrying such a banner. "Pray, beseech the governor of Setubal to hold his fire, or you will never see your precious woman again."

"You will approach the man named Mord in our stead?" Kamar al Zamen asked somewhat plaintively.

"I will indeed. . . . Have you spoken to anyone else about your search and how much you are willing to pay? And how did you get the banner of safe conduct you fly?"

Ajib smiled. "We purchased the flag with one gram of gold at Dublin harbor."

"Hah! Excellent."

"We have spoken to many men along the coast of England and Ireland as we sought these isles."

"If Mord hears of the price you are willing to pay," Dan said with a scowl, leaving the thought unfinished. "Ah, well, the bargain is mine and none of his."

Ajib warned, "We will pay whoever brings her to us, whether it be the devil himself."

"Then I shall have to be clever."

"Indeed," Aisha's son coldly replied.

The two Muslims remained the night and set sail for Setubal with the next morning's tide.

When Kamar al Zamen was gone from his *odel,* Dan danced about the house like an excited child, taking Freydis into his arms and swinging her into the air.

"My love, a special place exists in the heart of Odin for your husband! I will buy you a king's palace before winter comes again."

"A *toad,* that he is!" Gudrid shouted. She never spoke in normal tones. "Left this poor babe upon the high cliff. Now I ask you, what ails the little lad, eh?"

"Gudrid Mother," Freydis scolded patiently, wiping her hands on her apron. The smell of fish was strong in the cookroom; a thrall girl was cleaning salmon near the fireplace. "We have no room in the house for one of your strays. In your eyes every exposed child is perfect. You must return the infant to the cliff."

"Murderer!" Gudrid shrieked, stomping back and forth across the room, holding the swaddled infant tight to her bosom as if she were its distraught mother. "I will become a *Christian,*" she threatened. "Bring to me the babies, I will say."

"Now, stop it," Freydis laughed, turning back to her fish stew.

Gudrid came to a halt and leaned against the wooden chopping block. She scowled at her son's wife, grimaced and chewed her lower lip. Freydis was her master; she wore the keys in this house. She decided to change her tactics. Smiling, she said, "Harald is gone. I do miss him. Do you not miss your little son, Freydis Housewife?"

Freydis closed her eyes and sighed. "Yes, Gudrid Mother, I miss Harald. But it is good that he is knee-seated with so great and brave a man as Thorfinn Jarl, as his father was before him."

"It is . . . that is true. But this lad here in my arms, he—"

"No, Gudrid Mother!"

Freydis was as tall as Gudrid, as strong and as prone to overbearance. She was seldom if ever overruled in this house and never by Gudrid; it was a matter of principle. She flatly said that the freeman's decision to expose his son was good enough for her. There was a fault in the child, whether visible to Gudrid or not. Exposure was a sensible, humane practice; it kept the race excellent and prevented human anguish. "To allow a child to grow to manhood an inferior is the worst kind of cruelty, Gudrid Mother. Let the child return to the All-Father that he may live again soon in better flesh."

"How can you be so cruel? . . . Ah, poor thing."

Freydis paid no attention, determined to ignore all further protestations.

Harri entered the kitchen by the rear door. His boots were muddy and Freydis wailed in despair. Gudrid swept out the open door before the lad could close it, weeping and violently cursing the gods for their stupid errors.

"What ails her?" Harri asked, grinning at his foster mother.

"She is a mother again . . . fleetingly."

"Another stray? Is that what she had in her arms?"

"Yes, and for the second time in the past five weeks." She said charitably, "I think she always longed for a great litter. Birthing only Dan, my husband, has left her longing, I suppose."

"Perhaps. But I think she simply likes to cause a fuss. She always returns them."

"Have you finished your exercises, foster son?" Freydis asked, deliberately changing the subject.

"I won the swim—over Ingimund, Halfdan, and Gylfi."

"Did you now?"

"From Highcliff to Egilsay."

"That far! My—"

"In full armor," Harri persisted, hoping at some point to really impress her. But she kept her eyes on her cooking pot, stirring the stew energetically. The fire had made her pretty face rosy. Her exposed bosom rose and fell deliciously. "I said, in full armor."

"Dan, your foster father, can swim from Highcliff to Main Island," she said, swallowing laughter.

"And so will I, when I am fifteen and of age!"

"Ah, but you are already fourteen and some months."

"Tomorrow I shall try it."

Freydis turned to Harri, studying him closely. His hair was white-blond, his eyes hazel, his height near three ells. He was broad of shoulder and narrow of waist, a good promise in him. His deeds would be a thousandfold. It was a rare privilege to raise such a son. But she had given Harald to receive this one, and she was not certain the trade had been equitable. To be of noble birth was sometimes hard. It was easier for a man . . . to give his son as a gift to another; hard for a woman to release a child of ten years. But Harri's mother now suffered the same regrets. At least one did not have to remain without a son. Harri was fine. She loved him well. And she did have her three girl children.

"No, not tomorrow, Harri," Freydis said warmly, putting an arm over his shoulder affectionately. "You will swim to Main Island when your foster father says you are ready."

"I can jump higher than my own height."

"Can you *truly*?" she exclaimed with satisfactory amazement.

Harri smiled and reached for a loaf of fresh baked bread, breaking off half of it.

"You had better take yourself to your harp," Freydis said. "The body is not all. You must know nine *indrotter* if ever you would be a chief."

Talking around a great bite of bread, Harri said, "Play chess with me, instead."

"I am busy, Harri. Practice your harp."

"I think I will call on Svafa."

"Go to the south of Skylli! You will not. March into the hall and play loudly so that I may enjoy it from here."

"Svafa will choose *me*," he said pridefully, taking another bite of bread into his mouth.

"Only if you are the survivor. She pits you, one against the other, will see her suitors die one after another. You will have to be Odin's equal to win Svafa, Harri."

Harri ceased his chewing and thought hard upon what she had said. He moved toward the inner door, then turned back to Freydis and said solemnly, "Actually, Svafa is too fat . . . surely not worth killing Gylfi for. Gylfi wants her. I shall let him have her."

Freydis laughed delightedly. "Exactly how we discover who truly loves us, and who does not. Dan killed five brave men for my hand. How proud I was. . . . Cruel lout, you but toy with Svafa. When you find the right woman, you will be willing to die an hundred times over for her hand."

Harri shrugged and went to his harp.

While Freydis prepared the day's food, outside the compound Dan was launching the *Sea King's Deer*. She rolled into the fiord with a great splash and bobbed on the surface like a giant naked nymph, without masthead or trappings.

The deer's head was tenderly brought to the shore on a wagon. Much shouting and cursing ensued as ropes were rigged to lift the mammoth head into place. Dan shrieked more than once when he thought to see his precious piece fall to earth or sea. It was finally bolted into place, its jewel eyes socketed in. A new oak mast had been made during the winter and took its proper place. Then new sails of bleached hide, striped black and white.

The *Sea King's Deer* was being readied for another viking season and for a strange search.

CHAPTER NINE

Gudrid Dansdøtter, the widow of Thorstein Ericsson, who was the brother of Leif Ericsson, had received the small island of Ransay as part of the settlement when she divorced her second husband, Thorfinn-Karlsefni. With her child of six years of age, she arrived in the Orkney islands determined to build a kingdom for her son, Snorri Thorfinsson.

From Dan, her father, Gudrid had inherited two good ships and many *aurar;* her dowry was intact when she left her husband on grounds of religious incompatibility. Thorfinn-Karlsefni had blasphemed Odin by embracing Jesus Christ. Gudrid had declared herself separated so that her husband had heard her voice, as had three witnesses. She had said the words three times and then it was done.

The Christians of Greenland thought Gudrid had disgraced herself and should be outlawed. Greenland, then under Eric Jarl and his son Leif, both Christian men, held a Thing and agreed that Gudrid should be exiled, banished forever from Greenland. But she was of such high spirit and manly courage that they allowed her to keep her worldly goods and Karlsefni's son, and all properties save those on Greenland, which were given to her husband in the settlement.

Gudrid was very beautiful in those days and she won the heart of Thorfinn Jarl, prince of Scotland, though she was some years older than he. This prince, out of honor to his wife, would not seek a divorce, but he accepted Snorri, called Dan, upon his knee as balm for Gudrid's fury at losing her bid to win him as a husband.

While Dan grew and was trained, his mother fought to keep that which she possessed, taking to the helm as captain and as warrior. In full armor, her yellow hair flying, she was in the eyes of her enemies as Hel, daughter of Loki, risen from the lower regions to do battle with Odin's enemies. Spear and sword were comfortable in her hands, her arms barely aware of their weight. Dan, fastened Sea-Kingsson by his foster father, returned to Ransay at the age of fifteen and earned for himself the admiration and homage of the northern Orkneys.

The island upon which Gudrid had built temple and compound was part rolling hills, with a flat land situated just inland from the curved bay, some five miles in length and two miles in depth. On three sides cliffs reared upward like waves before a gale, sloping steeply to the sea. A fiord had been dredged to let the sea in up to the compound walls. Hollow cliffs, to the east and west, confronted the open sea that in a passion of wind broke high in great veils of spray to fill caverns with an eternal, echoing thunder. Far inland, miniature cliffs ribboned the island's hillsides like braids of rock.

The Orkneys were treeless, so that winds blew harsh-voiced without break. No leaves scattered in whispering, wild dances. No bows bent and creaked, the music of Nordland forests so often longed for by the settlers here. But the land was fertile in the valleys, offering fruitful harvest and lush grazing.

This had been a day of sun and rain, of clouds and moments of transparent visibility. The water of the fiord was rippled glass over gray slate upon which eider ducks swan idly to and fro. Over the crest of Highcliff flew a noisy screen of herring gulls. Smoke rose aimlessly from the houses of Dansfiord, explosive gusts of wind disintegrating the long trails as they reached listless arms over the compound barricades.

Dan stood back and admired the *Sea King's Deer,* now fully regaled and gleaming. Twenty men surrounded him. All were champions and loved Dan Sea-Kingsson more than their lives, for he could jump twice as high as they, throw twice as far, wield a sword in either hand; no man could best Dan Sea-Kingsson in wrestling, in swimming, in snowshoe running, archery or saga telling. They would trustfully follow him to the ends of the earth, forsake their families, for he was a man of nine indrotter and deeds a thousandfold. He was not chief by inheritance, but by the virtue of his accomplishments, chosen at the Thing when he was not yet twenty years and three.

When the *Sea King's Deer* was launched, Dan was satisfied. With his men he repaired to the temple at the center of the compound to give thanks to the gods. An *arrow* had been sent to the seven islands under Dan's Godiship, and before nightfall more than two hundred odel-men filled the sanctuary, having arrived by sea in many ships and smallboats. The time of sowing was near at hand.

The temple was a large, rectangular building with a rounded addition at one end, like the apse of a church. Timbers from the shores of far Vinland, brought to Greenland upon the ship of Dan's blood father, Thorfinn-Karlsefni, had gone into the construction of this temple. The inside was of two parts, inner and outer. The inner part housed the images of the gods. The outer section and larger of the two was reserved for the *Blavitsa*. In this large hall of the sacrifice, only one man was seated, Dan Sea-Kingsson, Godi. All others remained standing. Gigantic wooden totems rose on each side of Dan's highseat, and before him was a low altar of stone. The walls were splendidly adorned with rich tapestries and brilliantly ornamented shields, axes and swords. Over the door rested a golden key. No weapons were brought into the inner sanctuary. No man who had committed an offense punishable by law was allowed to enter in, and no act of violence was permitted within.

Dan was dressed in a purple cloak lined with white bear fur. The silver hood of the cloak was jeweled and bore oxen horns. Now he lifted his voice to Odin and a hush fell upon the assembly. No head was bowed, all eyes lifting and bright with faith.

Two oxen were brought forth on wooden slabs, their throats already cut. Their blood was caught by large horns that, as each was filled, were consecrated with the sign of the hammer of Thor. Each man held out his horn to receive the blood.

The horn of Odin was drunk first, for victory and power. Then Thor's horn, by those who trusted in their own strength and power. Frey's horn, for a good harvest and peace. And a memorial toast for dead kinsmen.

Blood had also been collected in a copper *hlaut-bolli* and was now placed upon the stone altar. Into this blood a sacred broom was dipped. The altar, the walls, the men and the idols were sprinkled with this consecrated blood.

The flesh of the oxen was cooked over a fire burning in a pit at the center of the hall, and the men sat upon the floor all around the walls, eating the sacrificial feast.

All departed from the temple with hearts filled with hope for a good year. They had much faith, and they had marked many good omens.

The fields were sown, the seed bosomed in the rich earth. Dan was now prepared to set sail for the island of Norn and Borgarsfiord for a conference with Mord Baptized-One. It was the season of the long-voyage, but he would comb home waters for a thrall woman. Many jests were being directed at Dan by his comrades about his woman hunt. He had told no one except Gudrid Mother and his wife how much the woman's husband was willing to pay for her return.

Freydis Housewife remained closed-mouthed in regard to her husband's quest with a determined self-restraint. Within a week of her husband's departure for Norn she would sail to Main Island for the purchase of household goods. She would barter for foodstuffs that Ransay did not provide, such as honey, flower seed oil, salt and choice Saracen sugar. She needed wool for the spinning of thread, and cotton, and she was of a mind to have a large urn of glass or amber, baked to retain its color, from which she would serve the good wine of England which she also would purchase. She kept her mind busy so that her thoughts would not linger on her doubts as to the rightness of Dan's woman hunt. But it was difficult to avoid such thoughts when Gudrid Mother screeched from morning to night against Dan's foolhardy venture, in tones louder than the sounds of battle horns; Dan should keep the gold he had already gleaned from the Saracens, go a-viking and forget this *thrall* woman, this common *foreigner*.

Gudrid despised the inferior peoples of all other lands, would have every foreigner blood-eagled, their hearts torn from their breasts. A world populated by the Asar and only Asa men was Gudrid's idea of utopia. She had no answer to the question of who would do the menial labor performed by the many thousands of foreign-born thralls.

Despite Freydis' obvious disapproval and his mother's tyrannical predictions of doom, Dan set sail at daybreak on a course for Borgarsfiord, the odel of Mord Baptized-One. His sword was peace-sheathed. He had sent an *arrow* notifying Mord of his coming, in the hands of Thorvald, his standard bearer, as well as gifts.

Dan had disliked the verdict of the twelve Lawmen at the All-Thing that had refused him a fair retribution from Mord, for the losses he had suffered at Cairo City, but he had accepted it. To go against a decision of the Thing was punishable by banishment. He had taken the one third of the value of the silks from Mord and had tried to forget the anger that had stirred him that day in Cairo City. But it was not easy for him to forget a slight. With great difficulty he would now bow and scrape before Mord, but he *would* scrape, for Mord was the only man who could tell him what he needed to know, the whereabouts of the most valuable female on this earth.

Harri's foster father had been gone two days. The lad stood at the edge of Highcliff, sucking wind into his lungs with deep breaths. He had run from the compound, around the cliffs to the grazing land and back again, only just having come to rest. His flesh was wet under his shirt, the sun exceeding hot to him, but he would not open his shirt and bare his chest. Only women exposed their breasts. If a man exposed himself thus he would bring much disrespect upon himself; a wife could divorce him for the offense, on grounds of perversity. If a woman wore breeches, she was treated the same, as an outcast. Even those women taking to sea and sword wore gowns with trains and bared their breasts upon the forecastle. Still, he wished that he could enjoy nakedness here upon the cliff, but nudity was allowed a man only when he was wrestling. He sat down on the rock ledge, dangling his legs over the side, entirely careless of the hundred-foot drop.

Harri sat and let his thoughts ramble aimlessly. At the next viking season he would man an oar for his foster father. He had decided not to return to Hylmir, his blood father, who was an odel-man, but with no ship and only four men to work his rocky land. Hylmir was a man of only five indrotter. Dan Sea-Kingsson had accepted Harri Hylmirsson to be knee-seated because Hylmir was a poet and philosopher of much accomplishment, his lines quoted by all men of Orkney and by some in the far lands. Harri admitted that it was a good thing to be a poet, but to do great deeds was better.

Harri's blood father was a dreamer. He was an atheist and a passionate anti-Christian. Often he was quoted vehemently by the Asar: "If I could lay hands upon that God who out of one thousand men whom he has made saves one and damns all the rest, I would tear and rend him tooth and nail as a traitor and would spit in his face!"

Harri agreed with that sentiment, but he did not agree with Hylmir's equally vehement disavowal of Odin and Thor as wish-figures created by men to serve as balm against their fear of death. He respected his blood father, but not as much as he respected his foster father, Dan.

Harri leaned forward, looking at the rocks far below, laughing at the fury of the sea, the exploding waves, the arms of spray reaching up for him. Suddenly his eye caught sight of a ship moving round the isle of Skylli in the distance. It was a long-serpent. He leaped to his feet, his face alight. Turning toward the compound far below, he cupped his hands round his mouth and let a bellowing cry fall into the wind. From where he stood the fiord looked like a thread of silver, the houses like toys. His voice did not carry. The little people moving about down there did not look up, or out to sea.

Harri sprang into a run, following the cliff edge, leaping from boulder to boulder. Gradually the rock descended, to a rise of some fifty feet. He crawled down from niche to niche, finally letting himself drop twenty feet to earth. He called again and men heard him. By the time he reached the fiord, the dragon ship was in sight, turning into the bay.

It was one of the ships of Ingolf Jarl, Nordland, called the Gull of the Fiords. Thralls and freemen, children and their pets, swarmed excitedly to the shore.

At the compound gate, Gudrid sat upon Fleet Raven, scowling fiercely. *"Veum!"* she shrieked, kicking the stallion hard so that it reared and exploded toward the shore. When she came to a halt beside an excited Harri, she spat hot words down at him. "Wipe the joy from your face, stupid boy. A wolf enters in. I foretold this day with stones and chips.—*Veum*!"

Harri instantly sobered; he had forgotten that Ingolf Jarl was an enemy even if his men were peace-sheathed, even if the shields upon his ship were inheld upon entering the bay. His hazel eyes gazed respectfully up at Gudrid, and he smiled and shrugged in apology.

Veum—*Wolf in the Sanctuary*—she had said, and it was true. To be called *veum* was to be named the worst of offenders, for you would have entered the sacred temple with a weapon in hand, thereupon doing violence. No quarter was given. Exile was immediate, if not a quick death after having hel-shoes put on your feet. He turned his eyes back to the approaching ship and saw a red banner with the white Christian cross upon it. Indeed, the mighty Ingolf Jarl was a wolf in the sanctuary, having taken up the sword against the temple in a war of baptism, as were all Christian priests wolves in the sanctuaries. A coldness disturbed the pit of his stomach as he recalled Gudrid's warning of doom; she had recently read death and destruction in the stones and chips. He believed in the spirits of the dead and in their ability to foretell. Dan's mother was a chosen one of the dead, to whom they spoke freely.

The anchor of the *Gull of the Fiords* was lowered and soon many men got into smallboats, rowing toward shore. Harri noticed two dark-haired women sitting beside a thrall man of slight frame and womanly beauty.

Gudrid also saw David of Saint Monica, and knew him. She had expected him, for the chips had shown him to her two nights past. "Ho there!" she called out, rising in the saddle. "Return to your ship. You are not welcome here!"

"Gudrid Mother!" Freydis shouted, having just arrived upon the scene. She sat a brown mare, her head arched back, her forehead creased with anger. She shouted to the approaching boats that she was master in the absence of her husband, and welcomed the people of Ingolf Jarl. Then she turned an icy glare upon Gudrid and said, "Hospitality, Gudrid Mother. How could you dishonor Dan's name with such rudeness? You could bring great despair upon our hearts. If Ingolf Jarl were to declare war, justified by the vileness of your tongue toward the men of his retinue . . . well, watch your tongue, I say."

"These are *my* lands," Gudrid cried, writhing in the saddle, "and I will not have—"

"No! This is *my* land . . . and you have no say!"

Gudrid shot a glance at the longboat now hitting shore, then reared her stallion and dashed toward the compound, vowing to set a curse upon Freydis and upon all Christians. Thor would come upon a black thundercloud and dissolve his enemies.

"Greetings, Captain," Freydis said coldly to the nobleman striding through the surf toward her.

"I bring good wishes for peace and contentment from Ingolf Jarl," the captain said, smiling warmly upon Dan's wife.

"You are most welcome. Come. Enter our homestead and we will feast this night."

The captain turned to David, who was wading with difficulty out of the surf onto the rocky beach; his smile vanished, his expression evidencing his contempt for the fragile priest. He said to Freydis, "I have brought David of Saint Monica, Egypt, to your odel. He seeks hospitality on this shore. Ingolf Jarl has sent with me his wish that this priest of the True Faith be given shelter and charity here."

Freydis frowned. She looked long upon the priest, then at the thrall women moving through the surf to stand beside him. One of the women was very young and heavy with child. Both women were haughty. They did not wear white *vadmal* to mark them, as thralls should, nor was their hair cut short over the lobe of the ear. They wore the dress of noblewomen and Freydis was offended by this. And veils over their lower faces.

"At Dansfiord hospitality is our pride," Freydis said tightly to the captain. "I can, of course, offer the priest bed and food for the night."

"Dan's Wife," the captain said warningly, "we must immediately return to the land of the fishes. We were commanded by Ingolf Jarl to leave the priest, and his wife and daughter, here."

"*Leave* them?" Freydis exclaimed, her delicate skin flushing. "For how long, Captain?"

"For as long as the sun continues to rise, good woman."

"Why am I expected to give charity to *thralls*?" She was at the end of her patience. Gudrid Mother had been right. She was painfully uncertain as to what Dan would want her to do.

"They are not thralls, Dan's Wife."

"They are to *me*!"

Many men backed up the captain now, and Freydis noticed how their swords were glinting in the sun. Their shields had been inheld as they entered the bay, but their swords were not peace-sheathed.

"I come in peace," Freydis heard the priest say, carefully enunciating the words in her own tongue. She frigidly ignored his presence.

"They are not thralls," the captain insisted again, "they are Christians."

"That is *worse,*" she shouted at the man. "I would rather give charity to thralls than to Christians!"

"Foster Mother—"

Freydis looked at Harri and saw that his face was pale, saw a message in his eyes. He warned her to tread carefully. He had stepped back and stood with his feet planted wide apart, set for an attack.

"Leave them, then," Freydis cried impatiently.

"They are to be treated as freemen, not as thralls," the captain warned her. "The priest brings with him the words of Jesus Christ that they might be passed among the people here, so that all Orkney may become Christians as under the law they are required to do."

Freydis sucked in a breath. From Highcliff came a shrieking cry of "Veum!" Gudrid Mother was up there on Fleet Raven calling Thor to bring his thunder down upon the priest. Freydis waited, hoping the call would be answered. But Thor did not come. The priest stood before her like a rock—unmoveable.

"As a freeman," Freydis whispered, nodding agreement.

The captain knew that she was as good as her word; she would not have agreed unless she meant to keep the vow. He turned and went to the smallboat, getting in and departing without a word to David.

When the smallboat was back alongside the *Gull of the Fiords,* Freydis at last spoke to the priest, ignoring the foreign women. "The young man before you is my son, priest. His name is Harri. He will see to your needs." With that, she spurred her mount and rode fast to the compound.

Taken aback by his foster mother's abrupt shifting of the responsibility to him, Harri could only glare upon the three standing dumbly uneasy before him with their feet in the rushing and receding surf.

Aisha sighed impatiently. Her eyes cast up to the cliffs, which were formidable ramparts and dreadfully enclosing. David seemed tongue-tied. Nur al Huda had been in the throes of silence for five days, forsaking temper tantrums for speechless pouting. Patience and fortitude were all well and good, but she was near the end of her endurance. Another miserable, long sea voyage, and now this Allah-forsaken island. She had begun to suspect that she would never see Cairo City again, and the fear lay like Nordland winter ice round her heart, immeasurably deep.

Pulling her shoulders back, Aisha stepped forward, holding her head high, and spoke to the boy who was staring at her so rudely. "Do you speak Arabic, boy?" she demanded to know.

"I do," Harri replied sourly.

"Well, that is a blessing. . . . If you would please see us to a warm place where we might find comfort for the body and soul, it would be much appreciated. We are exhausted and very hungry."

David added quickly, somewhat apologetically, "We do not expect luxury. A humble man requires only—"

"You are a *humble* man?" Harri asked sarcastically, his mouth twisting into a rigid smile.

"Yes."

"Then you have my sympathy, priest."

"Sympathy?"

Harri pointed toward a high cliff, where a turf shelter stood at the base, ancient and falling in. "There is a house for you. It is a humble abode built for a *very* humble man—a *dung* man."

"*Dung* man?"

"He who occupies himself with collecting the droppings of horses and cows, then drying it for our fires," Harri replied with a smirk.

"I see," David said sadly. "That house will be fine. You are most generous."

"What is it?" Aisha asked, turning to frown at David. She had followed the boy's arm and had seen the mud house, but her eyes slid right over it because it was impossible for her to conceive of living in such a hovel.

"The lad has directed us to a house," David replied uneasily, avoiding her eyes.

"*That* one?" she wailed, throwing an arm in the hovel's direction.

"That one," David whispered, flushing.

"*Never!* I will not step a foot into such a place. I will

die of exposure first . . . or leap into the sea and *drown*!"

"Please," David begged her. "We cannot expect any more . . . so soon. They are wary and understandably so. Patience, and—"

"I have *been* patient!" Aisha shouted at him, close to tears. "I have been abducted, raped, ogled, dirty, hungry and frozen. I have withstood it all knowing Allah has willed it so. But I cannot bear any more; I cannot!"

David's face blanched, his heart made heavy by her anguish. She had not wept once in all these months. He had come to greatly admire her strength and her acceptance of God's will. She would not turn to Christ, but she believed in God and adhered to the commandments so that he had come to think of her as in a state of grace; she would see Heaven.

"You have no better place?" David asked Harri. "My wife is used to comfort. For myself it is enough, but . . ."

Harri arrogantly inspected Aisha, from the toes of her leather shoes to her black hair wound in braids and fastened in a knot at the back of her head. Most of her face was hidden by a veil of silk, but he did not have to see all her features to know she possessed uncommon beauty; her eyes were magnificent, of an unusual gold color. The spirit was in her yet; no one had been able to break her. Her hands were soft; she had not worked in the fields or on the bleaching of linen.

He then turned to the other woman, who kept her chin high and her eyes cast to the sky. Her dainty feet were hard-set into the sand. Her belly bulged with child, but he saw a sensuality in her and was attracted by it. Little she was and dark of skin, with eyes the color of midnight. For a long time he had studied the Saracen language, but he had seen only a few eastern women, never one as lovely as this one, who did not hide her features under a veil. Irish thralls had a tendency to blotchy skin and pudginess. These women were soft as cat fur, with skin the color of dark honey. But he was not so attracted by the pregnant wench as to forsake his iron determination to put them in their place.

"It is a freeman's house," Harri said firmly. "Being Christians, you cannot dwell within the compound, near the temple. That is the only house available outside the barricades."

"So be it," David said wearily. "Will you provide us with some food? We will also need quilts and straw for our beds."

"Do you have *aurar*?"

"I do, yes." Ingolf Jarl had given him but one thing toward establishing a parish here, a small leather bag full of silver coins which were to last half a year, at which time the same amount would be forthcoming. No more aid than that. The parish must be self-sustaining within one year.

"Then you will have food, priest."

"God bless you, my son."

Harri stared rudely at David, then turned and left the three to their own devices.

David took hold of Aisha's arm gently and said, "Bear with this, please. I promise you, I will do all I can to see you home to Cairo City."

"I will never see my home again," she said hoarsely, swallowing a rising lump in her throat.

"Do not despair, please."

"Great Allah, no! I must not despair. Look! See how splendid is the house I will have, with silk curtains and satin mattresses. See the lovely view of the sea from the balcony. The grand . . . open . . . sea!"

Nur al Huda turned surprised eyes to Aisha, who had always been dominating and impatient, but never truly lost her temper, her self-control. She was stunned by the weakening and made a little uneasy by it. If Aisha crumbled, who would she lean upon for support in these dark days? Impulsively she stepped forward and put an arm round Aisha's waist, offering consoling words. "We must trust in Allah, First Wife."

Dejectedly, in a single-file march, the three moved toward the hovel. Wind screamed around them, as if the Asar gods cursed them at every step. They found the hut even more miserable than it had looked from a distance. In the past it had been used as a duck coop; foulness was an inch thick on the earthen floor. The turf roof had collapsed at one corner, so that snow had entered in the winter, rain in the past week. The inside space was about fifteen steps by twenty steps. Feathers mixed with the mud and dung on the floor to create a ghastly, slimy mess. One window, in front by the door, without enclosure of any kind, was the only source of light except for the hole in the roof.

Aisha stood silently in the entrance, staring wide-eyed at the fetid place. She turned to David and asked in a rough whisper, "What were the words your prophet said on the cross?"

Bewildered, David thought a moment, then said, "Father forgive them—"

"No! Not that! . . . I remember. 'Why hast thou forsaken me?' " She sucked air into her lungs and on an outrush of breath cried, "Great Allah! Why hast thou forsaken me?"

CHAPTER TEN

Three days after the arrival of the priest and his women, a ship flying the banner of Thorfinn Jarl anchored in the bay of Dansfiord. A smallboat came ashore bearing a messenger who delivered a letter into the hands of Freydis Housewife.

The letter was addressed to Dan, but Freydis did not hesitate to open it, for it might be grave news, or a command to arms. She could not read the runes, so had Gudrid speak the words to her. She would have preferred anyone else for the task, but Gudrid was the only person left on the *odel* who knew the runes. The old woman held a *sax* in one hand, the letter in the other. She had been practicing with the weapon for days, swearing she would once again take up arms against the enemies of Odin, and the priest in the hovel under Highcliff would be the first to have his head roll. Harri stood back, listening interestedly to the letter.

"Greetings to you, Dan Gudrid's Son, beloved son of my knee," Gudrid read sourly, slowly so that Freydis would catch every subtle meaning. "Word has come to me in Caithness that Ingolf Jarl has set upon the conversion of my lands. He will send servants of Christ to our odels.—*Will* send," Gudrid shrieked, interrupting the flow of the letter. "Thorfinn is behind the time. He—"

"Just read the letter, Gudrid Mother," Freydis insisted sharply, anxiously intent upon hearing it all quickly.

"He will send servants of Christ to our odels," Gudrid repeated bitingly. "I command you, as my son and as a chief of my jarldom, to accept with patience this unfortunate circumstance. Long past, and we can hope forever past, are the days of Olaf Trygavsson, days of murder and terror, when men were forced to speak falsely to save the lives of their sons and daughters. Ingolf Jarl, as bishop, seeks to peacefully convert us. He thrashes a sword in air, but does not send it home. So I ask you to ignore any priest entering upon soil under your *godiship*. Ignore him as if he were a boil upon the backside, confident that it will eventually burst of its own accord and go away. It can, of course, be opened with a knife, but such a course would only bring two more boils where before there was only one. Maintain a policy of abeyance and firm noncompliance. I know that I can trust you to uphold my wishes in this, for you are an honorable man and a good son . . . a true descendant of Odin. —*Fool,*" Gudrid roared, swinging the sax in her hand to send it whirring over Harri's head so that the blade stabbed into the wall just behind him; the weapon trembled and rested in place there.

Harri ducked and laughed, shaking his head good-naturedly.

"Calm yourself!" Freydis shouted. "Look back at the

letter and see if Thorfinn Jarl has said something about my Harald."

"Of course he has," Gudrid shouted back at her. "Thorfinn *Fool* is telling us to—"

"*Will* you go on," Freydis exclaimed, losing her patience.

With equal impatience Gudrid returned to her reading. "A word about our son, Harald. He was eleven winters on Thorsdag, and my good wife held feast for him. He drank much wine and fell prostrate before half the doings were done. But I gave him a boot and up he stood. I do not think he remembers much of what passed after that, but he stood on his two feet. Having had one year with Harald, I find much good in the lad and have high hopes for him. He will be the equal or better of us both."

"Ah," Freydis said happily, slapping her hands together.

"Harald will never go a-viking!" Gudrid screamed. "He will wear keys from a belt and fall on his knees begging like a thrall for mercy from above. A mock Christ, a beggar without stuff enough in him to—"

"Harald will *never* be a Christian!" Freydis protested, appalled. "Before I would allow such a thing to happen, I would slay him with my own hand!"

"Oh, would you now?" Gudrid snarled, marching forward to put her face close to Freydis'. "But you allow the Christian vermin to live on this very land . . . unmolested."

"You have just read the command of Thorfinn Jarl!"

"To Hel with Thorfinn! He has become a fool. For that matter, he was always a fool, proved by the fact that he turned from me so he could keep that mouse he called a wife."

Harri looked from one woman to the other, his heart heavy at the strength of their arguing that became more violent each day. He wished that his foster father was at home, for he was sorely needed now. He sighed and turned away, leaving them to go to his harp.

Harri softly plucked the strings and thought about the priest. He had given them bad food and threadbare quilts, but they dwelt in the hovel with seeming content. The priest wandered everywhere, but said little to anyone, smiling upon thralls and noblemen alike, laughing with the children. The Christian seemed to be a most harmless creature, a cat without claws. He did not speak against Odin, nor did he cry Jesus. He just walked and looked. He had brought no army to back him and carried no weapons. Harri could not help wondering what all the fuss was about; giants were trembling before a mouse. Confident in the ways of his ancestors, Harri thought that Gudrid and Thorfinn Jarl must have lost faith to so concern themselves. A loss of faith could bring on a famine, or worse. Truly this loss of faith on the part of his elders was more to worry about than a womanly man of Christ.

Aisha wielded a wooden plank, scraping it over the earthen floor to move the filth outside, where it belonged. Three days of shoveling and still the ooze and stench clung to this rat's nest. She had eaten dried fish and stale bread until she felt sick to death. Nur al Huda was close to her time. The child's fear was equal to her own. How could an infant survive in such an environment?

Suddenly Aisha's head arched back and she froze where she stood. A terrible thunder had sounded outside the house. Nur al Huda was at the shore looking for large stones for a fire pit. A scream wrenched Aisha out of her stupor and she exploded out the doorway just as a mountainous boulder crashed down the side of the cliff and caught the corner of the hovel a glancing blow that shook it badly, another section of the roof falling in. The small, plummeting mountain ricocheted to the right, flipped over a shore boulder and leaped into the sea.

Aisha heard a shriek from above. She looked up and saw a figure on the cliff top, a woman on a black, rearing horse. Then she vanished, as if the vision had been a dream. Now there was only cliff and sky.

"Aisha!" Nur al Huda cried, clumsily running to throw her arms around the older woman. "I saw her do it! She sent it over . . . tried to kill us."

"Bismillah," Aisha whispered, holding Nur al Huda's face into her bosom. "Allah protect us now from *witches*!"

Five days later David stood at the edge of the cliff, gazing across the sea inlets at the scattered islands. The stark, majestic beauty of this land was breathtaking. Already he loved the Orkneys. They were strong, somehow eternal in their persistence against the sea that seemed intent upon smashing them to bits. He breathed deeply of the salt air. Clean air, so different from the dusty, hot breath of Egypt. Saint Monica seemed as far away as the sun, as dim as a forgotten dream. This was the only life, the only place, where God had intended him to serve.

David did not hear the sound of hooves, for the wind was strong and blowing inland, pushing the thundering away from him. The black stallion was upon him before he heard the old woman's shrieks. There was no direction he could move except over the cliff, so he stood frozen, his eyes wide with shock. The horse's rearing hooves barely missed him as they returned to earth. The old woman laughed viciously down at him as she roughly jerked on the reins. As it turned, the stallion's hindquarter caught David and flung him down, rolling him over. His heart leaped and his throat closed as his fingers dug into bits of earth that filled the holes in the cliff rock. His legs slipped over the edge, but he was able to pull himself forward, flattening himself, legs included, upon the stone rim of the cliff. He lay there breathing hard, clinging, thanking God over and over again for His mercy. The wind carried the old woman's accusing cry of "*Veum*" back to him, and he shivered, chilled to the soul.

David pressed his forehead against the stone and whispered, trying to believe it true, "Father forgive them, for they know not what they do." He strongly suspected that the old woman had known precisely what she was about.

Defying anyone to deny her entrance, Aisha stormed through the open compound gate in a rage. That foul old woman had tried to kill them twice now, and she would not stand for this.

She saw a group of young men occupied in leaping a raised pole and recognized the white-haired lad who had so *generously* given them the hovel and the rotten food. She called out to him as she approached, commanding his attention. All six boys turned and gaped at her.

"Come here to me, boy," she shouted at Harri, at once the harim matriarch again.

Harri grinned sheepishly. His friends were nudging him, suggesting he bed the spirited thrall in a hayloft.

"Give her a strong son," Gylfi gibed. "She wants you. See how she beckons to you. Svafa holds out for a marriage contract. This one has only a womanly one for comfort. Show her how an Asa man makes love, Harri."

Shoved by Gylfi, Harri stumbled forward, laughing uneasily. Then he walked jauntily toward the woman. Indeed, she was good to look at, her breasts large and uplifted. He wished he could see all of her face. When he and the woman were at a stand, facing each other—spurred on by shouts from behind—Harri reached out and jerked the veil from her face.

"Curse you!" Aisha cried, scrambling for the silk scarf. But he refused to give it to her. "Son of a termite and a whore, give it to me!"

Harri was as pleased by her fury as by her features. Her lips were full and pink, as if she had bitten them hard to make them so. She had to be as old as Freydis, at least thirty winters, for she had a daughter with child, but she looked quite as young as Svafa. She lunged at him to catch hold of the cloth, and he held it from her, so that she fell against him. He caught her tight and held her to him, laughing and very satisfied by the shouts of praise coming from his friends.

"Let loose of me," Aisha wailed, struggling valiantly. "Great Allah! I have a *son* older than you. —If I must be raped again and again, let it be by a man, not by an *infant*!"

"*Infant!*" Harri barked, his pride sorely wounded. "In two months I will be of age." He easily held her so that she could move only her head. Moving his face close to hers, he nuzzled his nose into the hollow of her neck and nipped her earlobe with his teeth. "At fifteen winters an Asa man is equal to any Saracen man of twenty and five." Weary of wrestling with her, Harri took hold of her hair and jerked her head back, looking hard into her golden eyes. "You have insulted me, have forced me to prove my manliness."

"*Alhomdolillah!*" she exclaimed, wincing against the pain of having her hair pulled so roughly. "I admit it. For the love of Allah, you are a *man*." But he pushed his nose against hers and his breath was warm against her mouth. He pressed his face into her neck again and she bit his ear. He hollered loudly but did not let her go. Swinging her into his arms, he started off at a run with her.

"*Harri!*"

The lad halted in his tracks. He turned with Aisha tight against his chest, kicking furiously, and guiltily faced Freydis' anger.

"Put that woman down, Harri."

He did so, without a moment's hesitation.

As soon as Aisha's feet were firmly planted on the ground, she swung an arm and caught Harri across the side of the face with an open palm, jarring him and leaving a red handprint on his cheek. "Curse the lecherous pig who brought you up!" she screamed, choking on rage.

Suddenly Aisha found herself again caught up. The

old one that she had come to confront had grabbed her up under the armpits in a vice grip and held her with her feet off the ground, her craggy face pushed close to her own.

"Curses you fling, thrall woman!" Gudrid spat into Aisha's face in excellent Arabic. "Strike your superiors, will you?" With that, Gudrid dropped her to her feet and smashed a fist against Aisha's jaw, sending her sprawling to the ground.

Aisha lay there, face in the dirt, a brief blackness overcoming her, a darkness filled with lightning flashes. She lifted her head, then her shoulders, then got to her feet and stood swaying before the old woman. She gnashed her teeth tight together in a blind rage. No one had ever struck her. No woman had ever bested her in *anything*. With brilliant swiftness she threw up a leg and kicked the old woman in the midsection.

Caught off guard, Gudrid doubled over. But she was quickly upright. Aisha received a second blow, a fist flying toward her chin, but she ducked her head away and it caught her on the shoulder. Aisha swung wildly, missing, but swinging again, occasionally connecting with a good blow. The old one did not move away from her, but stood fast, giving a blow for every one she received, until Aisha collapsed to her knees without strength enough left to lift an arm.

Breathing heavily, her face bloodied and bruised, her clothes torn, Aisha raised herself to hands and knees and turned her eyes up to the old witch. "Leave us be, old woman, or . . . so help me . . . I will *kill* you!"

"The little fish, gasping out of water, speaks strong words," Gudrid roared, laughing roughly.

"Gudrid Mother," Freydis asked, coming between

Dan's mother and the fallen thrall woman, "why did she come here?" She sensed a special grievance between them, something more than normal antagonism.

"Can I help it if rocks fall from Highcliff?" Gudrid shouted defensively. "Or if the priest was in the way when I rode fast to the cliff edge. Poor thing, he nearly tumbled over. Can I help that?"

Freydis was visibly shaken. Her blue eyes rounded, anger so strong in her that she could not speak. She reached down and roughly pulled Aisha to her feet. She looked to Harri and to Dan's mother, shattering at least the boy with the sharpness of the look in her eyes. Harri turned heel and ran from her. It had been quite some time since she had taken a stick to him.

At last finding her voice, Freydis said to Aisha, "Go, woman. No more attempts will be made on your life."

"Speak not the Asa tongue to *this* one," Gudrid snarled, "shc was bred to speak *foreign*."

"Go!" Freydis shouted at Aisha, making an arm toward the compound gate.

Aisha wasted no time. She ran, tripping over her skirts, ran until she was safe inside the hovel, which suddenly looked like Allah's Paradise to her.

Mord Baptized-One sat on mound, a rise of earth constructed over the ashes of the ancestral pillars of his father, Borgar the Tall. He sat alone, far from the compound, as he was required to do an hour or more each day, that he might be approached for guidance, comfort or favor by his subjects. So far he had heard only one plea. Sancho, the Spanish thrall, had worked for himself, as many thralls were allowed to do, and had saved sufficient *aurar* to purchase his freedom.

Mord had listened to Sancho's true tale of bravery in battle, and had examined the coins in his bag. He granted the man freedom, but warned the blacksmith not to leave the *filjke* without permission, for he would only be brought back and then it would not go well with him. Sancho left the mound a free servant, and Mord was very pleased with his magnanimity. By the justness of his master, Sancho was now *fridheilag,* or peace-holy. Like all freemen he was sacred of person, inviolable of body and honor, and for every breach of this he could now claim redress.

Today Mord had also settled a case of fornication with a brother's wife, a runaway affair. He slew the man, for such a pervert was irredeemable, and he told the first man he saw after he had killed the offender what he had done and why, so that it could not be called a murder. If he had failed to immediately tell of this act of justice, he could have been outlawed, deposed as chief. And he had not failed to cover the body with earth, as he also was required to do under the code. He felt as justified as a Christian as he had as an Asa chief; Christ abhorred incest.

His time on mound completed, no other claimants approaching him, Mord rose and walked swiftly along the rocky shore of Norn. With a seething hatred he thought upon Dan Sea-Kingsson. His success at the All-Thing in obtaining a verdict favorable to himself had only slightly cooled his war fever. Now Thorfinn Jarl's favorite was en route to Norn, preceded by overtures of friendship, and he asked himself why. He did not like the smell of it. The *bonder* had been arriving since sunrise for the feast being prepared in Dan's honor. He had sent the *arrow* with an invitation to all his odel-men not a-viking, more from a desire to be strongly represented and armed by retinue than out of sociability. It had happened before that a chief was slain in his own hall under cover of peaceful intention.

Men called to Mord as he strode solemnly through the compound gate, his head bent against the brisk wind. A festival atmosphere had prevailed all day. A horse race was in progress, a good crowd lined along the *gard* to cheer on their favorites. Mord ignored all calls to join in the pleasures.

The house was humming, a veritable hornet's nest of frenzied activity. Twenty servants rushed in every direction, obeying the cheerful commands of their mistress. Five hundred persons must be fed this night and provided with "bottomless" horns of ale and wine. Musicians were practicing in the great hall, and poets stood in corners rehearsing their lines. No one seemed to notice Mord's scowling entrance. He moved swiftly, throwing open the door to the passageway that led to his private chamber, a separate building affixed to the house and reached by this enclosed walkway.

The room was large, with high, beamed ceilings. Light holes, enclosed with the stretched afterbirth membrane of a cow, were numerous along three walls. An open gap in the ceiling let out rising smoke from the blazing fireplace. The bed was of stone, covered with a mattress of straw. A clay-lined wooden bathtub stood near the fire. Many richly carved chairs of oak were set about, and the walls bore mementos of Mord's illustrious career—a singing sword that had downed a famous warrior Dane—a golden shield with a spear hole at exact center; the arm of Thorald Wolf-Slayer had been as mighty as Thor's when he wore the iron gloves, but Mord had prevailed against him, running the champion through at the last.

Two thrall men aided Mord in dressing for the feast. Absentmindedly Mord stepped into a trailing white gown seamed with threads of silver and gold. The sleeves of the gown were ten feet long and so tight that a thrall set himself on each side of Mord to pull up the sleeves with leather thongs, jerking them over his herculean shoulders. Under the gown Mord wore long white hose to which soft leather shoes with fringes were sewn so that hose and shoes were one piece. Bare legs was a Scot and Irish fashion. The Asar wore trousers or snug leg-hose even under formal gowns.

Over his hands Mord wore skin-tight leather gloves stitched with gold and lined with down. He placed a *hot* over his shoulder-length brown hair, bowl-like in shape, made of silk and ornamented with lace. Finally, a flowing mottled cloak covered all, held at the neck by a clasp of precious stones.

Mord heard the sound of horns and loud cries at the shore, but he made no move to go and greet his honored guest. He would meet Dan Sea-Kingsson sitting upon his highseat, looking down at the man from that imposing height. After a last-minute check of his whiskers and mustache, his Irish thrall man clipping a stray hair or two, hastily combing and patting, Mord rose and regally stepped into the bedlam of his household.

The great hall was also affixed to the main house by passageways and was by far the most splended room. The hall had two doors, one for men, the other for women. It was so vast that five hundred guests would not crowd it. Mord's highseat rose on a platform at one end of the room, and before it had been placed, down the length of the hall, one behind the other, intricately carved and richly appointed benches. Benches for the women lined the tapestry-hung walls. A platform rose at the opposite end of the room, where musicians would play and poets would recite throughout the festivities. The bench closest to Mord's high-seat also bore a raised center seat, for the guest of honor. When sitting on the benches, men would fan to right and left of the nobler man at the center—those at either end were placed there with deliberation, to point out their low status or inferior character. The end of the bench was a humiliating place, and the women took relish in seating their rivals accordingly.

As Mord entered the hall, several hundred people milled about. Hands slapped him on the shoulders, and many coarse jokes passed from man to man. Mord was only just seated when Dan Sea-Kingsson swept in, followed by ten of his champions in full regalia, and ten odel-men of high rank, and behind all these marched five lawmen of North Orkney and five priests of the Temple.

Mord's champions immediately gathered around his highseat platform, so as not to allow their chief to be outdone in a show of strength.

Dan and Mord met each other's eyes with smiles and warm greetings, each covering well the ice beneath. Dan had many friends among the gathered, and some enemies. He was called and he turned, moving easily through the crowd, pounding backs and laughing jovially.

Adorned women were as numerous as men in the hall. They clung to the arms of their chosen escorts and vied with each other for the eye of the bravest champion. Wives, with hair piled high in intricately twisted braids and rolls, watched their husbands closely, for the unwed girls with flowing hair and eyes bright under the influence of wine might clutch a forbidden arm and have to be hastily unattached.

Harpists played, and singers sang bawdy songs of battle and romance. Poets spoke dramatic lines of love, glory and folly. Few paid any attention to the entertainers. Ale flowed into horns and thence into welcoming stomachs, and the hum turned to thunder, laughter becoming sharper and quicker.

After two hours of drinking and talking, food was brought on enormous silver trays, carried by an hundred thrall men. Cooking had never reached epicurean standards in the north. Roasted fowl, mutton and beef in great slabs were heaped in mountains on the trays. Bread, boiled onions and dried fruit completed the menu. The guests chewed and talked at the same time, juggling slabs of meat in one hand, bread in the other. Bones were tossed to the floor, or waved in a comrade's face in the heat of an argument. Ale horns sat at their feet, under bench, clumsily lifted to be gulped from, then returned.

Within two more hours the entire company was tipsy, and manners became even more coarse.

Wiping his mouth against a sleeve, Dan approached his host, who had not left his highseat, as if glued there. He elbowed through determined hangers-on and shouted for Mord's attention.

Mord's chin dropped to his great chest and he fixed his blurring gaze upon Dan. "Ho, Dan Sea-Kingsson," he roared, his head wobbling slightly. "I drink a toast," waving his horn in air, "to your continued good fortune."

"I will gladly drink to that," Dan laughed, and drained his horn, tossing the empty cup to the littered floor. He stepped to the platform and sat down at Mord's feet, a gesture of subservience and homage. "Tell me, Mord Baptized-One, why are you not a-viking? *Raven of the Wind* is fully regaled but anchored in harbor."

"You sent an *arrow*, wished to pay me a visit," Mord yowled by way of explanation. "Tomorrow I set sail for Greenland on a trapping venture."

"A good viking."

"And you. To where do you sail from here?"

Dan sobered and his eyes veiled over. He glanced at his hands, then forced a thin smile and answered, "I return to my odel, having sufficient wherewithal that I do not need to go a-viking this season." Unwilling to lie, Dan added, "But I will take the *Sea King's Deer* for a good run before I return."

"Hah!" Mord barked rudely. "Here comes someone you must listen to. He has interesting information for you, Dan Sea-Kingsson."

Dan turned his head and saw a surly man in black, clean-shaven and purse-mouthed, pressing through the crowd toward them. Dan grew sour, slowly rising to his feet. Thengil was his name. Once he had been a *berserker,* now he was a Christian priest. But Thengil's insane fervor for the fight had not been dulled by conversion. Now he plunged bare-breasted and crazed into wars he called "holy," breathing his hot breath and wielding his blazened sword against the sons of Odin, without any excuse save a perverted righteousness. To

Dan, Thengil was the worst kind of outlaw, but though he was banned from both the Temple and the Thing, he had not yet been forced out of Orkney, protected by the law of Nordland as overseen by Ingolf Jarl.

"Thengil Peace-holy," Mord shouted down to the priest, "tell Dan Sea-Kingsson the news. He has no knowledge of it, or methinks he would not be here before me, eh?"

Thengil turned an insincere smile upon Dan, his pink tongue slicing out over his thin lower lip. His palms were wet and he slowly wiped them up and down over his black robe. "Greetings, Dan," he said, deliberately avoiding the use of Dan's proud title. When Dan merely nodded in greeting, sternly eyeing him, he continued with, "I have sent a priest to reside on Ransay."

"You . . . *what*?" Dan exploded, stunned.

"I said, I have sent a priest to—"

"On Ransay! How dare you take upon yourself—"

"Calm yourself, Dan. It was done by order of Ingolf Jarl, under whose authority I rule the Orkneys for Christ, and with the knowledge, if not the blessing, of your foster father, Thorfinn Jarl."

Dan sucked in his breath and held it, his chest bulging with his fury. He said between clenched teeth, on an outrush of breath, "My good wife will not allow him to step foot on Ransay!"

Thengil tightened his mouth into an even thinner smile. He met Dan's eyes for long moments, then deliberately turned his back on him, to say something polite to Mord about the goodness of the feast.

"I will cut his foul throat," Dan muttered under his breath.

Thengil whipped his head round and said over his

shoulder, "No! You will become a Christian, Dan Sea-Kingsson."

"Never! I say I will cut his throat and I mean it. No Christian will ever settle on my shores!"

Mord laughed. Leaning forward in his seat, he said mockingly, "Thorfinn Jarl has sent word to all chiefs to abide any priests who—"

"I do not believe you," Dan exclaimed. His foster father's opinion and command made all the difference to him. Out of love and duty he had never gone against Thorfinn the Mighty.

"You will either restrain yourself," Mord continued with a smirk, "and tolerate the priest, or see yourself outlawed."

"I would prefer exile," Dan growled, utterly frustrated.

"Or an ignoble death?" Thengil put in sarcastically, a definite note of threat in his tone.

Thorvald, Dan's standard bearer, moved close to his chief, and put a warning arm across Dan's shoulders. He leaned and put his mouth close to Dan's ear, whispering a reminder as to the purpose of this visit to Norn. Dan stiffened and set his shoulders straight.

Ignoring Thengil's presence, Dan said something vague to Mord about managing somehow to bear with the situation. Then he turned the conversation, saying nonchalantly, "I have heard that you took women in Cairo City. Did you keep one or two for yourself, eh? One wife is not enough. A chief must show his prowess in all things, satisfying a set of three wives as he juggles three dirks while running the oar blades."

Mord laughed appreciatively, but his eyes showed a small regret. When he had taken the baptism he'd had to choose between his three wives, giving up two. "Look who talks of three wives, he who has never had more than one."

"Ah, but I have not been fortunate enough to discover, or capture, such maidens as that one which approached me on the Cairo City wharf. Was she one of those you took from the house of the Golden Gate, or did you sweep up only concubines and—"

"You could have had her," Mord said sourly. "You refused to risk it."

"Indeed, you are braver than I, Mord Baptized-One."

Mord swelled at the compliment and his eyes cast quickly about him, to see if his champions had heard Dan's admission.

Dan added smoothly, "A pity you are a Christian and could not keep her. . . . Where is she? Did you sell her in Dublin, or give her to a friend?"

Mord opened his mouth to reply, then abruptly closed it. The conversation had suddenly become suspiciously pointed. He severely eyed Dan, then his glance slid to Thorvald's impassive face. They were being too matter-of-fact. Something more than curiosity lay in this turn in the conversation, probably the underlying reason for this so-called friendly visit. He had dumped the women and their foolish protector onto the wharf at Dublin, not caring what befell them. The women were valueless. To Saracens women were as drops of water in an ocean, one as good as another, one traded for another. . . . But what was that he had heard, something about a Saracen ship sighted in North Orkney waters recently? Only a few weeks past.

Mord scowled at Dan. "Are you regretful, eh? So much so that now you seek this woman out?"

Dan threw his head back and laughed, indicating that he appreciated the joke, the idea being absurd.

"How did you know that I took her?" Mord asked suspiciously.

"I did not know. I just asked you if you swept up only concubines and you—"

"Yes," Mord said irritably. "Yes, I took her. And I think you knew that before you came here today. You do seek her, right?"

Dan made a noncommittal face and shrugged. "When I heard that you took women, it occurred to me that one might have been her." Grinning wide, he added, "I have been considering taking another wife. I clearly recall that she had the most extraordinary eyes, quite as yellow as a cat's."

"I released her to the priest who took passage with me."

"The *monk*!" Dan exclaimed involuntarily, recalling the pale, effeminate creature hovering about the Street of the Flowers wharf. Of course, the monk would more than likely have taken her under his wing. In fact, her physician husband had mentioned a priest, but in his excitement he had not made the association. Where had the monk been headed? Nordland, he had said; yes, that was it. To Ingolf Jarl, then.

Dan met Mord's eyes squarely and he said bitingly, "You gave such a creature to a *priest*? How intense your faith must be. And how fulfilled must be the priests who protect such lovelies."

Thengil entered into the conversation, snapping, "Lustful heathen! Men of God have better purposes than—"

"Thengil *Man*-lover!" Dan spat out, cutting off the

priest's protestations. "You did not have to forsake a lust for women, did you? Pervert! Thor's contempt! Odin was relieved to see your vile face turn from him!"

Thengil's face blanched and the tendons of his neck constricted. Speech was impossible for him; he could only sputter and gasp. A gleam of purpose shone in his eyes. In the moments of silent hatred that passed between himself and Dan Sea-Kingsson, an imaginary death warrant was signed. By any means, fair or foul, he would see this arrogant, heathen chief dead. He had the law on his side. God stood beside him. Fuming, he turned heel and strode away.

Dan asked no more questions about the Saracen woman. Mord was obviously suspicious of his interest in her. He would repair to Nordland and search the fiords for her, looking now for the womanly pretty face of the monk that was quite clearly etched in his memory. First, he would approach Ingolf Jarl, though he doubted the Christian bishop would say anything more to him than "Take the baptism or it will not go well with you and yours."

Dan remained the night under Mord's roof. He did not want to make his purpose seem too urgent or obvious. While he briefly slept, in quarters suitable to his station, Mord set his standard bearer and beloved brother of the turf to the task of questioning Dan's drunken followers. The information was easily enough extracted, in bits and pieces from several loose tongues. A Saracen ship had indeed entered Dansfiord bay, and Dan Sea-Kingsson had made a bargain with the resplendent passenger, for an unknown but fantastic sum in gold. Dan Sea-Kingsson did indeed seek the woman, but not out of an urge to possess an exotic new wife.

When the news was brought to him in his chamber, Mord doubled over, tears of laughter running down his cheeks. He could not control his glee. Thengil had not mentioned to Dan that the priest on Ransay was accompanied by a wife and child, that the monk on that Cairo City wharf was one and the same. She was now sitting in residence on Dan's very own doorstep.

"On his doorstep," Mord giggled, choking on sobs of amusement. "She sits on his doorstep and he sails the seas searching for her! Perhaps ten thousand grams of gold, maybe twenty, and it will all be mine. Can you imagine! The Saracen chasing after his woman when he probably has twenty more just like her in his harim? I would never have believed it possible."

Mord abruptly sobered and began shouting fierce commands right and left. The *Raven of the Wind* would not set sail for Greenland on the morrow, but for Dansfiord, where he would sweep up and carry off a king's ransom from under Dan Sea-Kingsson's nose.

Mord did not know where the fool Saracen husband lay in wait, but he wagered it was somewhere in Muslim Spain. When he had the woman, he would hold her snugly and wait. He would send couriers to Spain, seeking news of a husband anxious to pay a high price for the return of his wife. He could not believe his good fortune, or that Dan Sea-Kingsson could be so easily duped.

Mord convinced himself that the Saracen wench was his by right of war in any case. She had been part of the loot, as much his property as any other of those confiscated goods he had sold on the wharves of Dublin. Dan had no legal right to make a bargain for another man's property. Mord was certain that if it came to a matter of judgment at the Thing, the woman would be awarded to him.

Mord did not sleep that night, his mind filled with visions of gold, and a stupendous victory over Dan Sea-Kingsson. Not only a victory over Dan, but a complete humiliation as well.

CHAPTER ELEVEN

Aisha lay wakeful on her straw bed, shivering under damp, ragged quilts. The sea pounded against the nearby cliffs and shore, a constant thunder in the night. She could hear David's steady breathing to her right. Nur al Huda groaned in her sleep, and Aisha pushed herself to a sitting position, her heart hesitating in her breast. When the girl remained quiet, she relaxed, falling back and pulling the quilts over her head. "Allah most compassionate," she prayed, "let the infant not present itself in the middle of such a night as this."

She lay in total darkness, could not see her hand before her eyes. No sound now but the thundering sea. Her right cheek burned and her jaw ached from the blows she had received five days past. Her entire lower face, up the right cheek to her forehead, was purple, red and black. The pain and swelling was so extreme that she had been unable to abide even the weight of a veil over her face. She thought that the beating she had taken might have been worth this pain and disfigurement, since the old harpy had not so much as shown her face to her since their battle, but, thinking again, she wished she had simply waited for an opportunity to push the witch over the highest cliff on this island.

A dog howled mournfully from somewhere far off, and Aisha hugged herself with both arms and shivered. She had not slept deeply since landing on this monstrous shore. How could Dan Sea-Kingsson, the man she had thought to be so regal, so astonishingly civilized in his bargaining at the Inn of the Nightingale, so handsome as he strolled the paths of her garden at the Golden Gate, be the product of that hideous old woman, a resident of this dreadful land? This was not the land of a *prince*. Not even *dogs* were content on such a shore. Two or three dogs were howling now, sounding as if their hearts were broken. So cold. She had not been warm since passing the Pillars of Hercules.

Nur al Huda rolled over and awoke with a start, clutching her abdomen. "Aisha! A cramp. I feel as though I must . . ."

Aisha sighed and irritatedly threw the quilts away from her. "It is time," she said, unable to prevent annoyance tinting her tone of voice.

"Great Allah!" Nur al Huda wailed.

"Do not become hysterical, for the love of Allah! Lie quietly and tell yourself that you are a woman now, and you must be brave and patient. The sun will rise before the climax is reached."

"Do not lecture me *now*!" Nur al Huda protested, groaning and pressing both hands against her ponderous middle.

Aisha impatiently crawled out of her bed and stumbled about the hovel, moving her arms before her like a blind person to find her way in the blackness. David grumbled where he lay, but did not fully wake. She stepped out into the cold night and noted that there were red coals left in the stone fire pit. Fortunately, it had not rained, to make rekindling the fire nearly impossible. She tossed dried dung onto the coals and sullenly watched it catch and create a pleasant glow and warmth.

Looking about her, Aisha noted the flickering torches burning on the barricades of the compound in the near distance. A thin thread of water spilled over the cliff to her left to form a miniature stream that ran the few hundred yards to the sea. She thought she should take a bucket to the small pond formed by the waterfall, but she could not bring herself to step alone into the dark. There was time. She would wake David soon and he could fetch the water. Resignedly, she reentered the hovel.

The night seemed eternal. Nur al Huda found bravery to be beyond her capabilities, screaming at the least little pains. Fully roused, David fluttered nervously about, embarrassed by his ignorance and helplessness.

When the contractions became more frequent and urgent, Nur al Huda enthusiastically embraced hysteria, cursing, screaming and wildly thrashing about. Aisha commanded David to hold the girl's legs apart while she attempted to see how far dilation had progressed.

"Dear God!" David cried, his voice breaking with pity. "This is terrible!"

"She makes it far worse than it need be," Aisha gasped, trying to grab Nur al Huda's thrashing arms to prevent her from inflicting injury upon herself. "If she would aid the process . . . but she fights. Damn you, Nur al Huda! Curse you, will you cease. I say, stop it!" But the girl did not hear her, or paid no attention.

Dawn brought with it a gray light. The day passed and still Nur al Huda writhed in agony.

Worriedly, Aisha said to David, wiping perspiration from her brow with a forearm, "Perhaps the infant is wrongly turned. She may be in more pain than I had thought."

David stared at her, bewildered. Nur al Huda lay momentarily inert, her face ghastly pale and wet; she seemed barely able to breathe. "What can we do?" he said in a whispering voice.

"Get help. David, you must go to the compound and seek a midwife for her. I . . . David, she could die, if . . ."

He lurched to his feet and began running before even reaching the door.

Aisha touched a moist cloth to Nur al Huda's cold forehead and whispered words of encouragement and comfort to the girl. After an amazingly short time she heard sounds behind and turned to see Freydis looming in the hovel doorway, her blue eyes filled with sympathy and a steel purpose.

Freydis held a thin-bladed knife in one hand and gleaming white linens in the other. She quickly stepped inside and knelt down beside Nur al Huda, reaching to feel the woman's brow. Then she ordered David to hold one leg and side, Aisha to hold the other.

Nur al Huda began to thrash, harsh groans and screeches escaping her bitten and bleeding lips. Freydis took up the knife and with a single stroke sliced flesh, ignoring the woman's reflex lunge away from the knife.

Sickened, David did his best to hold his side of Nur al Huda's body still, but it was a constant catching, losing hold and catching fast again.

Freydis put both hands into Nur al Huda, straining and biting her lower lip in concentration. She eased, gently pulled, moved her bloodied hands from side to side in a rhythmic motion. Suddenly Nur al Huda bore down, as she should have hours before, for there was no complication. An explosive gasp erupted from her throat, and Freydis cried out as the infant slid into her hands and lay there like a crumpled, dead thing.

"A miracle," David said, awed, his face wet with tears.

Freydis jerked the infant up by its heels and smacked it sharply on the backside, until the infant squawked and sucked in a breath.

"Does she have red hair?" Nur al Huda demanded to know.

"No . . . *he* does not," Aisha replied, laughing and collapsing to the earthen floor.

"Thank Allah," Nur al Huda said, a smile cracking her drained face.

"Witch! Will you never cease being a trial to me?" Aisha laughed and cried at once.

Freydis wrapped the infant snugly and thickly in the linens, then lay the bundle in the crook of Nur al Huda's arm.

Nur al Huda turned her head and looked questioningly down at the infant. Only its red, pinched face was visible to her. Her head snapped back and she shouted at Aisha, "Take it away! I do not *want* it!"

Ignoring the girl's tantrum, Aisha whispered, "Thank you," to the northwoman who towered over her where she sat.

"She said . . . thank you," David repeated in the Asa tongue.

Freydis sourly studied Aisha for a long moment, then turned and without a word left the hovel, striding along the shore toward the compound, her golden head gleaming in the sunlight.

The *Raven of the Wind* arrived at Dansfiord just after dawn. Mord was not welcomed warmly, but he received the full hospitality of Dan's house. He talked amiably with Freydis and cheerfully ignored the vitriolic harangues of Dan's mother. He showed no signs of hurry or urgent purpose. While he ate a good meal, outside the compound his men let their eyes roam the shore and the odel for signs of the priest and his women. But David and Aisha had kept to their beds all morning, exhausted by the ordeal of the day before.

Mord was finally forced to outright questioning. Over his ale horn he carefully said to Freydis Housewife, "Where is the priest sent by Thengil? It is his office I seek on your shore. It is a holy day and I did not wish to pass the day without the blessing of a priest. We are on our way to the Isle of Man."

"He dwells in the hovel below Highcliff," Freydis said uninterestedly. "I aided in the birth-journey of his daughter yesterday. . . . Do your priests impregnate their own daughters, Mord Baptized-One?"

"No, Freydis Housewife, they do not. At least not any priest I have ever known."

"I think that they do."

Enjoying a rush of triumph, Mord did not respond, but rose to his feet and made easy comments on the fine meal and his extreme gratitude to her for the hospitality. Freydis obviously loathed the women, Gudrid as well; they would not fight to keep her on the island. They were as ignorant of her identity as Dan was ignorant of her existence on his odel. The ease with which he had succeeded in locating the prize amazed him. Now he had but to take her aboard the *Raven of the Wind* and . . .

The sound of a ship's horn startled Mord. He rushed outside, then across the compound to the gate, and, to his chagrin, saw the *Sea King's Deer* drawing into the bay, about to lay anchor. Standing dead in his tracks, his mouth fell open in stunned incredulity. He watched the smallboats swiftly ride the swells toward shore. Dan Sea-Kingsson stepped ashore and his face was as much a mask of bewilderment and consternation as Mord's.

Dan's return had been instantly acknowledged by a flood of people pouring riotously from the compound, including his wife and mother. But he did not falter in his stride toward the gigantic man standing in the sun before the *gard.* When he stood facing the man, he said, "Mord . . .?"

Mord drew himself up. "I pay a visit to the priest," he muttered, his mind fumbling for a more convincing excuse. "It is a holy day."

"No, Mord Baptized-One, it is not a holy day."

"I thought you were taking the *Sea King's Deer* for a run."

"I turned back, thinking I should first remove the Christian pestilence from my shore." Dan turned and scowled severely at his anxious wife, who stood back watching and listening. "Did you allow a priest to invade my odel, wife?" he asked bitingly.

"She did!" Gudrid shouted. "I warned her. I ordered them to leave, but she would not listen to me."

"Freydis," Dan said huskily, "how could you go against me in a matter as important as this?"

"Thorfinn Jarl sent a communication, my husband, in which he enjoined us to tolerate the priest, rather, *commanded* us to do so."

He stared at her for long moments, frowning. At last he said coldly, "We will discuss it later." Turning back to Mord, he said testily, "What is it you seek on my shore, Baptized-One?"

"My *property*," Mord replied vehemently, certain now that he could not steal the woman away.

"Your . . . *what*?"

"The woman is mine according to the law of—"

"In the name of Thor . . . *what* woman?"

"The Saracen whore!"

Dan gaped at Mord as if the man had lost his senses. "You seek a . . . a Saracen woman—on my shore? Are you mad?"

Mord's glance slid past Dan to the distant hovel. Two people now stood in the doorway, curiously looking their way. He raised an arm and pointed at them. "Look for yourself. There she stands. Beside the priest."

Dan's head snapped round. His eyes focused on the figures, but still it did not penetrate. Absentmindedly he began to walk toward the hovel, then broke into a run. A crowd chased after him, and so did Mord.

When Dan was a few feet from the two people standing frozen in the hovel doorway, he abruptly halted and stared at the woman. She was ragged and filthy, had been badly beaten. The image he recalled was exquisite in every sense. This creature could not be the same person. "What is your name, woman?" he demanded to know.

"Aisha. Wife to Kamar al Zamen the physician, of Cairo," she instantly replied.

"In the name of all the gods . . . how did you . . . I do not believe it!" Dan gaped at her, then flung his arms in the air to express his astonishment. He began to laugh, doubling over, just as Mord had laughed when he presumed to have the edge.

"She is mine and none of yours!" Mord protested excitedly.

"Yours! Be gone, Baptized-One. She is my prize." Dan did not take his eyes from Aisha's naked, battered face.

"She is part of the goods I took, not a part of your settlement with me at the Thing."

"Be on your way, Mord," Dan said warningly. "I will not stoop to arguing with you about anything so foolish."

"I will call you to task before the—"

"You do that. Call me to a day before the judges, by all means."

Enraged, Mord stormed off along the shore toward his men and smallboats.

"Woman!" Dan shouted, brandishing an arm at Aisha. "Step here to me."

Aisha hesitantly stepped forward, desperately wishing she could hide her face from him, not only because it was indecently exposed, but because she did not want him to see how ugly she looked. With as much hauteur as she could manage, she stood before him and looked up into his face.

"Your grieving husband was here some weeks past. He is offering a magnificent ransom for you."

Aisha gasped, her eyes lighting. She whispered a prayer of thanks to Allah, then blackness overcame her and she stumbled forward. Dan quickly caught her up in his arms, holding her easily against his chest. She murmured softly into his shoulder, silently weeping in her happiness. Allah had not failed her; she would see Cairo again.

The three daughters of Dan Sea-Kingsson, age four years, seven and nine, hovered over the strange woman on the bed. They tittered and whispered to each other, speculating upon the status of their mother in this new situation. Their grandmother swore the thrall woman would take a place as concubine in this house, for all Saracen women were harlots, caring little about decent living. The woman continued to sleep as if dead.

Below the loft, in their father's chamber, a loud argument was in progress, their mother and grandmother being severely reprimanded for the beating this thrall had received. But all thralls were beaten on occasion. The girls did not understand the fuss, but delighted in it; it was great fun.

Aisha whimpered in her sleep, rolling over, and the three girls dashed away, squealing happily. One at a time, or in small groups, the entire household had come up to the loft to examine the female who had won the favor of Dan Sea-Kingsson with but a single glance, despite the ugly welts and bruises marring her face. Many a foreign princess had taken comfortable positions in northland households, causing much rancor among wives.

Hyrna Dansdotter, the eldest of the girls, chose to believe the woman was an oriental queen, and imagined her father to have entirely succumbed to passion. Had he not defied the power of Mord Baptized-One for the woman's sake? He would do many brave deeds, die if he must, for love of the sleeping queen. She had stubbornly refused to accept her brother Harri's blunt argument that it was a matter of monetary expedience, that her father was actually guarding several bags of *gold*.

As the girls entered the house below the loft, Dan's voice became thunderous, and they blocked their ears with their hands. The smallest girl stationed herself at the chamber door, an eye fixed to the keyhole, and the other two fitted themselves close behind her.

"But why try to kill the woman?" Dan roared at his mother. "The priest I can understand, but what harm could—"

"Foreign harlot!" Gudrid screamed. "I would even now send her straight to Hel. What do I care for gold? Greed has overcome your good sense, Snorri Thorfinnsson!"

Dan paced the room, unable to look upon his wife or his mother. Thorfinn Jarl's communication lay on the floor, where he had thrown it in anger after reading it. He could not comprehend the womanly tone of his foster father's advice. If Christianity had not gone away in an hundred years of resistance, how could it be expected to vanish of its own accord now? His heart raced as his fury increased. The monk dwelt outside the *gard* and represented ultimate defeat; *doom* was in his very presence. He groped for words but found none.

"Husband?"

Dan turned coldly to meet Freydis' anxious blue eyes. "What is it?" he snapped.

"The priest is . . . well, he is a rather harmless sort of man. No one has paid the slightest attention to him, and he does not threaten, or preach, or—"

"He is an intruder! A *wolf in the sanctuary,* Freydis. One who remains unchallenged and unmolested! His tolerated presence on my land constitutes a sacrilege, for which I could justifiably be outlawed!"

"Kill him!" Gudrid cried fiercely. "Kill the priests and you kill the sect."

"It is not that simple, Gudrid Mother . . . unfortunately." He began to pace again, furiously stomping back and forth before his women. Suddenly he shot his eyes to the ceiling and cried, "In the name of Odin, is not Enea enough . . . England and Eire? Must they rule the *world*? If Thor does not show himself to Christ soon, I will lose all faith in him!"

"Dan!" Freydis cried, stunned.

He swung about and dashed to the door. His three daughters fell into the chamber as he hauled the door open, but he merely leaped over them and ran from the house.

Dan mounted Fleet Raven and made for the hovel under Highcliff. When before the hut, he hauled on the reins and jumped to the rocky ground, storming the entrance.

Upon Dan's explosive entrance David quickly got to his feet and moved to stand protectively over Nur al Huda's bed, where she lay with the infant at her breast.

She had been weeping, because David had pushed the child upon her, saying Allah would condemn her if she let it starve. As Dan stepped toward them, she cringed, crying out in terror.

Dan glared at David. He put his hands to his hips and laughed contemptuously. "So! You think to make a Christian of me and mine, eh, monk?"

David's hands fluttered nervously and he found it difficult to meet Dan's eyes. His heart seemed to be skipping every other beat. He was not afraid of the man. His extreme discomfort rose out of his awareness of the fact that he could not possibly match wits with this proud chief, any more than he could match strengths or skills with the man. He met Dan's eyes now and said in a near whisper, "I have come to offer you Christ's mercy and love."

"I have all the love—and mercy—that I need! I refuse your offer of baptism, but you will not leave my odel in defeat, *will* you?"

"No . . ."

"I am considering a death for you called blood-eagle. We take a knife and split the back open in the shape of—"

"I know the death," David interrupted softly. "Ingolf Jarl was kind enough to describe it to me in detail."

"Ah! Like Christ, you would bravely accept such a death, never flinching or—"

"On the contrary. I would be terrified. I would probably cry out many times. I am not Christ. Nor do I pretend any likeness to Him."

"Hah! At least you admit you are a coward. Will you also admit you are a swine, a foul child killer . . . a war-mongering hypocrite with words of peace in your mouth?"

Once again David recoiled from the chilling bitterness of Dan's feelings about Christianity, made the worse now because he knew that at least a part of the man's hatred was justified. He thought upon Christ and imagined tears in His eyes at what had been committed in the northlands in His name.

"I will not abide your presence on my lands," Dan exclaimed. "I am giving you three days to remove yourself. If you are not gone by midnight three days hence, I will have you blood-eagled."

"If you never accept the faith," David said emotionally, "the loss will be yours and not mine, or Christ's. I will never . . . *never insist* that you—"

"Priest!" Dan roared. "You are *veum*. Unholy and detestable. *Veum!* Never have the Asar forced their faith upon any other race. It is our exclusive religion, the gods ours alone, and greatly do we love them. What manner of prince of peace is your Christ, to be so enamored with himself as to demand the homage of the entire world? He is the prince of conquest, of destruction . . . bent upon smothering the very spirit of man, so that *he* will never be questioned or called to task!"

David sucked in his breath, expecting to see the sky split asunder, the avenging sword of God striking Dan Sea-Kingsson dead. And at the same time he dreaded such a happening, pitying the handsome giant the terrible, eternal fires of damnation he would suffer.

Dan laughed and shouted, "You see hellfire at my heels? Know, Womanly One, that I have an honored place on high. No hel-shoes will ever cover *my* feet!"

"Why do you call me Womanly One?" David asked, perplexed.

"Because you are not a man."

"Must I be a slayer of mankind to be considered a man?"

"But you *are* a slayer of men, if you are at all Christian. To be a man you must be proud in your manliness, be strong of arm and of heart. Skinny you are, and lack-muscled. To me you are a joke, one of Odin's mistakes. If you had been born to me I would have exposed you, left you to the wolves."

With tears in his eyes, David said, "I will not leave."

"As you will. You have three days to live." With that, Dan spun about and plunged out of the hovel. He rode Fleet Raven at a furious pace to the compound. Taking the steps of a side staircase two and three at a time, he entered the loft, where the Saracen woman slept away exhaustion.

Dan stood over Aisha, sourly examining her relaxed face. Her bruised lips shivered a little, and her fingers fluttered as if she strummed a dream harp. He wondered if Saracen peoples were dream-wise, as the Asar were, and if they possessed guardian spirits. As he watched her, he thought that she was so deeply asleep as to appear to be running in another shape—her flesh under a magic spell that kept her body safe while her spirit ran the earth. She might take the form of a flyer, or a graceful deer, but her eyes would be her own; the eye never altered when magical shapes were taken.

Two thrall women entered the loft with huge piles of tapestries and linens in their arms. Dan had ordered the loft to be adorned as befit the chamber of a noblewoman. Eider down for the Saracen's bed and embroidered linens for her mattress covers. The walls should not be bare, or the floors cold and naked, and braziers were to be placed in every corner to warm the place. No chairs or benches, for Saracen women enjoyed cushions set upon thick oriental carpets. Dan was not altogether motivated by generosity, rather did he attempt to compensate for his mother's brutality. And he wished the woman to be favorable to himself, since Mord had threatened a Thing. If this woman held the bad treatment she had received against him, all sorts of complications could arise.

Because of his distrust of Saracens, Dan had decided not to take the woman to Setubal. A massive ambush might await him in that port. He would send word of her discovery and good health, commanding the physician to come and fetch her with the promised gold in hand. It would be a month, probably longer, before the old man could make this port. Meantime, he intended to do all in his power to please this living goldmine, never letting her out of his sight.

Finding himself in the way of the busy thrall women, Dan moved to sit down on the floor at a corner of the room, where he leaned back against the wall and watched the women at their work. Occasionally he made soft-spoken suggestions as to where a tapestry should be hung and at what height. One of the women's young son entered with an oak table that had just had its legs amputated to fit Dan's specifications. Soon the loft began to glitter. Freydis' treasured small wood carvings from the artistic hand of her father, splendidly glazed and jeweled, were placed on shelves along the wall over the bed. Lengths of silk were hung to create a division between living and sleeping quarters. Through it all the woman slept.

Carpets were scarce in the northlands, so heavy layers of tapestries were substituted, thrown upon the floor to add spectacular color and luxury that completed the decoration. The thrall women sighed wearily and departed, grumbling under their breaths something about Freydis Housewife not liking this one bit. Dan laughed softly in his shadowed corner. Here in the quiet he had been able to relax a little.

At last Aisha awoke. She opened her eyes a little, but the lids fell closed again. Wriggling and groaning, she stretched her body out, then snapped back into a curled position.

"*Auhashtani,*" Dan said softly, an effusive Muslim greeting used by friends long parted from one another and reunited.

Aisha's head snapped round and she saw him standing close beside her bed. Her hands instinctively flew up to cover her face.

"If you wish veils, I will have several made for you," he graciously offered.

She stared at him through the spread fingers of her hands, her eyes rounded in confusion, then in amazed recollection. Here was her savior. Had he not said that Kamar al Zamen had made a bargain with him? "You will see me home?" she whispered.

"I will. And very soon."

"Ah," she sighed happily.

"I sincerely ask your forgiveness for the brutal treatment you received here on my odel. If I—she had known, she—"

"That *witch*!" she cried. "If I had a knife, I would cheerfully cut her foul throat!"

"She is my mother."

"Allah console you, Saíd. Allah pity you for so unfortunate a birth!"

Dan took a deep breath and swallowed a compulsion to strike her for the insult. Angry as he was with Gudrid, he loved no one in the world more. No woman had ever matched her in his eyes, not even Freydis, who had been chosen for him by Gudrid. Freydis was of the blood of kings and brought with her strong alliances and many *aurar*. He had wooed and won her, and he took great pride in her, cherished her, but he had often dreamed of a woman of Valkyria proportions, daring as a man and as warm as the sun.

"What is done is done," Dan said tolerantly. "Look about you and you will see my good intentions. I put my life over you."

Aisha sat up, at last dropping her hands. Through the silk drapery surrounding her bed she saw what had been done and smiled, very pleased. It was not even close to Cairo City standards, but the intention was sincere and the luxury quite comforting. "Where is Nur al Huda?" she asked, turning a questioning eye upon him.

"Who?"

"The young wife who was abducted with me."

"Do you mean the wench in the hovel with the priest?"

"Of course! She will be brought to me immediately. The filth of that place. She will die of—"

"Ho, now. I made bargain for *you*. Your husband mentioned no other woman."

"Well, I mention her; let that be sufficient."

"You alone are enough bother," he argued, losing his friendly inclinations. "Shall I have a full *harim* in this loft?"

"Only two women is not exactly a *full harim*!"

"The bargain was for one."

"Then I shall personally guarantee a sum for Nur al Huda's safe return to Egypt."

His eyes brightened. "Oh? How much in gold?"

"Five thousand grams of gold," she said grandly, thinking to see his mouth drop open in amazement.

"Is that all? Your husband will pay one *million* for you alone!"

Aisha bolted forward on the bed, shrieking, "One *million*! Great Allah, he has gone mad!"

"Mad, indeed. But that madness insures my diligence as naught else would."

"Impossible. How *dare* he? A goodly portion of that one million is mine by right of law—when he is gone. How could he? One *million*? Great Allah, if such a sum is paid for me, when I return I shall be destitute."

Laughing at her dismay, Dan said, "Your husband led me to believe you have a goodly fortune of your own, so I think it unlikely that you will be destitute. . . . How much for the wench, hmm?"

"*Ten* thousand?" she asked weakly, certain Nur al Huda was not worth such a price.

"Make it twenty thousand and you have a bargain," he said, grinning down at her.

"Robber!" she wailed, but immediately agreed.

"I will have her brought to you."

"And the infant, of course."

"Infant! Now listen to me—"

"Would you leave the infant to die, for the love of Allah?"

"I most certainly would!"

"It is of your race by half. You should take the child and teach it your heathen ways. Yellow-headed he is, and brawny. I cannot imagine him in Egypt. But she has named him Kamar al Akmar, Moon of Moons. Can you imagine!"

Dan laughed appreciatively, envisioning a man of Asar proportions astride a thin-ankled Muslim stallion, the beast bending in the middle under the saddle and breaking in half. And handling the sharp toy swords of Islam. It was quite a funny picture.

Aisha sobered and became thoughtful. After a few moments she said, "And what of the priest, Dan Sea-Kingsson?"

"He departs in three days, or he dies," he said emphatically.

"Oh, no!" she wailed.

Before she could say more, he shouted down at her, "What do you care? You are Muslim and no Christian."

"Without his protection you would not have me to ransom," she argued heatedly. "He saved my life, my sanity and my body from further ravagement. I was raped by Mord. We all were raped. He saved us from more abuse by putting himself over us. I will not allow him to be tormented or threatened. Leave him be. He can do you no harm. He is the most kind and gentle man I have ever known. If there is such a thing as a true Christian, he is it."

"He must leave my lands," Dan growled stubbornly.

"Then I go with him."

"Ridiculous! You will go nowhere without my permission."

"If you kill him, I will kill myself and you cannot stop me!"

"What? Do you love this—this lapdog?"

"Yes, I love him. As a woman would love any man who has sacrificed and cared for her. He cannot be loved in a romantic or physical way."

"That I can believe."

"You will allow him to remain unharmed?"

Wavering, Dan said hotly, "Do you think you wield so much power over me that I will commit such a heresy against my faith in Odin and Thor? I can have you shackled and caged to prevent you from injuring yourself."

"I think you are terrified of him. If you are so strong in your faith, why do you insist upon his expulsion? Can so frail a man defeat your powerful gods?"

He scowled at her. There was truth in what she had said. By aggression against the priest he announced a fear of the sect the man represented. Thorfinn Jarl had known this. In his frustration at finding Mord and the woman he sought, she beaten and victimized in every way, he had not been able to think clearly.

"We tolerate Christians and Jews in Islam," Aisha argued excitedly. "We allow them to erect churches, to have separate countings of the years of civilization. They enjoy with us the rewards of living in a land as wealthy and as civilized as Egypt Land. Few of them choose to curse ways that have put silks on their backs and good food in their stomachs. We tolerate them and respect their right to believe as they choose. All converts to Islam are willing, and always have been. Islam took half the world by force of arms, but never pit that force against the minds of new subjects. Can you not do the same here? Tolerate him?"

"No," Dan replied firmly. "Because here the Christian is more often than not one of our own, a heretic; to vindicate his betrayal he slaughters those who choose to remain faithful to Thor. It is a revolution. We fight our brothers. Christianity does not soften an Asa man, rather turns him into a beast. Tolerance is not an Asar virtue. It astonishes me that Christians advocate accepting the unacceptable and call it a *virtue*. Turning the other cheek and patient acceptance are the traits of slaves, traits they quickly shed upon being freed."

"But David is not a man of your race, a brother, nor is he a heretic. Can the nonsense he holds to be fact harm you or yours?"

Dan threw his glance to the ceiling impatiently and thought a moment. "I will allow the priest to remain," he said at last. "I will build him a turf house on the high grazing plain beyond Highcliff, far from my people. There he can die of loneliness."

Aisha said no more, satisfied that David had an opportunity to do his work, even as he had given her a chance to live and return to Cairo City. She felt strong pity for David. He was fighting a losing battle. She could not imagine Dan Sea-Kingsson answering to any greater power than himself. He did seem to *be* that power, Allah come to earth as a man. She sighed and thought that man was a most peculiar species, insisting in these modern times that pagan peoples who worshipped many gods accept a single god, one who seemed to possess all the combined failings of the several pagan deities. The Dan Sea-Kingssons of this world would forever be at odds with the Davids, man the gentle philosopher and man the vengeful warrior . . . and in the middle there was woman.

Dan left Aisha, telling her that food would be brought within the hour. Then Nur al Huda arrived, escorted by young Harri and accompanied by a thrall woman with a ponderous bosom; the servant held the infant, Kamar al Akmar, to her breast.

Nur al Huda exclaimed happily at the sight of so much comfort. And when Harri was gone, she breathed, "Ah, was that not the handsomest man on this earth?" After inspecting the loft, she clapped her hands and cried, "Just think, we will be home within a few months."

"We can justifiably hope so," Aisha said flatly.

"Well, of course we will. And I will insist that the old goat divorce me. I will not abide the agonies of—"

"Agonies!" Aisha shouted at the girl, infuriated. "Perhaps you would prefer to remain here?"

"Great Allah, no! What a pigsty. How pathetically crude—a tapestry on the *floor*. Barbarians. They know nothing and have nothing."

"You had best be more grateful," Aisha said warningly. "And ingratiating. We are a long way from Cairo City. A very long way. Many pitfalls lie between here and there."

"Poo. What can happen now?"

"Only Allah knows," Aisha whispered, an ice of premonition chilling her heart. Indeed, Cairo City was not altogether a certainty even now.

CHAPTER TWELVE

At East Main Island booths had been erected on an open place called the Thing Plain. A Thing of all the Hosts had been called, a summons sent to every Orkney odel. Five days after receipt of the *arrow* all men who were right-thingmen were to appear, or their wives in their place, or a brother. Whoever failed to attend would be severely fined.

Between sessions of the legislative and judicial body, amusements would take place, saga telling, wrestling games and horse fights. The godi of the whole host had summoned a lawman for the instance of each defendant and each plaintiff. Each godi had to construct a booth on the Thing Plain large enough to hold all his thingmen; this would serve as a place of residence during the fourteen-day-long assembly.

The All-Thing began on a Thorsday, just as the sun began to set. A man-reckoning, or census, was taken, then all those present were told that they could not leave the confines of the Thing until the assembly was formally dissolved.

The ordinary judges stood for election once a year

and were the most influential, respected and loved men of the Orkneys. Great was the faith in their advice, for they were men full of knowledge and of ancient law and custom, thought of as living lawbooks. If a man was both godi and lawman, he could sit in only one capacity at a time. The place where the judges sat was holy, and its boundaries were marked off by ropes. The law court within the rope boundaries was covered by a timber roof supported by wooden pillars and three long benches were arranged within the circle, one behind the other. On the center bench sat forty-eight self-appointed judges who constituted the real judicial body; the ordinary judges could advise only those who were middle-seated. Thorfinn Jarl, chief over the whole host, was represented by the godi of Caithness and of Main Island, and he sat at the center of the middle-seated judges. This court held enormous power and was renowned for its democratic enactments of justice. Only one thing was above these individuals and that was the law itself.

The law was written and it was explicit in all things, even to the matter of biting. "It is not fitting that men should bite each other like horses or dogs. When a man bites another he shall have his teeth broken from his mouth."

A slanderer was to receive the punishment the offended would have suffered had he been guilty. Oath breakers were loathed and fined. Outlawry, or exile, was the common punishment for all but the most heinous crimes. A three-time offender was executed by sword as irredeemable. There were no prisons in the northlands. An enemy of society, a wolf in the sanctuary, was either slain or left to the wild beasts in the wilderness. A family's right and duty was to avenge a slaying of one of its members, and blood feuds were so common that an indemnity had been set for murder, called wergild, or the price of a dead man. The entire family worth was computed in gold, then the indemnity was fixed accordingly; the fine could be accepted if one did not wish to avenge the death with sword. But once the wergild was accepted, any act of revenge would be called murder.

There were many cases to be presented to the court, so it was not until the sun was at its zenith on the fourth day of the assembly that Mord Baptized-One was called into the holy circle to be heard on his accusations against Dan Sea-Kingsson. The accused stood outside the rope barrier with his thingmen, listening and waiting for his opportunity to speak. Only a man with odel, or owned lands, with at least three men working the odel, had a voice and was called a thingman. In Dan's booth on the plain to the south, Aisha, the goods in question, waited to be turned over to whichever man received the court's favor. With her was the priest under whose protection Mord had left her on the Dublin wharf.

Mord spoke confidently and heatedly to the judges, describing his pillage of the house of the Golden Gate in Cairo City, his escape and his reasons for leaving the woman to a priest of his faith—the priest had threatened to bring the vengeance of the Lord Christ down upon his head. He argued that the value of the woman was such that this could not be considered a petty case of thrall ownership. The woman was equal to a chest of gold and had been stolen from him by Dan Sea-Kingsson, who had used deceit to take her, coming to Borgarsfiord as a friend, fully aware of her value, intent upon extracting information as to her whereabouts with undisguised intention of robbery.

No one attempted to cut Mord's speech short. When he had finished, the judges asked him questions. Had Dan Sea-Kingsson been a part of the Cairo City sacking? How did the woman come to be on Dan Sea-Kingsson's odel? Since he had requested that the woman be considered more than a thrall, did Mord want her to be considered a free-servant and peace-holy?

Mord hesitated to answer the last query, but finally agreed, with some uneasiness, that the woman should be found to be a free-servant, but under his mastership. He went on to tell of Dan's dishonesty and belligerent manner when approached at Dansfiord as to this right of ownership.

When Mord had concluded his argument, the middle-seated judge spoke softly. "Certainly a wickedness has been committed, if your story is true, Mord Borgarsson, but a tale is always half told if only one man tells it, for most men are willing to take the worst side of a question if it will benefit them; therefore, as matters stand, we must hear Dan Sea-Kingsson's tale before rendering a decision."

It was a formal statement, but Mord's confidence slumped. The judges were prejudiced against him, evidenced by the use of his birth-fastening name, Borgarsson, rather than his proud Christian title, Baptized-One. He was being held in contempt for being a Christian. It was with much ill feeling that he gave way to Dan Sea-Kingsson.

Dan moved under the ropes and into the circle. He

spoke briefly about the sacking, recalling to the judges his earlier claim of thievery against Mord Borgarsson. He told them that this woman was the person with whom he had made bargain for silks that he had never received due to Mord's actions. He reminded them of his cheerful acceptance of their past verdict, though the loss to himself had been great in both gold and honor. He argued that by right of possession the woman was his to ransom. According to the law of free-servantry, if a master did not take after a runaway servant the servant became his own man. Since Mord claimed the woman to be peace-holy, she had a right to be heard, to tell the true tale from her point of view. If she could be called as a witness?

The judges considered the matter of whether the woman should be found to be peace-holy, speaking to one another in low tones.

"Call the witness," the middle-seated one said at last.

Aisha was quickly brought before the bench. David of Saint Monica stood by her side protectively, his eyes anxiously scanning the faces of the sober judges.

Dan's lawman stood forward to question the witness. First, Aisha was told that she had been accepted as peace-holy by this court, and what this meant to her. In precise Arabic the lawman told her the essence of the testimony so far.

"Is it true that you were taken in the Cairo sacking?"

"Yes," Aisha replied, worriedly glancing to Dan's impassive face.

A translator repeated the lawman's question and her reply for the judges.

"Was Dan Sea-Kingsson involved in your abduction in any way to your knowledge?"

"No."

"When Mord Borgarsson set you free, was it not an act of total releasing of ownership? He wanted nothing more to do with you."

"I . . . I do not know. I mean, I—" She was confused as to what Dan expected her to say, as to what words would ensure that she would not be placed within Mord's shadow again. Frightened, she threw up her hands in a gesture that expressed her helplessness.

The lawman turned to David and asked the same question of him, automatically reverting to the Asa tongue.

Rocking uneasily from foot to foot, David replied, "I made a claim on the women as a priest of Mord's faith. She was released to me without qualification."

"You did not steal her from Mord, or in any way coerce him, to obtain possession of this woman?"

David hesitated. He had used a kind of coercion. "I used my power as a priest," he admitted.

"With how many men to back you up?"

"No men, only the force of God's—"

"Enough," the lawman interrupted. "We are not interested in your gods." He turned back to Aisha. "Tell us, as a free-servant, which man, plaintiff or accused, you consider master over you."

"Dan Sea-Kingsson," Aisha replied emphatically.

The lawman then spoke to the benches. "Since this court, at the plea of the plaintiff, has agreed that this woman is peace-holy, the plaintiff admittedly releasing her and making no effort to bring her back as the law requires, we contend that her personal sanctity would be violated by a verdict in favor of Mord Borgarsson."

The middle-seated judge nodded and directed a

question to Aisha. "Are you not considered the wife of this priest, woman?"

"I am. But—"

"You have lived with him as his wife for the period of one year; yes or no?"

"Not a year," Aisha replied falteringly. "It cannot have been that long. Perhaps—"

"The time span is of no consequence. Have you lived with this priest as his wife?"

Aisha turned her head to look at Dan's stubbornly averted eyes for help. She cared not what they believed. The true or the false of it was of no matter. She only wanted to say the right thing. But Dan refused to so much as meet her eyes.

"We await your reply, woman. Hesitation hints at a need for time to think of a lie."

"Yes! We have lived as man and wife," she exclaimed on an outrush of breath.

David's head snapped round and he stared at her in shock. But he said nothing, praying they would not also put the question to him. He would not lie for her, nor did he wish to say that she had lied.

The judge sat back, apparently satisfied. Dan's lawman had no more to say, nor did Dan. The court was cleared of witnesses, and the judges turned on the benches to discuss what they had heard. The elected ones spoke first, giving advice to the judicial bench. Very little time was spent. Their opinion and judgment was given to the foreman of a separate group of twelve lawmen who sat outside the holy court. The verdict would be incontestable, for this was the highest court in the land.

The twelve jurors made a quick decision. The foreman rose and called Dan and Mord to stand before the jury.

"It is our decision that neither the plaintiff nor the accused has any legal claim to this woman."

Enraged, Mord yowled in protest, cursing and wildly thrashing his arms in threatening gestures at the jury. Dan's eyes rounded in surprise, his hands knotting into fists.

"Since it was agreed by this court that the woman is peace-holy, and since we recognize marriage to be a mutual pledge between a man and a woman, no ceremony or contract necessary, and since we do not recognize marriage vows taken in other lands under other codes of law, and since the plaintiff forfeited his claim by failure to follow after her, and since the priest is a freeman, not a servant . . . under the auspices of Ingolf Jarl, we hereby proclaim the woman in question to be wife and property of David the priest, to dispatch as he, her husband, sees fit. By the decision of this court, any ransom would be his. Let it be noted that the priest is not an odel-man and therefore has no voice in this assembly and cannot claim redress, but any infraction of his rights as her husband will be considered unlawful, he who steals from him a thief. Such is the verdict of this court."

Mord's rage was no more volatile than Dan's. The two simultaneously exploded. Each surrounded by his thingmen, they spat hot words that filled the air with overlapping curses and threats. The jurors were besieged, fingers poked against their chests, yowling protests directed at them, but they stood firm. Not a man accosted the judges within the rope boundaries; to do so would bring upon the offender immediate outlawry.

Mord finally managed to make his voice heard over the general clamor. He called the host's attention to this vow. "As an Asar chief and as a Christian, I disclaim the sanctity of this court! I herewith denounce the justice of this Thing. I refuse to respect this verdict!" He unsheathed his sword and tore the peace-wrapping from it, brandishing the blade high over his head. "With the power of Christ's bishop, Ingolf Jarl, behind me, I will have the woman and the ransom due me!"

Shouts of protest were loudly directed at Mord. Anger was not uncommon, but denouncement was blasphemy and intolerable.

Dan wasted no time. He rushed toward his booth, dragging Aisha along with him, shouting to his thingmen to follow. He hustled David and Aisha aboard the *Sea King's Deer* and set sail immediately for Dansfiord, breaking his commitment to remain throughout the assembly, for which he would pay a heavy fine. Mord had declared war against him. He could no longer concern himself with ransom; the homestead had to be protected from fire and pillage.

David stood alone at the crest of a hill, leaning into the wind. A flock of gulls flew overhead, dipping their wings and sailing effortlessly in graceful dances against the clouded sky. Dan Sea-Kingsson had thought to punish him with this aloneness, but it was very like Saint Monica on this high plain. The silence was profound, so his thoughts could take a snail's pace through any contemplation. There was no urgency. Life seemed to have become ordered and controllable again.

The turf house built for David while the All-Thing

was being held was well sealed and adequately outfitted with a stone bed, fireplace and washtub. Cooking and eating utensils had been provided, linens and good quilts as well. A stream was nearby. Fish was brought each day by small children, and fresh goat's milk, cheese and bread, for which he paid in *pennings*. No limitations had been placed upon his movements, but he had not felt like leaving the plain since returning to Ransay. He had much to think about and meant to take his time in coming to a decision.

Laughter rode on the brisk wind and reached David's ear. He turned his head to look in the direction of the sound, toward the distant, rocky ledges. All around him rose hills of rock and bracken. Dan's odel was an hour's walk away. Again youthful laughter bounced off the nearby hills, then echoed again, then again. David smiled when he saw Harri's white-haired head appear over the rise. Nur al Huda was with him, and the oldest daughter of Dan Sea-Kingsson.

"David!" Nur al Huda called across the field as she ran toward him, cupping her hands round her mouth.

David walked toward the young people, very happy to see them. Nur al Huda ran to him, her face flushed by the sun and the brisk sea air. "Great Allah!" she gasped, laughing. During the year of her ordeal she had adequately mastered the Asa tongue, and she now carefully used that language to communicate with David. "Harri said it was but a short walk from High-cliff, but I swear we left two days ago."

"Should you strain yourself so soon after giving birth?" David asked concernedly.

"Poo! I feel simply marvelous. It has been nearly eight weeks."

Harri carried a hamper weighted with foodstuffs. He smiled uneasily at David, moving past the priest toward the house.

David looked down into Hyrna Dansdotter's bright green and wary eyes and said, "How good of you to visit me. You are very welcome. My, how beautiful you are."

Hyrna flushed and beamed at the compliment. But she was shy of the priest and ran after Harri, her skirts flying.

"Are you well, David?" Nur al Huda asked.

"I am very well, thank you, child."

"I think it was brutal of them to put you way up here by yourself. It is a prison with cliffs for walls and bars."

"I am grateful to God that I have been allowed to remain on the island."

"Oh, you *would* be. David, you must learn to be more greedy. Harri tells me that the court decided you are Aisha's master—and that the ransom will be all yours. But you seem foolishly indifferent to the fact." It had not occurred to her that if David owned Aisha, he owned her as well; she had a sense of being as free as the gulls overhead.

David laughed. "I have been thinking along those very lines." He took her arm and held it lightly as they walked toward the turf house.

"I must say it is lovely here, David, in a stark kind of way. So green, and open."

"I agree. It is already entirely home to me."

Harri had deposited the hamper before the door. He stood sourly waiting for the two to reach him. Hyrna was chasing a rabbit across the back field; she was a child of boundless energy.

David approached Harri smiling. "It was good of you to bring me the food, Harri. My sincere thank-you." He extracted a bag from inside his shirt, taking out coins and putting them into the lad's hand.

"I was ordered to the task," Harri grumbled, pocketing the money.

"Nevertheless, I thank you. Will you eat with me? You must be hungry after so long a walk."

"No," Harri said quickly.

"Oh, he *will*," Nur al Huda exclaimed. "Stop being so silly, Harri. I have lived with David for nearly a year, and Jesus Christ has not rubbed off on me. Really, sometimes you can act quite stupidly."

Harri was angered by her gibe, but when he opened his mouth to object, he noticed again that she was the loveliest creature he had ever seen, the stuff of poets' fancies. He had never been so happy as since she came into the house, fairly making the rooms sing with her exciting presence. She had not chosen to separate herself, as the queenly one did, but took meals with the family. She gave orders to Freydis and Gudrid, which made their blood boil, but they indulged her for Dan's sake. He had spent many full days with her. Rarely was she out of his sight. When wrestling with Gylfi, he would look up and see her watching. She did seem to follow him wherever he went.

"I would be honored by your acceptance," David coaxed.

"I am hungry," Harri admitted. He added hastily, "But I will not stand still for preaching!"

David laughed heartily. "I swear to you, I will not preach. I will even say my mealtime prayer to myself, so as not to offend you."

Harri somewhat reluctantly smiled, nodding his head to indicate they had struck a bargain.

"Harri, I have a problem," David said solemnly, "and I would like your advice." When the lad merely curiously studied him, he went on with, "I am laughed at . . . called *Womanly One*. Not even a Christian enjoys derision." Harri laughed out loud at that but said nothing. "Even the little children make up jokes about me and call me terrible things, like Hel's Exposed One, or Odin's Mistake." David hesitated, his mouth twisting into a wry smile. "Now, if someone could teach me to be a man, then I might earn the respect I am hoping for here."

Harri gaped at the priest, uncertain if the man was joking with him. "A man is a man. It is not *taught*."

"But that is not true. I have seen men teaching their sons who are barely able to walk how to throw and swim and jump."

"You would learn to jump? And to *throw*?"

"Especially to swim."

"You cannot swim?" Harri exclaimed incredulously.

"No, I cannot. Desert surrounded the monastery where I was raised. We barely had enough water to drink."

"What fun," Nur al Huda cried. "Harri, you must teach him. And I will help. I am a good swimmer."

"A *good* swimmer can swim ten miles in rough sea with ease," Harri barked jovially. "Do you mean to tell me you can swim that well?"

"Ten miles! I do not believe you."

"I can carry a man on my back that far, and swim back again with him."

"Father of liars!" she teased, looking upon him wonderingly.

"I wish to be strong of leg, of arm and of heart," David said more intensely. He recalled Dan Sea-Kingsson's bitter tongue-lashing that day in the hovel and scowled. An iron determination had grown in him since that confrontation. He would gain the respect of that stubborn chief if it cost him his life. There was no other way to win these people to Christ. "I am thirty years and five. I appear to be frail, but I possess a vigor that is hidden and of the spirit. With luck and hard work I think I can develop one or two muscles. Hm?"

Harri looked dubious. His eyes scanned the priest from head to toe. He had a good enough frame, but no flesh or muscle on him to speak of. It was impossible. The man was bereft of his senses. "Come to the bay sometime," he offered unenthusiastically, "and I will give you a swimming lesson."

"Thank you, Harri. . . . Tomorrow?"

"I . . . Tomorrow?"

"Tomorrow!" Nur al Huda agreed excitedly. "What fun. David, you are the father of mystery and I shall never understand you fully."

David offered no enlightenment as to his character. He went to the food basket and removed bread and cheese, smoked salmon and an earthen jug of milk. Hyrna was called and the four enjoyed a pleasant meal together, David mostly listening to the young people, a contented smile on his face.

After the meal Harri took Nur al Huda by the hand and raced across the fields with her. She stumbled and fell. Laughing, he hauled her up in his arms and ran as easily as if he carried no weight at all. Hyrna followed their routeless chase for a time, then tired of the game and wandered back to the house of the priest.

Harri directed his feet toward a rising, jagged mound of rock. Someone had long ago planted a Nordland evergreen tree in the windswept earth that had filled a crag; the seedling had grown tall, but bent and twisted by constant winds from the sea. With the giggling wench over his shoulder, Harri scaled the rock and scrambled over the top, planting his burden under the spreading canopy of branches. The rock was slightly concave under the tree, in an oval shape about five feet by nine feet that had thickly filled with evergreen needles, forming a quite comfortable shelter under the dipped down branches. "You are so impossibly *strong*," Nur al Huda said breathlessly, sitting beside him, glowing with happiness.

"Yes," Harri agreed smugly.

"It has been the most wonderful day," she said on a sigh, hugging her raised knees with her arms. "I wish—" She bit off her words, looking wistful.

"What do you wish?" Harri asked, turning his head to study her now somber profile.

"Oh, many things. Particularly, that I had been born as free as your mother and—"

"What do you mean? Were you a *slave* in Egypt?"

"Great Allah, no!" She laughed delightedly at such an idea.

"Then, why would you wish to have been born free?"

"My father promised me to Kamar al Zamen, my husband, when I was five years old. I went to him when I was twelve. Harri, he was ancient! A foul old goat with shivering hands and wrinkled skin. He did not want me as a woman, but nevertheless, it was agonizing for me."

Harri's young face writhed in sympathy. "But he gave you a child," he said miserably, despising the foul person who had so abused this black-eyed dream of poets.

Nur al Huda flinched, but made no effort to put him straight; he might despise her if he knew how she had been ravaged on the ship. Better he believed the infant a natural result of marriage. How she had loathed all the heathen men of this land. Oh, but not Harri. She felt strange with him, not quite herself. His touch made her flesh writhe, and fire to burn in her breast. He was all her dreams of love of all those lonely days and years in Kamar al Zamen's harim. She had devoured the *Tales of a Thousand Nights and a Night*, wherein foreign princes stole away harim girls, rereading the detailed descriptions of their couplings and kissings over and over again until her eyes burned and she could not see to read the words again. Now Kamar al Zamen was en route to Ransay. Only this morning Aisha had said that it would not be more than a month before his arrival. The vile old goat would never die . . . never. Her entire youth would be wasted, and only tales of fancy would cheer her heart, when she was returned to the harim. Tears welled into her eyes and she began to beat against her knees with balled fists in frustration.

"What is it?" Harri cried.

"He will never divorce me, I know he will not. He intends to live forever." She began to sob, succumbing to tearful grief.

Harri hesitantly touched her quaking shoulders with

a hand. "But if he is that old, he must die soon," he said, trying to soothe her.

"I will be an old woman by then, like Aisha. I am already sixteen."

"Do not weep, please," he pleaded miserably.

"I cannot help it!"

"You are as beautiful as the sea," he said huskily, "even while you weep."

Nur al Huda's head lifted and her enormous eyes fixed on him. She wiped tears from her eyes with a balled fist and said, "Truly?"

He put a palm to her damp cheek, his eyes capturing hers. "To an Asa man there is nothing more beautiful than Ran's husband. To me, you surpass the beauty of the sea."

"Ooh," Nur al Huda said breathlessly, provocatively fluttering her thick lashes at him. "But I am without kohl and lip paint, my hair impossibly tangled by the wind."

His hand slid from her cheek to slide over the black silk of her hair, his eyes devouring her. Asar women were as cool as green forests and mountain lakes. Nur al Huda was like coal and fire, like earth and moon.

"Harri?" she whispered, leaning toward him. "Please love me."

Their eyes met and held. Harri sucked in his breath, at the way her lips shook for want of him, her face seeming to be dissolving before his eyes. He leaned slowly forward and put his nose against hers, sliding it over the delicate bridge, his breath mingling with her breath. His innards tightened and his arms ached to hold her, but he was suddenly frightened. Many kisses had he stolen from Svafa, and thrall women had received him and taught him the ways of love. But this was different. This was explosions in his head and in his racing heart.

Then Nur al Huda's arms were tight around his neck and he fell back, catching her tight to his breast and taking her with him. He kissed her eyes, her hair, his fingers digging into her waist. Gasping for breath, he took her mouth in his. She groaned and seemed to press into him until they were one. He pushed her away from him, so he could touch her where her flesh was exposed. With a cry he threw his face to her breasts. Her fingers took hold of his hair, and from her throat came pleas for more. Shaking, he reared back from her and began to remove his trousers. She struggled out of her gown. For an instant he knelt over her, unable to move, his hungry eyes roving the length of her. Then he fell on her and kissed every part of her, until he did not know where he was or who he was, only that he would love this woman all his life. He went into her and rolled over and over with her wrapped in his arms, crying out his love in her ear. At last he lay over her gasping for breath. But she was not satisfied; it had not finished for her. She urgently whispered in his ear a plea to gratify her. It was not difficult to do. The heat rose again in him quickly, and this time he made certain to please her.

Harri and Nur al Huda abruptly noticed that the breeze was chill, and they hastily clothed themselves, then lay tight together, whispering vows of eternal love to each other, oblivious of passing time. When it began to grow dark, Harri sat up, exclaiming that it was late. He leaped to his feet and dragged her with him. They scrambled down the rocks and ran laughing across the fields.

David had been looking for them, concerned for their safety. Hyrna had wished to return home alone, but he would not allow it. The sun was out of the sky. They could not return after dark.

When the young couple appeared, running toward him over a rise, David saw a newness on their bright faces; there was a softness of the eye and a trembling of the lips.

"It *is* late," Nur al Huda exclaimed, dancing around David, "but, oh, what a wonderful day!"

"I can imagine," David muttered. "I think you had best remain the night here. The cliffs are not safe by night."

"I know the cliffs as well as I know the lines of my hand," Harri bragged.

"But the girls do not."

"No," Harri agreed, grinning at David.

"Then you will stay."

Harri caught Nur al Huda's eye, winking at her a secret promise. "We will stay," he said playfully.

With paternal consternation David looked from one to the other. "Harri," he said softly, "do you know that Nur al Huda is a married woman?"

"David!" Nur al Huda wailed, her dancing about coming to an abrupt halt. She pouted at him severely.

"I believe your faith abhors adultery, just as my own does."

"Great Allah! Lectures again. I have but one life to—"

"And a vast eternity *after* it," David scolded.

"I care nothing for the afterlife," she protested, now very disturbed.

"Leave her be," Harri demanded, putting a protecting arm around Nur al Huda's shoulder.

"Rather it is you who should leave her be, Harri," David said emphatically.

"First *know* love, priest," Harri shouted at him, "then preach on the subject."

David's eyes rounded; he felt wounded. But he set his jaw and turned to enter the house. He threw coverlets on the hard earth floor, then took up quilts and carried them outside. "You are forever bragging of your physical hardiness, Harri," he said tightly, tossing the quilts in Harri's direction. "Therefore you will not be uncomfortable sleeping outdoors."

Hyrna thought that that was quite funny and began to taunt Harri, swearing she would tell everyone how the priest had put him in his place.

CHAPTER THIRTEEN

By the time David reached the bay of Dansfiord from the high plain he was utterly exhausted. Breathing heavily, he fell to his knees and clutched hold of a shore boulder, dropping his head against folded arms. He heard rousing cries to his left and weakly turned his head to look. Harri and his companions were playing at war, by attacking one another with swords. They leaped as high as eight feet in the air from a standstill, turning in midair, clearing the heads of their adversaries and lunging in for the pretended kill. The swords they held weighed perhaps twenty pounds. Chain mail added another five pounds of weight to each arm, yet the swords were as toothpicks to the young giants. They threw the swords high in the air and caught the hilts as they plunged to earth. Now they caught up spears of a unique design, eleven feet long and no more than an inch thick, the center of gravity marked by nails in order that the thrower might quickly get it in the right position in his hand—they were called *serpents of the battle*. The thin war serpents were sent slicing through air toward a raised wooden target, not one missing center. These boys were fully ready for the sea and for battle, for marriage and for deeds of valor.

David could not help smiling somewhat pridefully. God had been generous in sending him to such a place, to such a magnificent breed of men. For all their paganism, he loved them well. At times like this, beholding God's given strength and grace, he wished that he was like them, so exuberantly alive. Any feat of which flesh and muscle were capable these young men performed beyond the limits. They swam like fish, flew through air in great leaps like spirited gazelles; some ran fast as the fleetest horse. They were fierce as the fiercest lion, tender as the new-blooming rose—and stubborn as mules. Surely it was possible to worship Christ without destroying their uniqueness. God had intended them to be superior in these ways, for He was omnipotent and did not lightly dispense His gifts.

David patiently waited for Harri to come to him, grateful for the time to rest. Hyrna Dansdotter came along the beach and shyly hovered away from him.

"Come," David called to her. "Talk to me while I wait for Harri."

She cautiously stepped forward until she was two paces from him, then stood there staring at him rudely, refusing to say a word.

"Do young girls exercise, too?" he asked, smiling at her.

She merely shrugged in reply.

"I imagine you are very strong. How far can you swim?"

"From here to—to the fiord," her hesitation suggesting exaggeration.

"That far. You *must* be strong."

"Did you kill Dan, Gudrid Grandmother's father?" she suddenly blurted out, scowling accusingly at David.

David's heart rocked in his chest. Instinctively he stretched out a hand to her. "Child, I would not kill any man."

"Gudrid Grandmother said you took a snake and put it into his mouth. The snake went in him and ate through his side. Because he did not die bravely he could not see Odin in Valhalla."

"Dear God!" David sucked in his breath and closed his eyes against the accusation in her eyes. Then he took the child's hand in his and said unsteadily, "All Christians are not obscenely cruel, Hyrna. God's son, Jesus Christ, was gentle and good, and true Christians try to be like Him."

"Gudrid Grandmother will kill you," she said matter-of-factly.

"No. She suffers the pain of remembrance. One day she will know that I mean no harm to her or hers."

"You are wrong," the child insisted. "She always means what she says and does what she vows to do."

Nur al Huda's shrill voice prevented a response from David. She rushed up behind him and threw her arms about him, kissing his ear. "Aisha thinks that you and I are lovers," she breathed impishly in his ear, laughing delightedly to see his neck turn red, a flush that washed over his face to vanish in his long hair.

"Yours is a lost soul," David scolded, squirming away from her clutching arms.

Nur al Huda lifted herself to full height and called to Harri. The lad leaped round at the sound of her voice and came running.

"Here he is, Harri," she laughed, "ready for his first lessons."

Harri's mouth turned down and he scowled contemptuously. "I am occupied," he argued.

David got to his feet and met the lad's critical eyes. "An Asa man's promise cannot be trusted, Harri?" When Harri bellowed a curse in protest, he smiled and said, "Then, let us begin."

The lad turned and exploded in a run to the surf. A great spray of water rose around him as he dove under. He came up in a geyser and called David to follow his example.

"Go *on,*" Nur al Huda prodded as David momentarily drew back.

David raised his eyes to the sky and silently asked God to watch over him, apologizing if he seemed unduly foolhardy. As closely imitating Harri's plunge into the sea as he could, David stumbled over stones into the bay, hitting the water flat on his face. Sea water filled his mouth, nose and throat, frightening him severely. He lunged upward, gasping and spitting, lost his footing and again hit the water with his face.

Harri's strong arms lifted David out of the water as if he were a child, and he was put on his feet in waist-deep water. He could see that Harri was trying very hard not to laugh at him.

"What shall I do next?" David coughed, swallowing hard and squinting his eyes to see. He was freezing, his bones clattering. The sea was only nominally melted ice. His teeth began to clack and he tightened his jaw to stop their dance.

"Use your arms as oars," Harri instructed, demonstrating by fanning his arms in a breast stroke. "Lie on top of the water and kick your feet. It could not be more simple."

"Simple," David echoed sourly.

After extensive effort and much water swallowed, David had made no headway whatsoever, but he kept at it. The more he failed, the more determined he became. He thrashed and sank, stood up again, then madly fought the water again. Suddenly his ear caught shrieking laughter and he whirled around, swiping water from his eyes with balled, freezing fists.

At the water's edge Gudrid sat astride the black stallion, bent over the saddle horn in an agony of amusement. Her head back, laughter erupted from her throat like the shrill cry of the gull. Lined along the surf was an audience of grinning children, thralls and Asa men of all ages. For a moment David suffered profound embarrassment. But as he stood bent over, shivering, gaping at them, it slowly occurred to him that laughter had replaced jeering. Was it not better that they could laugh at him? And if he laughed with them, something would have happened to unite him with them as never before, even if only in a small way.

David happily waved to his audience and returned to his struggles. The crowd grew. Dan Sea-Kingsson watched sourly from a distance, standing high on the compound *gard*. Aisha had seen the spectacle from the window of the loft and had come out upon the shore. She stepped up behind Nur al Huda, shaking her head in maternal-like disapproval.

Harri finally insisted that David call a halt. Taking the priest under the armpits, he hauled him to dry land. When he let go David wobbled on his feet, his knees refused to hold him and he fell flat on the rocky ground. He was entirely conscious, but all sound had become hollow; he could not make his muscles follow the commands of his brain. He was numb, sinking into a dark pit.

"Carry him to the loft," David heard a familiar dream-voice say, and felt himself being lifted by strong arms.

David was carried facedown to the compound, one man holding his feet, another his arms. His head hung down and he could see the ground passing under him, a blur of stones and sand, hard earth and then a flight of wooden steps. He was unceremoniously dumped on the loft floor.

"Out . . . all of you," Aisha shouted at the lingering audience that had followed. When the loft was cleared of observers, she put her hands on her hips and said sharply down to David where he lay. "You silly, unthinking man! Would you kill yourself? For certain you will develop a lung congestion."

David tried to get up, but his legs and arms were useless, felt like cotton. He brought his hands before his eyes and gasped to see that his fingernails were purple, the flesh of his hand as wrinkled as a dried fig. He thought the disfigurement permanent and his heart sank. Aisha bent to aid him and he managed to get to his feet. He stumbled to a wall and leaned against it.

"Get out of those wet clothes," Aisha commanded. When he shook his head in refusal, she cried, "Do as I say, damn you, or I will remove them for you. You are too weak to fight me off."

Disgusted with him, Aisha went to the door, opened it and vanished from sight. Somehow he managed to peel off his soaked trousers, which clung to his blue flesh as if fastened to him. His teeth chattered and he shook violently. He was just naked when he heard Aisha's steps returning. He made a lunge for the curtained bedchamber, but he stumbled and fell.

When Aisha entered the loft she burst into laughter because David had just got himself to hands and knees and his backside was in the air. "David," she giggled, "you missed your calling. You should have been a jester."

David was certain he would have blushed if he had not been too blue to redden.

"Go away," he groaned, dropping flat on the tapestry that was spread out on the floor. He could only hide one side from her; he chose the front.

"Great Allah! I raised a son and I have been married twenty and three years." She said less patiently, "I wager Allah gave you nothing different than he gave every other man and dog."

A young thrall man brought two buckets of steaming water into the room and poured them into the tub at the corner of the loft. He repeated the water-lugging five times more. Then Aisha turned her face to the wall and ordered David into the tub. He made it without incident, but screamed in agony upon jumping in.

"I ordered the water hot," Aisha laughed. "It will warm you."

"It is *cooking* me!" he wailed.

Aisha moved to sit on a pillow near the tub. She soberly examined David's face. He had altered a great deal since she had first spoken to him on the ship. His mouth was more firmly set and his speech was less apologetic. Some of his shyness and humility had been replaced by a self-awareness that could ultimately lead to what he would probably consider pridefulness. But he was not yet proud. Still he retired from people, hovered back in every relationship. He was a man always in the background, a whisper, an undisclosed secret, a shadow under the trees of other people's lives.

"Have you been well, David?" she asked, smiling warmly upon him.

"Very well," he muttered, beginning to relax. The heat was slowly penetrating to his bones, to his great relief.

"It is not too lonely for you, so far from—"

"I have never known loneliness," he interrupted. But a tremor in his mind warned him that he had not been altogether truthful. He hastily added, "I have always been alone, but with God for company."

Aisha nodded. She watched his profile for long moments, then said, "Dan cannot understand why Mord has not attacked, or called him to battle."

"Mord is a Christian," David began, then thought better of it. "Perhaps he has decided to accept the verdict."

"Never. The pig! He will not rest until Kamar al Zamen's gold is in his pockets."

David glanced at her face. He had made his decision, but was uncertain how to press it.

"And the ship that carried word to Setubal has not returned," she added worriedly. "Mord has simply vanished. He took to sea with a fleet of four longships, and no one that Dan has questioned has any news of his whereabouts."

David fixed his eyes on the ceiling and blurted out, "I intend to take the ransom!"

"What?"

"It is mine by the law of this land and I will have it."

Aisha gaped at him in disbelief. He was deadly serious.

"Whatever has got into you? Dan will never . . . Do you wish to add to my torment with further delays? David, I must get back to Egypt. How can you do this to me?"

He sank deep into the tub. "With the gold," he said in a barely audible voice, "I can erect a church on every island of North Orkney. I can send to Italia, to Egypt, and to the Holy Land for men with true faith, to come and rightly show Christ to the people. Asar converts are not good priests; they are coarse shams and these people know them for what they are."

"Is it so important that they become Christians?" she exclaimed, exasperated.

"All men must become Christian," he replied heatedly, "if they are to redeem themselves."

"What nonsense! What utter foolishness. There is a far land called Chinaland, and there is deep Africa, and many places yet to be discovered, and all those far places are peopled by believers in different gods. David, it is an unmitigated conceit to believe yourself possessed of the absolute truth, especially loved by God. Do you make no allowances for error in the dogma, for what is merely expedient and ulterior in motive?"

"Do you make allowances in the practice of *your* faith?" he asked tightly.

"Yes! I most certainly do. I have read too many books, including your Christian writings, to do otherwise than tolerate other men's delusions. Allah receives all good men, no matter what their beliefs. And I think *Allah* to be only an Arabic translation of the word *Jehovah*. God is God."

"I have made my decision," he insisted stubbornly. "I will speak to Ingolf Jarl when he visits my parish, and he will aid me in the plan."

"But David, Dan will kill you before he lets you take the gold. You are being ridiculous!"

"Dan Sea-Kingsson will not go against the law."

"Are you absolutely certain of that?"

"I have learned much about the man. His honor comes before his life, certainly before gold. It would not be a matter of the lawmen not learning of his crime if he stole from me what is rightly mine. *He* would know of it, and Valhalla would be lost to him forever, for only the unfailing enter there."

"So. You place my life second to your personal ambitions."

"Yes," he said flatly. "I have given you all I can. Now I shall receive a thousandfold from the bread I cast upon the water. The decisions of the lawmen were God-inspired and have shown me the way."

"Alhomdolillah!"

"Any means that will convert without bloodshed, I will take," he argued, continually refusing to meet her eyes.

"No matter the cost in misery, mine . . . and these poor victims of your conceited aggression against them?"

"My first duty is to Christ," he insisted whisperingly.

"But Christ's first duty was to *man*!"

"To *God*," he contradicted.

"No. Christ came to redeem men and he gave his life for man, under the *command* of God. His duty was to man, his love and his hope—"

"What do pagans know of the son of God?" David barked, feeling strangely threatened.

"I want to know why you are forsaking *man*," she persisted.

"You talk in circles and make no sense at all!"

"If you were deeply concerned for the Asar, you would help to maintain their sublime faith rather than attempt to destroy it. Let them call Paradise Valhalla if they choose. Is God so petty as to demand only *Hebrew* words—names? You Christians! First prove bloodshed is not unalterably human by abstaining from it yourselves, before you preach the peace on earth philosophy. God made us. It entirely baffles me the way Christians argue so with God's intentions!"

"Will you take yourself away from here, please," David growled, "so that I can get out of this tub and dry myself?"

"No. Not until you swear to me you will be sensible."

He set his jaw and refused to reply.

"Name me one Christian," Aisha argued enthusiastically, "who can forswear lust as the Holy Church suggests, who does not *enjoy* war, who does not commit *all* the sins and break all the commandments—if only in their thoughts—just one who turns the other cheek, never steals, curses, or kneels before idols—and I will personally accept baptism from you."

"Myself," David exclaimed, his face reddening. "And eighty good men at Saint Monica."

"How *prideful* of you, David! And nonsense. I wager there are at least ten idols at Saint Monica, bowed and prayed to many times every day. Saint Mary. Saint Monica herself. Saint Joseph—"

"Idols!" David protested, rising so abruptly he caused a great wave that washed over the rim of the tub.

"Exactly. Idols. Muslims also say, 'That God should beget children, God forbid.' And I do not think you are saintly in your forswearing of lust, rather fearful of it in your ignorance. I wager your bowels churn and raging fires blaze there on still nights—"

"Enough!" David leaped from the tub in spite of her watching eyes, grabbing a sheet of linen up and wrapping it round himself.

"You have never thought to have a son, David?"

He did not answer her. Instead he said, "I must have dry clothes," refusing to look at her.

Aisha got to her feet and rushed to her bed. She pushed aside the curtains and fell on the mattress, highly irritated. "I refuse to get you dry clothes."

"Then I will take myself over the cliffs in this linen."

"Great Allah, you are impossible!" She thought a moment, biting her lower lip, then demanded to know if Nur al Huda was attempting to seduce him. "She spent last night under your roof. She said that you forced Harri to sleep outside so that you and she could—"

"She said *that*?" David wailed, bewildered and hurt.

She studied his flushed face, immediately discarding Nur al Huda's tale of fancy. If there was any truth in it, it was one-sided. "Then tell me what you were trying to prove by your display at the shore?"

His mouth turned up at the corners wryly. "That I can be fearless?"

"Respect, hmm?"

"Yes."

"The Asa man loves himself first, then his gods, his wars, and his women. You can love none of these. How then can you hope to gain the respect you seek?"

David hugged the linen closer to him and let a sigh escape his lungs. "I can only try," he murmured.

Dan heard from Aisha that David had decided to

claim the ransom. His expression did not alter. He seemed entirely uninterested. His days were fully occupied by the business of his godiship. Taxes were being collected for the support of the temple, and he was at his ledger pages a part of each day. Five legal petitions had been registered. A Thing was in preparation for Thorsdag next, over which he would preside as middle-seated judge.

Each chiefdom held Things that constituted lower courts; pleas could be made to the higher, All-Thing court if the plaintiff was dissatisfied.

The registered complaints ranged from murder to the settling of debts, and an insurance claim involving the loss of an entire herd of cattle to disease. Each odelman paid into a fund for insurance against a crop failure or death of livestock. Dan controlled the fund and dispersed to two thirds of the loss to those proving their claim with witnesses.

Freydis was at last able to set forth for the market fairs. But Dan had changed her destination. She would take a longer voyage and go to Dublin, to perform a double mission. Freydis would ask questions designed to learn the whereabouts and motives of Mord Baptized-One; all news eventually reached the great harbor. And she was to try to discover the fate of Thorvald, his standard bearer, who had taken a running ship to Setubal with the message to the physician.

Thorvald was now long overdue. Dan had sent him to sea the third day after Aisha's presence became known to him, four weeks before the verdict of the Thing. In the communiqué he had advised the physician to take all precautions, to sail by night as much as possible, and to lie in hiding during the day—easily enough accomplished by following the coastline of Enea, then crossing to Orkney parallel to the great firth. He had enclosed a directional map, and a letter in Aisha's hand to verify his claim. Now he wondered if he had made a mistake in not escorting her there, or putting her on board the running ship with Thorvald. He had considered it extra insurance to hold her at Dansfiord, minimizing the possibility of ambush along the ransom ship's route. As long as he held her, the ransom offer would remain, for the husband had vowed that he would, if necessary, renew the ransom until all his resources were depleted.

Mord was undoubtedly combing the seacoasts of Andalusia and the sea lanes en route to Orkney, meaning to have the gold in any case, with or without the abducted one. Thorvald should have arrived at Setubal before the occasion of the All-Thing, halfway home again before Mord set sail.

The partial payment in gold he had already received from the physician had offered Dan an opportunity to remain at Dansfiord during the viking season. In fact, with only that sum he could support his odel for many years. But he was restless. He had not missed a viking season since he had come of age. The prospect of war with Mord had stimulated him, but now it was a flat taste in his mouth. His enemy had chosen to attack on some other front—a coward's device, typically Christian and the shame of the gods.

In his free hours Dan paced the confines of his odel. He swam and wrestled, gave a feast every other night on any pretext, and in the ship-building shed he began construction of a new running ship. He drank more than usual and angered quickly. It was the uncertainty that plagued him. If Freydis returned without some definite news, he would set sail to search Ran's Husband, south, east and west, for his enemy, engage him and be victorious over him. The ransom had become secondary in importance. He could not let Mord Baptized-One best him.

The Thing was held and Dan's court dispensed Odin's justice as fairly as they knew how. The peculiar Christian priest was much discussed and many jests were made up about him. Dan's decision to allow the Christian residence was accepted by one and all. Not one convert had the priest made to date and none did the bonder expect to see, for great was their faith in Thor and in their chief. Harvest time was near at hand, so a sacrifice was made to the gods that the grain be good, the vegetables large and sweet. Many invitations were offered to Dan, for *arvels* (inheritance feasts) and wedding celebrations, but he declined them all, saying he was in a state of war. All Dan's odel-men reassured him of their homage; they would enter the fight without question on a moment's notice.

Ten days after Freydis' departure, Dan took himself to the shore to closely observe the priest at play. The man could now keep afloat, but that was about all. Each day those not occupied came to watch; it had become the favorite entertainment of his followers, who were as restless as he. For weeks he had heard nothing else, from Harri, the indolent Saracen mother, and from his own mother. Mealtimes were the occasions of much talk and hilarity in regard to the priest's antics.

Dan looked upon the frail thing thrashing in the bay and felt an impulse to rush in and drown it. Harri swore the priest had never preached to him. Then why was he here, if not to press his cause?

David stumbled out of the surf and began running, caricaturing the Asar long stride. He ran to the base of Highcliff and back again, coming to a halt before Dan, sucking in hissing gulps of air into his lungs, his chest heaving dangerously, his face blue and red at once.

"You puff and wheeze like a consumptive steer," Dan commented dryly.

"Yes," David gasped, trying to smile.

"Here! Catch it."

David leaped backward as Dan flung his sword at him. The blade stabbed into the rocky beach, vibrated on end, then collapsed.

"You— You might have cut off my toes," David wheezed.

"You are not a sword-wielding priest."

"I am *not*."

Dan stared at the man, then leaned and lifted the sword, replacing it in its sheath at his side. "Follow me. I want to talk to you." He whipped around and strode toward the compound, assuming the man followed.

David stood shivering in the center of the great hall, water a pool around his feet, waiting for Dan to speak from his highseat.

"I understand you are contemplating taking the ransom," Dan said at last, in a steady voice.

"I am," David replied with as much calm and force as he could manage, considering the trembling of his freezing body and his wavering confidence.

"There may be a reluctance in me to go against the law, but—"

"You will not break the law," David interrupted, hugging himself with his arms to try to warm himself.

"Exactly. I am no lawbreaker. So you can take your *wife* and your *daughter*—and house them under your own roof! Why should I take responsibility for them if I am not to profit?"

Stunned, David gaped incredulously at Dan Sea-Kingsson. "No. I cannot take—" He lost the sense of what he had intended to say.

"Now that you have full authority over and physical custody of the women, the ransom entirely yours, how do you intend spending the gold?"

"Ingolf Jarl will aid me in erecting churches of Christ on—"

"Not *one* of my odel-men will allow such a structure to be built! If you managed to somehow build a church, it would mysteriously burn down."

"And I would rebuild it."

"Take the women from my house immediately. I have no further interest in them. The matter is settled."

"But I cannot house them; you know that. Aisha is used to much luxury and—"

"What? You expect me to feed them, protect them, be in all ways husband and father to them as you are required to be under the law, but *you* are to take all the gold? That is not only stupidity of the worst sort, but unmitigated presumption! And a conscious effort to steal from me. You call yourself a Christian?"

David shivered in the severe drafts whipping through the hall. He glared at Dan's bemused face, then offered to pay Dan for the women's lodging.

"How *much* will you pay me, eh? Say, two thirds of the ransom?" A thin smile turned up the corners of Dan's mouth.

"*One* third," David said quickly.

"No. I am willing to accept two thirds, but no less—as my price for keeping the woman safe until she can be returned to her husband."

David wavered uncertainly. "How much gold would I receive if I accepted one third of the ransom?"

"Approximately three hundred thousand grams of gold."

David's eyes widened and a smile lighted his face. "A bargain!" he cried jubilantly.

Dan scowled at the man through squinted eyes. "Had you planned on receiving that much?"

"Oh, no," David exclaimed. "Far less. Much less than that. I thought perhaps I could persuade you to give me several thousand, if I were clever."

"So be it. Know that I do not consider myself duped. The law is inviolable. Once the verdict was in I had no intention of grasping it all. But we talk of dream gold. I wager we will never see that ransom ship in this harbor."

"But what is to become of Aisha?"

Dan shrugged and made a face, as if to say he could not be less interested in what became of her. Then a vision of her face shimmered before his eye—a Saracen delicacy to wet any man's appetite.

"The ship will come," David said hopefully.

Dan smiled. "I will continue to keep my eye ever on the woman, until the fate of her husband and his wild hope is determined. That I promise you."

CHAPTER FOURTEEN

David moved carefully along the now familiar paths toward his high home. The sky had gone black and threatened rain. Gulls flew in thick screens far inland, predictive of a storm. Here, the incline became so steep he usually went on all fours, but today his leg muscles were a good deal stronger and he managed to remain upright most of the way. For a week after his first day of physical exercise he had lain upon his bed unable to move due to an agony of the entire body. Now the effort was much easier. He would barely be winded upon reaching the plain.

A strange cry fell on David's ear. At first he thought it the call of a young gull and kept his pace. But as he drew closer to a deep impression in the rocky hillside, the sound became distinguishable as human. He discovered a swaddled infant in the depression, lying on the rock floor, which had been thickly covered with straw. A bit of pork fat had been placed in its mouth so that it might subsist for a time, long enough for a childless one to venture by and take it up.

He gingerly lifted the infant into his arms, combined

anger and pity stirring him. He took the child to his house, where he immediately baptized her. He named her Mary. The person who had exposed this child could not be expected to take her back. In the future perhaps this inhuman custom could be abolished. For now it had to be tolerated.

David wet a cloth in milk and squeezed the stuff into Mary's pinched little mouth, smiling and feeling a strong emotion in his breast. He had inspected her and found a livid birthmark on her back that spread round to cross her abdomen. God had marked her thus for a purpose. To murder the infant against God's intentions would be the grossest of sins.

Thereafter, carrying the infant in an improvised pouch on his back, David spent several hours of each day walking the length and breadth of Ransay searching for abandoned babies. He listened to the talk of the women, for great was the sadness among them all whenever exposure was demanded by a father. Destitute thrall women often took advantage of the alien custom, deserting infants that they could not possibly feed and clothe. When word had passed from mouth to mouth that the priest had taken in the infant of Gylfi with the Irish thrall woman Noreen, the hearts of several women grew lighter.

David found no more infants; rather, they found him. Within a month of discovering Mary, two infants, a boy and a girl, were left on his doorstep in the night, two weeks apart. The boy had been brought from Skylli, the closest island to Ransay, but David was not interested in from where they had come. He needed to know only that desperate women had brought to his door precious gifts from the Lord God.

Mercy, symbolized in the person of the priest, had been acknowledged by the people of David's parish. By accepting his Christian charity they had in a significant way accepted Jesus Christ. Heartbreak had been eased that late summer for two noblewomen and one young Irish thrall. Unable to deny the Odin-given right of their husbands to decide whether to refuse or to accept their newborn infants, the noblewomen gave the rejected children to the priest and to baptism, chose life for them in preference to death.

Aisha morosely worked at her embroidery. The loft was cold. A hint of winter was in the air. How she dreaded the return of snow and ice. How she longed for the sweet-scented warmth of Egypt. The seasons were sharply defined in this land. As soon as the fields were harvested summer came to an abrupt end, the sky turning surly, the winds becoming violent and ice-edged. She felt more isolated and despairing than ever before, had lost all hope. Still Kamar al Zamen had not come.

Nur al Huda had managed to fill the hours and days with adventures, learning to swim and exploring the nearby islands, but Aisha could not fit herself into this life. Too old to change, she thought petulantly.

She forced the needle into the cloth, carefully stitching gold thread over a silver stitch. She had been provided with the finest threads and material, which was some comfort. She rarely ventured out. Gudrid, the old witch, no longer harassed her, but she cringed at the mere sound of the hag's shrill voice rising through the floorboards of the loft, the memory of the beating she had taken sharply clear in her mind.

Dan Sea-Kingsson came to the loft each day, asking her to express her wishes or her discontents, then took himself away, always seeing to it that she had anything he could give to her. She did not like the way he had been looking at her lately, as if she were a stuffed fish on a platter.

Suddenly Aisha threw the linen across the room. She leaped to her feet and began to pace the loft. Her mind lingered on David—how foolish he was to maintain so stubbornly when defeat was inevitable. Then she told herself that she was no better than he. Stubbornly remaining Kamar al Zamen's faithful wife, reluctant to accept the fact that she was no longer the first wife in a harim. She was merely an unused concubine here. This good treatment was not destined to last. One day soon Dan Sea-Kingsson would stride in that door and order her out, because Kamar al Zamen was not coming for her. Ajib—

Aisha fought against tears. Her son had been so on her mind these endless weeks of waiting. The dangers were incalculable, a thousandfold. She shook her head hard, refusing to think that Allah would be so cruel as to take both Kamar al Zamen and Ajib from her at once.

Impulsively Aisha caught up a cloak from a wall hook, wrapped it about herself and purposefully left her quarters. She hesitated at the bottom of the outside stairs, then proudly threw open the door of Dan's house and entered his private domain for the first time.

The room she stepped into was large and drafty. No one was in sight. But she heard the low rumble of many muffled voices. Doors opened from the anteroom, six of them. She chose one of the doors and hesitantly passed through a short alleyway. Opening the next door, she stepped into the great hall, which was crowded with Northmen and their women. A wave of tumultuous noise washed over her and she froze in her tracks.

Sitting high above the sea of guests, Dan Sea-Kingsson saw Aisha standing dumbfounded in the entranceway and grinned in surprise. Pushing himself out of his seat, he strode toward her.

"To what do I owe this honor?" Dan asked, smirking down at her.

"I—" she began, but lost her voice. Fluster was not usual to her. She was astonishingly embarrassed, an emotion she had not experienced since discovering at a very tender age, while playing in a secret place with Armanus, that he had no male parts. Why she should think of such a thing at this time . . .? Armanus was dead. He had come to her as a gift at her birth, when he was only four. He was dead.

"Will you join us in feast?" Dan asked, soberly studying her faraway eyes.

"I . . . I was weary of being alone up there," she admitted, avoiding his glance.

"Then do join us. Soon there will be food. At the moment I can offer you drink. Wine?"

"Yes, wine," she muttered, absentmindedly allowing him to remove her cloak, which he threw to a nearby servantman. She followed him as he pressed through the crowd, growing miserably aware of her naked face; the back of her head felt prickly and hot. She had deliberately left her veils behind. It was time to fully accept Allah's will.

Aisha swallowed the bitter wine in gulps, hoping its

effects would relieve her tension. She refused any food, so that soon the brew caused her head to spin. The crowd around her was crude and boisterous, utterly without refinement. Music was strong in her ears. Suddenly she was abruptly hauled up in the air, held by Dan's arms and tossed roughly about in some kind of improvisational dance to the rhythm of the harps and wind instruments. Her backside was pinched and patted many times by different pairs of paws. Through the wine haze that clogged her brain she thought upon the extent of her own stupidity. These men had to be admired from a good distance. To get too close only served to disappoint and disgust a civilized person.

Dan put her steady on her feet after the dance, but she rocked tipsily forward, scowling at him belligerently. From behind, he took her arms and marched her toward a bench. "Sit down, drunken wife of the sweetest Christian since Jesus Christ."

She glanced irritably up at him and saw his head wobbling on his great shoulders. "You—are *drunk*!" she exclaimed accusingly.

"I am *never* drunk," he swore.

All around them men and women were swaying. One or two dropped and others used them for steps. Wine and ale spilled from horns and from loose jaws to dribble into beards and onto the littered, filthy floor. Blinking her eyes to clear her vision, Aisha watched a blurred orgy the like of which she never hoped to witness again and did not wish to further be a party to, even as an observer. She lunged to her feet, forcing her legs to carry her toward a door, any door leading out of this room, shoving angrily through the crowd, through a passageway, to find herself in the cook-room with five thralls staring at her.

Dan came up behind her and took hold of her round the waist, leaning to whisper in her ear. She thanked Allah he had spoken too low and fast in the Asa tongue, therefore sparing her understanding of his obscenities.

"Where is the loft from here?" she demanded of a gaping servant.

"This way," Dan said, laughing and once more steering her.

This time she entered a bedchamber. She whirled on Dan with eyes flashing. "How dare you!"

Ignoring her, Dan bellowed to his servants over his shoulder, "Wine and ale."

Small kegs were hastily brought into the room, and the door was closed behind the servants. Dan turned the key in the lock, then deposited the key into his shirtfront. He took himself to a chair and slumped into it, looking Aisha over from head to toe with a smirk.

"You are a magnificent specimen of womanhood," he said effusively. "A pity there is so little of you."

Aisha stood before him tapping a foot impatiently, glaring at him. "Was it in the bargain you made with my husband that you would rape me?"

"No—ooo," Dan protested with a broad gesture of the hands. "I would never rape you—no pleasure for me in that. But if you wish, I might—"

"Give me that key. I could never want anything from the likes of you!"

"Truly?" he grinned. "Am I so unhandsome?"

She examined him as he had looked her over, begrudgingly admitting to herself that she had never seen a man better designed by Allah than he, but she would never say so to him.

"Your husband is an old, old man. Have you never known the touch of a young man?"

"Never. And I have missed nothing, I wager."

"To wager implies a doubt as to the final outcome. Could you be wrong?"

"Give me the key!"

"Give *me* your *body*," he insisted, laughing at her.

"It is not mine to give," she cried. "With Allah as witness, I was given to Kamar al Zamen."

"But he is too old to enjoy you."

"That has nothing to do with it!"

Dan slowly lifted himself out of the chair and moved unsteadily toward her. She refused to back away from him. He put a hand round each of her exposed breasts and hauled her to him. His mouth moved against her neck. She stood rigidly resisting him, but a knife-like pain pressed hard at her groin, a spark kindled where no fire had ever burned. She felt slightly nauseated, drunk from the wine and sickened by it. She tried to pull away from him, but he caught her and kissed her face, his blue eyes close and scorching. He was young, and it *did* matter. It had always mattered to her that Kamar al Zamen was old. The realization struck her so hard that she lost her breath. Choking on tears, she uttered an agonized cry of denial. All the ordered purity of the past was crumbling about her. Those strange flutterings at first sight of this man—suppressed. Watching him for so long as he paced the garden court; a vagrant sense of longing had been denied acknowledgment.

"Please," she cried, beginning to panic.

Dan abruptly let her go, throwing himself away from her. "If you were any other woman," he said huskily, "I would take you and bedamned your ice."

Gathering her composure, Aisha lifted her chin and asked, "Why am I so privileged, may I ask?"

"You sound regretful," he said bitingly. "If you want me, you will have to say so. You are too beautiful to bruise. You should be treated as a rare jewel, kept in velvet and only occasionally used, never abused."

"Am I supposed to be *flattered*? A rare jewel, indeed."

Dan moved to drop into his chair. He said generously, "If it comes to pass that your husband fails to rescue you, leaving you stranded here, I would like to offer you the place of concubine in my house—in my life. I can promise you every—"

"I would prefer death to such a low status!"

"If you are *anything* to *me,* even thrall, you have reached the pinnacle!" he shouted at her.

"To the pig, all pigs are beautiful! Arrogant savage, I have lived like a queen, been first woman all my life."

"Not any longer."

"I . . . I will seek out Mord," she threatened recklessly.

Dan threw his head back and laughed. Then he caught her eye and growled, "Whenever . . . if ever . . . you return to Cairo, tears will fall from your eyes for loss of me . . . for you will love me, wait and see." With that, he reached deep into his shirtfront and extracted the key; he threw it to the floor at her feet. "Keep it. Use it anytime you like. I will welcome you to my bed any time of day or night."

"To think," she raged, "that I heard you say once that Asar men have a deep respect for all womankind."

"Hah! Evidenced by the fact that I am not in you this very moment!"

Aisha struggled up the cliff path, clinging to jagged rocks, cursing and near tears of rage and frustration. She had left Dan's loft at dawn and would never return. She had been thoroughly shaken by his attempt to seduce her. Her hands began to bleed a little, but she persisted. It took the better part of the morning, for she did not know the way.

The little house was snuggled in a valley, and smoke trailed from the roof hole. Rain had begun to fall. As she stumbled toward David's house she prayed to Allah for yet another measure of strength. Tomorrow had to be predictable, or today was insufferable.

"Aisha!" David cried, rushing to her when she stumbled through the doorway into his house. He put an arm round her and guided her to a chair. "In God's name, what has happened?"

"I want to be here with you," she said emotionally, not looking at him, gasping for breath.

One of the infants cried out, and Aisha's head snapped round. "A child?" she exclaimed.

"Not one, but three," David said with a weary sigh.

"*Alhomdolillah*! Where did you get them?"

"From God."

She rushed across the room to lean over a large woven basket filled with babies. Her eyes lighted and her arms reached for one of them. She picked up the boy and found him soaked. Investigating, she discovered that the other two were in the same condition. "They all need changing. And milk. They are not thriving, David."

He solemnly leaned over the basket. "I have no proper apparel. And they seem always to be hungry. Frankly, I am at the end of my rope. I have not slept fully in days."

"So this is why you have not given beach performances of late."

"I thought the entire world knew I was foster-fathering."

"Perhaps, but the information did not get to *me*. I have not seen Nur al Huda for two weeks. She flagrantly avoids responsibility for her infant son, which she left to me. The thrall woman who has been Kamar al Akmar's wet nurse for weeks today took him to her hovel, promising me she would take good care of him there."

"I saw her only yesterday."

"Who? The thrall woman?"

"Nur al Huda. On the rock mound, beyond the back field." He added cautiously, and somewhat critically, "She was with young Harri."

Aisha frowned but said nothing. She had been suspicious of the girl's unusually cheerful demeanor, but had not suspected Harri as the source.

"I would not like to forsake these children," David said sadly, reaching to touch little Mary's grayish face with a tender forefinger, "but I cannot continue to give them all my time and concern. There are things which must be done and can only be done by me."

"Wonderful. Then you need me. I will remain here and care for the babies. You can take yourself to whatever task that calls you."

David hesitated. He stepped away from the basket to

the window and studied the rain that softly fell outside. "What happened to bring you here?" he asked.

"Dan Sea-Kingsson, he . . ." She faltered. To anyone but David she could have explained it in blunt words.

"He wants you? As a man wants a woman . . . lustfully?"

"Yes."

He turned to study her. A strange light was in his eyes. Aisha became uncomfortable under his scrutiny. "What is it, David?"

For long moments he let his eyes rove her face. He began to rock from foot to foot, his lips trembling as his thoughts secretly turned; she had not seen this vulnerability, such a strong inhibition in him for a long time, reminding her of how much he had changed. "David?"

"I . . . I was wondering why God chose to give me no measure of desire. You were wrong about me. No fires rage in me, not ever. I do not forswear lust; I am never *tempted*." Flushing, he turned back to the window. "I look upon you and I am stirred, but no more than by a spectacular sunrise, or a rare, miraculously beautiful flower."

Aisha smiled and moved to stand close to him. She lightly touched his arm with a hand. "I think Allah designed you well, David, for the tasks he had in mind for you. Truly you are blessed. Lust can be a terrible curse. There is little joy in things of the flesh. The best of it is the children that result." She hugged the infant closer to her and her smile widened.

"But how Harri's eyes shine," he whispered. "I am disapproving of him, but cannot find any evil in his love for the girl. He is so innocent, utterly devoid of bad intention. On lust I am still baffled. I am uncertain as to where lust ends and love begins, perplexed as to what God had in mind for men and women."

"The Bible has told you."

"I vowed to seek truth for myself."

"Then experience would be the best teacher, would it not?"

He moved away from the window to pace the room. "No," he said at last. "I do not need to leap off Highcliff to know that the plunge will kill me. We cannot experience all things; we must accept many things on faith. I have never seen God, yet I could not be more certain of His existence."

"It seems obvious to me that to insist that lust is a sin . . . is a contradiction of Allah's intentions; he made us as we are."

David came to an abrupt halt in his pacing, raising his eyes to meet hers. "To overcome the more powerful compulsions is to develop great strength, which in turn purifies the soul."

"Forgive me, but I disagree with you again. Strength lies in unqualified acceptance of Allah's will, no matter how unattractive or brutal the circumstances may seem. I think acceptance is the greatest strength we can possess. What you refer to as compulsions that must be overcome are Allah's given traits that we all must learn how to live with."

"I would see all my people here in Heaven," he said emotionally.

"And they love life more than they could ever love your Christ, or his offered bliss in Paradise. You will never change them, David."

She moved to the basket and put the little one in

beside his sisters. She touched his face adoringly. A stir of memory warmed her. At thirteen years of age she had held her firstborn with a breathless happiness. A perfect son to live for. The secret longings could then be utterly dismissed from her consciousness.

Dan Sea-Kingsson came for Aisha on Fleet Raven, riding wildly across the high plain, the stallion, with ease and grace, leaping rocks and fences. He jumped from the saddle while the beast was still at a gallop, plunging into David's house.

Dan towered in the small room, his head brushing the timbers of the ceiling. Aisha stared frozenly at him from where she stood by the fireplace.

"You will take yourself back to the loft immediately," Dan commanded, glaring at her.

"No, Saíd, I will *not*," she said firmly. Throwing an arm toward the basket of infants who were all squalling, she said accusingly, "Pagan murderers! Three newborn infants left to starve to death. I have never heard of a more loathsome, sinful custom, a more vile form of murder. . . . How many of your own children did you leave in the cold to die?"

"None!" Dan roared. "Any child sired by me would not be less than perfect!"

"I have never known a man of such unmitigated arrogance and unjustified pridefulness."

"The priest does not want you here. He told me himself that he could not house you."

"That was before I found the children," David said uncomfortably. "I could use some assistance with the . . . my children."

Dan scowled at David, disgust a wounding sword

against the priest. "To preserve life in an unfit body is the vilest act a man can commit, priest, burdening the future adult with unnecessary sufferings all his days."

"What God has given only God can take away," David argued softly.

"You leave so much to your God, it is a wonder he did not forsake you in contempt long ago. Do Christians make no decisions for themselves?"

"We choose Heaven or Hell for ourselves."

"May I ask why *you* have chosen Hell? I understand it is very hot and unpleasant there."

"You will find out how hot soon enough," Aisha put in sharply.

"Hot or cold, everlasting life is everlasting life. I wager a man could get used to hellfire, so that he soon would not be terribly uncomfortable. To go to a heaven peopled only by Christians, what a prospect! Odin save me from such a fate. . . . Woman, I say take yourself to the loft where you belong."

"No," she snapped, standing firm.

Dan pursed his mouth and tapped a foot impatiently. He did not wish to press her on this relatively minor issue. She was not the kind of woman to be muscled, which only served to make her more antagonistic. He demurred, turning on his heel and leaving her. He leaped upon the stallion and rode off as furiously as he had come.

Before the day ended ten men surrounded the turf house. Each erected a tent and made himself at home. Aisha was still potentially very valuable The ten men were acting as Dan's watchful eyes upon her.

As the days passed Aisha became more content. The

hours were so frantically full that the sun seemed just risen when it began to sink in the west. She went to bed utterly spent. David was at his exercises from dawn to sunset, so she saw little of him.

One morning as she stepped out to go to the stream for water, she found an enormous bundle just outside the door. Inside the linen wrappings were baby clothes, all new and lovingly embroidered. Dozens of absorbent linen diapers. Little toy swords and axes for the boy and small dolls with golden hair for the girls. She could not believe her eyes. Who could have deposited such a store here, and why so secretly? Not one of Dan's men had any knowledge of a night visitor, or refused to tell.

A week later another bundle appeared, this time filled with knitted socks with shoes attached, blankets of soft wool, and freshly bleached linens. And that same day thrall men came and began to build a turf extension to the small house. Aisha was certain now that Dan Sea-Kingsson was in this way trying to win her respect. But when she spoke to David of her surmise he shook his head, a secret smile on his face. He absolutely refused to satisfy her curiosity, saying that he must respect the donor's wish to remain anonymous. He looked as though he had won a battle of some kind.

CHAPTER FIFTEEN

The ship's red sails appeared outlined against the frothy gray horizon like a great exotic bird, swiftly growing larger at the pushing hands of the northeasterly winds. For days Dan had suffered a nagging apprehension. Now, he ran from the compound, ordering men into a smallboat. They rowed furiously toward the approaching ship, fairly flying over the churning surface of the sea.

Dan was hauled aboard to be greeted by Freydis, who was thankfully glowing with health and joy in seeing him equally fit. He hugged her to his breast in a rough embrace. Over her high curls his eye caught sight of a ragged young man who was vaguely familiar to him . . . standing at the far gunwale staring sourly at the two.

Dan abruptly let loose of Freydis, his eyes widening in surprise. He shook an arm in the youth's direction, crying, "It is! You must be. You are her son!"

To be sure, Ajib was barely recognizable. He had lost a great deal of weight and his long black hair had been clipped short over the earlobes, his beard shaven. He wore soiled and tattered *vadmal.* All the marks of a thrall, and the humiliation showed in his dark eyes and the beleaguered slump of his shoulders.

"I brought him to you as a surprise," Freydis said guardedly, but with some pride.

Dan turned to her and said concernedly, "Mord succeeded."

"Not entirely." She tried to smile. "Let us get ashore. I am desperate to feel solid earth under me again. Then we can talk. The lad will tell you his tale."

It was an hour before Dan could extract the information from Freydis. She had insisted upon food, saying she was sick to death of stale butter, dried fish and unleavened bread. And she had had to kiss each of her daughters a hundred times, refusing to shoo them from her. Gudrid, sourly jealous of Freydis' opportunity to be at sea, kept interrupting with rehashes of her experiences as captain and warrior, of her narrow escapes on the shores of far Vinland. The Saracen was thoroughly occupied in ravenously eating several portions of freshly roasted steer, offering Dan no enlightenment.

"Curse you!" Dan finally yowled at Freydis. "I am exploding and will hear it all this minute."

He forced Gudrid and his protesting children out of the room, sat Freydis down and put himself across the table from her. "Speak," he commanded.

"Well," she began hesitantly, "I entered Dublin harbor and immediately began to question the wives. Never seek information of a delicate nature from men, who are fixedly tight-lipped. But women—"

"I know how loose-tongued women are," Dan complained exasperatedly.

Freydis at last sighed and set herself to the task of

telling him the bad news. With methodical attention to the sequence of events she told him how she had learned that Mord had attacked the ransom ship, which was on its way here to Ransay. She had met the wife of Thorstein Christiansson, Mord's standard bearer, at the silk bazaar and from the woman had extracted news of Thorvald, his crew, and the missing running ship that he had taken to Setubal with the message for the old Saracen husband. The wife had revealed that Thorvald was ambushed off the coast of Iberia the day after delivering the message, as he set a straight course for home. Every man was slain, the running ship sent to the depths.

Dan slammed a balled fist against the table top and groaned. His blood ran hot and he saw Mord Baptized-One dead.

Freydis continued, explaining that the wife did not know anything about the ransom ship, or pretended not. She had learned the fate of the husband from a Dublin slaver who had purchased the survivors of the ransom vessel. She turned to the morose Saracen youth, who had finally satisfied his hunger, and said, "Let him tell it as he told it to Gunar. I can only give the facts thirdhand, as Gunar told it to me."

Dan turned his fired eyes to Aisha's son. "Tell me your tale," he said in Arabic, "and pay attention to detail."

Ajib set his head proudly back. "Where is my mother?" he demanded to know.

"She is safe. In excellent health. When I have heard it all I will take you to her."

The sea had been rough from the very start. Kamar al Zamen was abed in his sumptuous quarters below deck, having recently suffered a heart seizure. The captain was ill-disposed to the command for night sailing. He did not know the waters. Each hour deeper into the northern hemisphere would multiply the dangers of running ashoal, or falling over the earth's brink. The captain who had sailed to the Orkneys on the physician's first voyage there had refused to tempt fate by repeating the folly. Another captain had had to be signed, an entirely new crew, and a motley lot they were.

It was difficult to read the map Dan had given the physician. The marked shore hiding places were invariably missed. When the hulking ship lay anchored during the daylight hours it was more visible than it should have been because the captain had not trusted the depths and dropped anchor well off shore.

On the second day at sea a dragon ship was sighted to the west. It sailed to within shouting distance, then veered northward and vanished where sky and sea met.

The leagues were carefully logged and slow indeed was their progress. The land of the Franks was not reached for three nights. The fourth day found them in open water off the Frankish coast, an easy target for the two dragon ships that steered a threatening course toward them, one from the north, the other from the west. The land mass was curved in such a way as to prevent escape by sea.

With little enthusiasm the Saracen captain had called his fifteen armed men to their battle stations. Horns sounded from the forecastle of the attacking ships and arrows flew over the mast, then grappling hooks whirred through the air, dug into wood and held. The fierceness of the attackers' war cries and the sight of their horned beast helmets so unnerved the soldiers that after a feeble resistance they flung themselves overboard and swam toward shore, the captain following their lead.

Men swarmed aboard with axes and spears in hand. They found slaves chained to the rowing benches below, and found Ajib and his father in their quarters, the lad standing close over the physician's bed, putting his life over his father.

Ajib was flung aside. A giant wearing a boar's head helmet with curved horns clutched up the physician by his collar and held him in the air, dangling, demanding to know where the gold was. Kamar al Zamen's eyes rolled in his head and he spoke deliriously, insisting that there was no gold aboard. Ajib cried out that it was true, there was no gold, because they had not been certain enough that Dan Sea-Kingsson was being honest with them; he could be pretending to have their wife and mother safe, intent upon taking the gold without fulfilling his part of the bargain. They had chosen to go again to Ransay and verify her identity, thereupon making new arrangements with her captor for payment of the ransom.

The giant had not believed a word of it. He threw the frail old man upon his bed and ordered the ship ransacked. Into the night the savages had hacked away with their axes, ripping out decking and sideboards, but to no avail.

Enraged, the dragon ship captain returned to his own ship. The next day he fixed lines to the Saracen vessel. All day and through the night they worked, hauling the cumbersome ship ashore, getting wooden rollers under it, heaving on ropes and chains to get it out of the water enough so that the hull and keel could be examined, the entire ship chopped to pieces if necessary.

Ajib and his father were bound with ropes and tied to the trunks of trees. Rain fell all that first day. Kamar al Zamen wept unrestrainedly. He had fought against death all these long months, refusing to remain at Setubal, vowing he would see Aisha safe before he passed on to Allah's Paradise. But on the second day ashore, without food or water, chilled by exposure, he died. His frail body suddenly went rigid, his heart stopped and his bearded chin dropped to his skeletal breast.

The ransom ship was taken apart board by board, each board chopped to bits. It took five days of stubborn, frantic labor. When the dismemberment proved fruitless, the giant went into a frenzy. Mad bull, he lunged with his sword against the mountain of debris, killing it, uttering unintelligible curses.

Many of the crewmen who had attempted to escape by swimming ashore had been scooped out of the water like fish in a net. Ajib was taken aboard one of the dragon ships and chained with the other captives at the stern. They were taken to Dublin and sold on the wharf as slaves for three marks of silver. Again he was taken aboard a ship, one that sailed to the Isle of Man, where he suffered whippings and menial tasks until the woman, Freydis, came and purchased him from his master.

For long moments after Ajib's story ceased, Dan's mouth remained agape in frozen concentration. Abruptly he caught himself up and said thickly, "There was no gold. I—"

"But there was," Ajib contradicted in a flat voice.

"Was," Dan echoed, rearing back on the bench.

"Naturally, we anticipated the possibility of such an attack. We devised a vault within the keel, fixed so that no eye could discern that the thick block was at any point hollow." Ajib sighed and swallowed emotion that rose to fill his throat. "I begged my father to allow me to tell them where the gold was, but he insisted such a confession would serve no purpose. The savages would treat us no less viciously upon gaining what they sought; we were dead whether they had the gold or not, and he did not wish to give them the satisfaction. I had to agree."

"But why did they not find it?"

"Only Allah the Compassionate in his sublime mercy saved it from discovery. They could not make toothpicks of every timber. Somehow the axes missed the cache. It is a relatively small package, not coin but gold powder."

"A fortune lying there on a Frankish beach!" Dan exclaimed, rising excitedly to his feet.

"That is the truth of it, Saíd."

"Praise Odin's name! Who have you told of the existence of the gold?"

"You are the first to hear of it."

Freydis interrupted with a remark that sobered Dan. "I have news that Mord will attack our odel, my husband. Coming as no surprise, I know."

"No surprise," he echoed impatiently. "Now that he has lost the opportunity to take the gold, he will have my head. I think he also covets the woman."

"He took himself home to Norn for the harvest. Unless winter is early, he will shortly attack in force."

"You already said that, woman," Dan protested irritably.

"Yes, but . . . I cannot help worrying . . . I mean, would it not be better if you took the war to him? The children, and . ."

Dan's eyes held hers for long moments. Then he nodded, his softened eyes telling her that he understood. He sat down beside her and reached out to put his hands over hers where they lay tightly clenched on top of the table. "How did you come by the fact of this lad's identity?" he asked softly.

"The slaver at Dublin. When he mentioned an upstart prince of the east as being among the captives sold, a lad who had shouted demands for safe passage to Ransay and the odel of Dan Sea-Kingsson, I put two and two together. I asked him who purchased the lad and to my amazement was told it was my uncle once removed, Raesnir of Man. I went to the Isle of Man, spending three days with my aunt and cousins, and finally persuaded Raesnir to agree to sell the lad to me."

"I cannot imagine why you were amazed to discover one of your uncles had purchased him," Dan laughed, squeezing her cold hands. "You are related to half the Asar, I think." He added warmly, "I am greatly proud of you, wife. You are the best of wives."

Freydis smiled broadly at that. But her blue eyes quickly became apprehensive again. "I hope that the ice and snow come early. My heart weeps at the thought of Christians attacking our odel. Dan . . . They will slay the children!"

Aisha was feeding the three infants at once, spooning bread softened with warm milk into one eager little mouth, then the next and the next. She heard the sound of approaching horses but paid no mind. The door softly opened behind her. She turned, but for a moment did not recognize her son. The dish and spoon dropped to the floor, and her hands flew to her mouth, a cry escaping her throat.

Ajib rushed to her and clasped her in his arms, holding her tight against him as she wept into his shoulder.

She drew back at last and devoured his gaunt face with her eyes. "My son, you have suffered greatly. You wear the mark of slavery. Tell me, how is my husband and your beloved father?"

"He is with Allah in Paradise," the lad said emotionally, tears flowing down his bronze cheeks. "I—I made him a vow . . . that I would not do anything for his sake that might jeopardize your rescue." He swallowed hard and hugged her tight to him, weeping into her ear. "I was forced to watch him die, Mother. He had said to me, 'I am very old and must die soon. To attempt to save my life for only a few days would not be worth the cost to your sainted mother. You must save yourself if you can.' His—his heart; he was too old for the strain of our ordeal."

Aisha wept too and held her son close. Over Ajib's shoulder she saw Dan enter the open door to stand waiting solemnly.

"What will happen now?" she shot at him, backing away from Ajib a little.

"A war must be fought, a winter spent under ice and snow," Dan replied apologetically. "In the spring, after the sowing, I will seek the gold."

"*What* gold?"

"The ship was ransacked, but the gold was not found; it lies on a Frankish beach."

"But what of my return to Cairo City?"

Dan hesitated, meeting her eyes coldly. "We will discuss that when I have uncovered the gold."

"*Alhomdolillah*! The better part of another year."

"Yes. At least another year."

"And you may never allow me to return!"

"That is a possibility," he admitted, a fleeting smile crossing his face.

"Men of honor you call yourselves!" she shouted at him sarcastically.

"I will see gold or you will not see Cairo!"

"Damn you, I am personally worth many millions," she argued heatedly, stepping angrily round Ajib to glare up at Dan. "If you take me to Cairo City I will put a million grams of gold into your hands. I will pay thrice that amount if need be. I am as valuable to you now as I was before my husband was slain."

Dan looked down into her exquisite, fired eyes and experienced a sharp regret at the idea of her departure . . . never to see her again. He said evasively, "I have to assume that Mord Baptized-One has reached the same conclusion. Since he unloaded your son on the wharf, it is obvious he now looks upon you as self-ransoming. If I do not defeat him utterly, you would get no farther along the path to Cairo City than your husband on the path here to Ransay."

"Let him come for me, then, and take me," she said vehemently. "If he is my only means of escaping this nightmare, so be it."

David entered the house, slump-shouldered and dragging his feet. He glanced questioningly from one to the other, waiting for one of them to explain the air of suspense and rage in the room.

Dan turned contemptuous eyes upon David. He said flatly, "On the morrow I will take a force against Borgarsfiord. Your *wife* will accompany me."

David's face blanched and he began to rock uneasily from foot to foot. "What possible motive could drive you to so risk her life? I do not understand you."

"What? What is it?" Aisha insisted anxiously. Dan had spoken in a low voice in the Asa tongue, as if purposely keeping what he was saying from her. "David, tell me."

David shook his head at her, keeping his eyes on Dan.

Dan argued, "I have let it be known over all Orkney that wherever I go she goes. To leave a goldmine on my odel for even part of a day would beg an attack while I am absent. I risk all I have, or I risk only *her*. And I choose not to let her out of my sight because I do not trust her, or you, or certain greedy men of my retinue. I must distrust everyone when a million grams of gold is at stake. She will be safer by far with me. I would not let pure gold slip through my fingers."

"Your enemy will know that she is aboard," David responded.

"Ah, that he will. What a fine drawing card she will be."

"But if you lose the battle—"

"Lose!" Dan exclaimed indignantly. "I may not be entirely victorious, but I will not be *defeated*!"

David turned to Aisha helplessly. "He will take you to sea with him tomorrow . . . into battle." He could no longer meet her eyes and shifted his glance to the floor at his feet. "I cannot persuade him to . . ."

"Battle! *Alhomdolillah*! Cannot? What *can* you do, priest?" She was so furious she could do nothing else but throw herself across the room and beat her two fists against the wall.

"For the love of God," David cried, "how could I change his purpose? With these two powerful arms, shall I restrain him?" He threw up his aching arms in emphasis.

Aisha whirled about-face and shouted at Dan, "I refuse. I will not be taken into battle with you. What a ridiculous idea!"

Dan said calmly, "If you are not at the bay shore by sunset tomorrow, my men posted here will escort you." With that, he turned heel and left the house.

Aisha sped after him, crying, "What is to become of my son?"

As he leaped astride the stallion and the horse reared to speed across the fields, he shouted over his shoulder, "Leave him to wet-nurse the exposed ones."

Numbed by yet another sudden and unpleasant turn of events, Aisha moved back into the house. David looked at her pityingly and apologetically. Ajib was furiously pacing the small room, cursing and beating a fist against a palm.

"It is of no use," Aisha said on a sigh. "It is fated. We are helpless in the face of Allah's intentions. I am for the rest of my life to pay for some grievous sin."

"You have not sinned, Aisha," David said to her comfortingly. "It is *original* sin for which we all pay in—"

"Do not *preach* to me!" Aisha cried in Arabic, pressing a balled fist against her mouth as if the gesture could somehow salve her rage and frustration. At David's bewildered, wounded expression, she said it again in Latin. "But pray for me. Your prayers and mine together might have some beneficial effect, but I seriously doubt it. Allah has forsaken me."

"I have never been so degraded," Ajib wailed. "The savages. You cannot imagine how base they are. I—"

"Not *imagine*!" Aisha shouted emotionally at her son, whirling upon him. "Oh, I think I could guess how base they are, Ajib. Nur al Huda has a child to prove it! And I suffer a ghastly memory of being *raped*!"

Ajib flushed. He went to her and held her, begging her to forgive his thoughtlessness.

"How did you ever manage to discover this place, or learn that I lived?" she asked wearily.

"Maymunah escaped and—"

"What?" Her eyes rounded in horror and resentment. "Are you telling me that woman found safety? But how, in the name of Allah? I thought her certainly dead."

"When she put her feet to land, she was on Muslim soil, my mother. You should have gone with her."

"Great Allah! Nur al Huda was so ill, I . . . To think, that that *bitch* is now enjoying my place in the house! Not as first wife, surely?"

"She is at home in Cairo City," he replied apologetically, "but no woman could take your—"

"Damn her eyes! Some people are blessed by Allah far beyond their due, that is the truth."

Aisha walked voluntarily to the compound and arrived there well before sunset. Ajib was beside her. He had sworn to go aboard with her or be killed, but she had dissuaded him from such a pointless gesture.

The shore was alive with men. A rumble and clamor of frenzied activity rose in a din, and Aisha was jostled and elbowed many times as she pressed her way toward the house of Dan Sea-Kingsson.

Inside the house, people were running in and out of doors in what seemed to be a crazy purposelessness, shouting and harried. Dan's followers wore the happiest expressions Aisha had yet seen on their faces. With childlike joy they looked forward to battle, little boys about to play their favorite game. Men.

"Saracen harlot!" Gudrid bellowed at Aisha upon sighting her in the midst of the anteroom hustle. "What business do you have in this house?"

Aisha instinctively cringed, but then took hold of herself, lifted her chin and said between tight lips, "I seek Nur al Huda."

The witch made a ferocious face and spat on the floor. "Who knows which of a dozen men she lies under at this moment? Seek a prone male, look under him, and you will probably find the slut you seek!"

Aisha's eyes widened and she swallowed her fury. Aggressively she pushed a path through the surging crowd and deliberately brushed past Gudrid, entering the passageway to the great hall. Ajib silently followed her.

Dan Sea-Kingsson sat on his highseat with many freshly washed and neatly combed noblemen surrounding him. The Asar went to battle as if to a feast, bathed, brushed, clipped and combed. Dan paid no attention to Aisha, if he noticed her entrance at all. She scanned the half-empty hall for the familiar dark head, but to no avail. She thought of the loft and immediately made her way outside, telling Ajib to wait where he was; he could observe the savages at their favorite pastime and perhaps learn something of the ways of heathens. Her mood was sour to the extreme. As she made her way up the side staircase, she told herself that such meanness of spirit only multiplied her distress, but the lecture did no good. She pulled the door open to quickly enter the loft, rushing toward the draped bedchamber to see if Nur al Huda was asleep there.

When the drape swung aside, Nur al Huda lunged forward on the bed, her face flushing. She was entirely nude. Beside her sprawled a very embarrassed Harri, who hastily reached for his trousers and put them on.

"Bismillah!" Nur al Huda said on a gasp. "You could have knocked on the door."

"The old witch was right," Aisha seethed. "You are a slut. Hell bent. I always said it and now I know it." It suddenly struck her that Nur al Huda was one of those people that the obedient of this world always wept for as damned, a liver of life as she found it, a follower of impulse and compulsion. Now she wondered if there was not a measure of envy in the curses of those who could not so easily set aside Allah's rules. But she threw off such thoughts and shouted at Harri to get out. He stubbornly hung back, saying he was to go to battle for the first time today and might not return. "Oh, I hope *not*," Aisha remarked nastily. "The thought that you might see your Odin prematurely pleases me greatly. . . . Now do as I say and get out!"

When the lad had taken himself from the loft, mumbling curses under his breath, Aisha paced before Nur al Huda, where she sat still stark naked on the bed, utterly disgusted. "I came here to see you, to tell you that your husband has died," she said belligerently. "But I can see that you were not very concerned about having a husband."

"Good riddance!" Nur al Huda snarled, turning her back on Aisha and beginning to pull on some clothing.

Aisha lunged forward, caught the girl by the shoulders and spun her round to face her. "Listen to me," she raged between clenched teeth, "and listen well. I offered Dan Sea-Kingsson twenty thousand grams of gold for your return to Cairo City. One more display of vulgarity and disrespect, and I will leave you to this place, these savages!"

"You can *keep* your precious gold," Nur al Huda spat in Aisha's face, her dark eyes fired. "I love Harri and—"

"Love? What do you know of love? Insane. How can you love a—"

"A man. He is so much a man I could die of him. And I am going to have his child. What do you think about *that*?"

"You little fool!" Aisha stumbled back, stunned. She could not find any more words. Nur al Huda's eyes were burning with a passionate defiance and sincerity. She truly meant to remain, to attempt to live her life on this Allah-forsaken island. "If I leave you, you can hope for nothing. A slave? You would accept the status of a slave, for the love of Allah?"

"Not slave but *wife*," the girl shouted. "Harri is going to marry me."

"Never. Do not be absurd. He will not and cannot marry you."

"He will," she shrieked. "Yes, he will. He has promised."

"Has he actually said as much, or have you assumed?

Harri will marry a Northwoman of means and noble house. Return to your senses, child, and—"

"Will you stop calling me a child!"

"Oh, certainly. I will stop calling you anything at all. You will be deserted here. A thrall woman serving Harri's meals and bleaching the linens for his shirts."

"Get out!" Nur al Huda screamed, moving threateningly toward Aisha across the bed on her hands and knees. "Mother of worms and maggots, may you burn in hell for ten eternities. Get . . . out!"

Aisha turned and ran from the room, her stomach turned in reaction to her intense disgust and anger. She plunged down the staircase and fell against Ajib, who had been searching for her. He held her steady a moment until she could gain control. At last she lifted her head and straightened her shoulders, then set out for the shore to put herself at Dan Sea-Kingsson's disposal. *Kuzia-Fakan—as it is decreed, so must it come to pass.*

CHAPTER SIXTEEN

"Better to offer no sacrifice at all than to offer too much," Dan said to his captains when they questioned him as to why he had not repaired to the temple before boarding his warship. "Offering smacks of compensation. I will worship Odin with my prowess in the battle."

Dan's prized *Sea King's Deer* was a long-serpent, celebrated for its beauty and power, but he left that ship in harbor and took to sea on the *Snake of the Waves,* a *skeid,* or swift sailor, a thirty-seater. Two hundred and forty men were aboard when he slipped out of the bay under a clouded sky that, at least for the time being, draped the moon to create a cover of complete darkness.

Dan wore a coat of ring mail, excellent in workmanship, hard of ring, and far thicker and more inpenetrable than Enean armor. A steel cap, the brim wide as his hand's breadth, covered his neatly combed hair, and a shining axe, the edge of which was two feet long, rested on his shoulder. Behind the *Snake of the Waves* a fleet of ships fell into line, some ironclad ramming vessels, others smaller and more easily managed types called *askar*.

Dan kept his position at the helm, below the rudder head. The woman had been confined near the highseat chest that held the weapons, third *rum* from the stern. She was safe enough there. The wind was fair, but for his purposes it was better to depend on oars. The skeid was light as he could make her by removing all save her very frame. Speed was to be his best weapon in the battle plan he had devised.

After rounding the curve of Ransay, Dan set a course due south. Leaving the helm to his newly appointed standard bearer, Dan went among his men, encouraging them, joking with them. Harri was happily amidship, brandishing an axe in wild swings and slashes.

"Your accumulation of great deeds begins, my son," Dan said to Harri, laughing affectionately, pounding the lad's back with the flat of a hand. "Do yourself proud. Let Odin know your name. Let Thor tremble before your thunder."

"Glory will be mine, have no fear," Harri assured his foster father. "I am Odin's equal."

Dan laughed and moved swiftly away from Harri to stop short before the weapons chest. Aisha sat there on a tied bundle of arrows, shivering and morosely leaning her chin into the palm of a hand, her elbow resting on her upraised knees; she was using a shield as a footstool.

"Before the battle begins," Dan said softly to her, "you will be brought to the helm, where you will be protected from missiles."

"*Thank* you," she purred sarcastically, "oh father of generosity and magnanimity."

He stiffened but did not turn away. "The night is chill," he observed, "but the clouds are clearing; it will be clear and starlit within an hour."

"A good omen, I suppose," she muttered sourly, sitting upright and at last meeting his eyes, if only fleetingly.

"Are you warm enough?"

Her teeth where crashing together, and he asked if she was warm enough. "If I were any colder, I would be *solid*!"

Dan rushed away, caught a cloak from the nearest shoulder and brought it to her. She took it without a word and wrapped it round herself, wriggling deep into its fur lining. He sat down at her feet, commenting that there was little to do now but pass the time.

After a long silence between them, Aisha asked, "Do you never weary of fighting?"

"Rather, I weary of the lapses between battles."

"You never sicken at so much death?"

"Death is a part of life. To die bravely is a good thing. I give my enemies the opportunity of dying at the instance of my sword, and consider them fortunate to have met with me, to have fallen in battle against a man of my fame and strength."

She sighed impatiently, finding it impossible to understand his reasoning. The men were quiet now, some sleeping in standing or sitting positions, all remarkably relaxed. "You are a strange man, Dan Sea-Kingsson," she said to his shadowed profile.

He turned his eyes to her. "You are no less strange to me." He thought a moment, studying her face. "Perhaps it is your strangeness that attracts me. Certainly, you are not the woman of my dreams; you were constructed on too small a scale. You are spirited, however, and I like that in a woman. But you are not self-wise, as I thought all womankind to be."

"Self-wise," Aisha echoed, shaking her head exasperatedly.

"Nor are you properly muscled. Nevertheless, I shrink from releasing you."

"I am too old for romance," she said flatly, more as a question than a statement.

Dan laughed, and that laughter could not have flattered her more, or better reassured her. She felt her face reddening in the darkness.

"By leaving this world and going to his gods, your husband has freed you," he said pointedly.

"Yes," she agreed wistfully, "I am free now." But it was not as she had dreamed it would be in those days long past. Somehow she felt still bound to Kamar al Zamen. She had not seen him dead, his death therefore unreal, difficult to believe a fact. She thought upon what her husband would want for her now, and heard his voice telling her to make the most of what she yet had to spend.

Dan got to his feet. He looked down into her eyes and said in a voice tinted with a peculiar emotion, "When the battle is won I will approach you again." His seriousness dropped away and he grinned wickedly. "Do not throw away a once-in-a-lifetime opportunity. A rare privilege indeed for a pagan woman of your years to know an Asa man's love. I am certain we will find our common meeting ground. . . . on a bed."

Aisha could not suppress a laugh. He was so preposterously conceited. No man on earth loved himself with the depth of feeling that he did. How could he love a woman when he gave so much affection to himself? He strode into the darkness and vanished from her sight. She hugged herself with trembling arms, contemplating the measure of her will against the measure of his. To know youthful passion. . . . Ach, she could seek love in Cairo City if that was what she wanted from her remaining years, and it was not. She would repulse him determinedly, she assured herself. But whenever she heard his voice on the wind that night, her heart quickened.

Just past midnight the fleet dropped anchor under the shadow of the northern cliffs of Norn. High waves broke upon the rocks, their thundering an excellent cover for the sounds made in landing men and weapons in smallboats. Seven hundred men went ashore with axes and bows. Ropes and grappling hooks were piled on the narrow beach for the scaling of the stone cliffs. Men immediately began to climb. From the high land above, they would have a bird's-eye view of the entire island and the bay of Borgarsfiord five miles to the south. Under the cover of night they would lie in wait.

With skeleton crews, three men to each bench, one for the shield, one for the bow and one for the oar, the five ships of the fleet eased out to sea again, allowing the current to carry them south slowly, round the curve of the island. Soon the torches of the alert Borgarsfiord compound gleamed in the blackness to port. Chains, with heavy anchors at end, were slung from ship to ship and caught fast, so that the ships became an unbroken whole. The line veered toward the bay and within an hour had completely blocked it, the curved formation presenting a formidable sight as the sky lightened in the east.

Mord Baptized-One had kept vigil on the gard throughout the night. In the Orkneys a surprise attack was rarely accomplished. The islands were grouped closely together, and word passed swiftly from odel to odel of any gathering of force. At strategic points on all high promontories, men were at their catapults, ready to rain stones upon any attacking warriors. Within the barricaded compound some nine hundred fighting men lay in wait. Mord had anticipated a landing by night, an attempt to burn his odel down around him. But it was dawn and the enemy fleet lingered at the mouth of the bay, showing no inclination toward an immediate attack. His own fleet lay in harbor, close in to shore, with skeleton crews aboard to watch for sabotage, prepared to set sail at a moment's notice.

The sound of horns pierced the air, and a red war shield was raised upon the mast of the enemy's lead vessel. Dan Sea-Kingsson was calling Mord to a sea battle, sending arrows over the host as a symbol of hostility. Shielding his eyes with a hand, Mord glared at the line of ships silhouetted against the rising sun. He saw shields slung along the sides of the ships, and could make out war helmets just visible over the gunwales. His experienced eye counted heads. The opposing host numbered at least a thousand strong by the look of it. Yet the vessels rode high in the water, as if lightly burdened. He turned and scanned the surrounding hills and cliffs. Gulls flew lazily in the brisk wind against an entirely tranquil background.

Mord cupped his hands round his mouth and let a cry fall upon the wind. From all his high positions echoed the prearranged responding cry, indicating all was well.

"Hah!" Dan barked from his position at the prow, "the big fish has taken the bait."

Men could be seen pouring out of the distant compound, a cataract of armed warriors, rushing to the bay and the anchored ships.

"Raise oars," Dan shouted, and his standard bearer repeated the command. Oars went into motion and the *Snake of the Waves* slowly turned in the bay. The ships behind, held in formation by the anchored chains, followed commands called from the stern of the lead vessel, then shouted them to the next ship, echoing, overlapping directives passing quickly from captain to captain, ship to ship. Helmets rocked on the spears that held them as decoys to convince the enemy all strength was aboard and not ashore. If they kept a proper distance between themselves and the pursuers, it would appear that they were indeed heavy-laden.

Now at the prow of the *Raven of the Wind,* Mord Baptized-One cheered on his crew. Three ships followed, but separately—one would steer east, another west, closing off Dan's line of skeids dead ahead. As the *Snake of the Waves* veered slightly to starboard, Mord caught a glimpse of the Saracen woman standing on the forecastle. He recalled the scent of her bronze skin, the softness of that flesh once against his in trembling dread. He would have her again and again, and squeeze from her a fortune that would last him a lifetime. He would sail to Cairo City again. Time healed all wounds; the Saracens were hungry for rare furs and live beasts. There, from the coffers of the wench, he would sap the gold. The wind slashed his face as he shouted at the oarsmen for more speed. No husband was required for this business transaction. Had not the husband ranted and raved about his wife's status in Cairo City, about more gold than Mord had known existed in the world? The close-mouthed youth he had sold on the wharf at Dublin was the son of the husband, but Mord had no inkling with which wife or concubine the physician had conceived the lout. The woman he recalled was far too youthful, surely, to be the mother of a full-grown man.

On the *Snake of the Waves* Dan also called for more speed, and the bowmen immediately dropped down to make two at each oar, the skeid leaping the swells to gain speed of almost ten knots, giving them the advantage over the heavy-laden enemy. Keeping just out of missile range, Dan led Mord farther and farther from the stronghold.

When the running and pursuing ships were only specks on the horizon, Dan's men swooped down from the hills surrounding Borgarsfiord. The catapults, high above, were simultaneously attacked and the machines turned to rain stones upon the homestead. Only an hundred men had remained to protect the *bor*. After a bombardment of stones and fire, the warriors ran toward the gard, set spears into the earth and vaulted over the timber wall, washing over in waves that no amount of arrows or stones could halt. Many fell, but the bor was quickly taken. Women and children were collected and herded into the church. Then fires were set. Axes hacked at the ship-building machines and tools. Foodstuffs in storehouses were carried beyond the compound, to preserve them for sale at the marketplaces.

When Dan saw the smudge of smoke rising behind the pursuing ships, he ordered his shield bearers to the oars and altered course to due north. The line turned on the sea, cut through the gap in Mord's strategic placement of ships, and raced back to the bay of Borgarsfiord. It was more than an hour before his fleet was stretched across the mouth of the bay, blocking Mord's return.

Smoke rose in black clouds and flames sliced upward as if the bowels of the earth had opened under Borgarsfiord. Men fell from the cliffs with arrows in their breasts. In his blocking position Dan waited for Mord's ships to arrive and make an effort to breach his line. His cheering men, having successfully fought their way from the high cliffs to the shore, now swarmed across the beach and dove into the sea, swimming swiftly to board their ships. Now the five ships were indeed well armed and could meet any onslaught at sea.

Aisha trembled in her hiding place, crouched deeply in under the helm. She could see only legs moving restlessly back and forth before her rounded eyes. Dan had put a coat of armor over her, but it was monstrously heavy and she had thrown it off. Smoke began to fill the air and she gagged, choking miserably. She could hear death cries now, as from a long distance, and the crackling of fire.

Suddenly the air was filled with a deafening roar, thousands of men simultaneously shrieking war cries. She sucked in a breath and grasped the coat of mail, struggling to haul it over her head again. The clamor was awful. She had never heard the like—groans, wails, screams of agony—intermingled with laughter, shouts of warning and the crunch of spear heads driving into flesh, bone and shields, the clang of axe heads striking against helmets, the dull cracks of splitting skulls.

Blood ran a thin rivulet along the helm rise decking, and Aisha's eyes fastened on it in morbid fascination, her stomach heaving. Then something struck, an explosive crash that quaked the ship and sent it listing to starboard, throwing Aisha hard against the wood of her shelter. The breath was knocked out of her. She screamed, terrified, as water rushed in and rose to her face. Then she was entirely underwater, thrashing and fighting to get out from under the heavy metal coat. The ship had been rammed, was sinking. She was drowning.

Her head abruptly broke out of the wash, and she was thrown in the other direction as the ship righted itself. Hysterical, she flung her arms and legs about, trying to get her footing. She reared out of her shelter. A warrior lay dead at her feet, blood spurting from the place where his head hung almost entirely severed from his body. She stumbled forward to see below her, amidship, a tangled mob, men hacking at each other with axes, soaring over the heads of their adversaries, using their feet as weapons, vaulting from the gunwale of one ship to the deck of another. From the height of the helm rise she could see the entire bay, filled with ships. Behind her was the burning homestead. The ship was listing badly, water was up to the knees of the men fighting below. She clung to the deserted helm and swallowed hysteria, whispering prayers to Allah.

Dan's voice rose above the din, a terrible, savage cry. Aisha's eyes flew to where he stood teetering on the gunwale, a spear in his gloved hand. He raised the thin spear, drew it back and sent it slicing across the expanse between himself and Mord Baptized-One, who stood in the prow of the *Raven of the Wind,* which was close alongside.

Mord whirled round at the sound of Dan's cry. He saw the spear being raised, but he could not lunge away fast enough. The head drove into his breast and he leaped in air, yowling like a wounded lion, then fell out of sight.

Dan had kept his balance on the gunwale. Now he stood high there and threw up both arms, bellowing a cry of victory. He leaped backward to the deck, bounced on his feet, leaped a scuffle of sword-wielding warriors, to land upon the helm rise beside Aisha. The *Raven of the Wind* eased away. Mord could be seen at the prow, several men leaning over him; the spear jutted from his chest and his face was a mask of rage and controlled agony.

"Another day . . . another battle, if you live to see it, Mord Baptized-One!" Dan roared fiercely to his retreating and wounded enemy.

Suddenly Dan clutched Aisha around the waist, hauled her up to the gunwale and leaped overboard with her.

Aisha's heart hammered as she fell, plunging deeper and deeper under water. The descent abruptly halted and she began to rise. Her head broke out of the bloodied, churning sea and she coughed violently. Dan swam toward shore with her, using one arm to propel himself, the other fastened under her arms and round her heaving bosom. When they were well ashore, he dropped her unceremoniously and ran away from her along the rocky beach, shouting commands to his captains.

Aisha sat there numb and shivering, her eyes fixed upon the bay. Bodies floated and rocked on the waves, then dipped under and sank from sight. Bits of wood and debris of all sorts littered the water's surface. Only two of Dan's ships had been badly damaged, the other three now steering toward shore to lay anchor.

The *Raven of the Wind* was sinking, her stern going under, the prow lunging upward so that the dragon head seemed rearing in agony, its jeweled eyes bright in death. Mord was going down with his ship. Dead. Dan had killed him, had killed the man who had destroyed the tranquility and predictability of her life, who had changed her anticipated destiny. A shocking exultation came with the thought, a triumph no less explosive and jubilant than Dan's.

Men began to collect the wounded on the shore. Litters were improvised of cloaks and spears. But Aisha noticed that certain of the dead and wounded were set apart, thrown cruelly aside. She dumbly watched from her crouched position on the rocks as the enemy dead were picked up and thrown like rubbish into scorched wagons brought from the compound and hauled away; the wounded of the enemy were ignored, left to die where they lay.

Harri appeared out of the darkness and stood before Aisha. His face was badly scratched, but except for the blood spattered all over him, he was in excellent condition. His eyes were glazed with excitement and the joy of victory.

"Come," Harri said, offering her a hand.

Aisha rose unsteadily to her feet, refusing any aid from Harri. Her wet clothing clung to her shivering flesh. Hair fell in damp strands over her face, into her mouth and eyes.

"My foster father wishes me to provide shelter for you," Harri said stiffly.

"How kind of him," she muttered nastily.

Harri proceeded toward the cliffs, and she followed him like an obedient child. After a short climb she was led into a shallow cave that was entered across a ledge that hung over the pounding sea. The ledge was positioned so that she had a view of the smoldering compound and the entire bay.

"You will be safe here," Harri said. "I will have someone bring you food and blankets." He added, after looking her over distastefully, "And fresh, dry clothing."

"You do that," Aisha commented sharply, falling to a sitting position just inside the cave opening.

Harri left her alone with the echoing thunder of the waves and the wailing of the gulls that winged noncommittally over the chaos below them. She thought, so this is the stuff of their dreams, the entire purpose of their lives. This was the Asar's sole aim in life, to kill and maim uninterruptedly until the predestined day of their own death in battle. Allah forbid that they should die of old age in a comfortable bed! They were not human. For the first time since knowing David of Saint Monica, she could imagine what might be driving him to such degrees of personal sacrifice. It was not smug or false to suggest that every one of these warriors would suffer hellfire for eternity for their sinful brutality against their fellow men.

She dropped her head against her upraised knees, weeping for a lost illusion; so many times she had thought to see a prince in Dan Sea-Kingsson, a magnificence that was almost superhuman. Hereafter she would see him soaked in blood, an axe in his hand. No woman could love a man with a heart so cold, with so murderous a soul.

At sunset Aisha sat at the cave entrance, warm in a wool gown and a fur-lined cloak, dry shoes on her feet. The wind pressed heavily against her and she leaned into it. Spray rose in a fine mist from the crashing sea below, settling on her lashes and dampening her face.

Something dropped from above and plunged into the sea. Aisha leaped to her feet and rushed out on the ledge to stretch her eyes up along the cliff face to the crest. She cried out and a hand flew up to cover her mouth as other prisoners and the slain of the enemy, their backs having been broken over sharp boulders, were slung like rubbish into the swallowing sea. Some had had their backs split open with knives in the form of eagle's wings, hearts and lungs torn out. A sacrifice to Odin, the final victory over the enemy. She stumbled into the far back of the cave and was violently sick.

A fire was set to finish the demolition of the compound. Women and children were herded aboard one of Dan's ships, which was set afloat with a man at the helm and the women at the oars. The ship moved sluggishly toward Main Island, following the wake of their fleeing warriors.

Soon after the flames in the distance died to a faint glow in the darkness, a figure loomed over Aisha where she sat, illuminated in the light of the torch he held. Dan stood silently over her, washed and combed, calmly studying her where she huddled far back from the opening.

Aisha slowly raised her head and coldly met his eyes. "You," she began huskily, her throat closing over her words with the intensity of her emotions. "You are, beyond argument, the vilest thing Allah ever created and must be ashamed of!"

"In what way *vile*?" Dan asked, unperturbed.

"If you need to ask, there could be no explaining it to you."

Dan moved easily into the cave and sat down beside her, leaning back against the cold rock wall. He turned to examine her stubbornly averted profile. "Vile, you said," he remarked thoughtfully, absentmindedly planting his torch in a crevice in the rock floor, forcing it to stand straight. "I have known vileness, but I had never thought of myself as vile; no." He cleared his throat, glancing again at her face, his eyes sliding the length of her. All there was to see was her face above the collar of the cloak, her shod feet below it. "I wonder if you think me vile because I shed no tears over those I have slain today." He waited for a reply from her. Receiving none, he shook his head, "Then, because I go into battle cheerfully instead of trembling? Should I, as Saracens do, according to their bible—what do you call it, Quran? Should I say, 'No war is right except in self-defense,' taking my war pleasures only after goading my enemy into attacking me?"

Dan swung his arms over his head, stretching and yawning exaggeratedly. To the roof above him he said, "You would have me weep over my dead enemies, pour guilt upon them after I have killed them; that is what you would expect of a right-man, I think. But would I kill them if I did not despise them? And if I despise them, I must kill them. I spit on their bodies, not ceasing my hatred for them simply because they are now dead. Why should I pretend I cannot help myself, try to convince myself that I am powerless to prevent their deaths, when I am a man of free will, committing no act without my own approval? Eh?"

He leaned forward and toward her, trying to see her eyes, but she snapped her face away from his probing glance. He sighed and patiently leaned back against the wall again. He chewed his lower lip a moment, reached up with a hand to smooth his neat beard thoughtfully, then said, "Praise Odin; he tells me to do what is most natural for me to do. —But *your* god, he has made you puppets to dance on strings for him, wooden men and women striking poses, committing vile acts under the guise of sanctification—'I was attacked,' you insist, or 'This war is *holy*.' 'I did not hate my enemy, for it is evil to hate; I killed him for my god who was angry with him.'— Then your god exacts his price, demanding guilt for the deeds you performed in his name. —I am *guiltless*!"

He sighed to express his contempt for the ways of her people. For long moments he stared at the shadowed rock roof over his head. Now he became urgent, his hands knotting into fists, his voice becoming sharper-edged. "Praise Odin. He gives me peace of mind. He knows me, for he created me. He loves the handiwork of his loins and would have me in no way different than I am. I am not a *pretender* to the throne of Dan Sea-Kingsson; I *am* Dan Sea-Kingsson!"

Aisha swung her head around to look at him. He did not move. His head was back against the rock now, his eyes closed. He had not spoken to justify himself but to gain her understanding. She stared hard at his tranquil profile and knew that he did indeed enjoy a rare peace of mind. She suddenly envied him his guiltlessness, and at the same time suffered a guilt of her own more severe than ever in her life before; she had partially forgiven him, had recognized truth in what he said, an unparalleled honesty. What he was he openly showed to the world, which could despise him or love him; the opinions of others had no power over his righteousness.

With him close to her like this, the warmth of him felt, she found that the horror of those falling, mutilated bodies was slowly ebbing, now difficult to recall. Now he was gentle, a calm sea after a storm—like a lioness licking her paws and rolling playfully in grass after the kill. Brutality was in him, as much as the raindrop was in the ocean, but you could not call the raindrop the whole sea, any more than you could say that brutality was the whole of this man.

"Harri slew Egil the Champion," Dan said emotionally, "slew him with a throw that Odin could not equal. I am swelling-proud of my son."

Aisha leaned back against the rock wall, relaxing. She made no comment.

"It will be a peaceful winter," Dan said, yawning wide. "Now Freydis will not live in fear for the lives of her children. The Asar do not slay children. —Speaking of vileness. Christians smother, disembowel, behead, and snake-slay women and children. Imagine! Little children!"

"Yes. It is good that Freydis need not worry about the children," Aisha agreed, closing her eyes with a sigh.

CHAPTER SEVENTEEN

The *Gull of the Fiords* limped into harbor on East Main Island shortly after sunset. Mord Baptized-One, rescued from the *Raven of the Wind* and unconscious, was taken ashore on a litter and put on a wagon. Two champions set themselves on the bench of the wagon and drove the four horses inland at breakneck speed.

By midnight the church of Thengil, fortressed with granite walls, was visible under the full moon. The church had been built like a miniature Frankish castle high on a cliff top, approachable only by one side over a moat and a bridge.

The champions identified themselves at the gate, and the drawbridge was lowered. Thengil was awakened by the clatter of wagon wheels over the wood and stone of the bridge. Enraged by the disturbance, he threw a black cloak over his sleeping gown and rushed out of his quarters along shadowed, damp passageways. A long, granite-walled staircase led to the lower floor of the castle. The two champions and their severely wounded chieftain awaited Thengil at the bottom of the stairs.

Thengil's ashen face pinched at the sight of Mord Baptized-One groaning on the litter, his great breast awash with his own blood. The spear had been cut, leaving the head deep in his body. The wound was livid and oozing. Thengil demanded to know the outcome of the battle.

"Borgarsfiord has been demolished," one of the champions said emotionally. "We played the fools in Dan Sea-Kingsson's scheme to defeat us."

"God damn you to hell!" Thengil spat down into Mord's twisted face. The chieftain had regained consciousness, but his eyes were glassy and his mouth drooped open stupidly. "Fool! Damned fool."

With that, Thengil sharply ordered one of the heavy-eyed servants who hovered back to give him a knife. He sourly jerked the blade from the hand that offered it, and, careless of Mord's suffering, savagely attempted to gouge the spearhead free, but it had penetrated at an upward angle and was imbedded in the man's shoulder bone.

Mord yowled like an enraged bull. Four men could not hold him down on the litter. He charged Thengil, sent the priest sprawling with a sidearm blow, then hopped off the litter to run like a madman round and round in circles, blood spurting and splashing around him as he whirled crazily, clutching his breast. His champions leaped upon him simultaneously and brought him crashing to the stone floor, where he lay panting and cursing, finally admitting to utter defeat. With a great release of breath he stopped fighting.

Before his glazed eyes Mord saw the Fates laughing at him; behind the Norns stood Jesus Christ with a sword in his hand. Christ was enraged and demanding an eye for an eye in a terrible voice. Then Odin appeared in a cloud of smoke and fire . . . not dead at all, but laughing with the Norns. Christ raged and the Asar gods, one after another, came to laugh. Laughter filled Mord's head, thundered in his ears, rising in volume to become a singular, unending shriek that threatened to explode his brain. The Valkyrias rode across the sky, laughing, but they were not coming to escort him to Valhalla, but flying away from him, disappearing behind the black clouds in the distance, leaving him, laughing at him. Thor sent a lightning bolt. It flashed in Mord's head, burned his eyes; then an inescapable blackness washed over him.

Thengil paced the dank halls of his miniature castle, cursing and muttering vows of reprisal. With the defeat and death of Mord Baptized-One, his Christian force had been reduced from nine hundred to approximately three hundred and twenty. Mord's standard bearer, Thorstein Christiansson, had temporarily been appointed chief over the survivors of Borgarsfiord and South Orkney until an election could be held.

Thorstein Christiansson could not plan an immediate reprisal against Dan Sea-Kingsson. Borgarsfiord had been laid waste, and rebuilding could not begin until timber was shipped in from England and, until winter was over, trees could not be axed. Already he was in debt to Thengil for the foodstuffs that even now fed the homeless under tents beyond this castle wall. When the snows came, the people could not continue to live exposed in tents. No system of banking existed in the northlands, so that all Mord had possessed, of gold and of goods, was invested or vaulted in the homestead. Dan Sea-Kingsson had impoverished the people. Thorstein would call a Thing and demand ships for his odel-men, and monies to pay the debts and provide for the families until rehabilitation was complete. He would get what he asked for, but he did not wish to wait so long, the better part of a year, to take his vengeance. Yet he could not command his men to a war in this season; they would call him a bad leader, refuse to fight, refuse to elect him as their chieftain. Cursed fools. Winter fire-sitting had been the custom of their Nordland ancestors simply because frozen fiords prevented sailing. But these waters were free of ice. Still the custom-worshipping idiots sat before fires all winter as if their bays were not navigable.

On the tenth day of his residence in Thengil's castle, Thorstein found himself the butt of many pointed remarks that questioned his rightness as a Christian. Since he had been Mord Baptized-One's chief counsel, in this castle-church he was considered equally to blame for the humiliating defeat. The dining table was long, the benches fully occupied. No women served or sat on the benches. Thengil allowed no women in his castle. Clerics did all the menial chores, of cooking and stitching, waiting on their superior most humbly and patiently. Thengil had twelve clerics in residence at all times, and not one chosen by him had ever been over the age of twenty years; all were smooth-shaven, graceful of feature and of limb.

As Thengil ate, his eyes flashed across the table to Thorstein Christiansson in sporadic stabs, then back to his plate, or to the lad sitting close beside him. Occasionally he reached aside with a hardly muscled arm and patted the boy's cheek with the palm of his hand, smiling indulgently.

"You have a new favorite today," Thorstein remarked distastefully, not looking at Thengil.

"Yes," Thengil smirked. "Of my twelve apostles I think this one is the fairest, do you not agree?"

"Apostles?" Thorstein asked, frowning bewilderedly.

"You have not read your Bible!" Thengil accused sarcastically.

Flustered, Thorstein shoved a slab of meat into his mouth and solemnly chewed it, hoping to avoid the subject; he had become a Christian out of love for and loyalty to Mord and knew next to nothing about the Bible. He had no idea what an *apostle* was.

"And you call yourself a Christian," Thengil scolded, scowling paternally across the table at Thorstein. "Allowing Christ's enemies to trick you that way. A child would have known better than to—"

Thorstein said defensively, "We had every reason to trust Dan Sea-Kingsson's appearance on the bay. He is—was supposed to be a man of strict ethics. He was the sinner, not Mord Baptized-One or myself!"

"You are a damned fool!' Thengil raged, waving his wooden spoon over the table. "Sinner . . . because you failed our Lord. You failed Christ!"

The boy beside Thengil leaned close and whispered in the priest's ear. Thengil laughed appreciatively and reached under the table to press the youth's knee with a moist hand.

"Christ will forgive us," Thorstein said hopefully.

Thengil's head shot round. "Oh, I would not be too certain of *that*. It is only through me that you can receive redemption, and I am definitely not disposed to speak to Christ on your behalf. To be frank with you, I am inclined to wash my hands of you, to leave you to an eternity in Hell."

"Hell! For losing a *battle*?"

"For failing and humiliating God and Christ, you fool!"

Thorstein stared open-mouthed at the priest. "I . . . I had concluded that I humiliated *myself*, but not—"

"A personal failure, indeed, in every way. I cannot imagine how you can rectify it, unless . . ." He deliberately let his words trail off.

"I do not have the wherewithal for the arming of a retaliatory fleet, you know that."

"You insult me, Thorstein Christiansson. As a priest of Christ I am charitable; I do not take . . . I *give*. In your time of need you can depend on my Christian generosity, I assure you."

Thorstein scowled, once more bewildered. Also, he was disturbed by the edge of hysterical or insane purpose behind Thengil's studied calm. He squirmed on the bench and made no comment.

"I am stunned to see that you are so bad a Christian," Thengil said around a mouthful of red wine, "that you will refuse to fight, to retaliate, for Christ. Do not deny it, I can see it all over you. Christ wants all men of the north in league with him, and you spit in his face with your reticence. The truth? Well, speak up! The truth, eh?"

Thorstein placed both palms flat on the tabletop and met Thengil's eyes squarely. The priest was not pressing for a retaliation, but a religious purge. "Ingolf Jarl, Bishop of Nordland, has vowed Christ desires a *peaceful* conversion of these islands," he said uneasily.

"Ah? Is that so? Who told you this? Your reluctant champions. Your pagan, Odin-worshipping vassals, I wager, who would, of course, prefer that you not use force."

"I heard it from Thorfinn the Mighty, a man who knows not the meaning of falsehood!"

"Hah!" Thengil laughed sharply in disgust. "Thorfinn Jarl does not splash blood upon pagan idols in pagan temples, I suppose? The pillars at each side of Thorfinn Jarl's highseat are false gods, yet his mouth speaks only truth?"

"What is it you want of me?" Thorstein exclaimed, leaning forward over the table in his intensity.

"Your aid," Thengil replied with a thin smile, "in a quick, sure conversion of that petty kingdom called North Orkney, ruled by Dan Sea-Kingsson, pagan."

"*My* aid! I have no ships, no monies! Half my force has been sent to the gods—to Christ."

Thengil shook his head and clacked his tongue, as he would with an incorrigible child. "A full-scale war will not be necessary, Thorstein. I can obtain ships from good Christians who are, admittedly, too few, but more than willing."

"Then let *them* convert Dan Sea-Kingsson. I am not a priest. You do your work and I will do mine!"

"Thorstein! I want Dan Sea-Kingsson on his *knees*, or his *head*!"

Thorstein's mouth dropped open in surprise at Thengil's passionately murderous word and tone . . . the Church hated blood.

Thengil repeated himself, "On his knees to me, or dead, Thorstein."

"Our desires, more or less, coincide," Thorstein said uncomfortably, "but—"

"But *what,* eh? You will reestablish a fleet and take it to Dansfiord."

Thorstein bit his lower lip, his glance sliding over, behind and around Thengil, never resting directly upon the priest. "We will slay only Dan Sea-Kingsson and those of his retinue that resist us," he said at last, questioningly.

"Oh, no, Thorstein Christiansson. That is not the way it will be. I want his wife, his children, his mother and every man, woman and child on his odel. I want them *all* . . . for Christ."

"No!" Thorstein shook his head violently. "No, priest," pounding his fists on the table. "If Christ is so hungry for the slaughter of the innocent and women who carry no arms, He can come to earth and slay them Himself. I do not slay defenseless children, or—"

"Slay!" Thengil shouted, looking pained. "Did I say a *word* about slaying anyone?"

"You said—"

"I said—exactly—that I would have Dan Sea-Kingsson on his knees before me, or have his head. He will kneel. Believe me, Thorstein, he *will* kneel."

Thorstein's face twisted as he considered the possibility of Dan Sea-Kingsson being forced to his knees before Thengil. "No," he said, shaking his head vigorously, "I know the man. Dan Sea-Kingsson is not capable of succumbing to threats. If any man is, Dan is the equal of Odin!"

"*Odin*? The equal of Odin, perhaps, but not of Christ. —There are ways—methods. And no killing will be necessary. A knife to the pretty young throat, eh?

No more will be necessary. He will drop to his knees and beg me to—"

"I would defeat him *proudly*!" Thorstein cried, greatly agitated now.

"Christ hates pride, Thorstein. But when Dan Sea-Kingsson has been baptized, I will allow you to play pride games with him. I can hardly wait to see him in Hell, and let it be sooner than later. But first he will be *baptized*."

"Since you have such a strong desire to do this thing, and have the wherewithal, then do it yourself and leave me and my poor beaten people out of it!"

"Ridiculous! I cannot step ashore at Dansfiord without a substantial force behind me, expecting to prevail against so many. Even with the number of men you can spare me, we will need to be full of tricks. . . . I will tolerate no warning in advance. Such heroic gestures may have pleased Odin and Thor, but Christ considers such warnings utterly stupid, if not sinful. . . . The plans have been made. I will go ashore with only my personal retinue. Your task will be to guard us against a large-scale onslaught when our real purpose is discovered. In this way you will pay your debt to Christ and save your soul from damnation. But if it is hellfire you—"

"You will be driven from the Orkneys as veum . . . a wolf in the sanctuary! Your men will not follow you on such a mission, never."

"You have forgotten, Thorstein Christiansson, that I have the might of King Magnus behind me, and that of Ingolf Jarl. Any means to the end. Any means."

Thorstein sucked in a breath and held it. On an

outrush of air from his lungs, he said, "I will think about it." He sourly rose to his feet.

"Yes, you think upon it," Thengil purred, smiling up at the man. "I will pray you do not die before you have made peace with our Lord. Hm?"

"What I seek is peace within *myself*," Thorstein snapped. "My mind swims. Why has Christ not struck me dead, I ask myself, if He is so enraged by my defeat at Borgarsfiord?"

"Because He has hope of you, Thorstein; he does. A man like you can cut a path for Christianity across these lands, win the Orkneys in His name. You, because you are now, with Mord's death, the most powerful man under Him in all the world."

"Now flattery," Thorstein complained, turning to stride out of the room.

"He will not expect an attack in the winter," Thengil called after him.

Thorstein called over his shoulder, "And in the winter you will not get men to leave their fires."

"We will see about that. . . . A good night's sleep to you, Thorstein Christiansson."

Snow began to fall in earnest the first week after Aisha's return from Borgarsfiord, and it did not cease for three days and nights. The addition to David's house had been completed in her absence and now served as private quarters for her and Ajib. The surrounding fields and hills quickly vanished under an ethereal white blanket that constantly altered shape at the creative whim of the wind. It became more and more difficult for men to bring food up the cliff and across the plain, the path for horses closed by deep drifts. Snow had also begun to pile up along the sides of the little house; it built up on the steeply pitched roof, then slid off in miniature avalanches until the cottage was buried in the stuff. Then it became necessary to exit from the house by a high window, and the only means of moving about outside was with snowshoes.

The babies were thriving, but growing pale from lack of sunlight, and fussy due to breathing the stale, smoke-filled air of the house. Smoke from the fireplace was a constant irritation to the eyes and the lungs; if the winds were wrong, and they usually were, the smoke was pushed back into the house through the roof hole from which it was supposed to escape. The two main rooms had become a veritable prison. At first David had attempted to keep up his schedule of four or five hours of exercise each day, but came down with so many wheezing infections of the lungs and throat that he admitted to partial defeat and resigned himself to snowshoe-running for an hour every morning.

The men who had in the autumn surrounded the house as guards of Aisha's person had dismantled their tents and taken up residence again at the compound. It was extremely unlikely that Aisha would attempt to go anywhere, or that anyone of ill-repute would venture to so lonely a spot to do her harm. All Orkney men of good repute or bad sat before fires, playing with their children, perfecting their chess games and harp playing, or snoozing lazily in their chairs before fires.

Ajib was passionately restless, incessantly pacing and grumbling about his fate. By now his wives would have forsaken him as dead. His property would be computed and dispersed equally between them and the children.

His entire life had been destroyed. How could Allah have done such a thing to him?

Aisha occasionally suggested to her son that no one had asked him to gamble his future for her sake, and he would effusively apologize, then be right back at complaining again. She began to study him closely; it was as if he were a complete stranger to her. She saw in him characteristics that she had never noticed before. It was apparent to her that she had badly spoiled him because he was often petty, selfish, inconsiderate, and always impossibly smug about his personal superiority over these "Northmen pagans." He had improvised a backgammon board and pieces, and she played with him whenever the children did not demand her attention, which was not often. When she left him alone at the board he would pout for hours afterward.

For herself it was not as difficult as it was for David and Ajib. For both men this winter hibernation was a cross to bear, but for her there was a certain tranquility, and the babies filled her days with joy. David felt stalled in his purpose. Soon an ecclesiastical mission would arrive to inspect his progress, and as of the moment it was nil—only three baptized infants and not one true convert. He had apparently been forgotten by the priest Thengil. No more silver coins had arrived to carry him through the remainder of the year, his money bag nearly empty. His lifetime in a monastery aided him in his adjustment to close confinement, but his mind held purposes now that strained at the reins of his patience.

One day blended into the next, indistinguishable from the other. A storm raged for an entire week, battering the land with intermittent sleet and rain. The rain turned the already high snow to slush, which seeped through the turf walls and roof to create a steaming dampness inside the house. Then the sky cleared and the temperature dropped severely, freezing solid all that had just been reduced to slush. The next day clouds came and dumped a foot of snow over the ice.

After a month of almost complete enclosure, Aisha was giving the babies their morning baths before the fire. The supply of dried dung was low, and she commented over her shoulder to Ajib that he or David would have to trek to the compound, or they would have no fire and freeze to death. Worst of all, they would have no warm baths.

"David can go," Ajib muttered sullenly. He was playing chess against an invisible opponent, sourly studying the positions on the board before him.

"I am not master enough of the snowshoes," David remarked from where he lay flat on his back with his head resting on back-folded arms. "I have an unreasonable fear of sinking. I was nearly buried alive yesterday when I was clearing frozen snow from the roof."

"Well! I hope you two are not expecting *me* to fetch the dung for our fires." She playfully splashed water into little Joseph's laughing face.

A cry sounded from outside. David jumped to his feet and stepped up on the chair placed under the high window. He opened the shutters and peered out the window through the membrane that enclosed it. "It is Dan Sea-Kingsson," he exclaimed in surprise. "He has brought what we need, I think . . . an enormous bundle of it. Food also, I hope."

"Well, let the man in," Aisha said crossly.

"Hark the conquering hero," Ajib remarked nastily. He got to his feet and stomped into the addition, jerking the heavy drapery closed over the entrance.

David clumsily struggled with the metal window frame that held the membrane fast. At last he loosened it. Wind from outside snapped the transparent stuff into his face and sent loose objects falling all over the room, odd articles of baby clothing fluttering about like gulls before a storm.

"Are you all well?" Dan shouted through the window hole.

"We are well," David shouted back. "Come in and get yourself warm."

"I am warm," Dan laughed, leaning his head down to peer inside. He wore a thick hood of fur and a voluminous cloak of rhandeer skin.

"Come in, or *go away*," Aisha cried. "The babies will catch their deaths."

"There is to be a feast," Dan shouted in to Aisha. "I thought you would enjoy a respite."

"No, thank you," she shouted, wrapping little Mary in a small wool blanket.

"She said, 'No, thank you,' " David called from his position at the window.

A canvas bag was thrown in, almost knocking David down. Then Dan's legs shot through the opening. He landed in the center of the room. David fought against the wind, managing to get the shutters closed and fastened.

Dan soberly inspected the small room, taking note of its neatness, the pleasant arrangement of the few pieces of furniture. Aisha kept her back to him as she dressed the baby she had just bathed. "I will have to insist once again," he said agreeably, stepping up behind Aisha. "You cannot hibernate here like a mother bear."

"I am perfectly content," she coldly assured him.

"Truly? Then I shall not have to concern myself about seeing you returned to Cairo City."

She whirled round to face him. "That is unfair! You know perfectly well what I meant."

Dan nodded and turned to David. "Get her a cloak and boots."

Aisha sighed exasperatedly. "Will this harassment never cease? Why do you not just leave me be?"

"Woman, if I forgot about you for two full days you would freeze to death up here, and begin to get very hungry. Eh? Anyway, you are not the type of woman to be so near to me . . . and forgotten."

"I must care for the babies," she argued weakly.

"They can manage for a day and a night without you. Besides, it is not only your charming company I seek. I have something of great importance to discuss with you. There is no privacy here, and this is a matter that is personal to me, that I would not discuss before strangers." He grinned wickedly. "It is likely that you will become angrier with me than ever before, and you would not want the sweetest Christ lover on earth to see you losing your temper, now would you?"

"You are definitely going to insist."

"Definitely."

"Did you bring milk and bread?"

"I did."

She shrugged defeatedly and moved to put her arms into the fur-lined cloak David already held up for her.

She struggled with the snug, heavy boots. Dan came to her aid, pushing them on and fastening the bindings.

Ajib stuck his head out of the addition door drapery, making a token protest that Dan frozenly ignored.

"I brought skis for you."

"What?" she wailed, pushing herself awkwardly out of the chair she had been sitting upon. "I cannot slide about on those slats of woods!"

"There has to be a first time," Dan laughed.

"You could have brought a sled!"

"I could have, but I did not," he grinned, moving to the window to open the shutters.

Aisha shivered at just the thought of going outside, drawing up the hood of her cloak and bravely stepping forward. Dan took her in his hands around the waist and hoisted her upward and out. She fell flat on the snow and clung there, not daring to move for fear of sinking deep into the stuff, though the surface was nearly as hard as the earth. Then Dan was beside her. He rolled her over and tied wooden slats to her boots. David said a cheerless good-bye and the shutters banged closed.

The sky was a brilliant blue and cloudless, the air electric. Aisha's breath left her mouth in clouds of smoke. When Dan had securely fastened slats to his own boots, he reached down for her hand, hauling her up, steadying her with an arm around her. He put two thin poles into her gloved hands, telling her to use them for balance. Then he put a rope around her, tying the other end around himself.

"I will tow you," he said optimistically. "All you have to do is steady yourself. You cannot slide away from me; the rope and my strength, which is limitless, will hold you. . . . Shall we give it a try?"

"No," Aisha said flatly, her heart thumping in her breast.

Dan laughed and set his poles into the snow so that his slats slid very slowly over the icy surface. The rope went taut and Aisha rocked on her skis, forward, arching back, bending at the waist against the pull of the rope. Miraculously she caught her balance and slid along behind him, teetering on occasion but remaining upright.

"Lift your feet . . . this way," Dan shouted at her over his shoulder. "Stepping, you see? Walk the skis, pointing the tips outward, ducklike."

She tried to imitate his effortless strides, but the point of one slat went east while the other went west, and her body fell into the middle. She screeched for help, thinking her legs were breaking; she was tied in a knot. Dan quickly put her upright again, with both slats pointing north.

"Just slide behind me, then," he said, amused, then set off across the field of snow at a slow pace.

Soon a hill loomed before them. Dan easily hauled her behind him, but when he halted at the crest, drawing Aisha up to stand beside him, she cried out, "Great Allah! You cannot be thinking of sending me over this *brink*!"

"You are not a very courageous woman, are you?" Dan grinned teasingly.

"You are absolutely correct!" she gasped, staring wide-eyed down the treacherous slope.

"It is not nearly as steep as it appears," he assured her as he loosened and removed the rope from round her. "You can see that it dips up again at the bottom. When you reach the gully, you can only come to a halt. . . . Give it a try, eh?" With that, Dan gave her a gentle push that set the skis in motion.

Aisha choked on a screech of protest that froze in her throat. She wobbled for an instant, fighting for balance. Her heart raced as she plummeted at an appalling speed. But before she reached the gully she was laughing excitedly, arms and poles flailing; she was actually managing to remain upright. She swept up the rise, halted in her tracks for suspended moments, then did two backward flips and nose-dived into a deep drift.

"Excellent!" Dan exclaimed as he dug her out and hauled her up. "Truly, that was very good. You have an excellent sense of balance."

Aisha brushed snow off her face, laughing. "It was quite exciting, really. But rather dangerous. One could break one's bones this way."

Dan smiled down into her rosy face, reaching to brush a bit of snow from her cheek. "The most exciting and rewarding things in life are often as not the most dangerous."

"I have known very little excitement," she said uneasily, avoiding his probing eyes.

"*Lately* you have not led an unexciting life."

"No!" she laughed. "I meant . . . before."

"Every hour of my life has been exciting," Dan said sincerely. "I harbor not a single regret, would not alter a moment of it. That I might never have strode this earth, heard Thor's thunder in the heavens, tasted the delicious tang of living on my tongue . . . is the only horror I can conceive. I would not have wanted to miss this existence of mine."

Aisha felt enclosed. He stood a mountain before her, and the snow rose a mountain behind her. Her face was flushed; it was painful to be so close to him like this. Again she was flustered, had lost her self-containment.

"Was it truly a good life for you in Cairo City, Aisha?" he asked, putting his hands on her amply covered shoulders, attempting to capture her eyes.

"Oh, yes, it was. I was never discontent. I was born to great wealth, you know . . . my father a jeweler and very good to me."

His blue eyes roved her face. "Within a prison, guards set upon you all your days, an ancient one to lie with and no other, but you were content?"

"Believe me, it is true!" she exclaimed, her eyes flashing up to meet his, then darting away again. "Is it so difficult to conceive? Our customs are as time-honored as your own. I was raised knowing what my future would be, and I looked forward to it. We have our codes of honor, as you do. I would not have dishonored my father by criticizing his choice of husband for me, or by bewailing. In truth, I never questioned that choice."

"How sad," he said, brushing her chin with a forefinger.

"Sad! If I were to talk about *your* ways, I would ask you . . . how can Freydis endure the loneliness? You are at sea more than half the year. And how does she bear the dread every time you go to battle, knowing you might not return? And giving her son away to whomever you choose."

"Muslim women lose their sons when the lads are the same age," he argued softly.

"Not so completely. At least our husbands see that they visit us often. Your son is entirely beyond his mother's love and concern. I think your customs are abominable. But then, contentment is truly dependent upon what one expects from life, what one is bred to."

"True, I suppose," he admitted. "But I set no guards upon Freydis. Her loneliness has been assuaged occasionally by other men. But you have lived like a silkworm, born in a cocoon and never released to fly; you have been neither worm nor butterfly. One is given a life and should live it to the fullest."

"I have lived a wonderful life! I harbor no regrets, either. What gall I would have to cry against a fate that birthed me in a palace, that offered me all there was of luxury, security and high status . . . while all around the world people live lives of abject want and despair. I could not have all there was; no one can."

"But *this*," he whispered, leaning down to put his mouth lightly against hers. She did not pull away. "This," he said again against her lips, "cannot be said to be a small thing." He moved his mouth to her eyes and brushed her lashes with his lips. "I would like to see you emerge, fly from your cocoon . . . to nest in my arms. On this altar of snow, life is making an offering to you. You cannot have everything, that is true, but you *can* have this."

He kissed her hard then, his arms tightening round her, until her lips parted and their breaths mingled. When he released her, Aisha whirled away from him, her head spinning, her stomach, too. "As Allah is my witness," she swore, "I will not love you."

"But you will. Any day now. I told you that you would and I still think so."

"I am going to return to my home . . . to Cairo City!"

"Perhaps you will. But in the meantime there is your life to be lived, and my determination to contend with. I have never known the body of a Saracen matriarch and have decided the experience would nicely round out my life. Willing or not, eventually I will take you. I prefer my women willing."

With that, he hastily refastened the ropes and proceeded up the rise. Within an hour the compound was visible from a promontory. Dan removed their skis and helped Aisha descend the icy, bare rock face that was so steep snow could not cling to it. Steps had been carved out. They made the slow descent without incident.

Snow had been cleared around the compound to a modest depth so that progress could be made without the skis. Dan led Aisha to the loft where she had first dwelt and left her at the bottom of the staircase, saying he would come for her in two hours. She would find gowns and jewels to be worn at the feast. A thrall would bring hot water and perfumes for her bath.

"Greetings," Nur al Huda said smartly as Aisha entered the room and stood at the entrance with her hand still on the door, as if she were thinking of turning and running away again.

Aisha glanced up and stared at the girl who was lounging on the bed. The child she carried was showing a little. She did not know what to say to her.

"Great Allah! Take off your cloak and boots; you are dripping all over the tapestry."

Aisha fumbled with the cloak. "Have you been well, dear?"

"Certainly," Nur al Huda snapped.

"I have not seen you . . . not since . . ."

"I told you; I have been excellent . . . extremely well."

"Yes, well . . . I am glad."

"If you are glad, Allah is a toad!"

"Nur al Huda!"

"I pity Dan Sea-Kingsson, I truly do." She lay flat on her back now, her arms folded back under her head. "Poor man. When he enters you, if he can ever break through the ice, he will freeze his tail solid."

Aisha squeezed her eyes closed and whirled round to avoid the sight of the bitter, snarling woman, a person she would never understand; never. With shaking hands she removed her damp gown. A green silk robe lay over a chair near the washtub, of Saracen design with vermilion satin trousers to wear beneath. Dan had either had the clothing made for her, or he had purchased it especially. She felt a warmth in her breast at the show of thoughtfulness.

"Exquisite, is it not?" Nur al Huda said behind her. "One pretty gown, the price he has to pay for you. An old woman like you playing the reluctant virgin. It just *sickens* me, it truly does."

Aisha could not maintain her studied indifference. She whirled on the girl and shouted, "No more than your utter lack of morality sickens me! When you are my age, as you say, old, you will find that there is more to think about than the moment—more to think about than the slot between your legs. Since I am not as stupid as you, I will not carry a brood of Asar brats back to Cairo City with me."

"Hah! I would rather have ten of Harri's children than *one* from that withered, disgusting prune that was our dear departed husband. Ooh, the ecstasy you must have enjoyed. Tell me, Aisha, how the touch of his wrinkled, quaking hands made you shiver to your very depths. Go on, tell me!"

Seething and red-faced, Aisha cried, "Kamar al Zamen was only forty years and five when I married him, and he was *not* disgusting in any way. He was a sainted man and I loved him dearly." Her voice broke and tears burned behind her eyes. "He was terribly good to me, and . . . and I will miss him the rest of my days."

"Go on, say it again; perhaps you might convince yourself." Nur al Huda laughed stridently, playfully kicking her legs in the air as if dancing on the ceiling she stared at. "You think me a fool. Well, I cannot think of a bigger fool than one who lives under a spell of self-deception. You have been whoring after Dan Sea-Kingsson since the first moment you saw him. I remember so well how you watched him in the garden, your mouth watering like—"

"I withdraw my protection!" Aisha shrieked, entirely out of control. "You—you can rot here on this Allah-forsaken island! May Allah curse you unfalteringly with tragedies and heartbreaks!"

Nur al Huda lazily got to her feet and strolled toward the door, the expression on her face one of extreme satisfaction. From a wall hook she took down her cloak. At the door she turned and said emotionally, "If I had to spend an hundred eternities in hell, I would do it, for just one more day with Harri, whether as his wife or as his slave."

CHAPTER EIGHTEEN

The great hall was not crowded. Fires burned with little success, sweeping drafts forcing the guests to keep themselves well shawled. The atmosphere was subdued, though cheerful. Men and women sat quietly together on benches in groups, pursuing mundane conversations. Odel-men, their wives and followers, had come in smallboats from the nearby islands. Feasts were relied upon as one of the few pleasurable occasions available to them in the fire-sitting season.

Dan had left his highseat to wander along the aisles between benches, halting to kneel before a friend and join in the conversation, then rising and moving on until another friend halted him or he was attracted by what was being said.

Freydis was, as usual, cheerfully bustling about, keeping herself ahead of the needs of her guests, directing her thralls with complete efficiency. She managed to avoid looking at Aisha with a determination that would lead her guests to believe she did not know the creature in the silk trousers existed; certainly, the Saracen was no threat to her. A passing fancy, no more; she had convinced herself of this and no amount of warnings to the contrary or predictions of doom from Gudrid Mother could persuade her to think otherwise. She herself had never matched Dan's vision of his dream woman. That puny Saracen was so far removed from his ideal that she was amazed he managed to desire her. Strange indeed were the ways of men. She would allow it to run its course and, in the end, have him all to herself just as before.

Gudrid leaped to the platform and silenced the harpists. A hush fell upon the assembly. She waved her arms and called for the attention of everyone and received it quickly. "I shall tell you a tale," she shouted to the crowd.

An encouraging hue and cry went up. "Tell us the saga of Vinland," someone shouted at her.

"Ah." Gudrid grinned, throwing her great arms over her head expansively. "Odin as my witness, those were exciting, brave days."

Dan smiled up at Gudrid. He had heard the tale at least a thousand times, he was certain. His eyes slid round the room and he noticed Aisha standing back near his highseat, looking lost and impatient. He moved quickly round the benches and strode to her side.

Aisha smiled stiffly at Dan as he approached her.

"My mother will tell the tale of her voyage to Vinland," he said, "the land where I was born."

She let her glance slide distastefully to the far platform, studying the beaded, jangling witch for a moment, then turned her eyes back to Dan. "How nice," she commented dryly.

"Truly, it is a pity you cannot understand our language. It is an exciting tale, the more so because it is all true, not a tale of fancy at all."

"Then you tell it to me in Arabic . . . translate," Aisha suggested unenthusiastically.

"I could never tell it with the flair, the drama that my mother gives to the tale."

"Try," she suggested flatly, sitting down on the floor of the highseat platform.

Dan sat down beside her and began to speak in low tones that would not disturb those nearby who were avidly listening to Gudrid's piercing voice, reacting delightedly to her.

Dan's father, Thorfinn Karlsefni, was the son of Thord Hesthofdi, who was the son of Snorri, who was the son of Thord. Karlsefni, a wealthy chieftain of Nordland, had stayed as a winter guest with Leif Ericsson in Greenland thirty-three winters past. There Karlsefni met Gudrid, the widow of Thorstein, brother of Leif Ericsson. Their wedding took place that winter, for quick and great was the love between them.

Around the fire as they fire-chatted, Karlsefni learned from Leif the tale of Bjarni, who had been storm-tossed en route to Greenland and came upon a strange shore far west overseas. Not daring to stop, for his provisions were low, Bjarni sailed only a small distance south along the strange coast, then set a course north, then east, at last finding Greenland.

Leif Ericsson spoke of his own voyage west in search of the land Bjarni had discovered, telling Karlsefni about the wealth of grape vines there, for which he had named the land Vinland. And great forests on a land with no frost in winter, the grass losing little of its freshness. He had explored the land north and south for a full year, having built booths to house his retinue. Leif had returned to Greenland with wine from the sweet grapes and with much fine timber.

The next winter Leif's brother, Thorvald, had set sail for Vinland, only to be slain by *skraeling,* wild men who rode the sea and the rivers in skin boats. Then Leif's younger brother, Thorstein, sailed for Vinland with his young wife, Gudrid, now Karlsefni's wife, but was tossed upon rocks just off Greenland. Thorstein and his crew were rescued, but Leif's young brother became fevered and died soon after, widowing Gudrid.

Karlsefni was very excited about the new land and vowed he would seek that strange, far shore. He received a ship from Leif, which he manned with sixty men and five women, including his bride, Gudrid. He would equally divide all the goods he brought back from Vinland with Leif, as the price for lending the *ship.* He took all kinds of domestic animals, for he intended to settle there. Leif Ericsson said he would lend Karlsefni the booths he had built on the Vinland shore, but he would not give them to him, because he planned to claim the land under the booths for himself one day; he and his people would migrate there.

Karlsefni set sail, and after three days they lost sight of land. Fair winds ceased and northern winds with fog blew for many days, so that they did not know in which direction they were drifting. When the cloud cover broke and they were able to distinguish the quarters of heaven, they hoisted sail again and sailed west a full day before sighting land. They did not know if this was Vinland. Drawing nearer the land mass, they saw that there were no mountains and no grass, only glaciers like plains of ice—not a good land at all, nothing like Leif Ericsson's descriptions of Vinland. It must be that place which Leif had named Hellaland, the last land he had sighted and not the first, where he had constructed booths. So they sailed south and found better land. It was flat and forested, with a low beach covered with white sand. This was the place Leif had named Markland.

With a northeast wind they continued to sail another two days south before more land was sighted. Karlsefni was certain that this was Vinland. He threw anchor and put a smallboat over.

On that shore they found dew on the grass, touched it and put it into their mouths, thinking never to have tasted so sweet a dew. There was a channel between an island and the cape that ran north from the mainland. Karlsefni returned to his ship and sailed up the channel in a westerly direction. Eventually the channel became very shallow and the ship went aground. At ebb tide the sea was far out from the ship.

Karlsefni's men were so anxious to go ashore that they could not wait until the high water reached the ship, so they ran out on the beach where a river flowed from a lake. When high water did reach the ship, they towed it upriver into the lake. On the lake shore they discovered the booths built by Leif and used by Thorvald before he was slain by the skraeling.

Meaning to establish a permanent compound, Karlsefni began the construction of large houses with lofts. He had trees cut and laid to dry over rocks. Before the end of summer they were comfortable. The male cattle had been let loose and they quickly became wild, causing a good deal of trouble.

The skraeling showed themselves for the first time late that summer, a host emerging cautiously from the forest near where the cattle were. A bull began to bellow loudly and the natives ran screeching in terror, as if they had never seen cattle before; they took with them the furs they had brought to trade.

"To hear my mother tell it," Dan laughed softly, "those creatures of Vinland were a cross between wolves and demons . . . naked for the most part and face-painted."

"You were born on that strange shore?" Aisha asked, leaning forward with genuine interest now. "At the very end of the world?"

"The natural processes of life went on," he grinned. "It was not all exploring. But my father did explore the land more thoroughly than any man before him, or after him, for that matter. He sent men south in smallboats, and men on foot trekked far inland. No skraeling settlements were ever seen, but the savages began making regular appearances at the compound and were not easily managed."

It was never possible to predict the savages, Dan continued enthusiastically. Weapons were banned as trade goods, for the skraeling might turn them against the settlers. What the savages most desired was milk from the cows, which they took away in their stomachs, having traded rich pelts for the stuff.

The beginning of the second winter brought skraeling in a large host. One tried to steal a spear and was killed. The horde scurried away, but before nightfall skin boats were as dust covering the face of the lake. A raging battle ensued. The settlement had been fortressed with a high gard and was easily held against the onslaught. But the skraeling would not cease their attacks, coming in waves endlessly.

Gudrid became so impatient with the steady attacks that she put herself in armor, took up a weapon and in the midst of the clamor charged out of the compound gate. The skraeling saw a giant white-skinned goddess coming at them, her yellow hair flying in the wind behind her—they heard the fierce war cries erupting from her throat—saw the spear and shield in her hands—and this vision so terrified them that they retreated and never showed themselves again.

"I believe that," Aisha laughed. "She affects me the same way."

"The next autumn my father said he would not stay another winter. He wanted to see Nordland again. He loaded his ship with fine timber, furs, grapes and other fruit from trees. I was two winters old when I was brought ashore at Greenland. My father told Leif Ericsson that he thought the land good, but too isolated and the skraeling too fierce for colonization. It was a rich land indeed, but he would not go there again."

"But this Leif, surely he returned to Vinland?"

Dan shook his head. "Only Freydis, Leif's sister, made the voyage, and very unsuccessfully. She was a bad woman and had men who were against her slain so that the voyage was more a disaster than anything else." He sighed and his eyes became wistful. "I have always dreamed of returning to Vinland. Perhaps I will one day." He added bitterly, "If Christians become too thick here, a man might find peace nowhere else."

"Your people have explored and colonized more of the world than I ever knew existed," she commented admiringly.

"Our blood is like seed on the wind. From the Baltic Sea to Scatia, to Nordland and Denmark . . . then to England and west to Snowland and Greenland. Next, Vinland. I believe there is still more land to the west than either your mind or mine can conceive. My father, no matter how far south he sailed, or how far inland he trekked, saw no end to it. The poison sea, the brink, must be so far away as to be unreachable."

Aisha glanced across the torch-lit hall and gazed upon the old woman telling her tale so enthusiastically and acknowledged a new respect for the witch, for it could not have been an easy voyage or an easy life on that hostile shore. She disliked admitting that the shrew had even one saving grace.

Gudrid had taken a sax from the wall behind her and was now brandishing it carelessly, yowling and feinting, pantomiming her fearless onslaught against the horde of skraeling.

"Is there actually a woman's heart under that armor-hard surface your mother puts between herself and this world?"

"If I asked her, she would slit her throat and receive hel-shoes for me," Dan replied emotionally. "She has lived her life for me since I was born and risked it many times over for my sake." His voice quavered and he looked quickly down at his two hands. He cleared his throat of emotion and said, "When my mother was not yet fifteen years old, she ventured to the wood on a spring day to hunt for deer with bow and arrow . . . she and two young champions who were vying for her hand in marriage. They went far. At sunset they returned, to find that Olaf Trygvasson had come to her father's odel. Her father, Dan, had been snake-slain.

She found her mother hanging by her heels from a timber cross; she had been blood-eagled, her lungs torn out before her husband's and her children's eyes. Her younger brothers and sisters had been suffocated, beheaded and dismembered. No one was left except those thralls and followers of her father who had accepted baptism to Christianity."

"Bismillah!" Aisha gasped.

"My mother was very ill of the mind for a year following the massacre. Relatives in Greenland sent for her, and she went to live with them on that shore."

"In Andalusia it is the same," Aisha said on a sigh. "The Christians battle to push the Muslim farther and farther south. Soon the sea will be their only recourse. In that push southward I have heard that they slaughter our people with a brutality that I had heretofore thought grossly exaggerated. Perhaps the Andalusian tales of horror are true, after all, but it is difficult to believe that any people, particularly Christians, could be so brutish."

"Sometimes, in the night, the memory of that massacre returns to Gudrid," Dan said huskily, "and her screams tear through this house to rend my heart. For love of her, for love of my ancestors, my grandmother and grandfather, I hate that which she hates and fight the battle she raised me to fight. As long as the memory of Gudrid is in me or mine, the fight will continue. When my father, Karlsefni, accepted baptism voluntarily, having been persuaded to the faith by Leif Ericsson, it broke Gudrid's heart. Whatever heart was left in her turned cold, as you have seen it."

"But you have seen that all Christians are not like the brutes who slaughtered Gudrid's family . . . in

David." When Dan merely muttered something unintelligible under his breath, she insisted, "It is true! Admit it."

"I will admit only that, so far, he has kept his sword sheathed. I trust no Christian. Any man addlebrained enough to accept the concept of sin and punishment cannot have much good in him; certainly he is senseless, and only a senseless man would slaughter children in the name of a so-called *gentle* god and savior. . . . All men who are wise know that man is a killer of men, deep in his soul and never to be altered. *All* men, including David of Saint Monica."

Harri and Nur al Huda entered the hall with an arm about each other. As they moved past Dan and Aisha where they sat, Nur al Huda did not glance Aisha's way, but Harri met Dan's eyes fleetingly, a glimmer of defiance sparking in the glance.

Dan grimly followed the couple with squinted eyes, thoughtfully biting his lower lip. Abruptly he got to his feet and ordered Aisha to follow him; he wanted to discuss with her that business he had mentioned at the house of David. He led the way to his personal quarters, then motioned her to take a chair. He began pacing the room, his hands clasped behind him.

"Harri has asked my permission to marry that . . ." Dan was at a loss for words to describe Nur al Huda. "That empty-headed *pest* you persuaded me to protect with offers of gold."

Aisha slapped her forehead with a palm, exclaiming, "The young fool! I cannot believe it."

"He vows to love her with a passion that will outlast eternity." Dan halted his pacing before her and scowled. "Hylmir, Harri's father, is not a man of wealth. He has five other children. What little he possesses will be divided six ways, so that Harri cannot presume to call himself odel-born. I love the lad well, but what I might have given him must be saved for my son, Harald, and the dowers of my three daughters. Harri must marry well if he is to become an odel-man, with many men working his bor."

"Of course," Aisha agreed. "You need not explain the situation to me. I told the wretch that he could not marry her, but she would not listen. . . . She is with child, you know."

"I am not blind," he snapped. "It has come down to this. I waive all right to the ransom you set upon her. I want you to take her to the house of the priest and keep her there."

"Great Allah!" Aisha wailed. "Spare me such a punishment. No matter what other course you must take. To be confined within those four walls with Nur al Huda day in and day out would have the three of us slashing our throats, or each other's, within a week."

"Then I must demean her in Harri's eyes, enthrall her . . . clip her hair over the ears, put her in vadmal and set her to the emptying of chamber pots. She will soon enough lose whatever glow he sees about her, especially as she swells with child." He had said it quickly and now awaited her wrath.

"Excellent idea," Aisha said brightly.

Dan's mouth dropped open in surprise. He frowned confusedly.

"That young woman has some lessons to learn . . . about gratitude to Allah, and respect for her betters. I could think of no better way to soften the meanness in her."

"Well, then . . . it is settled." He was so taken aback by the fact that she made no protest that for long moments he could not find a single word to say to her. "Of course," he said at last, "if . . . when you return to Cairo City you may take her with you. I claim no actual ownership, you understand, since we did agree—"

"As far as I am concerned, you can keep her through eternity. Allah forbid that I should ever have to live in company with her again."

"I see. You will not be forced to share the loft with her tonight. I will have her enthralled immediately."

He strode to his carved oak chair and sat down, staring solemnly into the blazing fire close by. The silence grew between them and Aisha began to fidget in her chair. In an effort to break the uncomfortable silence, she asked, "When will you seek the gold?"

He looked over at her. Their eyes met and held. "When the snows are melted and my fields are sown."

"Will you take me aboard . . . on the search?"

"Yes. And your son, who must show me the place."

"When you have the treasure, could you not leave us on an Andalusian shore, which would be close by?"

"Possibly."

"Why are you so unwilling to promise my return? Why?"

His eyes caressed her face. "It is not yet certain in my mind that you will still wish to return to Cairo City—when this fire-sitting season is over."

"How can you even suggest such a thing to me? As a man you have offered me nothing. I will say this for Harri; he offers Nur al Huda all a man can give, his whole life put over her through the protection of marriage."

"Would you marry me if I asked you?"

"Great Allah, no!"

"Then it would be pointless for me to ask."

"It surely would! I would not tolerate even the smallest burdens that Freydis accepts without question. Frankly, you are not my idea of a husband, if ever I should marry another. Nor could this harsh land ever win me to giving the rest of my life to it. Allah knows how I long to be warm again, to smell the jasmine and the gardenias on soft winds, to sit beside perfumed fountains and pools, to see walls and floors of marble and illumined tile. Egypt Land is Paradise on earth. In comparison, this island is a frozen hell."

Dan raised his eyebrows and shrugged, looking back at the fire.

"I truly cannot understand," she persisted, glaring across the room at his profile, "your determined interest in me. I am older than you. I persistently reject you. I in no way fit your image of ideal womanhood. Surrounded as you are by women, you cannot be hungry for passion; you have been with your wife every night all winter. I think you long for what is withheld from you, like a child insisting upon having the sweetmeat his mother has denied him."

Dan swung his eyes around again, fixing a bemused gaze upon her. "You underestimate yourself. I have thought upon it a great deal, questioned myself along the same lines. It is not so much your beauty, which is as spectacular as a radiant sunrise, but the essence of you—intelligence, spirit, and a sensual, lusty quality that stirs my innards like Ran stirs her husband to froth. It is a thing of the flesh, of man and woman. Who can explain it?"

"I am *not* a lusty woman!" she protested. Faltering, finding the words difficult to say, "I am, in fact, rather . . . I mean to say, I am content to be . . . to be . . ."

"When lies are spoken, the tongue often stumbles," he commented dryly.

"It would be most foolish of me to indulge any—any attraction I feel toward you. I was taught to be a moral person. Within our code of religious ethics no allowances are made for women of sin; hellfire is all they can expect."

Dan eased out of his chair and stretched his arms and shoulders. Then he stepped to her and kneeled at her feet. He took her hands in his and held them lightly. "It has come to an end," he said firmly.

"*What* . . . has ended?" she asked unsteadily, trying to release her hands from his.

He laughed softly. "I suppose you could call it . . . the wooing period. I have waited long enough."

"I—I cannot fight you."

"I would not want you to fight me." He slid his arms around her waist, his head leaning toward her bosom.

"Not here," she whispered, her head spinning.

"Why not here, hmm?"

"Come to the loft . . . in an hour. I will bathe . . . and I wish to be properly . . ." She lost the gist of what she wanted to say.

He got to his feet and made a flourishing arm toward the door. She rose from her chair and stepped past him, feeling a flush burning her cheeks. It had been nearly ten years since Kamar al Zamen had ceased calling her to his bed; she had been only twenty and three years of age. All the way to the loft that thought sounded in her mind like wind in a cave—ten years . . . ten years.

When Aisha had left him, Dan marched iron-jawed through the house, striding purposefully into the great hall. His eyes skimmed searchingly around the room. He saw Harri's white head rising above the crowd near the fireplace. Elbowing past guests who blocked his path, he quickly confronted the young lovers.

Harri looked up and saw his foster father coming, instantly recognizing his expression as warlike. His arm flew out and caught hold of Nur al Huda, and he hauled her close to his side and held her tight. "No," he whispered to Dan when his foster father stood before him. "Please. Leave us be."

Dan studied Harri's stricken face, a hot pity for the boy surging in him. "Curse you, you young fool. Why did you drive me to this? I have no wish to hurt you."

"Harri?" Nur al Huda murmured, her black eyes leaping from one man to the other.

Dan stepped forward and caught the wench up in his arms, jerking her from Harri's hold with a violent twist of his body. Nur al Huda screamed, terrified, kicking and thrashing as Dan strode swiftly out of the hall with her.

Harri fell back against the fireplace wall, his eyes closed tight, his heart pounding against his ribs. He loved them both. He could not lay a hand on Dan Sea-Kingsson, or speak a curse against him. Odin knew how much he loved his foster father. Odin knew. He whipped round and beat his fists against the wall in a wild outburst of rage and frustration, his piercing cries causing the hum of the crowd to abruptly become a deep silence behind him. He felt the eyes of the multitude upon him, as well as the eyes of Odin and Thor. He whirled round and ran from the hall, following the sound of Nur al Huda's screams from the cookroom. He shoved the door open and stumbled inside.

"Oh, Harri!" Nur al Huda sobbed. "Oh, Harri! Stop them!"

She had been stripped of noblewoman's attire. White vadmal had been thrown over her head. Two thrall men held her as Dan took a sharp knife to her knee-length hair. Freydis moved out of shadow and stepped to Harri. She put a hand on his arm to indicate her understanding of his pain, and to warn him against any action that he might regret the rest of his life.

"I will love her until my dying day!" Harri cried, wrenching his arm from Freydis' hand. He rushed forward, shouldered Dan aside and put his arms around Nur al Huda's waist, laying his head on her breast. "No cutting of her hair or rough cloth will alter my feelings," he insisted against her bosom.

Dan paid Harri no mind. He kept on slashing the silken shawl of hair; pieces dropped upon Harri's head and back like great black tears, clinging to his shirt and trousers.

Nur al Huda wept hysterically, but made no further effort to prevent Dan's determined shearing; half her hair was gone already. She stroked Harri's head with a shaking hand, clung to him. Then he was pulled away from her by his determined father.

"If I cannot marry her, give her to me as a concubine," Harri pleaded tearfully. "I will love and protect her always. It matters not to me what she is called, wife, or slave . . . or concubine." Harri took hold of Dan's arm in his urgency. "My father . . . I implore you!"

Stone-faced, Dan jerked the girl to her feet by an arm and shoved her into the hands of a thrall woman. "Take her to the hovel of Jenny," he ordered, "and give her the chamber pots as task, and fish cleaning, and linen bleaching."

Harri fell back, horror and despair on his face. "Give her to me, please!"

Dan threw up his hands angrily. "Without aurar or odel, with only one deed of valor to your credit, you will take on the support of a concubine? Ridiculous! First, you will design your future, beginning by marrying well. Then you will build your fame and fortune. After all that has been accomplished, you may consider taking a concubine. . . . Now, take yourself to your quarters and praise Odin's name that you have a father as concerned about your best welfare and your future glory as I am."

Freydis stood back from it all, closely watching Dan's face. She saw detachment in his eyes in spite of his deep concern and urgency; the woman was on his mind. Inwardly she shook with a kindling jealousy, sensing the lust hot in him, but she held her face expressionless. He would not come to her this night. Gudrid Mother had made an accurate prediction. Dan had taken a concubine into his own life. Telling herself she had been extraordinarily fortunate in having him entirely to herself these twelve years, she tried to put out the fire in her breast, but it only grew hotter. She knew that he had taken a few unknown women in these years of their marriage on his long voyages, but they were exactly that—unknown, only shadows. This woman was under her own roof, and she could see the dark and exotic beauty that enticed him. For a moment she despised her own large frame and cool blondness. She could not divorce Dan for only one offense. A man had to many times commit adultery and witnesses had to be brought forth before it could be accepted as grounds for divorce. If a man was wealthy and powerful, a concubine was accepted under the law. But she would not divorce Dan for any reason—what a foolish thought.

Then Freydis' mind wandered to Thorvald the Black, who had approached her suggestively tonight, and she was cheered somewhat. It gave her comfort to think upon a spiteful union with the champion, even if she had no intention of accepting his offer.

Dan was unable to wait the entire hour out. He made a hasty exit from the cookroom, leaving the despondent Harri to Freydis. He moved swiftly through the anteroom, stepped out into the freezing night without a cloak and rushed up the loft steps.

Aisha was not there. Her cloak and boots were gone. Instantly he was in motion, leaping down the staircase. He plunged into the house, grasped hold of a torch and threw a cloak around him, then exploded out into the moonlighted night. Her tracks were clear on the hard-crusted snow. He found her sprawled at the base of the low cliff, shivering and weeping. Taking her up in his arms, he ran back to the loft with her, taking the stairs up two and three at a time.

Dan put Aisha gently down on the bed, hastily removing her boots and cloak, examining her for broken bones. He leaned back in relief; she was unhurt.

"What were you running away from?" he asked softly, kneeling beside the bed, gently brushing her cheek with a fingertip.

Aisha covered her face with her arms and shook her head, refusing to answer him.

Dan got to his feet and went to close and bolt the door. Then he put the torch to the braziers and blew on each bed of dried fuel until they flamed. He returned to the bed and stood beside it, gazing down on Aisha for long moments. She refused to look at him. He carefully eased himself onto the bed beside her, lying flat on his back and making no move to touch her. They did not speak. Soon the flames on the braziers began to warm the room. On impulse Dan got up, removed all his clothing, then returned to lie beside her again. His flesh gleamed white as ivory in the flickering light, except for his neck and face, which were bronzed by sun and winds, and his hands. Every tendon and muscle in his body was sharply defined; he was as carved from marble.

"It will be your decision," Dan said softly at last, his head turned to her, his eyes evidencing a tension that belied his studied calm. "I will lie here like this to tempt you, to show you what I am and what I have to offer. In all my life I have never taken a woman who truly loathed me, who truly did not want me."

Aisha remained rigid beside him. She felt him as ice feels a fire—the flesh closest to him beginning to melt, while the other side shivered still. Ten years. *Never* a young man. But Kamar al Zamen had been so handsome, so gentle; his kisses had been like the touch of butterfly wings upon her breasts, her stomach . . .

She started when Dan cleared his throat and moved slightly, thinking he was going to touch her now. But he remained like a statue there beside her, melting her; her heart was crazily dancing under her ribs. This was ridiculous. Did he actually expect her to make the first move? She could not, not possibly. Great Allah, she could not even look at him; if she did she would succumb.

Aisha slowly turned her head and met Dan's eyes, stunned by what she saw there—an almost blinding urgency that spoke volumes. He wanted more from her than mere physical contact, more than relief. In his desire there was a need to capture her very soul and hold it—not for just the moment, but for eternity. Kamar al Zamen had looked at her the very same way a long, long time ago. She tore her glance away from his, her mind stumbling to find an explanation for the tumult of conflicting thoughts and emotions that raged within her. She did not comprehend the quality within herself that caused a man to respond to her in this way, with emotions that transcended the physical. Was this tumult within herself also something more than physical? Love?

She turned her head to look at him again, catching her breath because the light was still there, even brighter now. She let her glance slide down the length of him. He was, as Kamar al Zamen had said, a Greek god come to life. Yet he was weak before her; see how he trembled in his hope that she would return his love. A power was in her that she had been only vaguely aware of with Kamar al Zamen. The conqueror, the savage aggressor, lay waiting for her to lay siege to him, to be stormed and ravaged. She could take him and drain him, utterly destroy him, he was so utterly vulnerable at this moment under her glance. The weapon and power of femininity and beauty, the age-old spell.

Aisha moved and put her forehead lightly against his cheek, then softly kissed the corner of his lips. She smiled into his eyes, and he fairly dissolved under the promise she was wordlessly making. She touched his warm flesh with her fingertips, moving them flutteringly, light as butterfly wings . . . down to his hard-muscled stomach. He lifted a hand and touched her breast, then her cheek. Delicately he touched the tip of her nose with his tongue, drawing her breath into his lungs with a deep, dizzying intake of breath.

"Dan Sea-Kingsson," she whispered against his mouth, "I have decided not to forsake a once in a lifetime opportunity . . . to love you." She pushed her mouth hard against his, her arms sliding around him, flattening her body along the length of him.

Dan groaned under her onslaught and bruised her mouth with lingering kisses, but continued to allow her full control. His hands slid over her back, fingers pressing through her gown into yielding flesh. She fondled him and kissed his neck and breast, breathing in the scent of him until the pain in her groin was more than she could any longer endure. She threw herself over on her stomach so that he could loosen the fastenings of her gown. His fingers fumbled with the clasps, then his hands were on her back flesh, moving down to her rounded, firm buttocks. His teeth bit her shoulder, and she cried out in the pleasure of it.

"In Odin's name," Dan whispered, his face buried in

her waist, "I have never known a woman like you. I am already drunk with you."

Aisha slid over and held his face to her stomach as his hands pulled the gown from around her, then removed her trousers. She let loose of him and his mouth tasted her flesh, teeth gently biting her inner thighs, then finding her heat and increasing it with the heat of his breath and the roughness of his tongue. Then up to her breasts like a starving infant.

Aisha writhed under him. At last he was in her and at the same time he was kissing her mouth and eyes, and she was no longer the aggressor but laid waste to, ending utterly spent and gasping for breath.

Aisha lay in Dan's arms all night. When sunlight entered through the light hole above them, she begged him to take her once again; a dread had come over her that there would be only this once for her, only this one fire in an entire lifetime. The night was so quickly escaping, already ashes.

"Later," Dan whispered in her ear, nuzzling his face in her neck. He had sensed the fear in her and in this way attempted to reassure her of many more nights and days to come.

Suddenly Aisha began to weep, surprising herself as much as Dan. She wept for all the years spent within a cocoon of delusion, and for all the future years wherein new illusions would need to be created in order to bear the emptiness. She wept out of happiness and despair, out of regret and some guilt.

"I am saddened, too," Dan said comfortingly, brushing her hair back from her face with fingertips. "It was so fleeting, after so long an anticipation."

"Yes," she sighed, pushing her face into his shoulder.

"But that is the way of life. We can only keep hope in tomorrow, begin to anticipate all over again. —I will leave you now. You can lie there and dream of me. —You *will* dream of me?"

She laughed at him and stopped her foolish sniffling. "I must get back to the babies," she said regretfully, having returned to reality and good sense.

On his feet beside the bed and looking down at her, he said, "I will not insist that you remain here, but it is my wish that you would. Let me send two thrall women to the house to care for the infants."

"Then we would have the remainder of winter together," she said, tasting the sound of it on her tongue and relishing it.

"An hundred days—at least."

"It will pass like the wink of an eye."

His eyes roved along the length of her. "You are fashioned of the stuff of goddesses, an artful, breathtaking tapestry of line and curve and color. How shall I ever let you escape from me, hmm?"

"You will, because I will entreat you, and, now that I have you completely enthralled, you will be powerless to deny me."

"Hah! Not far from the truth of it, I wager."

With that, he took up his clothing and hastily dressed himself. He strode to the door, turned and shook a warning finger in her direction. "For now, do not try any more foolish escapes. I will only drag you back by the hair. For one winter you will be mine, if it cannot be for the rest of our lives."

CHAPTER NINETEEN

Thorri-manud, the month of declining winter, had come and passed, yet blizzards ravaged the islands to heap more snow upon the already consuming drifts and ice that clogged normal activity.

Dan Sea-Kingsson spent the better part of his days working under a shed on a running ship that he would use for the seeking of the treasure. The length of the ship was seventy-five feet, the width ten and one half feet. It had fourteen benches and twenty-eight twelve-foot oars. The rudder was ten feet long. The bottom plank, which was not a keel, measured forty-five feet three inches, a solid piece. The ortholes, fastened with ropes, had a general shape, but no two were alike. The ship was being clinch built, held together with iron bolts with round heads outside and clinch plates inside, at a distance of five inches from each other. The space between the planks was filled with woolen stuff and a pitchy, sticky mass; the boards were joined with bast ropes. In the frame were holes which corresponded to elevated pieces on the boards, which were also bored through, not nailed but hewn, thus having lost half their thickness, giving the ship great elasticity which would serve well in heavy seas. In both stems, which were fastened to the bottom plank, there were two holes through which ropes would be drawn to drag the ship across land at the end of winter, and back again to the shed when winter came again.

When the running ship was completed, Dan name-fastened her *Rhandeer of the Breezes* and had her painted above the waterline in stripes of gold and black. He took himself to the *hof* and made a sacrifice to Odin that the new ship would be blessed with all good fortune and ever favorable winds.

Nur al Huda gave birth to a second son soon after a melting of the snows began. She had the child in a turf hovel separated from the main house. The thrall woman who had nursed her first son attended the birthing. Nur al Huda did not shrink from Harri's son, as she had from the child of rape. She wept with happiness when the infant was put into her arms.

Harri came to the hovel to see his son. The thrall woman had laid the infant on a cloak at the center of the earthen floor, for Harri had told her he would come to inspect the child. He walked round and round his son, searching for deformities. Seeing only perfection, a dark-haired, blue-eyed combination of himself and the woman he loved, he kneeled down and took the boy into the crook of one arm. He smiled, nodding his head at the thrall woman, who brought him an urn of consecrated water from the temple. Harri dipped his fingers into the water and sprinkled his son in the ancient custom, naming him Gunar Harrisson. If he had not acknowledged the infant within three days, the child would have ever after that been considered a thrall. He put a tiny wooden sword in one little fist, a miniature axe in the other, and he asked Odin aloud to always smile upon Gunar Harrisson, and the Fates to weave a thousand deeds for him to perform so that a place would await him in Valhalla.

"Gunar Harrisson," Nur al Huda whispered adoringly down into the infant's wizened, pink ear after Harri placed the child in her arms.

Nur al Huda would not let the infant out of her sight, carrying him on her back in a sling through the unending chores she was forced to do all the light hours of each day. Harri relieved her by taking loads from her arms, by hovering near and cursing anyone who spoke harshly to her or asked too much of her. He slept in the hovel on some nights, close beside her, asserting again and again his unfaltering devotion. To his eyes she was more lovely than ever. Short hair suited her heart-shaped face, curling now over her brow and ears in a beguiling way.

David soon showed himself on the shore, determined to begin again on his program of physical development. He swam in the icy sea, then ran a mile to warm himself. Occasionally he suffered strange chest pains, but he attributed them to chills and continued without giving way to them. Only once did the pain become severe enough to halt him in his tracks. A few minutes' rest and they went away.

Before the snows David had taken to throwing a spear at a target, to develop his eye as well as his arm. Now he was lifting a weighty axe daily, swinging it overhead and round in circles. He had acquired a bow from Harri and set himself to learning its way with a grim purpose. He no longer drew an audience. Men no longer laughed at him. He was respected for his strong will and for his uncompromising demand for perfection in his performances. He felt strength growing in him daily. Now he could swim from Highcliff to the fiord and back. He strictly adhered to the Asar dress, never bearing his breast, affecting more easily the long stride. He bathed each Thorsdag and never came upon the shore in other than fresh clothing, with his beard and hair combed. The handling of weapons was essential to being accepted as a man, so he steeled himself against the suggestion of violence in his actions, seeing only wood at target and not the heart of a man. Spear throwing was used in hunting for food. The axe was used for any number of humane purposes. He avoided only the sword, which was designed specifically for the slaying of men.

Harri remained faithful to his promise, continuing as David's instructor, but now taking a far more respectful attitude toward the task and the man. He cheered enthusiastically if David came even close to the target, and leaped joyously in air if the spear caught the edge of it, slapping the priest on the back and congratulating him. Patiently the lad would fix the spear in the priest's hand from behind, balancing it, swinging David's arm and down, ordering him to relax the tension in his arm. He would set the man's stance, then order the weapon slung.

More often than not Harri wearied of the lessons long before David did; he would throw until the sky began to darken, only then trudging away from the shore to his house on the high plain.

On a gray afternoon when the snows were only a dirtied slush on the ground, Gudrid rode to the shore, hauling in the reins to watch David, scowling fiercely. He became nervous under her critical eye and the axe he was swinging over his head shot from his grasp and splashed into the surf.

"You will slice off your head!" Gudrid shouted at him contemptuously.

"Or a leg," David agreed, laughing at himself.

"Take your grip higher on the handle," she suggested sourly.

David rushed to retrieve the axe, took hold of the handle carelessly, and asked, "Like this?"

"No. Higher still."

"Thus?"

"Now swing it."

He did so and with much greater expertness. The old woman made no comment. David let the axe-head drop to rest on the ground. He smiled at Gudrid, but her expression remained severe . . . unreadable.

"The exposed ones are thriving," he offered softly, so that only she would hear him.

"Indeed. And what exposed ones would you be talking about?"

"The two mysteriously brought to me, and the one I found in a cave."

"Huh! Fine world it would be if the deformed were allowed to people it!"

"My folly," he said lightly. "I am far too tenderhearted. I should have left them to the elements, I know. You are wise in age. Tell me, do you think I should cease my shameful indulgence and set them out to die?"

Gudrid's eyes closed to slits. She squirmed in the saddle, fairly agonized by conflicting emotions.

Abruptly she kicked her heels into the horse's sides and screeched, "If you expose them, priest, I will have your head!" She was away along the shore in an instant.

David cast his eyes to the sky, silently telling God that progress had been made, even if it was not obvious to Him. There was a Christian charity in the old woman that she was willing to indulge at least secretly, a charity she would rather die than admit to. Packaged food and clothing had arrived at regular intervals throughout the long winter. Gudrid knew that he was aware of her philanthropy. He hoped she would begin to trust him because he had not spoken out and shamed her for giving charity to a *Christian.* If he could win her complete trust his remaining years on this island would be far easier, his success far greater.

Dan, Aisha and her son boarded the *Rhandeer of the Breezes* in the dead of night and slipped out of Ransay harbor a week after the sacrifice of the sowing. Because of the possibility, though small, that Thorstein Christiansson, Mord's successor, would attack his bor, Dan was taking only the one small running *ship* and a skeleton crew, thereby leaving the bor under heavy guard. His odel-men had been alerted and had sworn to keep watch over and to protect Dansfiord during his absence.

Dan departed with the tide under a shield of darkness, so as not to announce his absence. His odel-men would frequently mention his presence at a feast, or at a horse fight, telling that Dan Sea-Kingsson did not go a-viking in this season because he was a wealthy man by virtue of the one third of the ransom that he had already received from the Saracen physician. The *Rhandeer of the Breezes* was southeast of the Orkneys before daybreak, setting a course south by southeast for the Frankish coast.

Dan had kept good account of the movements and apparent intentions of Thorstein Christiansson. The defeated chieftain had kept residence with Thengil Man-Lover for a month, then had taken himself to the ruins of Borgarsfiord, where he set up booths for winter protection. His people had spread out over the southern Orkneys, had been taken into the homes of relations, friends and the charitable.

Thorstein had made a winter voyage in the merchant *ship* of one of his odel-men, bringing back from Dublin harbor supplies to last them throughout the snow season. Now Thorstein occupied himself with reconstruction of his bor, having received a shipment of timber from Eire. He seemed to have no intention of seeking vengeance in the immediate future. Nevertheless, Dan felt compelled to be cautious.

The *Rhandeer of the Breezes* lay at anchor close in to the curving shoreline. Ashore, the debris of the Andalusian vessel was being systematically sifted. Winter storms had not disturbed the wreckage greatly. The wreck had been combed for an entire day without success. The hull and keel had been axed, the pieces carefully inspected, then flung aside. Ajib had said that the particular block holding the gold was marked in tar with the shape of a Greek letter L; no piece was discarded before Aisha's son had thoroughly inspected it for the mark. They were five days, one week, out of Dansfiord.

Immediately after dropping anchor, Dan had gone ashore and seen to the erection of a tent for Aisha's comfort. She had gone ashore with intense misgivings. It could take many days, even weeks, to find the gold. Foodstuffs for a fortnight had been brought ashore. Aisha had spent that entire first day of combing the wreckage wandering up and down the shoreline, feeling restless and sad.

Kamar al Zamen's body had been left tied to the trunk of a tree. Dan had seen the monstrous corpse before her eyes had moved in that direction, and he had quickly shielded her eyes from the sight by drawing her head to his shoulder and holding her fast. Now Kamar al Zamen was buried and she was alone, terribly alone.

The frantic search through the wreckage for gold unsettled and depressed Aisha even more than the cruel death of her husband. It was as if Dan sought a potion for the death of their love in that debris. The gold was payment for her release and for an end to their idyll. She felt suspended between the past and the present, her mind teetering, uncertain which way to go. Dan had spoken the truth when he bragged that if she left him it would be with bitter regret. What she hoped for, in delinquent moments, was that this search would be fruitless, thereby giving her a little more time with Dan before they had to part. A failure to find the gold would give her an excuse for delaying her voyage home. Not under any circumstance, not even for a lifetime with Dan, could she bring herself to refuse passage home—to Egypt Land. Confronted with a choice, a ship in harbor waiting for her to board, she would not, could not refuse the opportunity. She was a caged bird in this place.

The sky had begun to darken. Surrounded by the ribs of the dead vessel, Dan halted his labor to call a warning of closing day to the men. Ajib moved sullenly through the debris, kicking aside sticks and slats, his eyes desperately searching for the mark that indicated the gold that was as much his passage home as his mother's. Suddenly he reared upward with a triumphant cry and dropped to his knees to dig into the debris with trembling hands. "The mark!" he cried out. "I have it! The mark!"

The men set up a cheer and Dan bounded over to Ajib with an axe in hand. Ajib put the block down on a boulder. Dan carefully took aim and cracked the block open with a controlled swing of the axe, letting the steel box fall free.

Aisha shivered and hugged herself with both arms as Dan took the box into his hands. His eyes darted round in search of her, and when their eyes met his face sobered and he smiled no more.

A bowman brought a deer from the wood. After a brief, high-spirited celebration that involved the draining of many horns of ale, Dan set himself to the skinning of the small beast so that they might have a feast. He had piled up stones to form a butchering block. Now he leaned his axe, the metal box that held the gold, and his sword against the rise of stones. He had just removed the deer's head when his eye dropped and he cried out, a terrible shriek, as if he had mutilated himself.

"Dan!" Aisha exclaimed, running to his side. He

lunged back from the block, the cry now caught in his throat, apparently gagging him. She thought that he had badly cut himself with the knife, but there was not a wound on him. He stood there white and horror-struck. "Dan! What is it?"

Men moved up behind Dan and they followed his stare, then sucked in their breaths. Blood of the deer had dripped upon the blade of Dan's sax, and upon the steel box, an omen of death. Death would touch Dan Sea-Kingsson.

"Dan?" Aisha pleaded, pushing herself before him, trying to force him to look at her, to explain to her what was wrong.

He shook off the spell with a shudder and met her eyes, tears of grief sliding down his cheeks. "I am dream-wise," he said in a breaking voice. "They are all dead!"

Before Aisha could speak he had whirled away from her, shouting orders to his men.

The *Rhandeer of the Breezes* raced full speed toward Ransay. Dan ceaselessly paced the forecastle, cursing Odin with a ferocity that chilled Aisha to the bone, throwing spears at the sky, raging . . . demanding Odin come down and show himself. Brandishing his sword in air, he called Thor to task as well. Enraged by the reluctance of the gods to do battle with him, he beat his fists against the neck of the ship, wailing in despair.

One week after Dan's departure, David was at his shore labors. As he swam energetically in the high swells, he noticed a ship rounding the island curve. It was a small vessel, a fourteen-seater, seven oars to the side. From the masthead flew the red cross of Ingolf Jarl, and below that flag flapped the white flag of peace. He sucked in his breath, turning in the sea to swim to shore. The year was at an end. Now he must face inspection by Thengil. He expected severe criticism and probably dismissal.

David was at the shore when Thengil got out of the smallboat and arrogantly strode through the surf. A line of Dan's champions stood coldly questioning the priest's purpose in coming to Dansfiord. Drenched and uneasy, David stepped up to his superior and greeted the man.

"Will you please explain my purpose here to these heathens?" Thengil said nastily. "Pagans. Always only too eager to cut someone's throat."

David frowned at the harshness of the man's tone and manner. He turned to Dan's men—they all knew him—and explained that his accomplishments here as a Christian priest were to be investigated by Thengil. They believed him, but remained guarded and watchful.

Thengil had with him ten men of great size and strength who were unarmed. "I could not hope for charity on this shore, I suppose," Thengil said bitingly to Dan's standard bearer, who glared at him sourly, a hand on his sheathed sword. "We will need to remain the night. This man to my right is cousin to Freydis Housewife; he would like to visit with her, if it please her."

A hundred fully armed warriors stood in protection of the bor, so eleven men did not represent a great threat, and Olaf the Tall was recognized as the true enough first cousin of Freydis Housewife. Thengil demanded beds and food, saying he and four of his men would spend the remainder of the day hours with this priest in investigation of his merits and achievements. He had his way in respect of the dictates of Thorfinn Jarl.

David led Thengil and his men to his house. The robed priest seemed to take great pleasure in the rugged trek over the cliffs, never once hauling in a deep breath. When the little house was visible in the valley, Thengil halted and examined the site and the surrounding fields and slopes. "Where is the cross, eh? I see no cross!"

"I have not erected one," David explained, "because the people are distrustful of all symbols of—"

"Are they really? Imagine that. A frail excuse, to be sure. Let the crosses fall and we will raise them up again."

"I will erect a cross," David said unhappily.

Thengil strode across the spring green field and shoved open the door to the house. "This is a home, not a church," he shouted, turning on David accusingly.

"Little use I would have for a church," David muttered, staring at his feet.

"The number of converts. How many?"

"Three baptisms . . . of infants. No converts, Father."

"Hurrah! You are a fine one, are you not? Bishop Hoskuldson was out of his senses to send such as you to me. The situation will be corrected, however. You will begin the construction of a church immediately."

Something in the man's tone chilled David. His eyes darted up to examine the face of Thengil, and he saw madness there. "May I ask how you will correct the situation?" he asked tightly, his entire body tensed, his mind storm-tossed.

"Almighty God has lost his patience and has chosen me as His champion. I expect your full cooperation. You will aid me in the baptisms."

"*What* baptisms?" David exclaimed, backing away from the man toward the door. One of the babies started to cry, and the sound shattered him like a stone striking glass.

"Did you come to Ransay for a swim, David of Saint Monica? traveled halfway across the world to play with spears, did you? Oh, yes, I have heard about your games, and I am, frankly, inclined to send you back where you came from."

"What *baptisms*?" David insisted. "Force would only increase their hatred of us. It is the way of Christ to love our . . . to do good to those who—"

"For the love of *Christ*!" Thengil screeched, throwing his powerful arms in air exasperatedly. "You are the prize fool. Christ said, 'If you are not with me, you are against me.' The moment of triumph over these pagans is at hand. God is on a rampage. Name your side. Either you are with Christ or you are against Him."

"I am only against force," David said emotionally, pain sending a tremor through his entire body that unsettled his knees. "I am against *you*, not God or Christ!"

"Are you saying that God is with you alone, and not with the hundreds who are coming after me?"

"No! I merely say that—that you are exercising a personal vengeance here, not in any way carrying the banner of God."

"Well spoken. That adequately clears up any questions I might have had as to your loyalty." With that, Thengil motioned to the men behind him and they rushed at David, taking him in hand. The thrall nurses screeched in alarm and were also taken. When knives were put to their throats, the two women pleaded for mercy and were told that only acceptance of baptism to Christianity would gain them mercy. Before a gag could be pushed into David's mouth, he cried out to the women to accept the baptism, and when they held back, commanded them to do so, even if insincerely . . . they could recant tomorrow. Christ would understand the lie and forgive them, for he was good. Christ was *good.*

David was left bound and gagged on the floor of his house. In a state of terror the like of which he had never known, he struggled against the bonds that held him. Before his mind's eye he saw faces —Hyrna Dansdotter smiling winsomely, Harri with his eyes filled with love for a girl, Gudrid's fierce visage masking a tenderness for little children that Christ could not help but note. He saw them hard before Thengil. He knew that not one of them would accept the baptism. From time immemorial the Asar had been water-sprinkled at birth, and David had come to accept this sprinkling as baptism, but the Church refused to give it sanction. Perspiration wet his face, and tears of rage and frustration ran from his eyes to the mud floor under him. He could not lose himself.

The house became dark. The babies wailed with increasing hysteria in their baskets; they were hungry, cold and wet. The muffled groans of the thrall women hummed in David's ears. All humanity was moaning, eternally moaning against persecution. Then it was dead of night and he slept fitfully. He awoke with a start to see a faint glow in the sky through the door that had been left open. Then, like a miracle Harri's white head appeared over the far rise, visible to David through the open door.

David uttered muffled shouts against the gag in his mouth and wildly struggled on the floor. He managed to roll over and over until he was in the doorway. An eternity passed it seemed, before Harri bounded in and jerked the rag from his mouth.

"Dear God," David choked, clutching at Harri's shirt, "go and warn them . . . warn them . . . forced baptisms."

Bewildered, Harri cut the bindings on David's legs and arms with his knife. "Is this how you priests treat one another, eh?" he asked with a laugh. "Thengil sleeps like a baby in my foster father's house. He brought only ten men with him. . . . Why has he tied all of you up like this?"

David was on his feet, rushing to release the thrall women. He commanded them to take the babies into the far hills, to find a cave and hide there. Then he turned on Harri, who was smiling uncomfortably at him as if he thought he had gone mad. "I refused to aid Thengil in the baptisms," he shouted. "*That* is why I was bound and gagged!"

Harri stood there frowning uncertainly. Eleven men could not overcome one hundred. Thengil had some grievance with this priest and had chosen to leave him tied like a sack of meal until he could dispense with him. "I could not sleep. I thought to take some early exercise." He studied David's anguished face. "All was quiet and right when I left; everything."

"Curse you! Odin damn you with hel-shoes!" David lunged at the boy, taking him by the arms and shaking him. "Go to your family. They will need you. Go, I say, damn you!"

Harri looked deeper into David's eyes, searching for sanity. He saw it and exploded out of David's hands, running, fast vanishing across the field and over the far rise.

David rushed out of the house and stood there in the light of the rising sun indecisively. Thengil had said that men followed him. Then ships must have come by night, hiding under cover of darkness. Now that it was getting light, secrecy was no longer possible; they would strike. But by which approach? By the bay? Or over land, which would bring them across this plain? He turned heel and ran in the opposite direction that Harri had taken. He clawed at the ridges of the rock-ribbed hills, his strength doubled by his desperation. His chest began to pain him again with every gasping breath he took, but he did not allow his pace to slacken.

When David arrived at the crest of the low cliff, he could see the southern curve of Ransay. Just rounding it, moving in the direction of the bay, sailed a long-serpent flying the banner of the dead Mord Baptized-One, bearing the white shield of peaceful intention. To the west rode another warship with shields inheld and white shield flying. Across the narrow inlet the tiny isle of Skylli lolled in a rosy haze. He cupped his hands round his mouth, teetering on the cliff edge, and let a blasting war cry fall on the wind. Again and again he shrieked the cries he had heard so often emerging from the throats of the practicing young warriors. His throat became hoarse and he ceased his cries, straining to see across the water to the compound of Skylli, barely visible now through a moving mist. A small figure appeared on the shore, looking across the inlet in his direction. He thrashed his arms, sucked air into his ravaged lungs and let another fierce cry explode from his throat. The figure waved, then turned to run in the direction of the compound.

David flung himself into action again, running along the edge of the cliff, following the curve of the island until he sighted the bay below to his left. One of the ships had just moved into the bay, had dropped anchor there, lying in wait at the mouth as if to stand as a blockade. Smallboats clinging to the coastline so as not to be seen from the compound moved swiftly from around the northern curve to enter the bay. A third warship sat in northern water in a defensive position, to hold off any would-be defenders.

David could not see the compound, which was hidden by the rising Highcliff. He put a hand to his heaving chest, felt his heart pounding in there in wild jumps and sporadic hesitations. He fell to his knees on the rock ledge, his heart and the sea throbbing in his ears.

"Holy Mary Mother of God," he prayed, his eyes squeezed tightly closed, "pray to God for me. Let Him smite the devils that have come to this shore. Save my people!" He offered his own life. He would accept Hell. He would commit any act, sacrifice anything—everything if God would show him the way that these people might be saved from torment and a cruel death. "God! Let them live!" he cried out, lifting his stricken eyes to Heaven.

David stumbled to his feet and left the cliff, cutting across a stretching plain of rock. He leaped a ravine and was in a grazing field, stone fences blocking his path every few acres. He vaulted the fences, ran as fast as he could considering the swift weakening of his legs. When he reached Highcliff he came to a gasping halt. Below him raged a monstrous assault. Many of Thengil's men had gained entrance to the compound. Dead men hung over the gard, lay at the base inside it and outside. The gate was wide open. The men who had accepted Freydis' charitable offer of beds for the night must have opened it from within while everyone slept. Women and children ran flailing toward the shore, only to be caught up by men and carried off screaming.

David screamed. He ran, lunging over boulders, falling and picking himself up again. He dropped thirty feet, falling flat on his face, the breath knocked out of him, but in an instant he was up again. As he approached the compound the struggle seemed to quiet. Then he heard an awful shriek, like that of a wounded beast, or as someone in the throes of a ghastly nightmare. As he sped around the gard, he saw Gudrid on Fleet Raven, charging headlong against men who held the women and children in a circle near the shore. She swung an axe round and round her head, then cut it into a man, then another.

David saw a man leap up to the gard, saw him raise the spear, his arm pulling back for the throw. *"Gudrid!"* David screamed in warning.

Gudrid's head whipped round. She instantly saw David, saw in him the loathsome Jesus Christ, saw the murderer of her mother and father. With a cry of "Veum!" she dug her heels into the horse's sides, hauling the stallion around to charge David with the axe whirring over her head.

The spear was thrown and its head plunged into Gudrid's breast and came out through her back. For an instant she remained erect in the saddle as if untouched. Again she screamed "Veum!" then she slumped over Fleet Raven's neck to hang limp there. The stallion reared in terror and ran with her, plummeting toward the base of Highcliff.

Tears blinding him, David stumbled into the midst of the clamor. Only a few men were left to fight, the struggle reduced to isolated incidents, men dueling one against another. Then Thengil appeared high on the gard. He shouted down a cry for peace. He had come only to receive them into Christ. If they would cease their resistance no deaths would be necessary.

"Lay down your swords!" Thengil yowled to those outside and inside the gard, turning in circles that all might hear him. "Fools! We did not come to slay you!"

David rushed through the compound gate, his eyes wide and staring, his mind unable to absorb what he saw; it was a nightmare. Bodies lay everywhere, blood soaking into the muddy earth. Thengil was still bellowing, now above and behind him. He did not know what he sought, or whom, only followed the lead of some indefinable instinct. He plunged into Dan's house. It was still as a tomb.

Freydis lay in the entrance of the cookroom, blood a pool around her, her midsection gaping, her intestines spilled out like a bloodly tangle of heavy twine. A sax was clutched in her stiff hand; her eyes were open and filled with an indescribable agony.

"Oh God, no," David wept over the body. Then he

spun round and ran outside with a scream caught in his throat, a rage building in him like an earthquake in the bowels of a volcano.

The struggle was over. Thengil leaped down from the gard with a broad smile of satisfaction on his face. He saw David come to a halt outside the gate, falling back against the gard post, breathing heavily with both hands against his chest as if he were trying to prevent his heart from exploding. "Come aid in the baptism of your people, priest," he shouted at the stupid man who apparently did not hear him; he leaned there staring into space like a madman.

All the survivors were herded together before the gard. David saw Harri's white head among the men. The lad's hands were bound behind him, his face a mask of devilish hatred. From beyond the shore rose the sound of horns as ships approached from Skylli and from Wyre. But the *dreki* of Skylli gave the huge warships at the mouth of the bay a wide berth, vanishing into a low, sea-clinging fog.

Harri was the first to be brought to Thengil. A heavy post had been driven into the soft ground and the lad was tied to it, round the neck, waist and ankles.

Nur al Huda exploded out of the circle of men that held in the women and children. Her infant son was, as always, on her back in the sling. She ran sobbing to Harri, throwing herself on him. Thengil's eyes lighted at the look of adoration Harri's eyes showed the instant he saw the woman coming. The priest laughed and strode over to haul Nur al Huda back. He held her roughly by an arm, smiling at Harri.

"Will you accept baptism, Harri Hylmirsson?"

"No!" Harri shouted, spitting at the man.

Thengil deliberately wrenched the soft arm he held, causing Nur al Huda to scream in pain. "I ask you again. Will you accept baptism?"

Harri did not waver. Again he spat in the direction of Thengil's face.

With a toss of his head Thengil motioned to the infant mewing on the woman's back, and the child was wrenched from the sling that held it, then held high in the air in two bloody hands. "I wager this infant is yours," Thengil said ominously to Harri.

Nur al Huda hysterically thrashed and clawed at the man who held her back from retrieving her son. Then she whirled on Harri, screaming, "Say you will do what he wants! Say it!"

Harri shook his head, his teeth biting into his lower lip, a sob quaking his chest.

"After the infant we will slay this thrall woman," Thengil warned. When Harri kept his eyes fixed on the sky, he gave the command.

The man who held the infant drew his arms back and sent the child crashing against the wall of the gard. Nur al Huda's eyes widened in disbelief, a stifled scream caught in her throat. She broke free and ran toward the smashed infant that lay facedown in the mud. An arrow sliced into her back as she ran. She fell. Whimpering insanely, she slowly pushed herself up and crawled on hands and knees. When she reached the child she clutched it to her breast, then fell on it and did not move again.

An agonized wail erupted from Harri's throat. Tears filled his eyes and ran down his face into his thin beard. "Christ be damned. Be *damned*!" He choked on his spit and coughed violently.

Hyrna Dansdotter was now brought before Harri. Through clouded eyes he saw her standing there. Hoarsely he said to her. "Hyrna, if—if I could not say it for—for them, I cannot say it for you."

"Yes, Harri," Hyrna said tremulously, looking wide-eyed up at him.

"We shall put the snake in her," Thengil warned. "The horn into her mouth, the little red snake into the horn, a torch to send the creature diving down her throat. Slowly he will eat his way out of her, our hungry little reptile."

Thengil gave the signal and a stick was forced into Hyrna's mouth to hold it open. A wriggling, thin snake appeared in a hand and was dangled before the child's terrified eyes.

Suddenly a wild cry erupted from behind him, and Thengil whirled around to face a charging madman with an axe swinging over his head—so powerfully that it sang in the air. Before Thengil could blink and absorb the significance, the axe split his skull open down to his shoulders.

David screamed again and again—could not stop. He swung the axe left and right blindly, ferociously. "Eye for an eye!" he shrieked, slashing with the axe, men scrambling out of his path, "tooth for tooth!—hand for hand!—foot for foot!"

The men of Thengil stumbled back and away, their eyes frozen on the crazed priest who was renowned as next in gentleness to Christ himself. Then cries rose upon the cliffs above, and the men of Skylli and Wyre, having come over land, showed themselves armed and coming to fight. All joy in the slaughter had left the men of Thengil, running from them as the blood that spurted from the crack in Thengil's skull.

David could not cease his wild slinging of the axe, having lost his reason. A man ran close behind him and he swung viciously, sideswiping the runner with the blunt edge of the axe. The weapon flew from his hands with the blow, as if wrenched from them by someone unseen. He stood immobile, staring straight ahead, gasping for another breath.

"David," a voice said as from far, far away . . . behind him. He slowly turned and looked up into Harri's stricken eyes.

"They have gone, David," Harri said softly, his eyes filled with grief, pain and gratitude.

"Oh, my—*God*!" David cried. "My God—my God!" His voice broke and he raised his eyes Heavenward. Throwing his arms up to make his plea, he shouted in a terrible voice, "God! Strike me dead for what I have done! Send lightning and strike me dead. Thou shalt not *kill*!"

For an instant David stood there unmoving, his arms held up to Heaven, tears washing down his cheeks. Suddenly his eyes widened, he sucked in a breath, raised a hand to his heart; then he dropped as if struck in the breast with a spear.

"Cut me free!" Harri shouted to the men of Skylli, who rushed through after the escaping attackers.

When Harri was free, he ran to where Nur al Huda lay. He gently rolled her over and saw her eyes wide open and staring. He clutched her face to his breast and crumpled into uncontrollable weeping. For a long time he held her. Then he numbly turned his head to see Hyrna sitting in a pool of blood, holding David's head in her little hands, sobbing and choking on grief.

Harri ran to the child and knelt beside her.

"His god came," Hyrna said questioningly.

"I think that he did," Harri said huskily, reaching to brush a hand against her cheek.

"But why? Why did he have to kill him? He was only trying to help me."

"Because he broke the law of his god."

"But—but his god did not kill *them,*" she sobbed, throwing an arm in the direction of the bay, where Thengil's men scurried away in smallboats.

"With David's strength, his god slew Thengil," Harri said, frowning confusedly. "David was a brave man. Very brave. He was Asar brave. He was a man."

"Maybe Odin will accept him in Valhalla?—if his god does not want him in *his* place?" Her eyes searched Harri's face, pleading for his answer to be yes.

"He died bravely in the fight."

"Oh, I hope he goes to Valhalla," she sobbed, dropping her face to the cheek of the dead priest from Egypt. "I will pray each day to Odin. Each day!"

Harri took Hyrna up in his arms and began to walk toward the compound with her. He took her to the loft of his foster father's house and left her there. He searched for her two sisters and, finding them, had a thrall woman take them to the loft. Gylfi was dead. Freydis and Gudrid were dead. Only twenty men had survived, and all save himself were wounded. He had been taken before getting a weapon in his hand by two men attacking from behind as he entered the compound gate after David's warning.

Harri took up Nur al Huda and his son and carried

them to the shore. He placed them in a smallboat and covered them over with many cloaks and trousers ripped from the backs of dead men. The men of Skylli stood away as he lit the rags with a torch. When the flames were good, he shoved the boat into the surf, following. When the water was over his head, he swam, pushing the little boat out to sea, farther and farther out to sea. Then he turned back and swam to shore, where he sat on a rock and watched the boat bob on the far waves, becoming a raging inferno, hissing and smoking, finally sinking deep into Ran's bosom.

CHAPTER TWENTY

Dan had driven the rowers mercilessly for three days and nights without rest. Ransay was reached on the third day after Thengil's attack. From the forecastle of the *Rhandeer of the Breezes* as she rounded the island curve, all seemed in order. The compound stood. Smoke trails rose to be caught and disintegrated by swift winds. But as the ship sailed into the bay a deserted, deathlike atmosphere overwhelmed all on board.

Unwilling to wait out the lowering of a smallboat, Dan dove overboard and swam to shore. He struck out for the compound, calling Gudrid's name. The gate was open. Not a champion showed himself, only thralls and sad-eyed children of freemen. Then, from the Isle of Skylli, rose the mournful cry of a horn and Dan froze in his tracks. He rushed the gard and climbed to the walkway, straining his eyes across the bay. Smallboats approached.

Dan met Harri at the bay shore. He stood stone-faced before the lad, awaiting an explanation.

"The Christian Thengil came," Harri said emotionally, finding it difficult to meet his foster father's eyes, "under the protection of Thorstein Christiansson—came and—and slew Gudrid Mother, and Freydis, and sixty beloved, brave men."

Dan sucked in his breath and let it out again in a hissing sigh of despair. His hands knotted into fists and he fought against tears. "Where is he?" he demanded to know. "The Womanly One. Now I will cut his throat and draw out his innards, as I should have done long—"

"David of Saint Monica," Harri interrupted roughly, "is dead also. He slew Thengil with a single blow of an axe. We put him to sea on the burial ship . . . with Gylfi, Gudrid Mother, Freydis . . . the other brave dead. My father, the priest saved the life of Hyrna, and my life also."

Dan stared incredulously at Harri; the enemy was absolutely defined and it was Christianity—Christians.

"I speak the truth. His god came and he saw the deed that he had done, Thengil dead at his feet, which was a sin before the god that he knew. From heaven an invisible arrow was sent and it pierced his heart. I saw it with my own eyes, for I was tied to a post not two feet from where he stood. His god has great power."

Dan's throat had closed and his stomach was heaving. He ran from Harri, vanishing round the gard, then soon was seen scaling Highcliff. He disappeared over the crest. Harri did not follow him. It was better to be alone with so profound a grief.

Aisha went to the high plain the next day and entered the little house. It was empty, but David's presence was strong. She felt his eyes warm upon her as she touched his Bible with a lingering fingertip, as she gazed upon the brown robe hanging on a wall hook, the deserted monastery in its very presence—and all the vows forsaken. Hanging there, the robe had been a constant reminder to him of life in its perfect state, purely good like an unruffled sea, without temptations, or life quakes that slashed gorges in its base and set it on fire. She took the robe down from the hook, folded it neatly, then placed the Bible into a fold. This was all that was left of a sainted man.

As she stepped outside, Aisha saw Harri coming across the field. She waited for him, pity for him bringing tears to her eyes. He had truly loved Nur al Huda and she admired him for that; the child had not been the easiest person to love. The lad carried a heavy burden over his shoulder. As he drew closer, she saw that it was an enormous cross, and hanging over the cross bar—a white shield of peace. The cross was made of wood, apparently, and had been gilded and embossed with figures of a warrior with angel's wings and a golden halo.

Harri halted before Aisha, letting the stake of the cross rest on the ground before him. "My foster father and I," he began huskily, "made this cross as a memorial. All this day an artist worked upon the figures. If there had been more time—" His words broke off, and his hollow, red-rimmed eyes closed for a moment.

Aisha could not speak. She reached out a hand and touched Harri's sleeve, fighting back tears.

"I thought to place it atop his house," he said at last, glancing at the steeply pitched roof.

She shook her head and said softly, "Follow me, Harri."

She led the way across the fields and hills, toward Highcliff. Harri followed close and they did not speak. Rain began to fall softly, and Aisha recalled how the Asar said that rain was the tears of the clouds. It was a long walk, but she ignored her weariness.

At the edge of the cliff Aisha halted, looking across the inlets to the scattered islands. "Here we will bury a saint," she said. "Men of Christ must be interred to receive Heaven. The Asar burn their noble dead, but David would have wanted to be in earth."

Harri's face fell. "I did not know," he groaned.

"Ach, do not fret. No god could turn from the sainted one who fell here, certainly not out of pique that he went to his reward on a flaming dragon ship."

Harri laid down the cross. Following Aisha's instructions, he went and brought earth for a mound. She put the brown robe and the Bible on the rock ledge and covered them with earth. Harri drove the cross stake into a crevice nearby, deep in until it was firmly set.

"May he rest in peace always," Harri said earnestly. "Let all men know that a man is buried here. He was a man of peace, but most of all a man." He lifted up the white shield of peace and hung it over the bar of the cross.

Aisha closely examined the boy's drawn face. "Harri, I am so sorry about the loss of your child, and—"

"What is your paradise like?" he interrupted urgently.

"Oh, quite serene and luxurious," she said, smiling at him.

"She is with Allah?"

"Oh, yes, Harri. I am sure Nur al Huda is with Allah in Paradise."

"Will Allah allow my son in Paradise, too? He must be with her. She—she would not want him in Hel, away from her. Why, she would rage . . . something fierce." He lost his voice, choked on a sob and spun away from Aisha, running along the cliff edge toward the path to the compound.

Aisha moved away, slowly walking along the path Harri had taken. The sun came from behind a black cloud, and the tears of Heaven ceased to fall. No man sailing these waters would fail to note that Christ had come to Ransay, for David's monument rose high and white against a blueing sky. The winds pushed hard against it, but it would not fall.

After four days of isolation in his quarters, Dan came to Aisha in the loft. His eyes were swollen and stricken. Wine was stale on his breath. He sat sluggishly in a chair and stared at his boots.

"My beloved son of the Sea King," Aisha said softly, "I am deeply sorry for what has happened to you and yours."

"I will slay every Christian in the Orkneys, beginning with Thorstein Christiansson."

"And a thousand more will come to take his place," she said on a sigh. "His men will attack you in counter-vengeance, and on and on it will go, until you are dead."

He threw a leather bag at her. It landed beside her on the bed and she stared at it, bewildered.

"I want no gold that is stained with the blood of my mother and my wife," he said heatedly, as if she had been trying to force the gold on him. "For lust of that gold I caused the death of Gudrid and Freydis and many good men. Buy jewels and plant gardenias to perfume your garden; take it with you to Cairo City."

Aisha sat up on the bed, staring at him. "You are sending me away?"

"With the tide tomorrow. War will rage, and this place will be under fire. You are not safe here. I will not stop until I am dead or completely victorious."

"You fight your king, the very law of the land! Dan, you will be outlawed."

"A law that protects butchers is not fit for the honor of an Asa man!"

Aisha rushed to him and knelt on the floor before him. "Dan Sea-Kingsson, I deeply love you. I am reluctant to depart. Please . . ."

He leaned forward and took her face in his two hands, searching her eyes. "I am too full of hate to love anyone," he said huskily. "Perhaps we will meet again one day. Perhaps I will set sail for Vinland in search of freedom and peace. I cannot say now what I will do in the end, if I live. But you will sail for Cairo City tomorrow, of that I am sure."

Aisha moved and brushed his cheek with her lips. "I will dream of you all the rest of my days," she whispered emotionally.

Dan got to his feet and moved to the door. "I leave at midnight for the fight. . . . Goodbye, Aisha. It was good, the winter. It was good."

When he was gone the tears came. But on the morrow Aisha cheerfully stepped aboard the *Rhandeer of the Breezes*, a weighty bundle in her arms, Ajib, grinning happily, close beside her. Ajib was happy, yes, but there was strong disapproval behind his eyes, behind that smile. Three more wrapped bundles were carried aboard by members of the crew.

"You will come into my house," Ajib said firmly as the running ship moved out of the bay.

"No, my son," Aisha flatly disagreed, "I will not come to live in your household."

"But after this ordeal. You are getting old, and . . ."

Aisha's head snapped round and she glared furiously at him. "I am not old!" she informed him. "I will keep the manor house of your father, and I will have many gay feasts and gatherings of friends there. Some of my friends will be male, you can rest assured. I may not even wear face veils before my company. And it is likely that I will tell anyone who will listen to me the tale of an Asar prince and how he loved me."

"Mother!" Ajib protested.

"By the mercy of Allah, within certain limits, widowed women of age are free to do as they damned well please in Islam, and, my son, that is precisely what I mean to do . . . whatever I damned well please."

The lad swallowed his horror and disgust. Unable to keep still, he argued, "And what do you propose to do with the—the illegitimate ones, the pack of orphans you—"

"Kamar al Akmar?" she asked, loosening the blanket from around the toddler's impish face. "Why, raise him for Nur al Huda, of course. A fine lad he will be. Already he walks with the stride of a prince, and barely one year old. Mary, Joseph and Monica, David's little exposed ones? I will try to raise them with a Christian conscience. Perhaps Joseph will return here one day and continue his foster father's work that was begun so nobly."

Ajib stared at her open-mouthed. He did not know her at all. "You have changed," he said accusingly.

"Oh, yes. Indeed, I have, my son. You will never know how much."

The ship turned and Aisha saw the white cross gleaming in the sun at the crest of Highcliff. She watched it until it was no larger than a gull against the sky.

Gardenias and jasmine scented the morning breeze that softly entered the harim through the open pavilion doors. Servant girls were busily rolling sleeping mattresses and putting them away in their closets. The music of fountains surging in the garden and the songs of birds added to the overall tranquility.

"Grandmother?" ten-year-old Hasan said sweetly to Aisha, his dark eyes examining her jeweled hair and radiant face adoringly.

"Yes, my sweetmeat?"

The boy sat on pillows at her feet. *The Book of the Thousand Nights and a Night* was open on his knees. His comely face was bright with stimulated imagination. He seemed to have lost the question he had wanted to ask her.

"Keep reading, sweetmeat. Sindbad's adventures never fail to stir excitement in me. I look forward to your visits as much for our reading of the tales as for your sweet company."

"I want to hear *your* tale," Hasan said eagerly, "of how you were abducted by the cruel pirate, and how the handsome prince saved your life and loved you."

Aisha laughed brightly. She opened her mouth to speak, but Kamar al Akmar came running from the garden and threw himself against her bosom, nearly unsettling her on her pillows. A servant girl chased after him, blood in her eye.

"What has our prince done now?" Aisha smiled up at the furious servant.

"He deliberately pushed Mary into the pool . . . deliberately! Impossible, the child is incorrigible."

Kamar al Akmar's round face lifted and his tongue flashed out at the servant. He quickly hid his face again in Aisha's shoulder.

"He takes after his mother," Aisha said, amused. "What can we do? Such is the will of Allah. He is not quite four years old. Perhaps we can civilize him before he is a man; we can only try."

"Grandmother," Hasan protested, "tell me the *tale*!"

The servant woman turned and huffily returned to the garden.

Aisha held Kamar al Akmar close to her and smiled happily at Hasan. "Oh, those were days, my grandson. And the excitement was real, not letters on a page. But you know, such events are only exciting when we tell of them in reflection. At the time one is too impressed with the terror, and the mind is too confined to just the moment. Now I can look back and see it all, and enjoy the thrill of the adventure as I could not do then."

Hasan squirmed on his pillows. "Tell me," he squealed excitedly.

"Ach—they are giants, the Northmen, rising seven feet tall and broad through the chest as a wine barrel.

And they have white hair and eyes the color of the sky on a summer's day. And all are kings."

Aisha moved Kamar al Akmar aside and got to her feet, wandering to the window. She leaned her forehead against the iron grillwork, looking wistfully out over the gray Nile. "I stood exactly where I stand now, gazing out . . ." Her throat closed and her head arched back.

"*Alhomdolillah!*" Aisha fairly screeched, gripping the ironwork with both hands.

Hasan ran up behind her, craning his neck to see around her.

"A dragon ship!" she cried. "Hasan! A dragon ship approaches!"

Aisha whipped round and sped past the boy, racing through the harim, silk veils fluttering a trail behind her.

Hasan shook his head. As his father always said, his grandmother was far too giddy for so old a woman. Why, she was thirty years and six.

The lad turned back to the window. He watched the ship come into clearer view. It passed close along the river. Its prow bore a deer's head with laced horns. The mast flew the banner of a black horse. It was the *Sea King's Deer*.